Secrets of the Past

BERNARD IRVING

Gail:
Hope you enjoy a peek
into my imagination

Bernie

To Liz, Alison and Gail.
Always an inspiration.

ONE

He felt out of place the moment he stepped into the room. Looking up at the high ceilings, the sounds echoing off them and resounding in his ears, he felt himself shrink, becoming smaller with each step into the restaurant.

He didn't belong here; he felt his clothes shout as he self-consciously walked toward the end of the entrance hall, his hands trembling as they gripped his tattered hat. He felt coldness come from the walls and from the stares of the people around him as he continued to walk. He began to shiver at the frozen looks and felt himself cringe and huddle as if he were a child entering a room full of adults for the first time.

"Can I help you?" a stuffy voiced man asked him as he stopped at the edge of the main dining room. He looked up at the face that owned the voice and saw a look of disgust cross the man's eyes. How dare you enter my restaurant, the face seemed to say. How dare you come in here?

"Can I help you." the maitre d' sneered again. There was anger in his voice blaring in Helmut Schorner's ears. The voice and the look on the mans face made it seem as if a dirty, wet dog had come into his presence.

Helmut cleared his throat, choking to find some moisture to coat the dryness on his lips as he struggled to speak.

"I...I have an...." but Helmut had trouble forming the words.

"Come, man!" the maitre d' chided him for his stumbling. "If you have something to say then spit it out."

Spit it out! Helmut thought he was going to spit out his entire breakfast on the man's shoes. He was almost too nervous to speak. Damn, he thought, this is what he deserved for expecting a favor.

"This is your last chance," the maitre d' said. "Or shall I call the police."

"I...I have an appointment," Helmut stammered on. "With Herr Albert Freyberg."

The maitre d' crinkled his nose again at Helmut. "You do?!"
Helmut nodded.

The maitre d' looked over his list. "I believe you are correct. Please follow me."

Helmut began to walk behind the maitre d' and took in the sights around him. He had heard about this place, one of the finest restaurants in Northern Germany, they had said. Helmut doubted that he would ever have the opportunity to eat here, especially on his first day in Bremen, not expecting Albert to ask him to join him for lunch when he called his old friend.

The restaurant was a strange place, a place where even the depression didn't enter. Its mirrors glimmering their reflections and didn't lie. The more he looked around the more out of place he felt in his old and faded suit. Even the busboys seemed better dressed than he. Yet Helmut knew his clothes were the best that he could afford, times being what they were. He only hoped that Albert was picking up the check for lunch and doubted if it could be otherwise.

The maitre d' stopped at a table. "Your guest has arrived." he announced crisply before departing.

As the maitre d' left his form passed between Helmut and his old friend, revealing him to Helmut for the first time. Helmut immediately realized how long it had been, for he barely recognized Albert Freyberg. It had been fourteen years since they had seen each other and Helmut realized how much both of them had changed.

A hand reached out to Helmut. "Good to you see you, my old friend." Albert's his voice still had that deep, crisp quality. "Sit down. We've a lot to talk about."

As Helmut sat he stared at the figure in the chair across from him. He didn't look like Albert Freyberg, but the years can change a person. The eyes still seemed the same, their soft brown hues showing concern, but the rest of the face had a fullness that was strange, as was the crop of gray hair that rested atop Albert's head. He had always been so thin, almost gaunt at times, but now he had the roundness of prosperity; not fat, not muscular, yet well kept in his fine tailored suit.

Helmut remembered that Albert always looked older than his years back then, but he had aged well. He still looked older than his forty-two years, rich and confident as one would expect from one of the most successful bankers in Bremen.

4

"You know, Helmut." Albert began to speak. "You don't look any different than you did in 1918. You haven't changed, but I can tell by the way you're looking at me that I have."

"Not at all the same person," Helmut said, looking around the restaurant, his nervousness probably showing. Helmut wondered where to put his hat.

"Don't let this place intimidate you." Albert said. "The food is excellent, but the climate here is terrible. I hoped that you don't mind that I treat you to a meal. I seem to remember that I owe you one."

Helmut squirmed in his seat.

Albert smiled at him. "Is this place making you nervous? Relax, please! I felt we'd both be better off talking here than in my office, but maybe I should have picked a different spot."

"No. No." Helmut replied. "This is quite an experience."

"Then relax and enjoy it. If you act like you own the place, they'll treat you that way."

Helmut and Albert both laughed. The ice had been broken.

Albert began to pour some wine into Helmut's glass. "Let me see," he began to say. "I guess we'll need to refresh each other's memory on the happenings in our lives the last few years. Tell me, how are things going for you?"

Helmut smiled. "Except for money problems of running a farm, I'm doing well."

Albert poured more wine. "I seem to remember a French woman you were quite stuck on back during the war. I seem to remember nearly getting shot for her. Do you still think about her?"

"Yes," Helmut smiled. "I'm married to her now."

Albert eyebrows lifted, his startled look surprising Helmut.

"I was a little ashamed of myself at first, especially so quickly after my first wife died, but then, as I grew more accustomed to it, I realized how happy she has made me."

"Touching," Albert smiled. "I'm glad that you found your happiness."

"And you, Albert?" Helmut asked.

Albert's face grew serious. "Our plans don't always work out as we would expect, but I'm happy. Although the plans I set forth back then didn't happen, I found a woman who loves me and I'm very happy also."

Somehow Helmut felt he saw remorse in Albert's eyes, as if his talking about the past had rekindled an old hurt, one his friend had hidden in the back of his mind for a long time.

5

Helmut quickly changed the subject. "I see you have made something more of yourself than the old weathered Hauptmann I remember."

Albert nodded. "That's more the doing of my wife, and for the happiness of my children. I think that I would have been happy being a simple shopkeeper. If you remember, I have never been the kind of man who takes on burdens he doesn't want to carry. But, when things were bad at my father-in-laws bank, I was asked to step in and have been there ever since. They say I have a nose for such things, but I'll tell you, I've just been plain lucky."

Helmut saw the shadow of sorrow cross Albert's face once more and was more determined than ever to change the subject. "Tell me of your children." Helmut eagerly insisted.

Albert smiled. "Yes! Yes. I have three children: a son and two daughters. You will have to come out to the house while you are in town. My son, Willi, always asked about the war, about my old friends then.....I am afraid to tell him."

They both nodded.

"I don't think about it much anymore, but the danger wasn't with me all the time. The death, to me, was a distant thing." Helmut said. "You had to live with it everyday."

"It never enters my mind." Albert went on. "Even when the pains come back...and they do come back now and then....I blot out the war. I don't see why the politicians keep bringing it up. It wasn't anything glorious, anything to be praised as the Nazis do. I lost my youth there. I lost my health and almost all my friends. I lost nearly everything by the time the war had ended."

They stared silently at one another for a moment, remembering the past.

Albert sighed. "I'm sorry, Helmut. I don't talk about what the war did to me very often. I never mention it a home and most of the people I know don't seem to understand. I guess, talking to am old comrade like you brings the anger out. I don't mean to be so depressing."

"You and your wife never talk about it?" Helmut asked. "Marie and I do from time to time, but then, though it may sound strange, we had met during the war and it brings back good memories as well as the bad."

"Mina and I also began during the war, but our circumstances were so different. Our relationship never did turn out as we had planned. Between us, our love, is not the same kind of love we had felt for other people."

"Yet you are happy." Helmut told him. "You have a beautiful family. You have a good business."

Albert smiled. "That too isn't what I expected it to be."

"How do you mean?"

"Since the day I got married I think Mina always wanted me to join her father's bank. He had died in 1919 while in Holland and the operators of the bank wanted a family figure to put in charge. Min was, and still is the president of the bank, but I was foolish. I was determined to make a go of it as a baker, just like before the war. I was a fool. After the inflation I grew much wiser. I went and took over the business. I learned it very well."

Helmut interrupted. "So I have heard"

"You know, Helmut. All that I ever did wrong prepared me well for this game of banking. I learned how to be ruthless. I learned how to be cruel, but it serves me well when it comes to protecting the little man."

"That's why I'm here." Helmut said, getting down to business. "I need your help."

Albert nodded.

"Things have been so difficult the last couple of years. I have watched all my savings drain away. Marie and I decided we would need some money to get ourselves back on our feet. Yet no bank would give us money. We had seen your name mentioned in the newspapers and she suggested I come to you. At first, I didn't want to. I guess it was my own pride. I thought that with the children grown I might have been best to just sell the farm and try to find work in a factory or something, but I don't know anything else. Marie finally convinced me to come here and see if you could help."

Albert had listened intently to Helmut as he spoke, his expression unchanging. Now Helmut waited for an answer, hoping that his old friend wouldn't turn him down. Albert was still for what seemed a lifetime, finally raising his wine glass and taking a sip before speaking.

"I may have difficult times convincing some of my people to loan a broken down old farmer money, but I'm sure there is something I can do." he flatly told him.

"Thank you," Helmut sighed.

Albert nodded as he took another sip of wine. "Are you sure you want to go through the bank. I'd happily lend it to you myself."

"Absolutely not! Sir, I don't want any charity."

"Have it your way." Albert smiled as he raised his glass. "After lunch we'll go to the bank and put the paperwork through."

7

Helmut nodded, relieved that his problems may be solved.

After another sip of wine, he changed the subject. "Remember when we broke into the Colonel's private wine cellar and drank ourselves silly."

TWO

Joseph Strauss hated doing street duty. Maybe it was touch pride and ego that made him feel it was beneath him to put on riot gear and work the streets just like a uniformed policeman, but when the department got a demonstration call all the officers that were available went out to control the crowds.

There would be trouble, Joseph knew, there was always trouble now when the Nazis and the Bolsheviks crossed paths these days. It was becoming a matter of course that once a week the two political groups would send out their faithful to intimidate the other. Today it was the Bolsheviks turn to start the trouble.

In the old days, when people were working and the money was around, the demonstration would have been peaceful. Joseph had always viewed the radicals as a bunch of angry children and before the trouble most of the people in Bremen felt the same way about them, but now their voices were being heard more loudly. Desperate people tend to listen to other desperate people.

As a detective, with a secure salary and the benefits of civil service, Joseph wasn't swayed by their rhetoric. As a detective he seldom had to deal with either group, except when one gang member murdered another. Now, when each day is filled with news from all over Germany about the depression, about the politics in Berlin, when each week there is another incident between the two radical groups, it was becoming tougher to remain uncommitted to either group, or to those that opposed them.

It was a typical beginning to the demonstration and the riot that would surely follow. The Bolsheviks had set themselves up near the entrance to a closed shipyard in the poorest waterfront neighborhood and one of the spokesman, a Red affectionately called Crazy Max by the police, had been hoisted on the back of a truck and was condemning the Weimar government, the press, the Nazis and just about everyone else in the country. As he spoke the crowds of unemployed workers would gather, and the police would muster their forces anticipating the inevitable arrival of the opposition.

It would come, Joseph knew, after the crowd was large enough and the Bolshevik hard-liners had worked them up into a frenzy. It would come because the Nazis were in the crowd too, watching, waiting for the right moment to bring in the brown-shirted gang members lucking a few blocks away.

As Joseph watched and listened he grew angry that he and the rest of the police stood around for so long and did nothing. He knew that they had the power to stop the battle before it began, but the power of both sides was feared by the city government and nothing would be done until both sides had the outcome they wanted. It would have been easy for the police to stop the Nazis march on the crowd. It would have been so easy to break up the Bolshevik demonstrators before the Nazis came. Yet he knew this would not be done because each side had friends in City Hall and in the Police Office.

"There will come a time." Crazy Max was shouting to the crowd that stirred below him. "There will come a time when the people will rise up and shake off their oppressors. The rafters of the money hoarders and food hoarders will shake when the voice of the people is heard."

Joseph mumbled to one of the other police. "I give them five minutes more."

"Watch that little man over there, near the edge of the crowd. He'll be the one to fetch the other side." the police sergeant replied.

"We must remain organized against the corruption that threatens our lives." the Bolshevik shouted. "We must not let the forces of the right, of the rich, of the corrupt delude us from our mission and goal.

"Someday the world will be united in the teaching of Marx. Someday the workers will decide their own fate. It is our mission to see that that someday happens soon in Germany."

Joseph listened as the crowd began to shout, the agitators among the ordinary workers shouting louder, swaying even the most docile of men to hate and anger. He watched as the little man in the corner of the crowded drifted from the rest and walked slowly around the corner.

"They're on their way." he told the sergeant and both of them circulated among the waiting police, spreading the word.

Joseph continued to watch the crowd and listen as he prepared himself, tightening up his gloves and wrapping his fingers around the nightstick in his hand. He would be lucky today: it was his job to put anyone arrested in the car behind him, not to wade through the crowd when the fighting started.

He began to hear the sounds of marchers coming, their voices singing loudly their party song. He watched as the crowd sensed their coming as well and some heads turned away from the speaker.

"The enemy of the people comes!" Crazy Max raised his fist to the crowd. "Meet them with the iron fist of the worker!"

All faces now turned up the street as the singing and the sound of boots against the cobblestones grew louder. As the brown-shirted youths rounded the corner the scurrying began. Those that feared the Nazis ran from the crowd while the Bolshevik stalwarts drew their hidden clubs from beneath their coats and braced themselves for their enemy.

The young policeman next to Joseph took a step forward. Joseph reached out and took his arm. "No, wait." he ordered.

As both sides screamed and shouted the two groups collided. The workers in their black coats decorated with red ribbons merged with a sea of brown shirts and Nazi armbands.

Joseph pointed. "You! Make sure those children don't get hurt." he shouted to the young policeman. The man ran over to a group of children standing away from the brawling crowd and pushed them out of harm's way.

Joseph watched the fight once again. The Nazis would get the best of it today, he quickly assumed. They were stronger, more organized, and they had been growing in strength each week. The Communists, on the other hand, never had seemed to lose their street gang tactics. It was easily seen who prepared for these riots more. The Bolsheviks were getting their asses beaten badly.

The police began to wade into the crowd. It was time to break it up before someone got badly hurt. Several men on each side were already drifting away from the brawl holding their heads, blood oozing from between their fingers. Others were on the pavement, rolling in pain from the blows inflicted by the other side.

Joseph concentrated on Crazy Max, who was beating the hell out of one Nazi. The orator fought well, Joseph knew, but within a moment three other brown shirts came to the rescue of their comrade. Crazy Max was quickly on the ground, the three youths above him with their sticks pounding the man's flesh.

Two police came to Crazy Max's aid, but the Nazis began to fight with the policeman as well. It was something Joseph Strauss had never seen before. Both gangs usually left the police alone.

"Let's go." screamed the police sergeant.

Joseph rushed, with several other officers into the crowd. He grabbed one of the brown shirts by the arms and wrestled him to the ground. He pulled the club from the youth's hand and kicked him in the side.

Suddenly Joseph felt a sharp pain in the side of his head and the world around him began to spin. The next thing he knew he was staring up at an angry blonde haired boy, no more than eighteen, and the club in his hand looked about the side of a man's leg.

Joseph rolled away from the club as it slammed into the cobblestones next to him.

When he looked up again the boy was gone.

The pain in his head ached as he gently felt his scalp and rose to his feet. It was sore to the touch, but there was no blood.

"Are you alright?" the sergeant questioned.

Joseph nodded as he focused on his surroundings. The crowd had almost dispersed. Only those who couldn't run away remained, their bodies writhing on the pavement and in the street, some caked with blood.

"That was really something." the sergeant said.

"Yes." Joseph groggily replied, "The worst one yet."

"Seems like they think they're above the law now."

Joseph shrugged his shoulders. "Maybe they are."

He could hear the whine of the ambulances now, finally arriving to take the wounded away.

Joseph felt dizzy and began to stumble. He felt a hand on his arm and knew he was being helped, almost dragged to the ground.

"You'd better go to the hospital." his sergeant told him.

Joseph shook his head. "I'll be alright."

The sergeant offered him a cigarette.

Joseph refused it. "How about we get some lunch?" he asked the sergeant instead.

THREE

He would sit in the park and wonder about the world. He would sit there, watching the people go by, sandwich in his hand, and look at the despair in the eyes of the passersby. He would feel happy that his soul was calm and at peace with the world. It was nice to have a job, to work and earn money at a time when so many were out of work and had nothing.

He knew that the crowds that passed by the park bench that he had turned into his lunch table were searching for a way to survive until tomorrow. It was something he didn't have to worry about, at least not for the moment. He wondered what they thought about him as they walked by and stared at him and his sandwich. How hungry were they? How desperate were they? How did they feel when they gazed at him? Did they feel envy, or hatred? Did they even really notice him against the fall landscape, its greenery turning slowly to rust?

The depression had hit everyone hard, he knew. It struck down the old, who struggled on what little they had saved from the good times to survive. It struck down the young, who searched the city desperately for work, finding none for them to do. It stuck down the common worker worst of all, his skills now unused at the idle mills and docks that dotted this riverfront city. He thought about and watched all these people wander by and hoped that he would never join their ranks. He hoped he would never become that desperate.

His eyes returned to the tasteless sandwich he was eating, but soon he felt the eyes of one of the desperate people prying into his mind. Slowly he lifted his head up and began to stare back at a pair of cold eyes. Even more cold and hateful was the scowl on the face of the bearer. He was a dirty, middle-aged man in a dockworkers garb, his weather beaten face showing age probably beyond his years. As he stared back at the dockworker, his eyes grew equally cold until he forced the man to turn his head, to look down at his well worn shoes. He too watched the feet wearing the shoes until he saw them begin to move as the man went on his way.

"Well, Martin." he whispered to himself. "There goes another one who will hate my guts."

Martin Bock then thought about himself. Thinking about himself in the way others saw him and how he saw his own being, as if he could be outside his own body, up in the trees watching someone else eat lunch alone in the park. To Martin, he would see a simple man, someone who had worked himself up from the slums of the city. He thought of himself as someone who these common people should be proud of, as one of their own kind who rose above the squalor of the slums, but he knew otherwise. These people would look at him, in his well pressed suit and shinned shoes, at his clean, classy look and see an enemy. To them, he was one of the prosperous few. He was one of those people that the radical politicians, the Communists and the Nazis alike, called the enemy. He was what the common people were beginning to think of as the enemy. He was working, making the money that they weren't.

He felt another pair of eyes staring at him and began to feel uncomfortable. He loved eating his lunch outdoors. He loved the park and the cool gentle breezes it carried in autumn, it was such a welcome change from the cramped, stuffy office, but he was beginning to realize that the stares were making it too difficult to sit there and peacefully eat the meal he had prepared for himself.

He finally looked up to search for the eyes that were pounding into his brain. He found the stare coming from the eyes of a young girl sitting on a bench across the park. She looked very relaxed on the wooden bench, her legs crossed and one arm resting against the back of the bench with a cigarette squeezed between her fingers. She appeared to be a pretty girl, maybe twenty-two or twenty three, with curly golden hair and a sweet smile on her face. To Martin, she seemed to be admiring him, not envious at all. She seemed to be viewing him as he would view the passersby.

Martin continued to watch her as she puffed away at her cigarette, the smoke circling her head only a moment before the breeze whisked it away. She couldn't take her eyes off him either, and it didn't seem to bother her in the least that he was looking back at her. He could have sworn she liked it.

Now he was becoming self-conscious and broke his eyes away from hers. He decided he didn't like to be stared at and went about

14

finishing his lunch quickly. He had an urge to get out of there and away from all the prying eyes.

As he gobbled up the remnants of his sandwich his mind refused to look upon the girl, but knew she was still there. As he finished he collected his things and was ready to go. It was time to get back to the office anyway, he reasoned.

"Hello," a voice called out to him. It was a woman's voice.

Martin Bock looked up from the ground and saw the girl standing before him. He realized how beautiful she truly was with her etched cheekbones and gentle eyes. He also realized that she was dressed and made up very softly. She was just as appealing up close to him as she had been from afar.

"May I sit with you," she questioned, "or are you leaving?"

Bock could change his mind quickly and adjusted to the situation. "I'm not leaving yet. If you want to sit here, it's fine with me."

"I notice you come here everyday." she said as she sat down. He saw a smile crack across her pretty, freckled face.

"I hadn't noticed you before."

"Maybe I haven't been here everyday, but I do come here fairly often at this time. You have always been here when I am here." she explained.

"I must be slipping. I should have noticed you" Bock joked.

"I'm Greta," she introduced herself. "What's your name?"

"Martin. Martin Bock."

"Well, Martin Bock." she went on, "What do you do other than sit at lunchtime in the square."

"I work at the bank offices across the street."

"I thought so."

"So, what do you do?" he asked her.

"I wander the streets." she giggled, it seemed to Martin that she was self-conscious about herself.

"It's not unusual in these times." Martin told her. "You're not the only one out of work."

"No, you don't understand." She explained. "I truly do wander the streets. That is my work."

Martin smiled at the girl. "You expect me to believe you are a streetwalker or something."

She leaned toward him, smiling broadly. "I am."

He leaned toward her as well, playing along with her teasing. "Prostitutes don't look for business in broad daylight in the middle of the business district."

"Maybe it's time we did." She laughed. "I'm not looking for business, just walking around town."

"And taking any business you can get, I'm sure."

The girl lit another cigarette, digesting his words carefully as the first puffs of gray smoke circled her head. Finally she spoke, "Are you interested, Martin Bock?"

He shook his head. "No."

"I thought not." she said as she rose from the park bench. "Work first, pleasure on your own time."

"I don't need a prostitute." he said as he watched her begin to walk away.

She turned back toward him, talking as she walked away. "Maybe I'll see you here again. If you change your mind, you know where to find me."

He watched her walk away from him, her body swaying as she went as if she had worked hard to learn that rhythmic walk. He knew she didn't look like a whore, but she was only clowning with him anyway. Some of the young girls will lead on a man like that at times. He guessed she felt it was a daring thing to do.

"She couldn't be....." he began to mumble to himself as she walked out of sight. She was, to Martin, too pretty to be a whore.

* * * *

Martin barely got his foot in the door to the bank offices when he heard his name being called. He felt like ignoring the distant voice calling him, but turned to search for the bearer of the voice. It was no easy task in the crowded, noisy office. There were a multitude of workers scurrying about the floor, making loud clicks on the hardwood floor as they walked in front of his scanning eyes. The ever constant echoes and the chatter of the secretary's typewriters made working conditions poor, but only made Martin work harder. The harder and faster he worked the sooner he could leave the noise behind and leave.

He heard his name being called again, but still failed to find the owner of the voice. A bit disgusted at himself, he shrugged his shoulders and began to walk toward his desk, dodging a phalanx of clerks as he went. A third call became louder and he realized that it was Lucy Wagner who was calling him and turned toward her desk.

She looked rather anxious as he approached her desk. Lucy was an attractive girl, her wavy brown hair hanging freely on her shoulders, her darting eyes looking at him and then quickly away. Her face seemed strained to Martin, as if she needed his help to work out of a crisis that had arisen.

"I'm glad you're back." she said as he took the last steps up to her.

"What's wrong?" he asked, not really wanting to handle any major problems today.

"There are two problems. One is that there is a man here to see Herr Freyberg, but wants to see him immediately." Lucy told him, her eyes shifting to her right in a gesture that forced Martin to glance over at two men sitting on a hard bench. "I have been told by the 'boss' not to bother him. The other man has a loan application you must see."

Martin smiled hearing her mimic calling Herr Freyberg 'boss'. Albert loved using the Americanized term, even if it made the more staid employees cringe.

When Martin looked over he realized why Lucy, who was the boss's personal secretary, was so upset. The stiff little man in the chair was wearing the armband of the Nazis. It was something he seemed to see more and more people wearing lately and it made him nervous as well. These people, Martin knew, were always obnoxious little martinets.

The other man, a shabby looking old peasant, could wait, but the Nazi had to be attended to immediately.

"What should we do?" Lucy asked, her eyes probing into Martin's for help.

He smiled at her. "I'll take care of them."

Martin took a deep breath and turned to face the stuffy little agitator. He felt instantly repulsed by the Nazi, his angry face and bearing staring up at him. He searched his soul for some inner courage and extended a hand to the man.

"Good!" The Nazi announced. "It's about time."

"I am Martin Bock, the assistant manager of the bank. Can I help you?"

The Nazi seemed displeased. "I came here to talk to Herr Freyberg."

"He is unavailable." Martin explained. "Can I help you?"

17

"I need to see him on an urgent matter." he said, his stuttering, clipped voice sounded almost military.

"Won't you come into my office, Herr....."

"The name is Dietz." the man blurted as he walked beside Martin into the small office. "I am here on a very important matter."

Martin sat showed the Nazi to a chair and took his place behind the old desk he called home. Martin's office did not give the appearance of importance, and he liked it that way. He felt that visitors felt less intimidated when they saw the barren office, furnished with only a chair, a file cabinet and his small, simple desk. It usually made the visitor more likely to speak freely than when faced with a pompous, elaborate office.

"Now," Martin started, trying, despite his nervousness, to be cheery to his guest. "What can I do for you?"

"It has come to our attention that your bank has been practicing employment policies contrary to the policy of the National Socialist Party. We have evidence that you have no party members in high ranking positions in your organization and that they show favoritism to people who oppose our views." The man sounded as if he were reading to speech, which was probably more true than not.

Martin smiled at the man. "I don't quite understand."

Dietz frowned at Martin's puzzled look. "I....uh..." he stammered, probably not expecting such a response. Martin figured that the Nazis, their power growing stronger each day, were used to people jumping at their barking commands. He had no intention of giving the arrogant little man that satisfaction.

"Herr Dietz," Martin went on to say after an appropriate moment of silence. "This institution shows no bias toward anyone in its employment and advancement practices."

"That is just the point." Dietz interrupted, "You haven't shown any cooperation with us and put any of your people who are members of the party to any rank of authority. You employ Jews and Bolsheviks. You do not encourage participation in any National Socialist activities."

Martin sighed. He had heard all this before. "The last time I looked this was still a republic, Sir. The last time I looked we were not a Nazi bank, but a bank of all the people of Bremen. I see no point in your argument."

"When we come to power....."

Martin interrupted. "When you come to power you will have the right to do what you wish. As of now, this bank still reserves the right to run its own business."

18

"When that day comes, Herr Bock," Dietz scowled at him. "Your Jewish owners will be stripped of their money and position and all who side with them will fall as well."

Bock stood up from his chair, anger swelling in his body. "Don't threaten me, Sir. I have no political preference. I am only following the policies of the bank and its officers. Those policies show bias toward none and not preference toward any one group of people."

"Our day will come, Herr Bock." Dietz concluded, rising himself and rigidly standing up to the taller man. "You tell that to Albert Freyberg and his Jewish friends. You tell them that."

"Good day, Sir." Bock growled.

Dietz stood at attention and extended his right arm high and stiffly in the air. "Heil Hitler!" he shouted.

Martin watched the man strut out of the office and thought about the angry words that he had said. He was right when he told Dietz he had no political preference, but he did believe in all the things Albert had taught him. Albert Freyberg, the manager of the bank, had always tried to help the poor. He had taught Martin that the only way to be was honest and totally fair to all, yet still uphold the bank's principles. He, as Martin's mentor, had steered him toward an ideal that Martin could only agree with. Not the shortsighted, radical rhetoric that was sweeping the land.

Martin knew one thing, though. If Albert didn't change his mind and start working with these people, he would be in trouble. Martin could see the day fast approaching when neutrality would no longer be a virtue.

As he stepped out his office Lucy glanced at him coldly. He couldn't read her thoughts, wondering if the cold stare was due to the stress of the day or something personal. Lucy seldom talked to Martin anymore, not since he had broken off their relationship, something he felt he had to do.

For more than a year he had been attached to Lucy. Attached was the word he used because he felt she never felt quite the same as he about their affair. He never viewed it as a permanent relationship, though she obviously had. She proved to be very affectionate and a lot of fun, but much too possessive for Martin. At times, since he had broken it off, he felt angry at himself for being cruel to her, but something inside him told him she wasn't the girl for him.

At first he thought it wouldn't affect his work, but now he wasn't so sure. Their work relationship while they were going together had begun to crowd the workday, which was one reason he ended it, but still, two

19

months after ending it, it still seemed to come between their working together. Both of them tried, and seldom succeeded, in keeping their personal feelings out of the days work.

"That was quicker than I thought." she said as he neared her desk.

"You just have to know how to handle these people." he replied to her.

She mumbled. "I guess you know how to be cold and heartless."

He glanced up at her with a cold and disgusted look.

She stared back and switched their thoughts quickly to business. "I can't believe this man has the nerve to come here for a loan." she said as she handed the application to Martin.

His eyes scanned the paper, jotting the facts into his mind as he looked alternately at the paper and the shabby little man squirming on the bench.

"Tell him I have to review his application and ask him to wait a while longer." he ordered Lucy.

Obviously she didn't like the tone of his voice today. "Jawohl." she crisply answered as he turned and returned to his office.

FOUR

As Martin scanned the application of Helmut Schorner he felt anger and a small amount of respect for the man's courage. The respect came from the feeling that it took courage to apply for a loan with a situation like that which the farmer described. The anger because Martin knew he would have to turn him down.

The application Schorner had presented was pitiful. Schorner was a forty-eight year old veteran who owned a small farm near the Dutch border. Like many farmers during the depression he was faced with little market for his goods. He seemed to be able to either grow or barter what he needed to keep himself and his wife alive, but what he tried to sell for profit was not enough to keep him going. He made no profit since the people had no money to buy his produce at fair market value. He would never produce enough to repay the loan.

Aside from that Schorner was working the farm alone. His children were grown and had left home which left only the aging farmer and his wife on the farm. Therefore, the bank had no security should anything happen to Schorner and would have no alternative except to take the property if the loan defaulted and one thing the bank didn't need was the liability of another farm.

For all those reasons Martin knew he was going to turn the man down, but he admired the courage Schorner had shown, or was it simply audacity.

Martin sighed as he flipped through the credit references attached to the back of the application. There were letter from the officials in the village near Schorner's farm. Then he saw the last one. It was a simple office memo, from the boss. It instructed Martin that, if the loan was not acceptable to come and see him.

Martin looked the application over again and came back to the same conclusion. This farmer was an absolutely atrocious risk. He would have to see Albert Freyberg.

"Sit down, Martin." Albert cheerfully said as Martin walked into Albert simple office. Despite the authority and position he held, Albert decorated his office rather plainly. Martin walked up to a plain clerk's desk and placed the application upon it.

Albert picked up the application and glanced down the first page. "No good, eh." he smiled as he turned the page.

"I think you knew that when you sent him to me."

Albert gently put the application down. "Do you want a drink?"

Martin shook his head. "I take it that you want the loan approved since you attached that little note." he stated, there was a tint of anger in his voice.

Albert rose from his desk and walked quietly toward the bar, his limp seemingly more pronounced than usual. Martin knew, as he watched him pour a glass of water, he was going to get one of Albert lectures about responsibility to the people.

Martin started before Albert could sit himself down again. "I realize that every little man deserves a loan if he has a reasonable chance of fulfilling his debt, but this farmer's chances of that are slight. He's too old, first of all, he's got no one to pick up the debt, and he's not got modern equipment. And if he defaults, we have no use for his property."

Albert slyly smiled. "I know all that, but I want you to approve the loan anyway."

Martin felt back into the corner. "Why?" he sighed.

"During the war," Albert began, "Helmut Schorner was my sergeant, my chief mechanic in the section of observation planes I commanded."

The boss paused as if he was shuffling through the pages in his mind recalling a time Albert seldom spoke of. Martin knew Albert had been an officer, a flyer, during the war, but, unlike many of the old veterans, never talked of those days. It was as if it were a time he would rather forget.

Albert continued. "We spent three years together in France and during that time our relationship was more than officer and conscript. He was also my friend. When things got rough and equipment was scarce, he always kept the planes flying. When someone needed something Helmut always found a way to get it. In short, he was a resourceful man, and I feel he is a good risk for the loan. He has my personal recommendation."

"That's not enough." Martin responded. "You have always taught me to keep my personal feelings apart from business, and the facts are he doesn't have the credit or the resources to repay the loan."

22

"Sometimes, Martin, we must forget business. This is one of those times."

"Will you countersign the loan?" Martin coldly asked.

Albert thought about it a moment, wrinkling his brow and running his hand through his gray hair. "I will," he finally said, "but you mustn't tell him I'm doing so. The man has a lot of pride."

Martin kept his businesslike approach. "Very well, I approve the loan based on your signature."

Martin took the application from the desk and turned quickly. He was disappointed in his mentor, a man who had never mixed business with personal feelings, yet had just let his sound business sense desert him.

"One moment, Bock," Albert sternly said.

Martin turned on his heels to face Albert once again. He realized he had made him angry.

"I believe you don't think my explanation is sufficient." Albert said, his deep voice echoing in the room. "Sit down." he ordered.

When Martin had returned to his seat Albert went on. "There are many things you don't understand about the war and the comradeship of the men there. It is something I hope you never have the need to understand or to experience. Many of us felt we were living on borrowed time, but Helmut was one of the few who sensed his own survival when all around were dying. He may have been a mechanic stationed at a landing field far from the trenches, but he sensed the death all around him and kept his spirit and instilled that spirit in all of us.

"There was also the feeling of self-sacrifice in the man. Late in the war I was returning from a mission, my Albatros was shot to hell and I was limping in for a landing without the aid of even an undercarriage. I had somehow put the plane down and walked away from it, but only a few steps. The plane exploded and I was injured. Helmut and another man, both of whom I cherished as my closest friends, pulled me from the fire.

"If it weren't for Helmut Schorner," Albert concluded. "I wouldn't be alive today. That, if for no other reason, makes me insist that the loan be approved.

* * * *

Martin sat staring across the desk from Helmut Schorner and tried hard to see inside the man. He didn't look courageous; he looked rather ordinary in fact. He looked older than his years and his suit was

23

threadbare. The man nervously gripped the old felt hat on his lap, not the picture of resolution that Albert had described.

Schorner's huge mustache was not groomed properly and his face had a shadow of a beard. His sad brown eyes nervously glanced around the room as if anticipating someone else was lurking in the office. He was not the picture of confidence that Albert had described either.

"Your loan was difficult to approve." Martin explained. "But we got it through. I'm having them write you a check now. Congratulations."

Schorner seemed to be relieved, but then his expression turned to concern. "Did Herr Freyberg have anything to do with my getting the money?" he asked.

Just as Albert had said the man had pride.

"His recommendation does have weight here." Martin explained, "But I approved the loan based on your past record. Herr Schorner, you have never had financial troubles before and I expect that you will repay the loan as quickly as you can. You don't strike me as the sort of man who likes being indebted to anyone."

Helmut nodded. "Good. I didn't want Herr Freyberg pulling strings for me. He had done enough for me in the past."

Martin was confused. "Just how well do you know him?" he asked, his mind deciding to probe the farmer for facts, though not knowing why. He had heard Albert's explanation, but that didn't seem good enough for him. He knew so little about his boss, even though he has worked closely with him for five years, but had always craved more. Now he had a perfect opportunity.

"Herr Freyberg and I go back a long way." Schorner explained. "I doubt to say that I know him well, however. Up to the time we met for lunch today I hadn't seem him since 1918, as a matter of fact. He and I spent the war together. He was my superior officer."

"I see." Martin tried to look interested although the story was the same as Albert had said.

"The Hauptmann and I had many adventures during the war. We became very good friends." Helmut continued. "Being a flying section we tended to spend more time together than the infantry. They didn't die as quickly or in such large numbers. One or two men would go and someone else would replace them, but there always seemed to be a group around that never changed. Albert and I were two of those, most of the others never made it to the end."

"I wouldn't know." Martin interrupted. "Albert, I mean Herr Freyberg, never talks much about the war."

Helmut smiled, his weather-beaten face cracking into thick creases. "That's just like him, but he was one of the most inspiring men I had ever met back them. I would have followed him into hell. I would have done anything for him. He, I guess, made my life what it is today."

Martin half expected another lifesaving story. Why did it seem that these old veterans were always indebted to another for saving their life?

Helmut leaned over closer to the desk. "My present wife is French, you see." he whispered toward Martin. "I became involved with her during the war, but she killed an officer in self defense and was put in jail. The authorities didn't see it her way and it was Albert and another flyer, Willi Reinhart, who got her off. So you see, if not for Albert, she and I would have never gotten back together, would have never been married. In that way, among others, I owe him my life."

The man looked as if he was about to go into another story, but Martin to cut him off. "That's all very interesting; Herr Schorner, but I have another appointment." He rose and showed the farmer the door. "Good luck and I hope everything works out for you."

Martin watched the man leave, he walked with a confidence he hadn't seen in him while he sat in the office. He began to think that the nervousness hadn't been an act to gain sympathy within the bank. He wondered if Albert knew his old friend that well after all.

He had learned something today, Martin realized. He had learned that the icon that Albert Freyberg was human after all. That he was more than a businessman and had a soft spot in his heart for old friends. He learned a little about the past that Albert himself never spoke of. He learned more in one afternoon that he had in five years with Albert, and his still felt there was a lot more to learn.

* * * *

The sun was setting as Martin left the office and the coolness of the late September air penetrated his body with the sharpness of a knife. It was unusually cool for September, making him think it would be an early winter. The leaves had already begun to turn in color and the fall winds were already kicking up. The streets of the city looked cold and uninviting too, but Martin felt the walk to his flat would be pleasant enough, no need to take the tram. He looked up at the towers of the

25

central cathedral and realized that the sky was clear, I was going to be a pleasant evening as well.

"I've been waiting for you." he heard a voice behind him as he began his walk. It was Lucy's voice.

He continued to walk, now with her beside him, slowing his pace down only a little.

"I don't feel we have anything to say." he told her, his voice a cool as the breeze.

"Well, I do."

He stopped to face her and coldly stared into her blue eyes. They were pretty eyes, for she was a pretty girl. Lucy was attractive, her round face enveloped with straight brown hair cut short as was the style of the day. Her thin lips and petite nose fit her face well and her complexion was fair and reminded him of clear crisp fall days like the one today had been. Her figure was just enough to perk his imagination, even under the cloth coat she wore. He remembered how fine a body she had: how her breasts curved so perfectly. It was a shame their personalities clashed.

"I can't go on like this." she said.

"How do you mean?"

"I can't see you everyday and want you, but know that it's over." she explained.

He began to walk again. "Well, unless you leave the firm, that's how it is going to be."

"You're making it worse." she said as she began to walk with him again, her feet scurrying to keep up with his accelerated pace.

"I'm not the one who wants me to make a commitment."

"Maybe I don't want a commitment anymore either." she said, causing him to stop again.

"No, Lucy. That's not true and you know it. Don't lie to yourself or to me and tell me you don't care about tomorrow when we both know that's all you think about. I'm not ready for the life you've planned and you're not ready for mine." Martin had said his peace and continued to walk.

She caught up with him again. "Maybe you're right, but we have to see each other everyday and that's not been easy."

"So quit."

"You know I can't do that." she almost shouted.

"Then adjust."

She stopped and screamed to him. "Why can't you just be pleasant to me!?"

26

Martin stopped, turned and walked back to her.

"All I want is for you to be nice to me. To talk to me like a person, not like a man with hate inside him. So maybe we weren't meant for each other, I think I can come to accept that, but at least we can exist in the same room." she almost had tears in her eyes. "Maybe you'll change your mind. Maybe you won't, but at least we can still be civil with each other."

Martin thought about it a moment. Maybe she was right; he had been more of a bitch to her than she had been to him. "Alright Lucy, I'll try."

The girl seemed relieved. "Friends?" she asked, or stated, her tone of voice implied it could be either.

"Friends."

She came close to him and wrapped her arms around him. He could feel every curve of her body pressing into his and was surprised that it didn't arouse or affect him in anyway.

"Walk me home?" she asked.

He stared at her curiously. What was she up to?

"Please, walk me home." she pleaded. "I won't ask you in. I promise."

He placed his arm around her and together they started down the street.

"Are you invited to the party at Herr Freyberg's Saturday night?" she asked as they walked on.

"Yes, all the inside staff are going."

"I can't wait to see the house." she giggled. "I've never been there before. Won't you take me?"

He felt somehow that Lucy was twisting him around her fingers again, but was powerless to stop her. Sometimes Martin Bock felt he was an ass.

FIVE

Martin Bock had been to the Freyberg home outside Bremen many times before, but each time there it was like his first visit. The house, located about five miles from town on a hill overlooking one of the canals, was absolutely luxurious.

It was a big old mansion, supposedly built by Frau Freyberg's grandfather, who was rumored to be a relative of the Kaiser. Martin didn't believe all those stories; he felt the house was magnificent and all, but it was not quite that regal.

It was ornate, in the style of the last century, and the sounds of the people echoed throughout the house, from the parquet entrance hall to the study, with tapestries lining the walls. Martin wondered if one could get lost in the house, roaming endlessly through its many rooms and never finding his way out.

Martin had been a product of the riverfront, with their clusters of cramped little row homes, each with the identical, typical German family bulging from the ceilings. He never knew what open space was, other than in his dreams. He could experience it in Albert Freyberg's home, for the huge house was surrounded with gardens and lawns that must have kept ten servants busy. It was a fitting place for the owners of the bank to live, but beyond Martin's expectations. But then again, Albert Freyberg had come from the docks. Maybe, Martin often dreamed when he visited the house, he, too, would marry into money.

You could tell what rooms were Albert's, Martin decided as he wandered about. The study and a small bedroom and dressing area had to be Albert's lair. Unlike the rest of the house it was sparsely furnished. The furniture there was newer, more plain that the rest of the house. They reflected Albert's taste while the rooms people usually saw reflected his wife's.

Martin liked the study the best of all the rooms in the house and tonight, while most of the guests gawked at the old, much too uncomfortable furniture and the priceless paintings on the wall, Martin sneaked into the study to admire its simple decor.

On the plain wooden desk that dominated the room, a desk identical to the one in Albert's office in the bank, there were four photographs. They were fairly recent pictures of Albert's family. Martin glanced at the closest to him, a double frame with the poses of Albert's daughters, Anna and Marta, age ten. They were fraternal twins, and really didn't look alike. Anna was dark, serious, and bore a likeness to her father. Marta, on the other hand, always smiled, her brown hair tinted with gold, her features like her mother's.

Martin picked up the next picture; it was of Albert's son Willi, aged 13. The boy's Germanic face stared out with a friendly smile, pleasantly welcoming anyone who looked its way. Willi, Martin decided, resembled neither of his parents. Both Albert and his wife were dark, yet the boy had blonde hair and a light complexion. It was as if Willi had picked up the genes of his ancestors and completely skipped those of his parents.

Lastly he stared at Frau Mina Adler Freyberg's picture. The face that stared back at him was one wouldn't expect of a matriarch. One always pictures German mothers as big, heavyset, wholesome women, like Martin's own mother, but Frau Freyberg was not like that at all. She was a thin woman in her early thirties, still attractive even after two pregnancies and three children. She had stylish black hair, untainted by gray and small petite features that denied her heritage. Yet to Martin, the face was not as cheerful as he had expected, a certain sadness around her small brown eyes showed through. She had power and money and a strong man to love. What more could a woman ask for?

Martin took his eyes off the desk and scanned the room. There were only five pictures on the walls. One was a family portrait of the Freyberg's when the twins were still toddlers. They looked the picture of happiness. The others were old photographs and Martin examined them whenever he came into the house.

The first was of two couples walking across the grounds of the park near the opera house in Bremen. He recognized Mina Freyberg as a young girl among them. The other woman, a tall, thin lovely girl had her arm around a soldier. The soldier, an officer in the service during the war, which is apparently when the picture was taken, looked faintly like Albert. The other officer, a very handsome young man, looked happy and jovial as he walked hand in hand with the woman who was to become Frau Freyberg.

It was on odd picture, to Martin, for the couples seemed wrong. Albert should have been walking with his future wife, not some strange man, who should have been arm and arm with the beautiful young girl. Someday, when the time seemed appropriate, he would ask Albert about it.

The second picture was also from the war. It was funny that Albert, who never talked of about it, would have a picture from his war experiences adorning his walls. The photo showed a group of men standing in front of an old airplane. There were seven men in the picture, all officers except one dirty looking and unshaved mechanic in soiled overalls. Martin scanned the photograph for Albert's face, it was just like the face in the last picture, and also found the other flyer that held Frau Freyberg's hand among the group. The rest of the men were a mystery to him, except one. A young man on the left of the group also had his picture on the wall.

He took his eyes from the old war photograph and stared at the young face of Felix Adler in the next picture. The painting was from his Gymnasium graduation in 1917. Frau Freyberg's younger brother looked a lot like her, but he was still just a boy when the painting was done. He never did get much older, having died in the last year of the war.

The last picture Martin had seen before. The stern face of Herr Adler adorned many walls within the bank he ran for twenty years. Frau Freyberg's father molded the small lending institution into one of the strongest banks in the Kaiser's Germany before he died in 1920. It was a shame that the old man had no man to hand his business over to. It was lucky for his daughter that her new husband proved to be the right man to replace him. Albert was nothing like his predecessor, some of the older employees had told him, and the man, which his icy stare exuding confidence from the painting, bore than out. There was no softness in the cold eyes, no compassion in the face.

"Why do I always find you here?" a voice asked him. It was a pleasant, unassuming voice that he knew belonged to Mina Freyberg.

"I don't know. Maybe I feel that spending time in this room helps me understand your husband better." he said without turning to face her.

"You'll learn nothing about Albert by staring at my father's picture." she told him.

He turned to face her, realizing that the photographs don't really do her justice. Her small, shapely frame and her young face made her appear more like a young girl than a woman with children. Her thin smile, radiating as it never did in the photos, was warm and friendly.

30

"Albert and my father are very different people." she went on. "Take my advice and don't emulate the old man, no matter what some of the old-timers say at the bank."

"I admire Albert very much, but he does run the bank just as sternly as they say your father did."

"I never really got along with him." she said as she too stared at the old man's face. "Maybe it was just being his daughter, maybe the responsibilities he forced me to bear. I don't really know, but my memories of him are not always fond ones."

That was another thing Martin liked about Frau Freyberg, she always was willing to talk. She always talked to you like she was an old friend.

"Do you ever come in here to look at the pictures?" he asked her.

"No." she shook her head, still smiling. "I don't like this room. It has bad memories."

"How do you mean?"

"For one thing, it used to be my father's library and this was his domain. This was the place he scolded us and put us in our place." she explained. "For another, Albert keeps these mementos of the past lurking here. I don't want to be reminded of the past as he does."

"They're just pictures."

She turned away from the wall of pictures. "They're reminders of another world, one better in many ways than today and one we will never return to. I can't afford to look back anymore. When I do I don't find fond memories, but anger and sadness. I don't come in here because I don't want to remember."

Martin took her hand and walked out of the study.

Frau Freyberg left his side once she they entered the parlor, excusing herself that she had to attend to other guests. She began to smile as he joined a crowd of people around the bar and quickly took a sip from a champagne glass. Martin didn't know if she really enjoyed these gatherings.

The crowd that had been invited to the Freyberg home was part business and part pleasure. Every year after the oppressive North German summer had drained their energies, the senior employees of the bank were invited to the mansion. The Freyberg's tended to make it appear a social gathering, rather than a reward by inviting several friends from Bremen's social class as well. It made for a strange mixture of guests; the landed gentry drinking champagne with secretaries and clerks. It sometimes made for amusing conversation, as a businessman

31

and gentleman tried to explain how his horses were doing to some teller whose only reason for being there was that he had put twenty-five years in behind a cage. It sometimes made for a fight, when one of the rich people realizes the person he is dining beside doesn't know how to use the silverware properly.

When these types of situations come up Albert usually laughs and talks his way around it, pleasing both the employee and his rich friends with his little joke.

Martin had never gotten into that situation, although it was a trap he could easily fall into. He learned after his first trip here that it paid to learn the ways of the rich. It made him fit in; it would keep him from being kept out of the inner circle as he rose in the business.

He now could wander around the room completely relaxed and listen to the conversations.

"I had to close it up, the way things are." he overheard a fat, impeccably dressed man say. "I can't make a profit anymore down in that section of town."

The woman he was talking to had been working in the office since Martin could remember. They affectionately called her Big Bertha. She was huge, and her voice boomed throughout the room as she replied to the fat man. "If you close your stores how will those people in the riverfront get their shoes?"

The fat man belched. "They don't need shoes anymore. They don't have enough to buy food, yet shoes. If I don't do something, cut back my losses, I won't have a business left."

"Did you ever think that you could barter with those people? Did you ever think that they might have something you need in the place of money?" she blared back at him.

"You speak like a Bolshevik." he sneered at her.

"I'm no Bolshevik, but some of their ideas are right."

"Just remember," the fat man told her angrily. "If they were to take over you'll be part of the bourgeoisie. They don't like them either."

Martin moved on.

* * * *

Surprisingly, Lucy Wagner found herself more fascinated by the people attending the party in the great house than by the house itself.

This, in a curious way, was not what she expected. The house was a sight to see, but, as with many great expectations, it didn't live up to here assumptions. Lucy had seen homes like this before. Not quite as big as this, but big and more tastefully furnished. The huge, old furniture in the mansion was quite out of date, almost antique, and she knew from the magazines that people with taste didn't decorate their homes with that kind of stuff anymore.

The guests at the gathering, those that she didn't already know from the bank, she found more interesting. They were from the best circles in Bremen, which, in the ship worker dominated city, made them a rare breed. They were generally older, heavily set, even somewhat pompous and most of the men liked to look at, talk to, and probably would love to paw a pretty young thing like her.

Lucy knew she looked good tonight. She had carefully prepared for this evening, choosing just the right perfume, setting her hair in just the right, most fashionable way, and choosing the most becoming dress. It showed off her figure well, as did most clothes, making men think that there was more there than there really was. Lucy hadn't reached the point where she dressed please herself; she was still trying to please the men in the crowd.

She had talked to several of the older men in the group during the evening. She found most of them weren't concentrating on really talking to her. They looked at her breasts, their eyes moving left and right, up and down when she moved her chest. It was as if she had nothing covering them and the men had one eye on each nipple, hypnotized. Sometimes that bothered her, this time it didn't. Sometimes, she knew, Lucy Wagner was a tease.

There was generally one big problem at a party like this, where she was a single woman and most all the men had their overbearing wives hovering nearby. As soon as she began to talk to the salivating men, their wives would give them a cold stare and they would drift away. Lucy never seemed to have to go find a drink, as it turned out, but she always finished the drink alone.

Someone else stuck a half-filled glass of champagne in front of her face.

She took the glass and stared at the face offering the drink. The man smiling back at her looked into her eyes, not at her tits. That was different. The man had a round, jovial face, decorated with wrinkles. He was not too fat, and had to bearing of a man who used to be muscular.

33

"You look as though you could use this." he told her in a resounded voice.

"Thank you," she chirped. She could never be truthful, telling these lecherous bearers of gifts that she was so tipsy that she couldn't walk away from the wall she was leaning on if she tried.

"I'm always glad to see there's someone else who's a stranger here," The man said. "And alone."

That was very perceptive of him, she thought. "How could you tell?"

"I've been watching." he explained. "For one thing, no gentlemen, and I use the term loosely, has talked to you for more than a few moments, and none more than once. For another no young man save one, and you looked at him as if he were a brother, has spent anytime here with you. Therefore you are here alone, as I am."

"That's very good."

"I take some pride in my instant analysis of the situation." he sarcastically said, the sneer on his face almost sinister. "What brings you to this occasion?" he then asked.

"I am Herr Freyberg's secretary." Lucy answered, and then quizzed the man. "And you?"

"My name is Karl Scheuler."

"I don't know you from the bank so I can assume you are someone of importance."

"No, not very important." she smiled. "Actually I'm not even invited here."

She looked at him strangely.

"It's very easy really," he began to explain. "Those that are from Freyberg's bank assume I am a businessman and those from that group assume I am from the bank. No one wants to pry so you tend not to get many questions."

"Why are you here then?"

"Secret mission." he whispered to her.

She was smiling, it was genuine. Usually she found that when she smiled in older men's company it was forced.

"Actually, I'm Albert Freyberg's old commandant and I had to see him. This party he was giving offered me the opportunity."

"Then the 'boss' invited you."

"The 'boss'?"

"It's a affectionate term." Lucy explained.

"Oh, I see." he nodded. "No. Not exactly. I just have this way of knowing about it, but I haven't even seen Freyberg yet."

"He's right over there." she pointed. "Why don't you go and say hello."

"Why don't you call him over, but don't infer who I am. Let him guess."

She waved at Albert, who slowly walked over to them. He stared at the man with Lucy as he approached his expression as if he had seen a ghost.

"Hello, Herr Freyberg." Lucy began. "It is a wonderful party."

"I'm glad you are having a good time." he said, his voice hollow and his eyes distracted as he stared at the man.

"This gentlemen asked me to introduce you to him." she said, watching the boss's eyes as the surveyed the stranger.

"Where do I know you from?" Albert asked as he took the man's hand.

"From a long, long time ago." the man who called himself Karl Scheuler said.

"I know, but I find it hard to believe." Albert answered, his hand still clutching the hand of the stranger. The look of recognition now covered his face. "Are you...... you......alright?"

Scheuler seemed as if he understood. "Quite recovered, thank you, Albert."

"What brings you here?"

"I need a few moments of your time. Not now, but later in the evening. I have a very important matter to discuss." Scheuler explained.

"Fine," Albert nodded. "A little later then. I'm sure Lucy will be able to entertain you until then."

"Yes, I'm sure she can." Scheuler replied as he took Lucy's hand walked with her out onto the patio.

"Well," she sighed. "That was very mysterious."

"Just two old friends a little frightened of what they might say to each other after many years of separation." Scheuler explained.

"Why did he ask you if you were alright?"

"Old war story." he said. "Someday I must tell you about it. But for now, let me learn a little about you, my dear."

* * * *

The night was getting long and some of the guests had had a little too much to drink. Martin wasn't one of them and he knew that he wasn't having a good time.

There was something in the air tonight, Martin realized, though he couldn't exactly figure out what it was. Was it him? Was it the way he felt? Or was it everybody else who made the air of the evening feel so uneasy, as if there was a summer storm brewing and the clouds swirled overhead and the wind had that peculiar hollowness as an uneasy calm settled over everything.

Maybe it was him. Maybe he was more upset at watching Lucy Wagner display herself than he would admit to himself. She looked wonderful tonight. Her face shinned, her smile lighting up that room, and her voice echoed brightly throughout the cavernous house. She was showing off herself, Martin guessed, her blue dress making her alluring as it hugged her body so tightly that there was no hiding what she possessed. Was she doing that for his benefit? Was she accomplishing her goal in making him jealous? Or was he reading more into it that there was?

She had latched only one older gentleman, if that term really applied, and they seemed to be having a really good time. He was a sturdy looking man, but, Martin had to honestly admit, he had to be twice Lucy's age. Yet they seemed to laugh as they talked to each other and in the recesses of Martin's mind it bothered him. Lucy and he always had a good time, but seldom laughed at things one another said.

Martin struggled not to stare at them, his eyes turning to scan the room and finding Albert and Mina talking to one of their more distinguished guests and his wife. The man was familiar to Martin; he was one of the banks largest depositors. Herr Lysk had been doing business with the bank since before Albert had taken over and was well respected in the city, were he ran one of the large shipping firms. He seemed upset as he spoke with Albert.

Martin eyes suddenly met Albert's and quickly Albert's finger beckoned him to his employer's side.

"Albert, please." Mina was saying quietly to her husband. "Don't make a scene."

"I'm making no scene." Albert dryly and furiously stated. "I just want to make my position clear to Herr Lysk."

"Helga," Frau Freyberg addressed the shipper's wife. "I'm sorry. The night was not meant to turn to business. Shall we leave them to talk over their business?"

"No," the woman said. "I wish to hear your husband's point of view."

"Herr Bock," Albert addressed him. "Will you kindly explain to Herr Lysk why we refuse to donate funds to political parties?"

"Certainly, Sir," Bock began. "Any donation would have to be accompanied by a similar donation to all political parties equally. I believe there are eighteen right now active in the Bremen-Hamburg area. That would turn out to be quite expensive."

"This is insane." Lysk bellowed. "I'm not saying give money to all of them, just to those that could influence bank policy."

"That would be unwise. I've no desire to back the wrong party and endanger the bank's future." Albert said.

"That's not what I'm asking." Lysk explained. "I say you back the one party that will help your bank."

"You mean, your own party, obviously." Albert retorted.

"The aims of National Socialism are to help business get back on its feet. A strong Germany can only help. We need to restore our position in the international sphere."

Bock was ready to add something, but chose to remain silent. He could sense that Albert was losing his patience. He knew anything he said could be taken the wrong way.

"You mean you need to bolster your shipping business and a stronger Germany gives you more outlets."

"A stronger Germany benefits us all." Frau Lysk interjected.

"An economically stronger one, yes, I agree," Albert went on. "But not one that is run by a bunch of hoodlums and warmongers."

"I take offense to that, Sir." Lysk, his face red with anger, grunted. "I'm proud to be a member of that party.

Albert looked at him as if in shock. The outburst by Lysk was loud enough to silence the clamor of the other guests. As the room went silent all faces turned toward them. Martin suddenly felt nervous and self-consciously wished he could remove himself to a corner.

Lysk went on. "If your father-in-law were alive he would be by my side. He was a man of insight."

"He had principles, Sir," Mina Freyberg interjected. She looked somewhat disturbed. "He wouldn't take sides politically for business reasons."

"He was an opportunist, Mina." Lysk glared back at her. He spoke to her as if she were still a little girl, contempt coating every work. "If I

37

recall, he took advantage of the situation, every situation. He would have seen the advantages of befriending the Nazis."

"I can't agree with what they stand for. I can't stand with men with whom I differ so greatly with in ideology." Albert stated coldly.

"Then you are fool, Freyberg." Lysk told him. "You will not find a friend in government when we take power."

"When 'we' take power?" Mina looked at the man, her face turning red.

"Mina, I'll handle this." Albert said as he took his wife by the arm and pulled her away from Lysk.

"I have every intention of being very important to the Nazis." Lysk went on.

"Then you are the fool, Lysk." Freyberg replied. His tone was callous. He was clearly being nasty intentionally. "You will be used by them. They need people like you now, but if and when they do have power they'll throw you out like a piece of used meat."

"Freyberg, that's ridiculous." Lysk laughed. "They're courting businessmen across the country. They're seeking our support and cooperation."

"And you," Albert pointed his finger in anger at Lysk, "think that once they gain power, you will control the strings. You and men like you! Don't you know that won't happen? The Nazis court your money, but tell the rabble on the street that you are the ones who ruined the country."

Lysk laughed again. "Brunning and the Social Democrats ruined the country. The Nazis realize that."

Albert's look turned to one of disgust. He waved his hand in front of the man. "Ah, what's the use? I can't reason with you. You're too far gone."

He turned his back on Lysk. The man's cheeks puffed up like a balloon, his face glowing red. As Albert turned his back on the man, Lysk reached out for him and jerked his body back to face him.

Albert angrily freed himself from Lysk's grasp. "You son-of-a........" He stopped. "Get out of my house!"

Lysk huffed as he stared at him. He didn't move.

"I said get out of here, you hypocrite."

"I consider your tone and attitude, and your behavior, an insult." Lysk snorted.

"Consider it anything you wish, you fat......" Albert's voice quickly tailed off.

Lysk seemed to exude smoke from his nostrils. To Martin he looked like an enraged bull, and Albert had waved a red flag in front of his eyes. The man reached for the glass of champagne his wife held in her hand and threw it in Albert's face.

Albert's hands dropped to his side. He lunged toward Lysk. As Mina reached out for her husband so did Martin, stopping Albert just as his hands raised up grabbing for Lysk's lapels.

"Albert! No!" Mina shouted, struggling to keep her furious husband at bay.

Lysk laughed. "Look at him now!" he seemed to be talking to the crowd. "We always knew you married a low-life, Mina. We thought you had trained him better."

Albert struggled to free himself from Martin's grip. It was all Martin could do to restrain him. "You scum!" Albert shouted. "Get your fat ass out of here!"

Suddenly a glass of champagne reached out in front of Martin's eyes. It turned and splashed against Lysk, the man's snickering suddenly stopped immediately.

The man who had been talking to Lucy had thrown the champagne on Lysk. He spoke, "There! Do you like it?" Lysk's expression turned to anger. "Sir, you have insulted your host in front of his other guests. Personally, I take offense to that. As Herr Freyberg so aptly put it: 'Get your fat ass out of here'!"

The two huge men glared at each other for an instant. Lysk then turned, grabbed his wife's arm angrily and stormed out of the room.

* * * *

Karl Scheuler had finally gotten Albert alone. It had taken that outburst to flatten the life in the party. It had taken that to make Albert realize that Scheuler wasn't here as an adversary. Karl liked that, he needed to get into Albert's good graces.

The party went quickly downhill after the incident. Karl had watched as some of the guests, he assumed they were from the snobbish business aristocracy, quickly gathered their ladies and left the home. He watched as the more meek members of the bank group excused themselves and shuffled off as well. He watched as the house drained itself, leaving only the staunch friends of the Freyberg's and their most loyal employees behind.

Karl felt sorry for Albert's little wife, whom he never had met. The little woman seemed quite upset at her husband. After the rats had left the ship she glared at Albert coldly and left herself. Karl could tell there was friction between them, but he knew that it would last only briefly. He had sensed an air of contentment and happiness between the couple. Actually, he admired them throughout the evening. Albert's wife seemed to love her husband and that was a rare thing after so many years of marriage, Karl felt.

It was then that Albert decided it was time for their little talk and had brought Karl to the study. He then excused himself for a moment while he cleaned himself up.

Karl admired the room. It was Spartan in appearance, decorated with simple furniture and a few pictures hanging on the walls. Karl studied the old photographs carefully. He had seen some of the faces before.

"I remember when that picture was taken." Karl told Albert as his host returned.

Together they stared at the old photograph of a group of men standing before an old Albatros C3. Karl recognized himself and Albert among the seven men pictured. He tried to place the rest of the faces as well.

"I remember when your wife took that shot." Albert said. "We were celebrating Helmut Schorner's birthday. I think she was happy to see us all having a good time and she wanted a picture to remember it by."

Karl smiled. "I had forgotten why the picture was taken. I only had remembered when it was. I should have guessed, you know. Schorner's the only one who's not an officer."

Albert grinned, as if remembering something else about the picture.

"There's Teglerhoff." Karl recognized another face. "Did he make it through?"

"No, went down in June '18."

"How about Adler?" Karl pointed to another face.

"No." Albert flatly, sadly stated.

"Ah-ha." Karl also frowned. "I'd guess Reinhart didn't make it either?"

"No, sir. October 1918, would you believe? He came so close."

Karl shook his head. "That's a pity. For all of them that's a pity. Such a fine group of young men we all were, even me."

Albert grinned. Karl had been the old man of the section and he had
left the war earlier than the rest in the picture. He realized it had been a
long time since he thought about those days.

Albert took his place behind a simple wooden desk and offered Karl
a chair and a cigar. "A lot has changed since that old photo was taken,
hasn't it." he began. "Are you alright?" Albert then glanced sideways at
his old commandant.

Karl smiled. "Oh, yes. I am quite recovered."

"Are you sure?"

Karl nodded. "My problem took a while to solve, but now
everything is just fine." Albert, he realized, was gently touching the
subject without actually addressing it. When one goes crazy from the
stress of combat, those that knew should be a little hesitant.

Karl decided that Albert needed an explanation. "It took about four
years before I regained control of my mind, Albert. That's a long time to
be considered quite insane. I don't think anyone really trusts me to this
day, but, honestly, I am very in control of my senses. I even solved that
other little problem."

"Oh?" Albert's eyes expressed curiosity.

Karl nodded. "Yes. I found that the groin injury wasn't what made
me impotent." he smiled, pointing to his head. "It's all up here, you
know."

Albert grinned broadly as he lit his cigar. "This is very interesting."
he said, apparently changing the subject. "Not more than a week ago
Helmut Schorner was in town to see me. He needed a loan for the farm
he owns. Now you're here. It's like a mystery story where all the old
things from the past come cropping up before your eyes, all the sins of
our past coming back to haunt us. Next thing you know the ghost of
Willi Reinhart will come walking through that door. What can I do for
you, Karl?"

"Curious you should ask." Karl smiled. "What makes you think I
need a favor?"

"Fourteen years!" Albert exclaimed. "You need a favor."

"Alright," Karl sighed. "I, since my release from the nut house, have
served as a civil servant in the government of the Prussian state. I have
worked my way up slowly into the ranks. It's funny how forgiving the
Social Democrats can be of an old monarchist with a little lunacy in his
past.

"Anyway, I came into possession of some information that disturbs
me and I would like to give it to you for safe keeping."

Albert looked somewhat confused. "What information?"

"Facts and figures on how the government is violating the Versailles Treaty and will do more so if the military gets its way."

"Why bring them to me? What do you want me to do with them?" Albert asked.

"I fear about the future, Albert. We were just talking about what happened to us and all our friends in the last war. We know what it did to our lives. I would do anything to assure that the same thing doesn't happen to another generation of boys."

"In many ways I feel as you do." Albert answered. "I lost almost everything then; all my friends, my loves, and nearly my life. I wouldn't want my son to face that."

"I feel the same way and maybe these documents in the hands of the English and the French could do some good in stopping Germany from rising from defeat to threaten the world again."

"You seem rather sure that we are the threat to peace in the world."

"I do." Karl flatly stated. "Whether you like it or not, Albert, the Nazis are just a short distance from taking power in this country. The Communists are on the decline. The Monarchists and the Social Democrats are done. It's only a matter of time before that group of angry little men takes over. Then, people like you and I are through. There's a lot of hate out there and much of it's coming our way."

Albert nodded. Karl knew he saw the clouds on the horizon and desperately wanted not to believe the truth.

"Then take the document to the French or the English." Albert stated.

Karl laughed. "Do you think they're going to believe me? I'm a refugee from an insane asylum? No, I can't take it to them, but you could, Albert. You're a respected member of the business world. You're important to them, I'm not. Why, I've got people chasing me across Germany right now. They'd kill me before I'd get across the border with it."

"They're that convincing?" Albert asked.

Karl nodded.

"I can't take them." Albert said. "I've got family to think about. I have children. I can't pick up and run away just because some group of radicals may come to power in the country. I can't run off."

"You're going to have to. Your wife's is Jew; your children are considered Jews in the Nazis eyes. You know that, don't you?"

Albert looked upset. "How do you come to know that?"

42

"I know more than you'd like me to know, but nothing that the Nazis don't."

Albert leaned forward and sternly looked at Scheuler. "First of all, my wife's mother was a Jew. My wife's never practiced the religion and my children certainly are not Jews. Even though I, too, have Jews in my heritage. My grandfather was one also."

Karl grinned. "I know that as well, but you know that to 'them' it makes no difference. You'll be branded with the rest of them when the time comes. Why do you think I'm here?"

Albert leaned back in his chair. "I'm not exactly sure. You could be one of 'them'. How can I be sure? I could take you up on your offer and wind up dead. Then who'd be here to look after my family."

Karl thought about it for a moment. "That's a good point, Albert. I never thought about it that way. Yet, you must make the decision to trust me or not to trust me.

"I've taken a leave of absence from Berlin. I'll stay in Bremen for a while. You let me know what you decide." Karl got up from his chair and extended a hand to Albert. "Remember, friend, I never lied to you back so long ago. I'm not lying to you now. Get out, Albert, while there's still time. Get to safety, for your sake and for the sake of your wife and children."

SIX

It had been five days since the incident at her house and Mina Freyberg was still upset at her husband. Albert has embarrassed her with his behavior, embarrassed her in front of her friends and ruined the party which she had planned so carefully and had enjoyed so much.

Now she was going to learn what his outburst was doing to her business.

Mina really didn't like going to the bank for meetings. Although she had inherited the principal ownership of the bank she realized that she was no businesswoman. She was perfectly content to have her husband handle the business matters in his capacity as general manager, letting him look out for her interests. After all, the prosperity of the Adler Bank was Albert's prosperity as well as her own.

This week she had been mad at him, but Mina truly loved her husband. She had wished he had restrained himself the previous Saturday, but couldn't disagree with his principles or the stand that he took. They were her views as well and that overbearing man, Herr Lysk, had no right to start and argument over politics at a social affair.

Yet, damn, she thought to herself, sometimes his rough, waterfront image came bursting out at the wrong moment!

Mina had married Albert for all the wrong reasons. Both of them were abandoned just prior to their marriage, the victims of bad luck and the horrors of war, and their love had been a shaky thing from the start. Min always knew that he had married her out of pity, as well as loneliness, but that was fine for she needed him badly and he was there for her. Both of them blamed the war for all their troubles, robbing them of the true loves of the lives, but both of them found solace and comfort in each other.

Mina knew it wasn't the best reason to get married, but their love for each other had grown these past fourteen years. From a bitter, young girl she had grown into a wife and mother, cherishing her children and the man who took care of her. From a woman who viewed her husband as protector, not lover, she and Albert had become partners in life, though sometimes she wondered if he was truly happy with the way things turned out.

It was the reminders of their past life that kept her wondering about him. It was those damned pictures he hung so proudly in his study. That shot of him, arm in arm, with Francoise, that made her wary of his love for her. She hated that picture, but dared not take it down. She hated what it meant to her as well, for she was in it too, her hand clutching Willi's with the look of happiness in her eyes. She knew she was happier then and that that kind of happiness would never return to her life.

She knew that she would never feel about Albert as she had felt about Willi, or he about her as he had felt for another, but there was a different kind of love between them now. No, Min knew, not great passion, but understanding and kindness and the familiarity that two people who genuinely love each other feel.

She loved him for his kindness. She loved him for the way he felt about their children. She loved him for the way he took on the responsibilities he maybe didn't want. She only hated him once in a while when his old habits would return.

"Meee-na." he would whine to her when his anger came out. He would stretch out her name, his guttural voice straining out the word as he explained. "Forgive me. I'm a bastard who doesn't deserve your love. I just can't help myself sometimes."

"Well, damn you Albert!" She would say to herself. "No matter what you'd do I'd still love you."

She had hardly spoken to him all that week, dreading to hear how things had gone at work because of the incident. She was upset when the office phoned asking her to come to a meeting of the trustees. She would hear the truth then, with Albert afterward apologizing continuously for what he had done. She hoped and prayed that the damage wasn't too great, but realized that they definitely lost Herr Lysk, a large depositor, a maybe some others who felt like he did.

On the drive into Bremen she thought about it, her mind firmly set to downgrade the impact of the setbacks. Her mind determined to not have a confrontation with Albert.

She felt a strange dread when she walked through the outer office as if all those there were staring, realizing that when she came to the bank there was trouble afoot. She didn't want to upset the employees. These were troubled times, many banks had closed already and too many people had been put out of work. She could sense the fear that was in the minds of the employees, a fear that the bank was in trouble.

She entered the board room with a fear herself, but hers was directed at the strained faces of the trustees. Some of these men viewed her as sort of a joke. To them she was a figurehead who had to be consulted when needed, but who knew nothing of the business she had inherited. She was, to them, the little girl who sat in the big chair. She was, she could always tell by their stoic faces, Herr Adler's little girl, not the president of the bank.

She took her seat in the gigantic leather chair and immediately felt herself shrink. It was a monstrous chair which made her seem smaller than she really was, and she imagined how little that might be in the minds of the trustees. Min was delicate and thin, her features rather plain in her own mind. She must have looked about ten years old in that chair.

A huge picture of her father faced her from the opposite wall. She hated looking at his face, staring back to her with his stern eyes. Watching her every move to make sure she made no mistakes. Why, she thought to herself, did he place this burden upon her small shoulders.

"Madame," the senior member of the board addressed her. "We have called you in on an urgent matter."

Min stared at the faces around her. All of them looked tired and stressed. All of the old men, many of who she remembered since childhood, had sadness in their eyes. There was also one face missing.

"Where is the general manager?" Min asked coldly.

The two eldest trustees stared at each other. Then one of them responded. "He was called to Hamburg this morning on a business matter."

She was being set up, Min realized. Damn these old men!

Another trustee spoke. "We called this urgent meeting because we must discuss Herr Freyberg's conduct and how it affects the bank's affairs."

"So you dare to do this behind his back." Min declared. "My husband is in charge here. It was his place to advise me if the bank is in trouble."

"Your husband is the cause of the trouble." the senior trustee said. "We chose not to have him here while we discuss it. We want to keep control of the meeting."

"You want to control me. You feel you have a better chance of that with him not around."

46

The trustee looked impatient. "We want to present you with the facts, Madame. That's all."

"I wonder, Sirs," Mina slowly replied, letting her words sink in. "I wonder if you realize the consequences of what you're doing."

The trustee ignored her remarks and presented a file to her. "Madame," he began to speak, his voice sounding well rehearsed. "In the past week eight of our largest depositors have withdrawn their funds from the bank. Among them are Herr Lysk, the Wilhelmshaven Shipbuilding Company, and the accounts we had with the Bremen city government. Your husband is away today trying to keep the largest Hamburg depositor we have from withdrawing also. If he fails we have a catastrophe on our hands."

She looked over the papers as he spoke. The total number of accounts that had left was high, but she realized that they were less important. Big depositors were what the bank craved, what the trustees needed to maintain their plush positions. That was their greatest concern. The loss to the bank was nearly seven million Rentenmarks.

"If this trend continues, we feel the stature of the bank is in doubt. We cannot continue with this kind of loss." the trustee concluded.

Min scanned the papers before her. There was something missing. "Where are the figures on the percentage loss to the bank?" she asked.

Several of the trustees looked curiously at one another. No one answered.

"I wish to know what we have lost in comparison to our assets?" she demanded.

The senior trustee finally answered. "The fact that the percentage is low is not important here, Madame. The important thing is the trend which had been set. Money will continue to flow from the bank under the present circumstances."

"I want those figures." Min adamantly demanded.

Several minutes silently went by while they waited for the figures to be produced. When she was finally presented with them her mind was eased. There was a significant financial loss to the bank, but it was not abnormally high. It wasn't good, nobody wants to lose money, but it wasn't the catastrophe such as the trustees painted it, either.

"Frau Freyberg," the senior trustee began after she had looked at the figures. She could swear his voice was trembling. "We, the members of the board, beg you to ask for the resignation of the general manager."

His words shocked her. "What! Why!"

"His conduct has endangered the bank. His business judgment has also not been sound."

Min tossed the papers across the table. "In what manner?" she angrily asked.

"Frau Freyberg." another board member said. "It's the position of the bank to maintain a good relationship with the community. The general manager's policy runs counter to the community at this time."

"What you are saying, gentlemen, is that my husband is not coddling up to the right political groups, in your view."

The senior trustee spoke. "Madame, times being what they are...." he hesitated. "Times being.....we feel that sometimes it is best not to fight these people. To bend with the wind, so to speak."

Min was growing madder by the second now. These old men were cowering to the hotheads. They were afraid.

"Madame," the jittery senior trustee went on. "The climate in the country is not good. We must court those that will..."

She cut him off. "I will not work in this manner. I'll not let my bank be run out of fear!"

Another trustee stood up and leaned toward her. "You too should resign. You too are the reason we are in trouble."

Min leaned back in her chair. No one on the board had ever talked to her like that.

The trustees began to talk among themselves.

"Let's not get out of control." the senior trustee said.

"But she's not helping." another said.

"It's all 'that man's' fault. She's just his wife."

"They're run us out of business if we don't get rid of her."

"I disagree. We owe it to Jacob."

"He's dead. We owe him nothing. Start thinking of yourself. They'll come and get you if you continue to associate with these kinds of people."

"They say we're in with the Jews anyway, whether we are or not. We must get her out of the bank."

"Gentlemen," Mina firmly said. "Are we holding a meeting of the board or trustees or is this a meeting of alley-cats?"

The trustees regained their composure quickly. The senior trustee sat himself down and one of the loudmouthed ones stood up. He was a man Mina knew little about. He joined the board after she lost interest.

"Frau Freyberg." he began. He also never politely called her 'Madame' as the other men did. "We are prepared to offer you a great

48

deal of money to sell your interest to us. We are prepared to make you a very rich woman and make all arrangements for your......"

Min cut him off. "I am already a rich woman, Sir. I also will never sell my interest in the bank. This is the Adler Bank and it will remain in the Adler family. I will not sell out and run like a beaten dog. I would rather lose the business than sell out of fear."

"Then at least get rid of him." the man demanded.

"And do what? Put you in charge?" she asked.

"I would be happy to assume that responsibility."

"You would be happy to cooperate with the Nazis even to the extent of selling me out, no doubt." she told him. "I dare say you'd probably betray your own grandmother."

"That was uncalled for, Mina." the senior said. "Herr Becker was volunteering his services."

"He would love to maneuver me and Albert out. He would love to maneuver himself in."

"I see not point in this argument." Becker demanded. "I see that the board has unanimously recommended that you and your husband resign from this bank and that you have refused."

Min stood up. In her mind the meeting was over. "First of all, I remember ten years ago when many of you told me that I had to close the bank down. I remember when you fearfully told me that I was out of business. I remember that Albert saved my and your skin by restoring the bank to its former glory. Yet now you come crying to me about his mistakes. The bank has prospered because of Albert Freyberg. In my mind it can't function without him.

"Also, gentlemen, remember that I am the majority partner in this concern. I will never sell my percentage to you."

Min turned and quickly left the board room. She had just adjourned the meeting. She could hear them arguing behind her, their voices muffled by the heavy wooden door.

She was proud of herself.

* * * *

Martin had been glad to get out of the bank. There was anger there today. There was something going on and he was more than happy to take a long lunch today.

49

It had been a tough week, and today crowned it off as he might have expected. Since the troubles began he had been waiting for the board to convene and he had been waiting for Albert to have it out with them. He was surprised they chose to have it out with Mina Freyberg instead.

She had come strutting through the office with an unhappy look on her face, but Martin doubted she knew that Albert had been called out of town. He was going to warn her, but decided against it. Whether she knew or not made little difference for she was going to have to answer to the board regardless.

When the meeting broke up he watched her angrily leave the office and heard that she had turned down all the boards' proposals, not knowing what they might have been. Now the rumors were running rampant through the office and that's when Martin decided to get out.

The autumn air was pleasant and the cool crispness of the day too nice to spend inside a stuffy office anyway, he reasoned. It was a great day for a walk.

As Martin turned the corner he came upon a crowd of people. There was another of those damned rallies going on. It was getting to the point were, he believed, you couldn't go a day without a rally in the streets. You couldn't avoid them anywhere in the city either. They used to confine themselves to the poorer neighborhoods, but not anymore. They now set up their banners, red ones this time, in the midst of the business district.

Martin, basically because he had nothing better to do, stopped and listened. He looked around self-consciously while listening, seeing the police patiently standing by, watching the others in the crowd as some hung in every word while others were simply passing the time as he was.

The speaker is a grizzled looking middle-aged man wearing rumpled looking clothes. He looked rather common except for the red ribbon he wore on his arm. He looked like many men he had seen on the riverfront. Martin wasn't even listening to his words today; it was as if they were going in one ear and out the other. He had heard Crazy Max before and the Bolshevik rhetoric impressed him even less than the Nazi rhetoric did.

"We must rid our lives of the money hoarding aristocracy." Max exclaimed.

Martin browsed the crowd again. They were collection of working people, some in stiffly collared suits, other's in old workman's clothes. There was a small section of men dressed as Crazy Max was, they must have been the Palace Guard, Martin reasoned. They looked anxious, looking for trouble.

"We must free the workers of this country from repression." Max went on.

There were few women in the crowd, Martin noticed. Most of the ones he saw were drab, hard looking women. The kind you saw in the offices cleaning the floors.

"We will prevail over the militarists and the reactionaries." Crazy Max continued.

Then Martin saw her. Her tiny figure was standing on its tip-toes, stretching to see Crazy Max from the back of the crowd. Her eyes staring at the man, her ears tuned to his words. It was the girl who said she was a prostitute from the park the other day.

Martin admired her as she trained herself on the speaker. Her slim figure attractively stretched to the sky, every curve glimmering in the sunlight. Her golden hair reflected the sun as well, shining as a beacon to him. Her elegant profile never turned from the speaker. He began to walk toward her.

"Hindenburg and his cronies are your enemies!" Crazy Max declared.

She seemed to shake her head in disgust as she listened.

He reached her side and spoke. "I'm surprised to meet you here. I didn't think you'd be interested in Bolsheviks." he said, hoping that she would remember him.

"Shush!" was her curt reply.

He studied her again, this time close-up. She was dressed in simple neat clothes that appeared to be of good quality. Yet he doubted she was a prostitute because the clothes were not a whore's attire. They were plain, yet attractive as if she were the stylish daughter of one of the middle class families of the city.

"The working man must rise against all who shackle him!"

"I can't believe you really believe that crap." Martin said to the girl. He needed to draw her attention away from the speaker.

"Will you shut up!" she demanded.

He was shocked by her reply, but didn't have time to reply back. Suddenly there were screams and shouts in the street. Rocks flew by his head as a riot broke out all around him.

He saw armbands with swastikas flash before his eyes and felt the swish of clubs behind him. He looked for the girl and she had vanished.

51

Martin ran off to the side of the crowd. He realized that the Nazis and the Bolsheviks were out there in the street fighting and also that the group of police were standing idly by and watching. But where did the girl go?

There she was, trying to make her way through the crowd toward the stand from which Crazy Max was speaking. Now that was strange, Martin thought.

He watched as she approached a couple of the fighters. It was Crazy Max about to get himself beat up by a much younger, much stronger Nazi hoodlum. Martin was amazed when the girl grabbed the man and pushed him away from the Red orator.

Then he watched as Max picked himself up and ran off, leaving the smallish girl to handle the attacker.

He threw her off him. She staggered back.

He raised his club to her. She cringed.

Martin felt himself racing to her. He felt himself grab the Nazi by the arm and twirl him around.

He felt himself grasp the girl by the hand and run. He ran blindly and as fast as he could.

The next thing he knew he was in an alleyway, peering back as the police finally broke up the crowd.

"Why did you do that?" Martin huffed at her.

She was breathing heavily, yet, as he gazed at her, she was still calmly beautiful. "He had no right to beat up on an old man." she told him excitedly.

"You could've got yourself hurt."

"I knew what I was doing."

Martin sighed. "I wish I did."

"Hey you!" a voice shouted behind him.

Martin nearly jumped out of his skin. He turned to face to policemen, one in uniform and one plain-clothes man. They already had the girl by the arm.

"Let me go!" she shouted as she squirmed, desperately trying to get away from the uniformed officer. "I've done nothing wrong. Ouch! You're hurting me."

"Hold it girl!" The uniform demanded. "We want to talk to you."

"If you let go of me, I'll talk. I won't run off." she told the police.

They let her go and the plainclothes policeman talked. "What do you two think you were doing out there?" he asked.

Martin replied. "She was caught in the middle of the fighting and I......"

"Yeah, I know." he smirked. "You wanted to rescue her."

"I'm no hero, but the girl needed help." Martin further explained.

"Card her, Detective Strauss." the uniform demanded.

The plainclothesman, Detective Strauss, looked curiously at the other policeman. Martin could see that she didn't look like a prostitute to him either.

"Go ahead. Card her."

He smiled at the girl. "Card?"

She looked disgusted. "Shit!" she said as she took her card from her purse. "I'm not working here. I've got the same rights as anybody."

Strauss looked the card over carefully and handed it back.

"I'm clean! Honest! I'm registered properly and I wasn't doing business." the girl continued to say.

Strauss looked curiously at her. "Greyer, huh. Greta Greyer." he gestured toward the patch of cobblestone where the riot had taken place. She nodded to him.

Strauss scratched his chin. "Alright, girl, you're clean alright. Just try to keep your family in line, if you understand me. Get out of here now and take your courageous knight along."

Greta nodded quickly to him, clutched Martin's hand and quickly walked out onto the now deserted street.

"What was that all about?" Martin had to ask.

"They like to harass whores. What else!"

"What about that line about 'your family'?"

She hesitated. "Just the crazy way cops talk to us."

Martin stopped her and faced her to him. "You really are a whore, aren't you?"

"I told you that before."

"I didn't believe you. You don't look like one."

"That's because I'm not working." she chirped back.

"I still don't believe it." Martin shook his head.

"I've got to go." the girl said.

She reached up and kissed him on the cheek. "Thanks." she sighed as she finished. Then she was off down the street.

"Wait," Martin called to her. "Can I see you again?"

She smiled when she looked back at him. "Down by the riverfront. Any night"

SEVEN

Greta dreaded seeing her mother. It was a task that she did out of love, but knew that her mother, who disapproved of the way she lived, would be as critical as she usually was. Greta never avoided her mother, but she never relished seeing her either.

Things always seemed to be tough on her and her family. All Greta could remember when she was growing up was poverty and the seemingly endless struggle to survive. Now, when she felt she could help her family out a little, her mother would always give her a hard time. It was all the suffering she had experienced as a youngster that made her the way she was, Greta realized, but her mother couldn't understand that, in these difficult times, she was only trying to help.

As Greta walked through the old neighborhood toward the home she grew up in she remembered the hard times. She remembered the dirty look of the streets and the battered walls of the houses and knew they hadn't changed very much since she was a child. She remembered the desperate look of the people on the streets and saw the same look on the faces that passed her way now. She remembered the ill-fitting cloths she wore as a child and saw the same unkempt and torn cloths on the bodies of the small children that played in the streets around her.

Didn't anything ever change here? She wondered as she drew closer and closer to her home if it could ever change. If it wasn't the wartime desperation she remembered as a small child it was the dragging everyday poverty of the people of the docks. If it wasn't the rampant inflation of her teens that kept the people down, it was this horrible depression that was happening today. She realized she was starting to sound like her father and maybe he was right. Maybe Communism could do better for the people.

She finally saw her house. It looked the same as always to her, only a little shabbier than before, like everything around it. If only her parents would take advantage of the things she could give them. If only she

54

could break them down to let her provide for them. It had to be better than struggling on in the endless cycle of the riverfront.

Her mother greeted her at the door, opening it before she was able to knock. To Greta she looked as if she wasn't even happy to see her, her face failing to crack even the faintest smile. She just nodded as she let her daughter pass through the doorway.

"How are you, Mama?" Greta asked as she tried to kiss her mother once they were both inside.

The woman drew away from Greta, refusing her child's gesture, and moved on into the kitchen. Greta followed, denying the anger that her mother's action had given her. She watched her return to sorting some laundry on the kitchen table, sitting down in a chair and searching for a way to break the silence.

Her mother looked tired. Greta remembered that she always looked tired and old beyond her years. It had been a tough life on her and it had really begun to tell on her mother's frail body. She had been alone so much, as Greta remembered. She had been forced to raise her alone when her father went off to war and then, reported missing during the Russian revolution, disappeared for two more years. Even when he did return Greta knew that her mother was the only one bringing her up since he was caught up in the movement. She seemed to watch her mother being dragged down by the years of loneliness and poverty and now, when she at last could help make things easier, all she got as coldness.

"I saw Papa today," Greta said, desperately trying to start a conversation.

Her mother shrugged, her sloped shoulders barely rising. "He's out with them, I presume." she began, emphasizing the word 'them' sarcastically. "Demonstrating and causing trouble."

"Yes. Their rally was broken up by the Nazis. One of these times he's going to get hurt."

"There's nothing I can do." Her mother said. "I guess he'll never change."

"Mama, I want to help you," Greta told her.

"If you want to help me," She replied. "Come home and give up that life."

"No thanks. I couldn't live this way."

"Then why do you keep coming back?"

"I want you to take some money. I want to help, but not by giving you another person to take care of. I'm making good money now, a lot of money. I want you to have some of it."

"I want money that was earned honestly." Her mother's voice was turning angry. "Not the money of sin."

"Is it a sin to eat, to have good cloths and a nice place to live?" Greta questioned.

"It is a sin to sell your body." her mother replied.

"If I stopped being a prostitute and came back here what would we have to look forward to? We would be poor and nothing anyone could do would change that." Greta kept defending herself, not making excuses for the life she had chosen. "I'm doing what I can to live now. Why can't you accept that? Why can't you understand that? Would you rather I turn out like you?"

Her mother looked up from her laundry, her face suddenly turning from anger to sorrow, her brown eyes staring at Greta as if she saw herself as she once was.

"That was wrong of me," Greta apologized as she realized what she had said. "I didn't mean to say that, Mama. I'm sorry."

"No," The woman shook her head dejectedly. "In that way you're right. I don't want you to end up like me. I want you to have a better life, better than I ever had. I just don't think you can get that by being a whore."

"I don't like being called that. Not by you."

"But that is what you are."

Greta wished she had never brought up the subject, maybe wishing she had never come.

"I want you to be happy." her mother said. "I doubt if you are truly happy."

"It's not so bad," Greta told her. "Look! No knight in shining armor is coming over the horizon to take me away from all this."

Her mother got a curious look on her face, as if some deep, dark thought had burst out from the back of her mind. Greta wondered what was going through her mind. Maybe she was thinking back to when she was young. Was there some knight in shining armor back there, in Paula Greyer's past that could have rescued her from this fate?

Greta's mind then thought back to today's incident. She remembered the man who helped her during the street fight, trying to remember the man's name, but only remembering that he worked at the big bank near the cathedral. In a way, Greta Greyer also wished there was a knight in shining armor for her. In a way she wished the handsome young man could be that.

Her mother finally spoke. "I wish there was, but maybe I can change that."

Greta looked at her mother, puzzled by her last statement. The curious, far away look remained in her mother's sad eyes. Greta felt certain now that events were passing through the woman's mind of an opportunity sacrificed, leaving her here on the riverfront instead of in some mansion.

"I don't know what else to say, Mama," Greta finally said. "I want you to take the money. I want you to use it to buy yourself something, to bring you some happiness."

"Leave it then," Her mother finally relented. "I will use it for your brother, or for your father. They won't even know where it came from."

Greta accepted the concession as the best she would get and placed the money on the table. She felt the urge to leave, not wishing to argue any longer with her. She silently rose from the chair to go.

"Greta," her mother called back to her. "I have to ask you something."

"Yes?" Greta asked as she stopped by the kitchen door.

"If I were to find a way to make your life easier, would you leave the sinful life you now have?" her mother asked.

Greta laughed, "In a minute, but you're no magician."

"Have some faith in me." she said. "Take care, Greta, and please be careful."

"Yes, Mama," Greta answered. "And I love you."

Greta stepped out of the house and stood on the stoop. Even the park across the street seemed shabbier that she remembered, littered with trash and its grass being edged out by clusters of weeds.

She looked to some children playing in the park, their faces red from running and jumping. She could see the childlike joy in their eyes and remember that she once had the same joyful, childish happiness. Those times were gone, she knew. Once you grow up there is little to be so happy about. Once you grow up everyday is sadder than the last, until the days melt quickly into weeks, then months and years.

She shook her head, trying to force the depressing thoughts from her mind. She was twenty-three years old, she told herself, and she had no reason to be so depressed. Things will get better.

"Hello, Greta." a cracking voice greeted her preoccupied mind.

She stared down the steps at her brother Gery. She saw more changes in him, as she noticed each time she came by her home. Twelve year old boys, it seemed, were constantly changing. Her little brother was no exception.

"I didn't expect to see you until next week," the boy said.

Greta was confused. "Next week! What's next week?"

The boy grinned at her. "My birthday! Don't you remember?"

Greta felt embarrassed. She had completely forgotten. "I'll be back to see you then. I'll bring you something nice."

"Yeah." he smiled, it was a sly smile, showing her he had thoughts in his head beyond what she thought a twelve year old should have. They were growing up faster and faster by the riverfront.

"You still working the waterfront?" he then asked.

"Yes. I haven't made enough yet."

Gery looked at her curiously. "I tell my friends you work at one of the shops downtown. I'm embarrassed to tell the truth. I'm waiting for one of two things to happen. Either one of them will visit the shop I say you're at and not see you, or one of them will see you on the street."

"I don't do kids."

"That doesn't mean they won't find someone to take the mark."

She smiled. "I'll be careful not to rob one of your friend's virginity."

"Thanks."

She reached into her purse and drew out some money, shoving it towards him.

He backed off. "No, Greta. You know Mama doesn't want me to take your money."

"Don't tell her. It's an early birthday present."

He took the notes from her and shoved them into his pocket without counting it. Greta wasn't even sure how much she had given him.

"I'd better go, Gery," she told him, stepping off the steps. "I've got to go to work soon."

"Yeah, sure," he grinned. "Maybe I'll come visit you at work."

"You do and I'll kick your ass all the way home."

EIGHT

Lucy Wagner seldom took extended lunches. As a matter of fact, Lucy seldom left the office for lunch. She had done so when she first began at the bank as one of the general secretaries. Then, along with a small crowd of other girls, they usually journeyed across the park to a little coffee shop and complained to each other over lunch about their superiors, or they're husbands, or their boyfriends.

Lucy quickly tired of the small talk and the whining. Lucy also managed to hook onto the prized job of being the management secretary, who served only the general manager and his immediate assistants. Then her lunch hour became less routine. Someone had to be there to answer the phones when the managers weren't in and usually that duty fell on her. She also felt that the other girls, many of whom had been there far longer than her, resented her quick advancement and her friendships among the secretary pool grew less. She always wondered why she got the job so easily. She knew she was an ordinary secretary and some of the other girls were far better, but, she realized, she had the looks. It was not that Albert Freyberg had ever laid a hand on her or even tried, but she knew he liked having an attractive woman sitting outside his office.

Today she was going to take the long lunch that had been promised her. She had a date and she was, surprisingly, looking forward to it. She didn't know why, but the gentleman impressed her, even if he was old enough to be her father.

It was turning colder, she judged even before she stepped out of the building. The flushed cheeks of those she passed on the way, their bodies wrapped tightly in their coats, told her the air was chilled and the winds briskly blowing. Winter was on its way and the fall was being pushed aside quickly. No manner of sunshine, and the sun was shining brightly today, could warm her body. She had suggested to her lunch date that they eat at the outdoor cafe three blocks from the bank, but she now expected that their meal would have to be taken indoors.

She walked quickly to the cafe, realizing she was already late, her pace quickening with each step until she had to stop herself from running. What did she see in Karl Scheuler? What excited her about the man? She wondered if he represented the father she could barely remember, or simply someone safe, unable to harm her as so many other men had done.

He smiled at her as she entered the cafe, his huge mustache turning up slightly as his eyes sparkled when they met hers. He was such a large man, not fat, but simply big. He was impeccably dressed; a sign of wealth, and all these things gave him a commanding presence.

"I'm sorry I'm so late." she apologized immediately upon sitting down.

"No problem. I have taken the liberty to order for you." His booming voice resounded back.

"Thanks." she smiled. "What are we having?"

"Coffee. Potato soup. A rather unimpressive roast beef platter." He rattled off. "I hope the food here is good. I've never eaten here before."

"It's passable."

"I had hoped to take you to a more exquisite restaurant."

"This will have to do. I do have to go back to work."

"Do they serve wine here?"

"Not that I know of."

"Then we'll just have to do without." He smiled at her. They fell into silence for a moment, both of them apparently struggling for something to say. He finally broke the silence.

"You know, Lucy, I was surprised you agreed to lunch with me. I would think a pretty young girl such as you would have suitors lined up anxiously at her door."

"You'd be surprised how seldom I get a chance to go out."

"It must be the times. In my day we chased after lovely young girls such as you. As a matter of fact I married a girl very much like you."

Her heart sank. She was sure she had been deceived. He was now going to tell her that his wife had changed. That she didn't love him anymore. She was going to be propositioned. Could she, he was going to ask, comfort an old man by giving her lovely, young body to him.

"But that was a long time ago. Many things have changed in the world since then."

Lucy decided to gently probe. Before lunch would drag on she had to get this conversation to the point.

60

"What brings you to Bremen, Herr Scheuler?" she asked, stressing the formality of his name.

"Please," he immediately corrected her, "call me Karl. Actually I had some business with Herr Freyberg and to renew my old acquaintance with him. I took some time off from my job for personal reasons and really had nowhere to go."

Lucy nodded. "Has your wife joined you?" she then asked.

Scheuler looked sternly at her. "Ah-ha. That's what you're thinking! I'm some lecherous old bastard who wants to sneak around on his wife. Well, my dear, don't let it worry you. My wife died many years ago."

Now Lucy felt bad. "I'm sorry. I've a bad habit of jumping to conclusions."

"Don't get the idea that I'm so safe, Lucy." he said, his face cracking a smile. "I have an affliction to younger women."

That brought a smile to Lucy's face as well. She felt a little confused. Was he a lecherous old bastard anyway? Was he just a lonely gentleman looking for some company while in a strange town? Was he the safe bet she had expected he would be?

Only time would tell.

* * * *

When lunch was over Lucy called the office. She informed them, quite politely excusing herself, that she felt simply dreadful and needed the afternoon off. It must have been something she had eaten; maybe it was a cold coming on. It was seldom that she lied to her employers, but she felt good at taking advantage of them. She also felt a little guilty, praying that no one would check up on her and discover that she was not sick at all.

The conversation over lunch was stimulating. She had found Karl to be a fascinating man, far more complex than most of the idle minded men she had known. Most of them had been so wrapped up in politics, or their jobs, or simply trying to get her infatuated with them that they would completely forget to show any interest in her aside from glaring at her body, their tongues nearly sticking out.

Throughout the long lunch they had talked and, although Karl had revealed many facts about his past, he had concentrated in getting her to tell her life story to him. She always wished to meet someone who was interested in her as a person, not just an object. He, with his prodding questions about her childhood, her likes and dislikes, had proved that he wanted to learn about her. Or was he just more skilled at beguiling a woman than the boys she had know?

She had decided, before the final cups of coffee were poured, that she liked Karl very much despite their difference in ages. She had decided also that she would let him do anything to her he desired. Maybe, she reasoned, it was time she learned more about life and love than she had been taught from the sex starved boys who had toyed with her body and her emotions.

Lucy often wondered if other woman were as lacking in virtue as she felt herself to be. Somehow, even as a teenager in the madly decadent age she grew up in, she knew that most of the other girls were tearing their souls apart, as she was, torn between the conservatism that was the way of their parents and the freedom that they felt around them. She had experienced sex early, speaking of it to no one, feeling that she may be outcast for it, but somehow in the unspoken language of her peers she felt that most of the other girls were going through it too. Have a good time, but keep it secret, the rules seemed to say. Everyone likes marry a virgin, but no one likes to date one.

She had discovered, as her teens melted away into her twenties, that most men expected sex. She realized that most of them did not expect their girls to be virgins, only to have been difficult with other men and easy with them. Most of the young men she had met seemed as torn between the past and the present as she was. Most of the men, it turned out, were asses.

She knew Karl wasn't like that. He was mature, guided by years of experience rather than years of hungry desire. He had long gotten over the need to see each woman he had known naked, their legs spread out before him as if she were a slave. He would never expect her to be reserved simply for him. He would, she believed, be tender and loving, and not demanding and cruel.

She allowed him to lead her from the cafe and onto the cold, wind blown streets, walking side by side, but never touching through the thin, mid-afternoon crowd.

She allowed him to take her to the small clothing store and allowed him to buy a silk scarf she admired. She watched the face of the salesman wondering by his looks what the man thought. She couldn't tell if he was glad to see a father buy his daughter such a trivial present, or if he glad that the man was nicely priming this young girl in preparation for bedding her. What the hell! Lucy thought to herself, what do I care what you think?

After the store they started to walk again, this time she weaved her arm though his and she was surprised when he didn't stop her from cuddling up to him. Maybe he thought she was seeking protection from the chill that grew more intense as the afternoon wore on.

She noticed that he probed the faces as they walked. She noticed that he nervously glanced behind him from time to time. What was he worried about? She wondered if he were nervous about being seen with her? She dismissed it, but there seemed to be in his eyes a wariness of the crowd. It was as if he was watching to see if someone was following him.

When they reached the street outside the Fredrickplatz Hotel they stopped. She was surprised when she realized that he was staying there. It was far from the best hotel in the city, old and a little on the seedy side, and she had expected that this finely tailored man would have only stayed at a place like the King's Court. Was he less wealthy than he had impressed her to be?

"Well, my dear." he began. "This is where I get off. I'd ask you up for a drink, but I feel I've taken up too much of your time already."

"Why I'd love to have a drink." she heard herself saying.

When they got to the room, Lucy was unimpressed. It was filled with old furniture and the wallpaper was peeling. There were cobwebs in the corners of the ceiling and spots on the well-worn carpets.

"Don't be alarmed by the look of the place." he explained. "Actually, it's a very clean hotel. Used to be one of the better ones in the city, I understand, back in the old days."

"You've stayed here before?"

He shook his head to indicate he hadn't.

"I'd have expected you to stay at King's Court."

"I didn't like the look of that place."

Lucy shrugged. If he felt more comfortable in this place, so be it. She could see by the jewelry he wore that he wasn't hurting for money. The watch alone, she guessed, must have cost a few thousand marks.

He had poured some schnapps from a bottle into two cheap glasses on the dresser and offered one to her. As she took it he raised his glass with a grand gesture. "To my lost youth!" he said his face cracking broadly with a wide grin. "Do I ever wish I had it back when I look at you?"

They clicked their glasses together and drank up quickly. Silently he poured another.

"If I were twenty years younger...." he began to say.

"I would be three." she interjected.

He laughed, but sensed nervousness in her laugh that joined his. "It's unfair of me to speak like that to you. I will scare you off from what could be a good friendship."

She finally realized that the thought of sleeping with her had never entered his mind, even though it had hers. She had to change that. She wondered how much of a fool she would make of herself for only an instant before deciding that it wasn't important. As she drank the second glass of schnapps down as quickly as the first she reasoned she could later blame it all on the liquor if he sternly reprimanded her for making advances toward him. She then realized that she had never had to seduce a man before. She didn't know how to start.

"Why are you looking at me like that?" he asked. She hadn't realized that she was looking funny at him, but maybe she was. "What's going through that mind of yours?"

Oh, what the hell! Let's get it over with! She had decided on the most direct approach. "I want to sleep with you." she declared.

Karl shook his head, drank a little bit more from the glass and turned toward the bathroom. "I'm an old man." he said. "Surely you can do better."

"I don't think so." Lucy heard herself saying as she lifted herself off the bed. She reached him in only a second and wrapped her arms around his waist. She climbed to her tiptoes and attempted to kiss him. He backed up and turned his head away. She began to feel foolish as if she was embarrassing him.

"I don't think I want this to happen." he told her.

She pushed herself toward him again, squeezing her breasts against him, reaching her hand down and cupping the bulge in his pants. Despite his pleadings she felt that he was aroused.

She smiled and kissed him. The unusual warmth of her own emotions coating her body with a tingling sensation she led him over to the bed and dragged his body down next to hers.

After a long embrace he drew away and turned his face toward the ceiling. She continued to massage him. "There is one thing I must explain before we go on with this." he panted. "There was an old injury that you will find. Some women find it uncomfortable to make love to me because of it. Although it's ugly it doesn't mean I can't make love."

64

She looked at him strangely. "Why are you telling me this?" She asked. "Don't you see that I want you?"

He laughed. "I'm old.......and not worthy."

She didn't understand, but realized that it wouldn't matter. "Let me be the judge of that." she told him as she slipped off her dress and lay down next to him again.

NINE

Although Min and Albert had frequently discussed the problems that were facing them, Min always felt that Albert had something spinning through the back of his mind that he was refusing to talk to her about. There was something lurking there tonight, Min decided, that he wanted to keep from her. She had also decided that she had to force it out of him.

All their discussions lately, you couldn't really call them arguments, had centered on how they were to cope with the situation. She had always thought that was the best way to approach it. After all, they had faced many problems in the past; the confusion just after they were married, the inflation, the depression when it first hit. They had survived all that, she reasoned, there was the likelihood that they would survive the threat facing them now.

Yes, she had to conclude, the country was a mess. The people were confused and scared as each day was marked with more plant closings, more bankruptcies, more people losing their jobs and their money. Yes, the bankers that they worked with were afraid, afraid of the radicals and the government's inability to handle them. It was a crisis, but it would pass and Albert and Min would still be where they were.

There was just a feeling in Mina's mind that he knew, or thought about something that he had not told her.

As she watched him dress for bed she wondered if she could get him to tell her the truth. As she sat up on the bed, her eyes peering at her husband from just above the book she pretended to be reading, she wondered, as she always had wondered, what was going through his mind.

She had known Albert for fifteen years, had spent over thirteen of those years as his wife, yet she sometimes felt she knew nothing of the man. Sometimes she was happy for that, because it added an air of mystery to their lives. Sometimes it made her angry.

She watched him as he stood, undressed, in front of the large mirror that hung from the far wall of the darkened bedroom. He seemed to be admiring his scars, though that was an odd way of putting it. Albert's body was covered with scar tissue, a remnant of his awful time in the war. Min remembered that it used to upset her terribly to look at him; his blotchy, creased body like something out of a nightmare, his skin rough and somewhat inhuman to her touch. She grew to accept it, but she knew he never did. Those scars reminded him of a life he used to have, and each time his other old injury to his leg pained him she realized that it too reminded him of something else, of someone else. He wasn't, she knew, admiring his wounds now, but remembering the past and what today could have been.

After he had dressed for bed and joined her, she approached the subject. "Are you still mad at me?" she asked, her voice squeaking out the words, making her sound vulnerable.

"No." he flatly stated. "I was under the impression that it was you who was still mad with me."

She sighed, "No, Albert. Not at you, just everything around us. What do you really think is going to happen?"

He lay back on the bed and looked up at the dark ceiling. He thought long and hard before speaking. "I don't know, Mina. The country will recover, but whether it shall mark us victims this time...I hope it doesn't, but I'm afraid it will."

"What do you mean 'mark us as victims'?"

"The way I see it, dear, it's only a matter of time before the government will give in to Hitler and his people. They have, for some odd reason, captured the imagination a lot of people. Their ideas, to people like us, are scary, but the out of work laborer and the angry peasant only hear the talk of better times and glory. Despite the racist, hateful things they say, people, good people freely vote these maniacs into the Reichstag. Soon, very soon, Hindenburg will be forced to give them control."

"Even if that happens," Min argued. "They'll need people like us. We have the real power. We have the money and the knowledge to use it."

"Mina, they need people like us, but not us."

"That doesn't make any sense."

He looked at her strangely, as if he was unwilling to say what he must. "Min, there are many people more likely to be trusted and used by them. We have been announced as their sworn enemies. Anyway you

67

look at it; we're the enemy whether they claim we're bankers, robbers, thieves, or Jews."

Min grew quickly angry. "I'm sick of that!" she shouted. "I'm no Jew. I've never practiced my mother's religion, you know that. All our lives we've been told to assimilate into the culture. Now, even with that, they're blaming us for everything! They blame us for all the troubles this country's in and that's not fair! They even blame us for losing the war! My brother died in the war, and look what it did to you!"

Albert shook his head. "That doesn't matter to them. They've made us the scapegoats, labeled us as a Jewish bank and me, despite what I was, as one of the Jew's lackeys. We know it's not right, but how can I fight them?"

"I don't know. I can't believe all the people we've helped believe that."

"It's a few quiet voices against the shouting of thousands. The masses always follow the ones who shout the loudest and tell them what they want to hear."

"Then what do we do?"

"We wait and pray." Albert told her as he turned away from her and snuggled up to his pillows. "Maybe we'll have to get out."

He had said that before in the last year, but those words frightened Min. "I'll never leave my home." she mumbled. He didn't respond. He was already asleep, or pretended to be.

* * * *

She felt very nervous as she entered the bank's offices. She wondered if she was doing the right thing. She wondered if he would see her at all. She wondered if he would help her after all these years, but she realized that the only one she knew who could help Greta was Albert Freyberg.

When she made up her mind to go to him she wondered how he would react. Albert was her brother-in-law, but they hadn't spoke in fourteen years, and he had made himself a new life, with a new wife who obviously had a lot of money. After all, the woman's family owned a bank and he had become protector of that fortune. He probably never thought about the life before that, about his life with her sister at the bakery down by the river. He probably didn't want to think about it. He probably didn't want to see her.

In her mind she felt that everyone was staring at her as she walked through the busy office. She looked old, she knew, and tired and poor in her worn out clothes. Many people looked poor these days, and older than their years, but few march through the halls of a bank and up to the manager's office.

The young woman at the desk outside his office looked at her coldly as she approached. She looked at her like she was going to call the guards and have her thrown out. Yet there was the look of pity in the girl's eyes too.

"My name is Paula Greyer." the woman proudly announced, trying to sound confident. She had decided that being confident would get her in to see him. "I need to see Herr Freyberg."

The young secretary looked at her strangely. "Do you have an appointment?" she asked.

"No."

"I'm sorry. You can't see Herr Freyberg without an appointment. Maybe someone else can help you."

"I must see Herr Freyberg. Is he in?" Paula asked.

"He can't see you without an appointment.'" the secretary repeated.

"I'll wait until he can." Paula told the girl. No matter what they told her, Paula had decided, she would wait around the office until he appeared. She hoped that once he saw her he would remember and talk to her.

"He is working. He'll not see you today." the secretary sounded annoyed. "If you wish to make an appointment he'll see you then." The girl began to look at a calendar on the desk. "He has an opening on Tuesday, two weeks from now."

Paula had an idea. She opened her pocketbook and searched through it until she found an old photograph of her daughter when she was a little girl. She handed it over to the secretary.

"What's this?" the woman asked.

"Show that to Albert Freyberg." Paula demanded. "I'm sure he will see me then."

The girl shrugged, but she did as Paula had asked and disappeared behind a door. The picture was of Greta when she was about two, a time when Albert was sure to remember.

Seconds later the secretary reappeared. She sat behind her desk and didn't say anything.

Her worst fears swelled up inside Paula Greyer. He didn't remember, or he did and wasn't going to help. All her hopes had been based on his coming to their aid, but he wasn't going to help.

A deep voice called out from beyond the door. "Fraulein, you may send her in now."

When Paula saw Albert she barely recognized him. Although she had read about him the papers and knew how well he had done, she only remembered the thin young man she knew from the docks. She only remembered the dark brown hair and the probing brown eyes. He had aged, which he surely must, but the well built, gray haired man was a stranger to her. Only the eyes were the same.

"What do you want, Paula?" he asked. The voice was the same too, she recognized. He seemed to be avoiding looking at her. Was he upset at seeing her? Or was she that terrible to look at? She knew she had changed as well over time, and not for the better.

"I need to talk to you about Greta."

He held a long pen in his hand and pointed it at her. "The last time I saw you I told you that I would never bother you about her again. I have kept my part of the bargain."

"I need your help." Paula pleaded. She felt on the verge of tears.

"I gave you help once before, remember. You ordered me to stay out of her life as a reward. I did just that. Don't come to me now and expect any more favors."

"But she's your daughter!"

"No, Paula. She's your daughter now. Yours and Max's. I gave up that right a long time ago. And, since I'm sure she's grown up by now, she has the right to live her own life. A grown woman doesn't need a mother's interference, or that of a father she hasn't known since she was three."

"We've not done that well by her, Albert. Only her real father can help her now."

He laughed. "She has a father...Max, if he can find the time between his condemnations of me to help her."

"Max is too far gone. You also have something that we can't offer her."

"Money?"

"No. A future. She can't find that down on the docks, but as the daughter of an important banker....."

He cut her off. "I have a family, do you realize that? I can't bring a grown woman into my home and say to my wife "here is the daughter I

70

SECRETS OF THE PAST

abandoned after my first wife died". Why, they have no idea that she even exists."

"But she does, and she needs you."

"Why? What has she done?"

"She's a prostitute."

He laughed. To Paula it was a cruel laugh. "That's just wonderful. I'm supposed to bring a whore into my house. I'm supposed to present her to my family, my son and my daughters, this.....this...."

She cut in. "She a good girl, Albert. Despite what she does, she's good. You know what life can be like on the riverfront. You know what it can force people to do."

He thought a second in silence. "What do you think she wants from me?"

"She doesn't know you exist. That's a secret I've kept from her. She believes she's mine. Up to now I saw no reason to tell her otherwise, but I want her off the streets and she won't listen to me. She wants things I could never give her. Maybe if you can give her some of those things....money...a future. Maybe she would give it up."

"Wait a minute." Albert gestured wildly with his hands. "I haven't seen her since she was eight. I haven't helped her all these years when I could have. As far as she's concerned her name is Greyer, not Freyberg, yet you expect her to welcome me, her rich, long lost father, with open arms! If that is how she is, then I don't want her for my daughter."

Paula looked down at the floor. "I don't know how she'll react. Probably with anger, I would guess. I only know that she's a lonely girl in search of something. I only hoped that you could give it to her."

"On face value, Paula, I can't accept this. I will not disrupt my entire life for some young little whore. Allow me to think this over. Tell her nothing. Please! I don't want her showing up at my door, suitcase in hand, ready to take her place in my family."

"I could never do that. I'll wait for your decision, but I'm sure you'll find it in your heart to help her.

Paula knew she had finished her business with Albert for the time being. She knew how tough things were going to be for him because she faced the same tough decisions herself. If he agreed she would somehow have to find the courage to tell Greta that her life had been a lie.

* * * *

71

Martin didn't like to go down to the riverfront anymore. It reminded him of his past, which was what he was trying to get away from. It was also a rather unsavory place to be, especially at night. It was a raw neighborhood, cluttered with poor, desperate people who lived amidst the filth, the smell of rotting industry and the crime and prostitution.

The riverfront had become the haven for all the bad elements of society and Martin wondered if he still could fit into this atmosphere. He felt he had long since elevated himself above it, but tonight, at Albert's request, he was wandering the litter filled streets just like the sailors, laborers and criminals who lurked in every passageway and who drank in every noisy beer hall.

His mind heard what Albert had asked of him, repeating like an old phonograph record playing in his head. "Go to the river," he had said. "Go for me, as a friend, and seek out a prostitute named Greta Greyer.

"Find her and learn about her," he had asked. "I have been asked by an old friend to help her, but I need to know who she is, rather than simply what she is, before I will help her. Find this out for me, Martin, and I will be in your debt."

How could he turn Albert down? How could he refuse such a favor from the man who had helped him so much? Yet Martin dreaded going down to the docks.

Martin seemed to remember doing this when he was a teenager. He remembered walking the same streets and seeing the same faces in the people walking toward him and staring at him in the shadows. He remembered the sounds of laughing, drunken men coming from the beer halls and the smell of sour beer and sweat and garbage rotting from every alleyway. These were reasons he had worked so hard to get away from this place.

But he owed it to Albert, if only he knew how?

How does one find one prostitute among hundreds? Albert couldn't even help him for he didn't even know what she looked like. He only said that she was young and that she worked the riverfront. Martin didn't know where to begin.

Many of the women Martin saw lining the street could be discounted right off. As they stood there against the brick walls of the buildings they looked old and used, their silhouettes coated with fat. These were the old hands, some of which he remembered when he roamed down here, and they looked then no younger than tonight. He saw few young faces on the girls carrying the umbrellas, and those he saw were occupied with the many loud merchant sailors who constantly approached them looking for a deal. Sometimes the men would get lucky. When business was bad they could get it cheap, or the girls would almost give it away to stop someone from bothering them too much.

"Hey! Martin Bock!" he heard a voice call to him. It was a guttural female voice. He turned to see who remembered him.

It was a woman he remembered vaguely from those days, but now she wore the garb of a streetwalker. She looked very unappealing.

"What brings you back here?" she asked.

He couldn't remember her name as he walked over to her. "Visiting the old neighborhood." he told her. He remembered her as living on his block and being no more than five years older than he. She looked thirty years older now.

"Sure," she said as she fingered the lapel of his coat. "You're looking for a good time."

He shook his head. "No. Believe it or not I am looking for nothing." He was trying to decide if he should ask this woman about the mysterious Fraulein Greyer.

"Let me show you some fun, Martin." she insisted. "I come cheap...for an old friend."

He smiled and withdrew a wad of money from his pocket. "Listen, I don't want you for that, but I'll pay you for some information."

She looked at the money closely. It wasn't a phony roll filled with blank paper meant to deceive. It was real money that Albert had given him.

"Goodness!" she exclaimed. "We have come a long way!"

He peeled off a fifty mark note and waved it before the woman. "Will you answer one question?" he asked. "Do you know a girl named Greta Greyer?"

She took the money, reached down and stuffed it into the top of her boot. "I never heard of her."

He waved another note in front of her face.

After she took it, her memory improved. "The name does sound familiar. I believe she works up the street near the Hopffbrau."

He handed the woman a third note and started up the street.

"Hey! Bock! She's just a little bitch, all beauty, but not as good as me. You'll see.....You come back."

In moments he was at the Hopffbrau. It was one of the seediest beer halls on the street, but also one of the busiest. It was well known around town and usually brought newcomers to the street. It was where the

SECRETS OF THE PAST

better whores paraded, since they usually could get more marks from the visitors.

There must have been twenty girls on the sidewalk in front of the large hall. They stood in clusters talking among themselves. When an interested party strolled by one or two of them would break off and work on the man. If they weren't bought they'd quickly rejoin their friends.

He searched around, trying to figure out which girl to approach first. It was an impossible job! Where does one start?

He saw a group of girls over by the alley and decided to start over there. He realized that his cache of money would be drained if he bribed them for information. As he came closer the eyes of one of the girls met his and sparkled at him. The face suddenly looked familiar to Martin. The girl from the park, who's name also escaped him for the moment.

"Well, Banker." she said. "Are you looking for me?"

She looked more like a prostitute now, Martin thought, but still she was too pretty to be a whore. She had decorated her face in heavy makeup which covered up her freckled complexion and she wore clothes that gave her shapely figure a cold, brassy look. The dress she wore beneath her fine woolen coat was bright blue and clung to her form so tightly he could see every curve. She had ironed the curls out of her hair and it shined a brilliant yellow against the dim street lights.

"Hello," Martin said as he searched his mind for her name, but realized that it didn't matter.

She took his arm and led him into the alley away from the crowd of girls. "See you," she called back to them. "I've found an old friend."

Once out of sight the girl hugged him around the neck and tried to kiss him. Martin backed his head away. He found her fascinating, but not as a whore.

"Oh," she pouted. "Aren't you glad you found me?"

"That's not why I'm here," he explained.

"I told you that you could find me here, didn't I. You came because you have decided to take me up on my offer, Banker. And I'll tell you what; I owe you one...so it's free."

"That's not why I'm here," he repeated.

"Why else would a man like you come to the river?"

"I'm looking for someone named Greta."

She smiled, her beauty glimmering through the heavy makeup in the half light of the alley. "Fine, I'm Greta."

He raised his hands and pulled hers from around his neck. "Look! Whatever your name really is, I know you're trying to be what I want, but I am really looking for a streetwalker named Greta Greyer."

"But I told you before that I'm her. In the park...remember." she was looking strangely at him. "Now quit playing around and let's go."

He thought back to their first encounter. He tried to remember what she had told him, but couldn't. He decided to play along anyway. Eventually she would tell him her real name and maybe the information he really wanted.

"I was just kidding," he smiled at her and let her kiss him.

* * * *

The prostitute who had assumed the identity of Greta led him to a rundown rooming house around the corner from the Hopffbrau. She walked past the desk manned by a muscular, hairy man as if he wasn't there and took Martin to what must have been her steady room. It contained only a bed, chair, table and a small bathroom over to one side. On the table rested two glasses and a bottle of schnapps.

"Why don't you fix us a drink," she instructed. "I'll be right back." She threw her things over the chair. She then disappeared into the bathroom.

Martin poured the drinks and then decided he had to find out who she really was. There was an identification card in her handbag, he remembered. He was still searching for it when she came out.

"Hey! What are you doing!" she shouted at him as she reached over and grabbed the bag from his hands. A good portion of what it contained spilled onto the floor. "What's wrong with you?"

He looked up at her, his mind stunned by what he saw. She was wearing only a bra and a slip, both black. She was magnificent.

"What'd you expect to find there?" she defiantly asked.

Martin couldn't think of anything to say. He just stared at her. She was the most gorgeous thing he had ever seen, even in her anger.

"I don't think you're a pervert." she went on, her voice still angry. "I know you're not from the police."

"I was looking for your name." He stammered out.

She looked down, saw what she wanted and bent over to get it. His eyes followed her firm, perfectly shaped breasts as she bent over.

75

She picked up a card from the floor and tossed it at him. "See! Greta Greyer is my name!" she told him.

He read the card. The coincidence was too great, but it was her.

By the time he looked up again the girl had cloaked her body in her coat. He was, he felt ashamed to think, a little disappointed.

"Now, you bastard!" she snarled at him. "What do you really want from me?"

Martin had been told to approach this task secretly. He was to observe and learn about her without revealing why. Those had been Albert's instructions, but it seemed a little late for that.

He stumbled around for the words. "I was given your...name by.....a friend!?" It almost sounded like a question, he realized, as if he were asking for approval.

"Shit on that!" she shouted. "Who ordered you to follow me, the party?"

He tried an explanation closer to the truth. "I was looking for you because someone...my employer had been asked to... look after your safety by an old friend."

She looked at him strangely. "Do you really work for the bank?"

He nodded.

"Then where do I fit in? How could he know me or anybody who knows me?"

He shrugged.

Greta looked at him disgusted. "Well, Banker, you found me. Now get out!"

Greta Greyer, enraged, looked ever more inviting to him. Damn, Albert, why?! He didn't understand what Albert needed to know and wasn't going to find out. Damn! He cursed the man in his mind and realized that, assignment or not, he wanted her.

"Get out!"

Martin reached into his pocket and withdrew the entire roll of money. He opened it and scattered the notes all over the bed. It was over two thousand marks.

The girl stared incredulously at the blanket of money. Martin doubted if she had ever seen so much of it at one time. She blinked repeatedly as if she were counting it.

"Oh, what the hell." she flatly stated as she removed the coat that covered her body. He was staring once again at the black underwear, but quickly she removed that too.

TEN

When Joseph Strauss was called into the office of the Commandant of detectives he didn't know what to expect. He was not in any trouble, he knew, and could only imagine that he was wanted for some sort of special assignment. After all, Joseph would immodestly think to himself, he was one of the best detectives in Bremen.

He was shocked when he entered the Commandant's office by the group of men he saw before him. He quickly reasoned that he wasn't going to like the assignment.

"Detective Strauss reporting, Sir." he coldly stated as he stood at attention before the desk of the commandant. He felt silly as he rigidly stood there. Sometimes the police force was just a bit too much like the army.

The men in the room eyed him silently, as if they were sizing him up and judging if he met their specifications.

He, too, was trying to judge these men and figure out what they wanted with him.

The commandant dominated the room. He was a large man with a jolly face, but today Joseph noticed the swastika pin on his lapel. Joseph had known the Commandant favored the Nazis, but he had always hidden the pin beneath his lapel. Among his present company he was proudly showing it off.

All the other men wore the brown uniforms of the Nazi party. There were four of them, each very different from the others and each decorated the unofficial uniform of their party a bit differently. Two of the strangers even wore their battle ribbons.

The commandant rose and extended his hand to Joseph. "How are you Strauss?" he asked in a friendly voice. "I hope I didn't take you away from something important?"

"No, Sir." Joseph replied as he shook the Commandant's pudgy hand. He didn't like the tone of the man's voice. It was all too friendly.

"Let me introduce you to our guests." The Commandant of Detectives went on. "This is Herr Pritwig." He gestured to a short, little man in the least decorate uniform. The little man stood up and meekly shook Joseph's hand. He smiled at the detective with a wide grin.

"This is Herr Beiser." the commandant introduced the second man, a heavyset older man who wore two Iron Crosses on his breast. When he shook Joseph hand he stood crisply at attention and clicked his heels together.

"This is Herr Schmidt of the City Banking Bureau." the commandant said as the third man stepped forward. "He is the leader of the local party." This man looked smugly at Joseph and simply nodded. He was a rather ordinary looking man and his uniform was very simple and without decoration.

"And this is the former Gauleiter of Dresden now Gauleiter of Bremen." The commandant said about the last man, an unsmiling soldier with several medals pinned to his chest. He also wore other signs of the war proudly; a patch over his right eye and an arm-less sleeve. He was younger than the rest of the men, but looked the most formidable. There was a certain evil about the man, Joseph felt as a very definite coldness and cruelty seemed to emanate from him.

"Are you a member of the party?" Herr Schmidt asked.

"As a civil servant I have felt it better to have no political affiliation." Joseph answered. It was a good safe reply, even though he knew he would never have anything to do with the Nazis. He didn't like the brown shirts; they seemed too often to be the center of problems on the streets. They beat people who were harmless and generally were no better than a gang of ruffians. He had always wondered if their political leaders condoned the violence, but figured they used the rabble as a tool. Still, he would never side with any radical group.

"I ask you here, Detective Strauss, because we have been asked to begin an investigation." The commandant explained. "You, by your record, seem to be the perfect man for the job."

"The commandant says you're an expert investigator." Herr Beiser added.

"Thank you, Sir."

"I have trouble giving this task to someone who may not agree with the principles of National Socialism." Herr Pritwig said, staring coldly at Strauss.

"Good policemen follow the orders of their commandants." The commandant assured his guest.

78

"And we are dealing with a crime." Schmidt said.

"What kind of crime?" Joseph asked.

"Crimes against the German people!" Beiser loudly proclaimed. He looked at Strauss as if he expected the detective to know the nature of the offense.

The commandant placed his arm around Joseph and spoke to him in his lyrical, father-figure voice. "There is no crime committed here in the pure police sense, Detective Strauss. In many ways we want you to do the job of discovering the crime."

"I'm afraid I'm a little confused."

"Strauss," the commandant went on. "We chose you because you have a bright future on the force. We chose you because you have a certain ability of dig deeply into the body of the case and find the motive. We chose you, and want you to help us, stop a man from harming the future of our country."

"And someone harmful to the goals of the Nazi party." Pritwig interjected.

"I doubt that, unless he has physically harmed a member of your party, he is in violation of the law." Joseph said. He didn't like the tone of the conversation. The Nazis had great power in Bremen's government, but their people still didn't control the city or the country. He knew that he would have to work within the framework of the law even if the Nazis sometimes ignored it.

"See!" Pritwig shouted. "It will take a firm believer in National Socialism to carry out or demands."

The commandant huddled close to Strauss. "See here, Joseph." He whispered. "These are powerful men and it wouldn't hurt you to get on their good side."

Schmidt spoke. "Maybe the detective doesn't have the imagination we need. Maybe he will resist following orders."

"I always follow my orders, Sir." Joseph stated.

"Then you will head up the investigation?" Schmidt asked.

Joseph looked at the Commandant of Detectives. The man seemed to be pleading to him to comply. It was as if he were their servants.

"Are these to be my orders?" he questioned the commandant.

The Gauleiter stood up. "They are."

Joseph stared at the commandant. He saw a feeling of resignation cross the man's face. Joseph realized his commanding officer was being ruled by this man. Neither of them had a choice. Joseph turned to the stern looking man who headed the delegation and nodded.

"Good." The Gauleiter went on. "How much do you know about the Adler Bank?"

"Only that it is one of the biggest in the City."

The Gauleiter began to pace the room. Joseph realized that the same fear of the man that possessed him also had griped the other men in the room. When he spoke everyone stopped and listened. "The Jewish owners and their Communist partners control much of the financial matters in Bremen. The Jewish owners and the corrupt general manager, Albert Freyberg, have deceived the people of this city and have put a spell over them. In many people's eyes the Adler Bank is a friend of the people. This is a lie. They are stealing from the good people of Bremen and pocketing the money into their greedy, Zionist hands."

"Is there proof of thievery by the bank manager?" Joseph asked. He then added. "If that is so I will put him under arrest today."

"They are too clever for that, these Jews." The Gauleiter went on. "They have covered their tracks well. The general manager is a clever man, but he is under the spell of the Jewess who is his wife."

"So what am I to do?" Joseph asked. He sensed that the other men were upset that he talked back to the Gauleiter. He too, he assumed, was to listen only.

"The only means left to us to bring an end to the spell the bank has cast over this city is to bring about the end of the Jewish control of the bank." The Gauleiter explained. "The Jews have not seen fit to sell to Aryan representatives and they have stood firm in their defiance of logic. They have cleverly disguised their dealings so as to even show a profit when the brighter, more realistic depositors have abandoned them. Our only hope is the discredit the ownership of the bank."

"By this you mean the owners and the general manager?"

"Yes. And that's your task, Detective Strauss."

"But you've said that they've done nothing wrong, Sir. Do you expect me to fabricate evidence against them?"

The commandant summoned up the courage to speak. "Joseph, everyone has done something in their past that is not quite legal. Everyone has a sin lurking in their past. All we want you to do is to find one in the past of Albert Freyberg and his wife. Something we can use to force them to relinquish control of the bank."

The commandant winked at Joseph. It seemed to be a warning. For his own good Joseph decided it would be best for him to cooperate.

"Detective," the Gauleiter spoke once more. "There must be something about them we can use against them. Something we can use to show the people of this city that these people are not their friends, but their enemies. Something! I want you to find me something!"

"I will do my best." Joseph felt himself saying. He also felt a sickness in his stomach. He knew he had no choice but to help the Nazis. He knew he would have no job if he didn't and it was a terrible time to be out of work.

He only prayed that this Herr Freyberg and his wife were faultless or clever enough to have hidden their past mistakes well enough so that he wouldn't be able to find them.

"Thank you, Detective Strauss." Herr Schmidt added. "Heil Hitler!"

"Heil Hitler." the other men shouted together.

Joseph Strauss nodded silently and left the office.

ELEVEN

Although he didn't know why, Martin Bock returned to the docks two days after he had first had sex with Greta.

Just after he had left her that night, despite the feeling of elation and joy that filled his body, he had resolved never to see the girl again. He had decided to make up some excuse to Albert; maybe to lie and say he couldn't find the girl. Possibly he could convince his employer that the girl wasn't worth helping, no matter who had asked. Maybe he was just embarrassed about having sex with the girl he was assigned to watch and learn about.

Yet he never said anything to Albert and he found his thoughts centered on the girl. He relived the night in his mind continuously and found himself drawn to the docks again, an insatiable desire drawing him there. It was as if she were a siren calling him back; back onto the rocks that could lay waste to his future and his career.

It didn't take him long to find her, leaning against a wall surrounded by the smoke of her cigarette and the mist of the chilled November night. It was as if he knew exactly where to look. She seemed amazed to see him, he realized as he gazed upon her beauty from twenty paces. She also seemed pleasantly surprised.

Greta quickly threw the cigarette down and crushed it with her boot. Martin seemed to watch her every move and time seemed to stop for him. She moved slowly, as if in a trance, and turned into the alleyway to disappear into the fog.

Martin dreaded that she was running away and rushed into the darkened alley to find her. He was quickly shrouded in the mist and could only hear her muffled footsteps on the bricks as it drew him further into the dark alley.

He followed, panting as he frantically ran toward the sound of the footsteps until they stopped.

He looked into the mist and saw only the darkness and the clouds created by his own breath. She was nowhere to be seen.

82

"Hey, Banker!" he heard the siren's voice a moment later. It seemed to come from right beside him.

He turned toward the voice and her form seemed to appear to him in the darkness. It looked as if she had materialized from the mist of the night.

"You come back for more?" the girl asked, her face smiling at him for the first time.

"Yes." he whispered, his voice breathless from his frantic run into the alley.

"How much?"

"Not as much as before."

"What the hell!" she smiled. "What you paid was worth two times anyway."

She led him again to her small room and stripped him of his clothes. She was a prostitute, yet he seemed to sense that she enjoyed him. He was more than just a job to her, he felt. He had always felt that prostitutes must be detached from those that pay for them, yet she seemed happy as they toyed with each other's bodies.

There was a passion between them, Martin sensed. He seemed to feel her body shiver as he touched her and as he kissed her. He felt a longing in her soul as he licked her small, firm nipples, stiffening them with his tongue. When he squeezed her firm buttocks she sighed and moaned as if she were a schoolgirl.

Together on the bed they seemed to melt in each other's arms. Her skin was warm against his as their lips pressed together and their tongues intertwined.

Quickly, somewhat forcibly, she pushed him onto his back and climbed on top of him. He saw in her eyes a rush of desire as she guided him into her. He felt her body moan as he reached up and squeezed her small breasts.

A moment later she lay down upon him and their bodies began to move together, their emotions cresting and falling together with each breath for what seemed to be forever.

* * * *

Though it seemed to last an eternity, for Martin it was over too soon. Though she had been all he ever desired in a woman, it was not enough. It could never be enough.

He was exhausted from it, yet he felt alive and filled with energy as he lay beside her in the bed. She was staring at the ceiling, awake, yet she seemed as exhausted as he was. As he looked over at her magnificent body he counted himself a lucky man.

He realized that Greta's nearly perfect form was not what many men desired. Most men want buxom women with far more roundness to them, but she was somehow what he had wished his perfect woman to be. Her smooth skin covered her thin, shapely body exquisitely. Her breasts were small, but round and firm. Even her rear was nearly perfect, not, like most girls he had known, either too fat or too flat. If Martin Bock were to design a woman, Greta Greyer would be the result.

Now he truly faced an impossible dilemma, Martin knew. He couldn't confess to the man who sent him to seek her out that he had sex with her. He couldn't face his mentor and confess that he had betrayed that trust. He wanted to share the joy he felt in finding the woman of his dreams, but not with Albert. He felt scared to admit that the woman of his dreams was a dockyard whore in the first place.

As he watched her silently staring at the cobweb covered ceiling he wondered who had put Albert up to this. Was it a debt owed from his youth on the docks? Was it a favor to an old friend or an old lover? Was she his lover as well? Could it be that the man he respected more than anyone he had ever known was making this girl also? Was Albert Freyberg, husband, father and honored citizen, keeping a prostitute on the sly? Could this be why he had sent Martin out to find her and to keep an eye on her?

What was his employer's interest in the girl? Could Martin ever tell him the truth about his lust for her?

"Hey, Banker!" he heard her haunting voice call.

He looked over at her. She had returned from her silent world of the ceiling and was smiling a radiant smile at him. She seemed to be glowing.

"What were you thinking?" she asked.

"Nothing much." he shrugged. "Just thinking."

"Hey! Banker! Want to go at it again?"

He smiled. "My name is Martin."

She smiled. "So, Martin! Again!"

He felt her hand against his body and as she touched him he felt aroused.

"Damn!" he shouted. "Go on!"

84

She looked up at him and grinned before she leaned down and kissed him.

* * * *

Lucy Wagner didn't know if she was falling in love with Karl Scheuler, but she knew something unusual was happening to her.

He didn't seem like a father figure to her, she knew. She certainly had no thoughts of having sex with her father, so he wasn't fulfilling that ugly vision. Yet he seemed more than a lover, and more than an older man whom she was paying back for showing her a good time.

Lucy had never had any qualms about whom she had sex with. She had kneeled down before a professor in school when she was sixteen and then turned around and did it with her lecherous classmates. Those were different times then, however, when money was freer and so were her morals. Now, older and wiser, she chose her playmates more thoughtfully, but Karl seemed more than a playmate.

As she waited in his hotel room for him, she wondered what he was all about. He seemed an aristocrat, but he seemed to be careful about where they went and how much they spent. He seemed to choose only secluded spots or the crowded streets, but not the places where the better people of Bremen spent their time. He seemed, sometimes, to be hiding. Was he hiding her?

Although she had learned something of his past, Lucy felt it was not enough. Although he spoke of his career as an army officer and of his position in the Weimar government, he always seemed to be hiding something from her. As she grew more attached and fond of him she also became more curious.

Did he have something to hide? Did he have another, darker side that he was keeping from her? These thoughts clouded her mind, but then she would reject them. After all, if he had something to hide would he give her the key to his hotel room?

As she stood alone in the middle of the room she let her own curiosity overwhelm her. All his things were in the room. Everything he had brought from Berlin was there. If, indeed, he had something to hide it would be hidden in this room.

85

Lucy felt no reluctance as she began to search through the dresser drawers and was actually disappointed when she found no hidden weapons among the neatly folded underwear.

She felt a little saddened, as she searched the drawer full of starched shirts, that there wasn't something hidden there either.

She became angry when it became clear that the dresser held no secrets from her.

Lucy walked over to the bed, discouraged and mad at herself for thinking such things. There wasn't anything secretive about Karl, except what she had made her mind think was secretive.

Something possessed her to take one more look, this time under the mattress where she did find a large brown envelope. No, two envelopes hidden beneath the bed on which she and Karl had made love.

She opened the first envelope carefully, not knowing what she would find and maybe hoping in her heart that it was nothing important, but if it were unimportant, why hid it under a mattress?

The papers to her were strange and Lucy didn't understand them as she read them. There were columns of numbers and lists of names and places which meant nothing to her. There were letters and notes from the Weimar cabinet to the Reichwehr staff and back, but all they spoke of were military matters. What did that have to do with Karl Scheuler, an official in the land office in Berlin? Why was he hiding them under the mattress anyway?

The second envelope she found more intriguing. It contained pictures of Karl in his younger days as an officer in the Kaiser's army. It also contained pictures of who appeared to be Karl's dead wife, a willowy young girl with long blonde hair and fair complexion.

There were also documents from a military hospital in Baden and a certificate of competency from a Bavarian mental institution. What, Lucy thought, was this to do with Karl? Was he some kind of......??

"Lucy!" Her thoughts were broken by the jolt of his voice ringing loudly in her ears. She self-consciously tried to hide the papers in her hand behind her back.

"Who gave you permission to ransack my room!?" he demanded of her.

She began to shuffle the papers together into a neat pile. "I'm sorry, Karl." she tried to explain. "I couldn't help myself."

He walked over and pulled the pile of papers from her hands. He looked angry, but not that angry.

"I'm sorry." she pleaded.

86

He looked over the top paper, the picture of his wife and began to smile. "She was lovely, wasn't she Lucy." he began to mumble, almost to himself.

"Yes. It's a shame she died so young."

He looked strangely at her as if he was engrossed in deep thought.

"That is your wife?" Lucy asked. "You did say she was dead?"

"It's about time you learned the truth, Lucy, about me and about my mission here in Bremen."

He offered her a seat on the bed and sat down beside her. He handed her several pictures and began to explain.

"Those are me in my better days, Lucy, Gretchen and I at our wedding. She was barely nineteen when I married her and her family was happy for it. We, my family, owned a lot of land in what is now Poland and her family were impoverished Junkers with only a title to their name.

"In the beginning we were very happy. I felt proud and lucky to have such a wife for I wasn't the most handsome of men. Then the war came along and everything changed.

"I was a cavalry officer in those days. See," he handed her another photo of young Leutnant Scheuler on his horse, "quite a specimen of Prussian manhood. That only lasted through August. At the Marne I foolishly led my platoon into a section of English machine guns and found myself wounded.

"The groin injury was quite severe and I was told than I may never be able to make love to my wife again. I took that to mean that I never could make love and never tried again in our marriage. Naturally, I grew bitter and our marriage sour and my wife depressed and torn between the emotions and needs of a twenty-four year old woman and the honor of an officer's wife.

"After time I let drinking and depression get the best of me. I did my job, Lucy, but I was an angry, bitter man. That's were your 'boss' met me. I became his commandant in the observation section. That is also were my wife met the man with whom she would have an affair."

Lucy looked over the pictures of the young girl. "Why are you telling me this Karl? How did she die?"

"I'm getting to that!" he went on. "I took liberties being the commandant and brought my wife to the front. Not to comfort me, but to show her off to my troops. It was as if I was saying 'look what I have, you bastards! Look how pretty she is!' She met a flyer there and had an affair with him and I found out about it."

"Then what did you do?" Lucy asked, her voice trembling.

"I went mad. I went mad when my wife was at the field and forced her to confess it to me. Then I chased the flyer, but he was young and fast where I was fat and old. Instead I took my revenge out on my wife and machine gunned her to death from one of my areoplanes."

He paused a moment to let that sink in. Lucy was suddenly frightened. There was a horror now in his eyes.

"I was sent to a mental asylum after that and spent the next six years there trying to bring my sanity back. It's back now and even my ability to make love has returned, but the price I've paid has been great. The guilt I feel at the slaughter of my wife by my own hand will be with me the rest of my life.

"That brings me to the other set of papers and my mission here in Bremen.

"I'm convinced that the war ruined me like it did so many others and I'm convinced that Germany is headed down the same path toward destruction today. Those papers you see, to the trained eye, indicate that the Weimar Republic is secretly rebuilding its military strength to challenge the world once again. God only knows what would happen when another, more radical group such as the Nazis take power!"

She looked over the documents. "You're going to sell them to the English, aren't you?"

"Lucy, I'd give them away, but no one would believe me. I'm a former mental patient and a murderer. I'm unfit to present these papers to the French and British, but Albert Freyberg is a respected banker and a war hero. I came here to convince him to take these out of the country."

"But Albert's not going anywhere."

"Believe me, Lucy, he will run. He'll have no choice. Sooner or later, he'll have to run away or lose not only his own life, but those of his wife and children."

TWELVE

"So, Mr. Steven Langley what brings you here?" Albert Freyberg asked his guest in halting, textbook English as they entered the office.

Freyberg was not exactly what Steve had expected when he first set eyes on him. His advance men had told him that Freyberg was as shrewd a banker as they come and that he, more than anyone else in Northern Germany would put his business before politics in the turbulent days now facing this nation.

Yet Steve was expecting an older man. He was expecting a wizened aristocrat, weathered by both the good times and the bad. He saw instead a man his own age, with the comfort of wealth to be sure, but with gentleness in his eyes and a smile on his face. There appeared no hatred against him as he had expected; no hatred against an American who could be held responsible for Germany's troubles.

Steve spoke to Freyberg in German, a language he knew well from his childhood. "I'm glad you have time to fit me into your busy schedule, Herr Freyberg."

Freyberg looked a little amazed at the command his guest had of the German tongue and quickly replied in his native language. "I've never been one to turn away business."

"I own a large financial clearing house in New York," Steve went on to explain. "I'm looking for someone to represent my interest in Europe. My financial commitments, particularly in Northern Germany are growing and I have been told that you're the man to protect those interests."

Albert Freyberg's eyebrows raised as Steve spoke the words. "Herr Langley, from whom did you hear such things?"

"I'd sent some of my people and ask them to find someone who could honestly represent me here. I wanted someone whom I could trust not to swindle me. They suggested you above all others."

Freyberg smiled as he rose from his desk and walked over to a table beneath the only window in the Spartan office. "What exactly do you know about me, Herr Langley?"

Albert quickly poured two glasses of wine from the bottle that sat on the table and handed one to Steve. The American took a sip before he answered.

"I know you're the head of one of the largest banks in the area. I know that you're a family man. I know that you have remained personally solvent throughout the world-wide depression. I also know that you've kept your concern just as solvent throughout it all. For me that's enough. I admire men who keep their wits about them in a crisis and who foresee impending disaster."

Freyberg had taken his seat at the desk once again. "That was pure luck, Sir," he explained. "I viewed the American stock crash as an omen and took measures to preserve my business immediately. I knew that Western financing bolstered our own prosperity. Unlike so many of my peers I didn't wait until the first business closed and the first banks went bankrupt to react. And, as you said, I didn't panic."

"All the more reason I want you to represent me here."

Freyberg took a gulp of the warm wine. "Do you realize that I don't particularly agree with the way things are going in this land? Do you realize that, if it were me, I would divest any interest I have in Germany?"

Steve smiled. It was an answer he expected from an honest man. "That's another reason I want you on my side," he explained. "You're too smart to be deceived by the rhetoric and politics. You're too much of a good businessman to allow those things to come between associates."

"Tell me a little about yourself, Steven Langley." Freyberg asked. Steve could sense that the banker's brown eyes were penetrating him, searching for the fiber behind the man.

"I'm an American of German descent, as you have probably guessed by now. My father, who was born here, made a lot of money in steel back before the turn of the century. I took over and found that there was more in working with the money I inherited than simply manufacturing. I found that I could easily turn money into more money."

"I see." Albert Freyberg nodded in agreement.

"I, like you, fought in the war," Steve went on. "As an aviator."

Freyberg's expression changed, his eyes widening as if he were suddenly alerted to a noise. "I, too, flew during the war. I was in an observation section."

"So I understood. It was another reason I felt you would find an association with me appealing. I was a fighter pilot."

Freyberg smiled. "I see. You harbor no ill feelings even though I was your enemy. That's good. I wish more of my countrymen felt that way and lost the bitterness of the war. Times have been tough here, but it does no good to hold a grudge."

"I like hearing you say that. Whether you'd consider me your foe was the one thing I couldn't predict."

"I was a soldier, as you were. I did my duty and paid for it in many ways. I lost four years of my youth and maybe most of my innocence. I nearly lost my life and saw my entire world change, but it wasn't your fault. It was simply the way things turned out." Albert looked down at the desk, lost in his thoughts. He looked sad, Steve thought, as if there were no pleasant memories of that time.

"Although I suffered less than you, I'm sure, I can understand how you feel. I had some trying moments then. We'd shut the possibility of death out of our minds and tried to hide the fear. I was never good at that." Steve added.

"Fear's not something you possess during wartime, my friend." Freyberg smiled. "Fear is something that overcomes you when you have something to lose. During the war I never realized all I had to lose. Today I do."

Steven looked at him curiously, not understanding what he had said but feeling he was going to be turned down.

"I have many powerful enemies now in my life, Herr Langley. I have many things to fear and many things to lose. I can't let you put your faith in me at this time. It's not a wise investment on your part. I think my time in Bremen as a man to be reckoned with is about over."

"Why do you say that?"

Albert shrugged. "The vultures of the Nazis surround me and my family, and my wealth, Sir. They are circling, waiting for the right moment to bring me down. You couldn't expect a man surrounded by enemies, fighting them off to desperately save his life and the life of his family...you can't expect me to give my all energy to your interests. I'm too distracted."

"Surely they need men like you, no matter what your politics?"

"This isn't America, Langley. In this country hatred and prejudice run deep. In this country you can't rise above what you were without feeling the scars and then only for a short time before you are beaten down again."

91

The banker looked upset, his mind apparently turning the trails he faced over in his mind, but Steven had to ask more of him. "If it's so bad, why stay?"

Freyberg shrugged. "This is our country. Where else do we belong?"

Langley had no answer. He probably would feel the same if the tables were turned.

"Ah!" Freyberg waved his hands wildly in the air. "Enough of this depressing talk! Steven, if I may call you that, let me at least be a host to you while you are here. Let me take you home and meet my family. Let's try to forget these troubled times and talk only of good things."

Good! Steve thought to himself. Maybe he could change Albert's mind if he were given half a chance. He rose from the chair and extended his hand to the man. "Okay, Albert! Show me a good time."

* * * *

Greta had met the mark where she always met her best marks, just outside the Hopffbrau. He had approached her cautiously, his youthful face looking pleased, yet self-conscious about seeking out a prostitute, even a young, pretty one like herself.

He had spoken hesitantly to her, his voice choking on the words as if his throat was parched and his lips dry. His eyes scanned her body, undressing it, imagining what she looked like beneath the coat, but seldom looking her in the eyes.

"What'll it be, Hans?" she had asked. She always called them Hans, and if they didn't correct her she assumed they wanted to keep their anonymity, or their name was really Hans.

"Can I buy you a drink?" he had asked at first.

"What for?"

"I didn't want to come out and ask..." his childish voice tailed off. He seemed to be apologizing, but she understood his shyness.

"Fifty marks, Hans." she coldly said, watching the cloud of smoke from her breath mingle with the first snowflakes of the season. "That'll be the price."

He nodded in agreement.

Greta had taken him to her room, but soon realized it was a mistake. The boy was inexperienced and he took his task too seriously. He acted excited, but didn't know how to have sex and refused when she tried to show him some of the finer points of the art. He wanted it fast and came too quickly.

In his haste she sensed anger in him and as he thrust himself into her she sensed a pain and a joy in his face as he recognized that pain. He seemed to relish each moment of agony he gave to her as she cringed more and more during the ordeal and as he squeezed her too tightly and clawed her too violently.

Thankfully it was over quickly, she felt. Thankfully he would be gone from the room shortly. She never liked men who looked upon sex as a chore. She felt a little ashamed when men felt no pleasure except when they gave her pain. The pain wasn't worth the price. Maybe her life wasn't worth the pain or the price she paid when she was with such men.

After he had gotten up from on top of her and ran into the bathroom she thought about her life as she lay on the bed. Maybe Martin Bock had the right idea, though she had rejected it so quickly when he had said it.

"This isn't the life for you, Greta." he had told her. "You're too beautiful to be here. You are too beautiful to give yourself to any man who can put up the marks. You're wasting your life here."

She wondered if he were the man to take her away from this. She wondered if he were the knight in shining armor she had told her mother didn't exist. She wondered why he had come into her life and wondered why she felt so alive when they were together. Greta had been with so many men, why was it so different with him? Was it love? Could she ever know what love was?

The young boy had come out of the bathroom and stood before her. He was a good looking boy, she decided, with his light brown hair and perfect, boyish body. He was muscular, but not muscle-bound. He was about twenty, she guessed, but it was a shame that he knew nothing of how to make a woman feel good.

Please go away, she pleaded in her mind. Go find some virginal girl who won't know how bad a lover you are. Go find yourself some poor girl who won't understand that all men don't enjoy hurting their women.

"You weren't worth it." The boy announced as he reached for his clothes.

Greta sat up in the bed, her soul growing angry. "You only get out of it what you put in."

"I'm not paying you what you asked." he announced.

"Fuck you, Hans!" she stated dryly. "You pay up or I'll call the man downstairs. He understands!"

93

"Don't threaten me, you little whore. I say you're not worth it." he sneered as he put on his pants.

She jumped out of the bed and reached for his coat, grabbing it away from his outstretched hands. She climbed back into the bed and searched the pockets. She was determined to find her money, or something worth keeping. All she pulled out was a Nazi armband.

"Shit!" she whispered to herself as she stared at the swastika.

Suddenly she felt his hand around her neck, pulling her from the bed. "Drop it, bitch!" he hollered as he shook her by the neck like a chicken. She released the coat from her hands and let it fall to the floor.

Don't hurt me! The words rang in her mind, but she was too frightened to speak.

She heard the sound of his hand striking her face and the pain as it crackled through her brain!

Suddenly she realized she was on the floor, her naked body at the young Nazis feet.

She felt a jolt of pain again as his foot slammed into her side!

Oh God! Oh God! Don't kill me! The thought rang through her mind.

The room began to spin around her. She realized she didn't know were she was, or where her attacker was.

She felt a fearsome pain on her scalp as she felt herself rise up from the floor. He was pulling her up by her hair. Greta screamed as loudly as she could!

Then the stinging as he slapped her face again!

She felt a wetness on her face as her senses returned, but realized it wasn't tears....it was blood gushing from her mouth.

"No more! No more!" she mumbled, but again felt the grip of his angry hands around her neck.

He pushed her over onto the bed and his hands tightened their grip.

Oh shit! She heard her mind shout. I'm going to die!

She felt herself suffocating as the man strangled her. She felt herself gasping for air!

Dammit! Greta! Her soul shouted. Fight back!

She felt herself growing faint, but summoned up the strength to move her legs. She slammed one into his groin!

She had stunned him just enough for him to loosen his grip. She could breathe again!

She slammed her leg into him again and heard him gulp for air. He completely let her go.

Greta stumbled from the bed and staggered from the room, she was so scared her heart sounded like a drum in her head. She had to get away from him! She had to run, but her legs felt limp and weak beneath her.

She saw the stairs too late and felt herself falling down them. As she rolled down the steps numbness overcame her. She should have felt the pain, but her mind blotted it out.

When she reached the bottom, dizzy and nauseous, she had enough energy left to point up the stairs.

"Help me! He tried to kill me!" she moaned.

The huge man who ran the boarding house grabbed a policeman's club he kept hidden behind the desk and started up the stairs. He was mad, she knew. He didn't want any trouble in his place.

She heard the noise and shouts from her room and felt safer, thankful she was alive.

She looked at herself, realizing that she was naked, realizing that she was covered with blood. She felt her head and her hand felt sticky. Suddenly the whole world went black.

* * * *

After waiting on the street outside the Hopffbrau for nearly two hours, shivering in the cold and watching the snow come softly down around him, Martin Bock grew angry.

Greta had promised to meet him there, cutting short her work that night to spend some time with him. She had seemed happy about it when he had suggested it, but, he thought, maybe she had second thoughts about forsaking the profits tonight for his company.

Still, he decided, it wasn't right to leave him stranded out there in the bitter night air. He deserved more than that. He was beginning to think he meant more to her than that. Maybe, he was wrong.

As his feet grew colder and the street less crowded, Martin decided he'd had enough. Whether she was working or not he was going over to the rooming house to demand an explanation and an apology from the girl.

He enjoyed the rush of warm air he felt as he opened the door to the rooming house. It quickly brought some feeling back to his frozen feet and hands. Although he thought the rundown place was unfit for human habitation, it was comforting for him to get inside, away from the biting wind and dampness. He barely noticed the blood on the floor near the step.

"Hey! You!" the slovenly keeper behind the desk called him as Martin began to climb the steps.

He stopped on the second step and turned to face the man.

"You Greyer's pimp?" the fat man snarled at Martin.

He returned the question with only a blank stare.

The heavyset, ogre-like man waved his fist at Martin. "If you are!" he shouted. "Get her out of here. Get her out, you hear me! I don't want any trouble!"

Martin ignored the man and continued up the stairs.

"I don't care how pretty the bitch is! Get her out!"

He was puzzled. What had she done?

He saw more spots of blood splattered on the floor as he neared her room. Now he was beginning to worry.

He knocked on the door gently.

"Get the fuck out of here, you bastard!" Greta screamed through the closed door.

"It's Martin."

"Shit." he heard her mumble. Then she called to him in a loud voice. "Go away. I'm sick!"

He turned the doorknob, but found the door locked. He pressed his weight against it until it opened.

She glared back at him from the bed of the room as he entered through the doorway. It appeared that a storm had hit the small flat and Greta looked as if she had been in the middle of it. She sat on the bed wrapped in a blanket, her face swollen and bruised. She held a bloodstained towel to her head with arms that were, like her face, covered with discolored bruises. She looked pitiful, but she also looked angry.

"Get the hell out of here!" she screamed, tears in her eyes, as she threw the blood soaked towel at him.

For a moment he couldn't move. He had never expected to see her like this, beaten and helpless. He grew angry as he asked himself who could have done such a thing.

"Go away." she pleaded this time. Tears filled her eyes.

"That bastard," Martin calmly said as he thought about it. The man at the desk, he assumed, had done this to her.

"It wasn't him." Greta's trembling voice replied after he asked that question. "It was a boy, a twenty year old, and wet behind the ears. He said I wasn't worth it and I was mad as hell. He....damn! It hurts."

Martin walked over and looked more closely at her. Her blackened eyes now poured streams of tears as she began to cry uncontrollably. Her body trembled and shook.

He noticed red creases in her neck and felt the welts with his hand, touching them as gently as he could so as to not hurt her further. She jumped as his fingers touched her skin.

"What did he do? Did he try to choke you or something?"

She nodded. "I thought he was going to kill me, but the owner saved me. He beat the shit out of him."

"The bastard deserved it." he said as he touched her shoulder. She cringed with pain.

"Oh! That hurts!" she cried out as he bent her head and peered at the wound that still oozed blood.

"We should take you to a hospital."

"No. They'll ask questions. I don't even know his name and when they find out what I am they'll just say I deserved it."

"Maybe they'd be right." he said, sorry immediately that he spoken the words that were in his head.

She pushed his hand away. "Sure! I'd expect you to say that. The little whore was looking for it, huh! If she wanted a good man she wouldn't sell herself on the streets."

"I told you that sooner or later...."

"Go to hell, Bock!" she shouted into his words. She quickly got up from the bed and walked toward the bathroom. He could see how much it hurt when she walked.

"You know you'd someday run into someone like that."

"Yes, I know. And it's not the first time either."

"Then why go on?"

She turned her back to him, the blanket dropping off her shoulders to reveal another cluster of bruises. "What do you think I could do, Martin?" she asked as she threw the blanket off her and reached for her coat. "This is the only way I could get out of the riverfront."

"There are other ways to rise up from here." he said. "Look at me. Look at Albert Freyberg, my employer."

Greta stared at him coldly. "Maybe men could do it, but not me. Women down here only grow old and shrivel up. Today I might be young and pretty, but I couldn't get out if I simply tried working for it. I'd turn out like all the women down here, like my mother, old before her time."

"If you keep this up you'll be dead, the victim of some maniac."

"It serves a purpose. Someday I'll have enough to start a new life in Berlin or Munich, or even Paris where no one ever heard of the Bremen riverfront."

"There are slums and bad neighborhoods in every city, Greta, and a place for whores."

"I won't be a whore then."

"You don't have to be one now!" he stated as he walked toward her. He saw her shy away as he reached out for her, but soon the girl melted into his arms. She began to cry again.

"Let me help you, Greta." he whispered as he tenderly touched her matted hair. "Let me take you from this life."

Greta trembled in his arms and continued to cry, her tears wetting his chest. She was like a child in his arms. Greta needed Albert's help, he thought, and his help as well.

THIRTEEN

"You know, my dear, I've never seen you look so radiant." Karl told Lucy as they walked down the snow covered sidewalk.

Lucy did feel wonderful. There was something about the cold, crisp air and the bright sunshine that glistened off the freshly fallen snow that excited her. She always liked winter, with its long, clear, starlit nights and sharp contrasting days of brightness and gloom. She loved this time even though most of her friends thought she was rather silly in delighting in a season that most of them hated, but there was something in her that welcomed the chill and the frosty weather.

She was surprised that Karl noticed it, however. Was her mood so much different today? Was it that way because of the weather or because of something else?

The first November snow had fallen the night before. It had showered the city with a light coat of whiteness which had remained glimmering against a cloudless sky as the sun rose on this cold morning.

As she watched the people scurry around in the still chilly afternoon, their coats and gloves shielding them against the wind, she was thankful that she had managed to get out of the office to meet Karl. She was worried for a while because Martin Bock had failed to show up that morning, but he came straggling in about noon and she took her leave to have lunch with Karl.

He looked quite happy, she realized as they ate a late lunch in the cafe where they had first dined together. He seemed more relaxed, as if a great weight had been lifted off his shoulders. Had his confiding in her all his past sins and his mission relieved his mind so? Was he glad that she knew all his secrets?

She had worried about what she had learned almost constantly since he revealed it all to her that night in the hotel room. She worried if he were truly as stable as he claimed and as he appeared. Could he return to the insanity that moved him to murder his wife? Could something she said or did trigger a violent, insane reaction that would make her a victim? She dismissed the wild thoughts; he was perfectly normal now.

His mission worried her more. It was dangerous to steal state secrets, even in the freedom of the Weimar. Yet, in his mind, the plague of war had altered his fate so dramatically that she could see his convictions overcoming his good sense. Things weren't that bad, she had always assumed. No matter who was in power, the Socialists or these funny looking Nazis with their Charlie Chaplin-like leader, the politics wouldn't really affect the average person. What could any of them do about the mess the country was in anyway? What difference would it make who was in power?

The average person, like herself, Lucy would always think, would be as well off or as bad off as they always were in spite of the government in Berlin. Hindenburg, after all, was no different than the Kaiser. Who could the next rulers of Germany hurt that weren't being hurt already by the depression?

"It's such a nice day for a walk," Karl interrupted her thoughts. "I love to walk on the morning after a snowfall. It reminds me of Silesia, when the fields I walked in my childhood always seemed to be snow-covered."

"I love this weather, too."

"It's a shame that when we get older we find ourselves less able to stand the cold," Karl said. He was warmly dressed in a fine woolen coat with fur lining and wore the thickest; most comforting muffler Lucy could ever remember seeing. For the season and the day, which really wasn't all that cold, he was overdressed.

"And it'll be good to walk after a meal. Burn up some calories," he went on. "That's another thing about growing older; you can't pack it away like you used to and get away with it."

She smiled. "I can't pack it away and get away with it now, Karl. Does that make me old? If I ate as I'd like to I'd be as big as a house."

"You, darling girl, would never be fat."

"That's only because I work at it," she said.

"Well, keep working at it. Never let that gorgeous body of yours go to seed. Always be as beautiful as you are today."

It felt good to hear words like that, Lucy thought. She seldom had men talk to her like that and then only when they wanted something. Karl really meant it. She wondered if he were falling in love with her the same way she was with him.

They huddled close to each other as they silently walked down the street, now deserted in the mid-afternoon chill. The wind whistled around them and Lucy felt happy. Who cared who looked at them! Who cared if someone thought it wasn't natural for a fifty year old man to be pawed by a girl in her twenties!

There were men watching her she realized as she glanced over to the other side of the street. She felt their penetrating eyes as she walked. She felt their cold, icy stare follow her and had to look their way. They were tall men in plain wool coats and wide brimmed hats. They looked like American gangsters as she watched them boldly follow the couple as they turned the corner.

Suspiciously, she turned her head to see if they would continue to watch them as they crossed the street. Instead of watching though, the men crossed over and began to follow behind Lucy and Karl. Their eyes never moved away from hers.

"Karl," she finally told him. "Someone's following us."

Karl turned and saw the men. He grabbed her hand and began to walk faster up the street. Lucy quickened her pace to follow, glancing behind her to see the men rapidly advancing on them, their arms now reaching underneath their coats.

"Hurry, Lucy," Karl pleaded, out of breath.

Lucy looked in front of her. The street was almost deserted. There was no crowd of people they could melt into.

Karl suddenly stopped at the entrance of a small street and turned into it, dragging Lucy behind him.

"Keep running," he ordered as he reached under his coat and withdrew a revolver.

"Who are they?! What do they want?!"

He pushed her away from him without answering and stared at the street, awaiting their pursuer's arrival.

Suddenly a gunshot rang out!

Lucy heard a ping as she thought she saw a bullet ricochet off a nearby wall!

Several more bursts of gunfire echoed in the small street!

Lucy screamed and dropped to her knees!

Another shot resounded in her ears!

"Get up! Get up!" Karl shouted as he pulled her by the arm, urging her to her feet.

101

He edged her down the small, darkened street, guarding their retreat with his pistol at the ready. In a second the small street ended and they were on a wider avenue across from a small park.

"Let's go!" Karl said as he turned, grabbed her arm and led her into the park.

They hid behind a small gardener's hut and watched as the two hoodlums emerged from the shadows of the small street, their guns cleverly hidden in their trench-coat's large pockets. She realized they had lost their scent as their faces searched up and down.

When the men realized they had lost their prey they slipped back into the cavern of the small street and disappeared.

"I'm sorry I got you into this," Karl said, puffing between the words as he caught his breath.

"Why were they after you?" Lucy asked as she herself panted for breath.

Karl slowly put his revolver back beneath his coat. "They've found me. They want back the papers I stole. They know I won't hesitate to use them."

"Damn," Lucy muttered. "They're from the government? Our government!"

"I don't know." Karl replied, his face seemed strained as he spoke the words. "Von Papen has many different groups associated with his government. Not all of them always work within the law."

Lucy noticed pain on Karl's face, "What's wrong?" she asked anxiously.

Karl reached into his coat and seemed to cringe. When he pulled his hand out again it was covered with blood.

* * * *

"Go and get Albert." Karl had pleaded with Lucy, his breath shallow from the exhaustion, pain, and loss of blood. "Get him and bring him here. And make sure you are not followed."

She had followed her instructions as she had all the others he had issued to her since the moment he was shot. She had followed; despite the pleadings from her heart that it wasn't right and that it wasn't the way things were meant to be. The tears had swelled within her and her mind told her to follow the rules, but she couldn't go against his desires. Karl wouldn't do what she wanted and no manner of arguing was going to change the course he wished to sail.

She had first wanted to take him to a hospital, but he had said no. No doctor, either, he had insisted. He had to keep them from finding him again, he said, and, although she saw the logic in his thoughts, her heart cried out against it.

He had begged her, coughing between each phrase that they go to her flat. There, he felt, he would be safe. What was she letting herself in for? She wondered what she would do if they found them there? Would they finish the job, killing both of them to stop him from his mission?

Damn Karl's obsession! Damn the need he had to steal those papers and his determination to get them out of Germany. Were they worth his death? Were they worth hers!?

Now he wanted Albert. Was he going to involve him as well in this insane quest? Her mind told her not to get him, but she once again did as she was asked.

She called Albert from the telephone in the corner store. Holding back the tears and choking on the words, praying that her panic wouldn't be noticed by the man behind the counter, she begged him to help her.

"What's wrong?" he asked her almost immediately. Her cries betrayed her easily.

"Karl!" she whispered into the phone. "Karl's been shot."

"Where is he?"

"He's in my flat. Do you know where it is?" she whispered.

"I'll be there as soon as I can." Albert said.

"Please, Sir, come alone. Karl says for you to be alone." she pleaded and then the line went dead.

Lucy rushed back to her flat and found Karl slouched over the chair. The wound, which she had hastily and clumsily dressed, was already soaked with blood.

Oh, hell! He's dead! She cringed at the thought as she stared at his limp body. What am I going to do with a dead body?!

She didn't want to move, but slowly mustered the courage to go to him. He wasn't dead, she discovered, just passed out from the pain of his wounds. She mustered all the strength she could and hoisted him back into a sitting position. He seemed to return to consciousness.

"Is Albert coming?" his voice no more than a whisper.

"Yes." She replied. She looked at her hands and realized that they were again covered with his blood. She looked at her dress; it was also painted with rich, dark splotches. "Oh God! What am I going to do?!" she finally cried.

"Albert will help me. He'll know what to do." she heard him say.

Lucy began to cry, unable to move or help the dying man. It seemed an eternity before there was a knock on the door and she returned from her world of tears.

"Who is there." she called as she picked herself up from the floor. She prayed it wasn't the police or some other unwanted guest.

"Albert Freyberg." the voice called and she ran to the door.

"Damn!" he flatly stated when he first saw Karl from the doorway. "What the hell happened?"

Lucy began to slowly explain the story as she watched Albert go over to the man and pull off the bloodstained bandages. He applied alcohol to the wound and cleaned it. Karl cringed with pain as Albert repeatedly dabbed the wound with the cloth.

"Thanks for coming. I knew you wouldn't let me down." Karl said as Albert began to probe the hole in the man's side.

"Shut up, you foolish old bastard!" Albert shouted as he looked deeply at the wound. There was a distressed look on his face. "Damn! Where's the bullet!"

"Lodged under all the layers of fat, I assume." Karl choked out. He tried to laugh, but coughed instead.

"Christ! It must be in there. Too deep! I can't do anything about it here."

"I wanted him to go to the hospital." Lucy interjected.

"No!" Karl shouted, his teeth gritting from a jolt of pain.

"It's either a doctor who can close this hole or you'll bleed to death!" Albert said.

"Oh God!" Lucy cried. "Don't let him die here!"

"Shut up, girl!" Albert screamed. He turned back to Karl. "Look, I'm going to call a doctor whether you like it or not."

"No, please!" Karl pleaded. "My mission is too important."

"To hell with the mission! Is it worth your life? Her life!? You'll never complete this insane mission if you're dead!"

Karl reached out with a bloody hand and grasped Albert's coat. "Listen, old friend, I asked you before and I'll ask you again, please take the papers and get them out of Germany. If you do that for me and my death with have meaning."

"Karl, I'm not going to let you die." Albert said as he clutched the injured man's hand.

104

"Take the papers!"

"Fine! Fine!" Albert relented. "I'll take your damn papers, but only until you're back on you feet and you can find another way to get them out. I'm not going anywhere."

"Fine, Albert. I knew I could depend on you." Karl sighed. In a second he was unconscious.

Albert continued to struggle with the wound, applying pressure with his scarf to stop the bleeding. He looked as if he knew if wouldn't be enough.

"Why did you have to get mixed up with him?" he asked Lucy.

"I don't know." she cried. "I was flattered. He was nice to me."

Albert shook his head. "He was so nice to you! Shit! Did he ever tell you he has a habit of ruining women's lives? Did he tell you the truth about those lousy papers?"

"Yes, I think I understand it all. But, you know, he's been kind to me. He's really been gentle and loving. He's not the same man you remember."

Albert laughed. "He's an old fool and he'll drag you and me to hell if he gets his way."

"What're we going to do?"

"Get to a phone." he explained. "Call my home and tell them to send my car out here. Tell them to put my two best hunting rifles inside. Hurry!"

"Hunting rifles? Why?"

"Accidents do happen, Lucy. A lot of things can happen when you clean hunting rifles." Albert grinned.

"No doctors." Karl mumbled as he slowly returned to consciousness.

Albert shook him frantically. "Listen, you old goat, where are the papers? Where are they?! I'll take them off your hands!"

"In the lining of my overcoat." he muttered.

Lucy grabbed the coat and tore open the lining. The two envelopes were hidden there.

"Now, go make that call." Albert told her as he took the papers and placed them in his suit pocket. "I'll keep these with me. I promise. I just hope it isn't the death of all of us."

FOURTEEN

Martin Bock had decided that the time had come to talk to Albert about Greta.

He had put it off long enough. His mind had mulled over the consequences long enough. She had suffered long enough. Greta had told him of her hopes and dreams of rising out of the gutter and Albert, more than any man Martin could think of, could help her achieve those dreams. Maybe that was why he had sent him there. Maybe someone else had heard the same wishes from the girl and had convinced Albert to help.

There was only one nagging question in Martin's mind. If Greta found her savior in Albert Freyberg, why would she ever need Martin Bock?

Martin knew he had fallen in love with her. Martin realized that the foul-mouthed little prostitute with the nearly perfect body had captured his mind, his heart, and his soul. There was something about her, he realized, something beyond the sheer joy of her body, of her passion, that had made him infatuated with her. There was something inside of her that he loved as well, something well hidden that was sensitive and worth his love. There was something sad underneath the brash words and curses, something that said she was looking for a love he was willing to give.

But what if he was wrong? What if she was just a sly little fox who was using him to reach someone who was a better prey? Could she have guessed his rich employer was whom she really had to please? Could she be using him?

It was unimportant, he realized. Either he told Albert about her or he would have to forget about Greta. He had an obligation to Albert to tell him the truth. He had to gather the strength to keep her love afterwards, if he could ever win her love.

He had arranged to meet with Albert at the bank first thing that morning, but the news from Berlin was all was on Albert's mind as Martin confronted him in his office.

"Looks like another crisis." Albert said as Martin closed the door upon entering. He was sitting behind a desk covered with newspapers from all across Germany.

Martin, preoccupied with his own life, was unaware of the news. "What's wrong?" he asked.

"Papen's government is on the verge of collapse." Albert explained. "They say that Hindenburg has called Hitler into conference. Maybe his turn has finally come."

Martin was surprised. "Two weeks ago the elections went against the Nazis. Why would Hindenburg let him try to form a new government?"

Albert shrugged. "Who knows? Politics doesn't have to make sense. I don't think it'll happen anyway. Not just yet. Von Schleicher hasn't played his full hand and Hindenburg despises the Nazis just as much as he does Bolshevism."

"What difference does it make anyway?"

"Martin! That's the kind of attitude that'll destroy this country. If no one thinks it'll make a difference, then the devil could come marching in and swallow us all."

Martin wanted to change the subject. It wasn't that he disagreed with Albert's opinions; he just had other things on his mind. "Sir," he began. "We have something more important to discuss than politics."

Albert looked up from his papers, puzzled. "In today's world, I doubt anything is more important, but let's hear it."

Martin took a deep breath and began. "You remember asking me to find a prostitute named Greta Greyer."

"Of course, I assume you've found her."

"Yes, but she wasn't what I expected."

Albert looked curiously at him. "How do you mean?"

"We're both from the riverfront and we grew up around the whores. I'm sure you'd expect her to be nothing but a slut, but she's not. She's.....she's something more."

Albert nodded. "Describe her to me."

"She's...." Martin felt himself stammering, unable to phrase the words the way his mind wanted them. "She's truly remarkable. She's beautiful. She's unlike any girl I've ever met."

Albert smiled. "It sounds like you're in love with her."

107

"I am."

There was a silence after that. Martin had admitted it and felt ashamed, but had expected Albert to laugh at him and was more ashamed when he didn't. Instead, Albert reached into his desk and pulled out a pack of cigarettes, lighting one and tossing the pack toward Martin. Albert seldom smoked anymore, and then only in times of extreme stress. Martin didn't smoke at all, but, at times like this, wished he did.

"I love her." Martin admitted.

"As a whore? As a woman? As a child?"

"I just love her?"

"Does she love you?" Albert questioned, his head now circled in a gray haze.

Martin shook his head. "I don't know that. I'm not sure if she feels the same way."

Albert grunted. "You young people! How could you think you're in love with a girl you've known only a day or two."

"I've found her the first day."

"And didn't tell me?!"

Martin nodded. "I had to learn more about her. That's what you said. As I learned more about her, I fell for her,"

Now Albert laughed. "I thought you were smarter than that, Bock. She's a prostitute!"

"There's something inside her, Sir. There is something better than a mindless whore."

Albert leaned back in his chair. "Fine! So you think she's worth any effort I put out in her behalf."

"More than that, I think she needs you're help."

"Have you told her about me?"

Martin cringed, wondering if he had disobeyed his orders. "Not exactly! Why, I'm not even sure I know what you're interest is in the girl."

"I've been asked to help her. That's all you need to know."

"Albert," Martin continued, unsure if he should try to persuade his employer or not, but charged forward. "She needs your help."

"Explain."

"It's a difficult life," he went on. "You know that. She really doesn't want to be down there. She thinks it's just a job, but only a few days ago she was beaten by one of them. If something isn't done she'll be killed by one someday."

Albert leaned forward, concern covering his face. It surprised Martin that Albert was upset. "How badly is she hurt?"

"She'll be fine, but then she'll be right back on the street."

"Then, if you love her so much, take her away from that life."

"Albert, I've begged her to stop, but she knows I can't give her a better life. She makes more in a month than I do in a year! Only someone like you can make a difference."

Albert crushed out the cigarette and quickly lit another. "That's what someone else told me."

"Who?"

"Her mother."

"I have to ask!" Martin shouted. "What is Greta to you?"

Albert inhaled deeply. "She's my daughter."

In the back of Martin's mind there had existed that idea, but he dismissed it every time it came forward in his thoughts. If a man like Albert had a daughter like that, he had assumed, he wouldn't have let her rot in the sewer. He had too much respect for Albert to think that low of him.

Albert could see a disgusted look on Martin's face. "Don't blame me for where she is today. I only knew what she grew up to be a day before I sent you to find her."

"Don't give me that, Albert. How could you ignore her?"

"How? It became easier and easier as time went by. We've all lived many different lives within our one lifetime. We've all had friends we've abandoned over time, and lovers, and relationships. We've all changed over the years and the old lives we once led have faded into the background like they were dreams."

"But not a daughter," Martin angrily told him.

Albert sighed. "I was nineteen when Greta was born. I was twenty-two when her mother died in a fire. I saved the child at the pleadings of my wife, but couldn't get back in to save her.

"I was too young, too unsure of myself to raise the child alone and gave her up to my sister-in-law and her husband. Then, with the war, I began a second life and the thoughts of her came back to me only for fleeting moments. By the time the war was ended there was no place in her life for me."

"How could you know that?" Martin burst in. "She was still a child."

Albert continued. "Near the end of the war I went and asked her mother, at least the only mother she had known, to give her back to me.

109

The woman refused and begged that I not press the issue. I agreed. I had another to love and a new life to build, you see."

"And Frau Freyberg agreed?" Martin questioned.

Albert shook his head. "That wasn't the woman I loved then. She, too, was part on another life that has faded into my dreams. Mina knows nothing of Greta."

"And since then, since the war, you've never thought about Greta until now?"

"Thought about her?" Albert questioned back. "Yes, I've thought about her, but I began a third life with Min, and the children and the bank. I had a happiness I never dreamt I could have and I assumed she had her own happiness as well.

"Then, her mother came to me and pleaded that I help her. That was when I first learned of her....profession. That's when I learned what my eldest child had become. Put yourself in my place, Martin! How would you feel to learn that a child you had loved as a baby was roaming the streets as a whore?"

Martin's eyes drifted down to the floor, unable to answer the question.

"That's why I sent you to find her and learn about her. Her mother said she's a good child. I sent you to find out if she's right. I sent you to see if she could become Albert Freyberg's daughter again."

"I understand."

"And what do you think? Should I deny her or accept her?"

"Accept her." Martin answered. "I don't know how she'll feel about you, but I'll do anything I can to make her accept you also."

Albert rose from his seat and walked around to Martin, placing his hand on Martin's shoulder. "Good. I may need you're help. I don't know how she'll feel about me."

"I can guess."

"She'll probably hate me." Albert added. "She'll resent that it took us this long to help her."

"No, Sir. I don't think so. She'll probably be happy. She's looking for something, I think. Maybe she always knew someone like you was out there."

"Well," Albert shrugged. "Only time will tell and the time is not yet right. Prepare her for me, Martin. Keep her away from danger until I can prepare my family for her. In a short time we'll tell her the truth."

Martin was puzzled. "Why wait? Why not now?!"

"It's going to hurt." Albert explained. "I'll hurt her and it'll hurt my wife when the truth is learned. I don't think she'll be able to deal with Mina's wrath unless I have cleared the path first."

"And what am I to do in the meantime?"

"Love her," Albert answered. "Think of her and protect her."

* * * *

They were already acting like they owned the place. They, the Nazis, Joseph Strauss thought, were too confident in the way they paraded around the police barracks. Yes, he had to admit, they did wield a lot of political power these days, but they still didn't control the government. They still didn't control him.

Joseph disliked them more and more as time passed, he admitted to himself and regretted it as often as he thought about it. These power hungry bureaucrats would someday be his employers, he assumed, but they could at least be nice to him while he was going about the business of doing his job.

"Well, Strauss!" the Gauleiter of Bremen shouted at him from the doorway to his office. He was repeating himself and this time Strauss couldn't ignore it. "Have you found anything out yet?"

"No, Sir." Joseph mumbled.

The Gauleiter swaggered over to Joseph's desk and hoisted one boot onto the corner of it. "I thought the commandant said you were a competent investigator."

Joseph suddenly wished he had an axe to chop off the foot that had interrupted his work. Then, he laughed to himself; the leg would match the empty eye and the empty sleeve.

"I would have expected you to have found something on Freyberg by now." the Nazi went on.

"It's difficult to uncover incriminating evidence on ordinary citizens." Joseph sarcastically explained.

"No matter," The Gauleiter said as he sat himself down in the chair next to the desk. He then began to remove his glove with his teeth. "If all goes well in Berlin we can dispense with the legalities and just throw the Jews in jail."

"You'll still have to act within the law."

111

The Gauleiter trained his one eye on Joseph. "We'll be the law, Strauss. We'll make the law. All Jews are criminals, especially Jewish bankers."

Joseph picked up the papers he had collected on Albert Freyberg and waved them at the Nazi. "You're wrong, you know. Freyberg is no Jew. And to blame all the sins of the past on the Jews is crazy anyway."

The Gauleiter laughed. "Don't you think I know that, Detective? I'm not a fool. The Jews are just tools to us, a force which we can use to direct the anger of the people. I personally don't hate Jews, but they do represent a foreign element in German society and they do have a subculture that works against the German people."

"I've no opinion for or against Jews, Gauleiter," Strauss went on. "Here they are a very small minority. I just feel you're picking on the Adler bank for a different reason. It's as if you have a personal vendetta against it. Freyberg's not your enemy, he's a good man. A Hauptmann in the war; several times wounded. He should be praised by you people."

"Sometimes the edicts from our party make no sense to us, even to me." the Gauleiter continued. "I hear what you're saying, but the aims of National Socialism and the aims of Jewish Zionism collide. It's as simple as us against them. The Adler bank is a Jewish bank. We are pledged to eradicate Jewish influence in Germany. Therefore, we are against them. War hero or no war hero."

Strauss shrugged. He didn't believe it. The intended victims this time were not criminals and Joseph couldn't bring himself to cooperate.

"So." the Gauleiter smiled. "Tell me what you have so far."

"Nothing."

"What do you mean 'nothing'?"

"I mean exactly what I said, Herr Gauleiter. The Freybergs have done nothing against the law."

The Gauleiter suddenly grew angry, pounding his fist onto the desk. "That's impossible! People that powerful have to have done something underhanded! Albert's hands can't be clean!"

"You sound as if you know the man."

The Gauleiter looked coldly at Joseph, as if a secret has been revealed. "Yes. Yes," he finally admitted. "I knew Freyberg a long time ago. You might say that I have a bit of a personal stake in this, Detective Strauss, but that doesn't alter the facts."

"Then it is a personal vendetta, as I said before."

"Yes, in a way, but your part in it doesn't change." the Gauleiter sneered at Joseph. "The fact that the Freybergs and I have crossed paths before isn't pertinent. The fact that they must be eliminated...and humiliated is! You're job remains to find me those facts to discredit them."

"I understand."

The Gauleiter rose and marched toward the door. He stopped at the entrance and turned to face Joseph once more. "It's for the good of Germany, Detective! Remember that!"

"Yes, Gauleiter Reinhart."

The Nazi pointed his finger sharply at Joseph. "You'd better come up with something soon, Strauss. You're time is running out."

If Wilhelm Reinhart, the Gauleiter of Bremen, only knew what Joseph thought he had, he would have been quite pleased. Joseph watched the man as he, at last, left the office and wondered exactly what made him hate Albert and Mina Freyberg so much. Joseph wondered how he would have felt had the detective revealed the theory that was forming in his mind.

It all stemmed back some 14 years, to the last day of the war. It seemed that Albert Freyberg, then of the Imperial German Air Service, had been romantically involved with an Alsatian nurse named Francoise Romberge. The nurse had a friendship with a young banker's daughter named Mina Adler. The two women seemed to be sharing a flat during that November, according to the records that Joseph had gotten.

Joseph also had to assume that something went wrong in the flat on the morning of November 11, 1918, the day the Great War ended. On that day Francoise Romberge was shot to death there.

All he had to figure out was who committed the murder; Albert Freyberg, or his wife.

FIFTEEN

For the first time in two weeks the sun shined over Bremen. The weather had truly been miserable since the first snowfall of the season had fallen on the city. It had been cold, windy and bleak, adding to the despair that covered Bremen as November melted into December.

The government crisis hadn't helped matters much either, Martin thought as he walked up the sunlit street, almost glowing from the glaring sun that sparkled up the old town. For two weeks, as the snow and rain fell over Bremen and the dark dreary nights shrouded the streets, the ministers in Berlin had haggled over who was going to form the new government. For those two weeks the newspapers all over Germany had heralded the latest speculation as to exactly who would to win out. It was only today, December 3rd, that the people learned the outcome. Papen was out, Von Schleicher, a soldier, was in. Not the Nazis, as everyone had assumed, but the conservative military would be called upon by President Hindenburg to save the land.

Martin wished he could gather the energy to really care, but he had too many other things on his mind. No, he thought again, he had only one thing on his mind. Greta!

She was feeling better, he knew as he glanced at her as they walked along through the wintry cold. Normally that should bring happiness to any man's heart, but it didn't to Martin. She had recovered quickly from the beating at the hands of the young Nazi and looked like a beautiful young girl again, but that also meant that she was destined to return to the riverfront. He didn't want her to go, but he realized he couldn't stop her if her mind was made up.

She'd already told him to mind his own business more than once, insisting that as soon as she was able, she was going back to the beer halls. If only he could think of a way to stop her short of tying her up.

Not today, though, he thought as he looked at her serene face, glowing pink as she walked against the breeze. Her eyes were sparkling and her smile brightened up even this shining day, but she had said that she would take one more day off. Only one more day! Then Martin would have to start worrying for her again, praying that another viscous patron wouldn't wreck her beauty beyond repair this time.

Damn you, Greta! Why can't you love me like I love you?

"So," her voice chirped as they reached the cathedral square. "What do you want to do, Bock?"

He pointed off towards the distance. "They're starting the Christmas sales in the shops. Maybe we'll window shop. Maybe we'll buy something."

"Maybe we'll eat first." she said as she walked ahead of him, beckoning for him to catch up.

The red scarf she wore flapped in the wind as she walked on, looking like a rich young lady out for a day with her man. No one looking at her today would ever guess what she was. She looked so pretty, even when dressed plainly, Martin thought. She looked more appealing to him like this than when she was decorated up to attract her customers. She looked like he always wished she would look.

"Come on, Bock!" she called back to him.

He ran to catch up and they locked arms as they continued across the square. The park was filled with people enjoying the refreshingly clear day, but most didn't notice Martin and Greta, or if they did they'd have assumed them young lovers. Oh, how he wished it were true! They, the people on the square, were too engrossed in their newspapers to notice the couple anyway.

As Greta and Martin neared the other side of the park the sound of music struck Martin's ear. In the icy silence of the day it rang out clearly, growing louder with each beat. It was military music.

His ears picked up another sound. It was growing louder as well, as if he was in the middle of a theater and two different symphonies were being played by two orchestras. In his left ear were the growing tones of the martial band, while in his right there was the sound of singing, and they were converging on them quickly.

The people in the square began to scurry. They picked up their newspapers and walked quickly out of the square. Some began to run.

"Let's get out of here!" Martin said as he grabbed Greta's arm.

"No." she said as she tugged back. "Wait."

The first group could be seen now. Storm troopers! Nazis! Their standards bobbed up and down as they entered the square, a sea of brown shirts and swastika armbands. In the middle of the crowd of storm troopers was a flatbed truck crammed full of men. The music blasted from a loudspeaker on the roof of the cab.

The second group came into view. Bolsheviks! Communists! They were dressed in grey and black workers suits with little round caps on their heads. They were lead by several men carrying long, flowing red banners and their voices, raised in revolutionary songs, tried to drown out the Nazi music.

Bock jerked Greta's arm again. "Come on! Let's go!"

Greta was searching the crowd of Bolsheviks, her eyes looking at the faces of the workers as if she expected to see a familiar face. She was biting on her lip as she searched, as if she dreaded to find that familiar face.

The Communists where the first to reach the statue of Martin Luther, that stood tall in the center of the square. Several of them climbed the statue and draped their banners around its giant shoulders. One had even climbed up to the head.

Martin was growing scared. The Communists were rallying around the statue, far from where they stood, but the Nazis still approached from the other side. The couple stood right in the line of fire.

The singing suddenly stopped! The loudspeaker finally stopped!

"There! There!" A Bolshevik speaker shouted towards the Nazi column. "There is you're enemy."

Martin grabbed Greta's arm and ran, pulling the girl along with him.

He saw the first rock fly by his ear! He heard the shouts of both groups rise like an earthquake in the silent air. He could only think of running away, but with each step Greta struggled to get free, struggled to keep him from safety.

Martin couldn't run fast enough! Soon they both were surrounded by shouting, angry men, fighting all around them. He let go of her arm and kept running.

A brown shirt blocked his path!

Martin saw the club the storm trooper carried only a moment before it whizzed past his head. He dodged a second blow and pushed the man aside. He kept running.

He heard a scream! Greta!

Despite the fear that swelled within him, Martin turned and searched for her in the crowd. He saw her fleeting image in the mass of men and started toward her.

The same brown shirt blocked his path again.

This time Martin grabbed the club as the man raised it toward him. He pulled it out of the Nazis hands. "Fuck you, bastard!" he shouted as he swung the weapon at the disarmed Nazi. He hit him in the back of the head and watched him wobble away clutching his wounded skull.

The sounds of police whistles and sirens began to grow in the distance.

He couldn't see Greta anymore. The crowd of battling men in front of him obscured the view of where he had left her. He dropped the club and struggled on, dodging pairs of fighting radicals as he walked.

He heard her scream again.

"Greta!" he shouted.

"Get away, you son-of-a-bitch." he heard her voice, but still couldn't see her.

She screamed again.

Martin climbed over the bodies of several brawlers and finally saw her. The girl was standing over the crumpled body of a Bolshevik, pushing with all her might against a large brown shirt who was trying to club the fallen man.

"Help!" she cried. "Bock! Help!"

The storm trooper shoved Greta out of his way and she staggered back, finally stumbling to the ground.

He took aim with his club on the fallen Communist.

"No!" Greta screamed as she quickly got back on her feet. She jumped at the Nazi and butted him with her head, upsetting his balance and making him stumble, with Greta in tow, to the ground.

The club, loosened from the man's grip, rolled away.

The storm trooper was mad, Martin saw as he grew closer to the scene. He was struggling to his feet with a pained expression and a firm grip on Greta's arm. He looked strong enough and angry enough to break it off. Martin could see the pain in her face as the Nazi twisted her arm.

Martin saw the club and felt himself picking it up. He saw the man's face and watched his eyes turn toward him. Martin felt himself swing the club and watched it smash into the brown shirt's face. He watch the man's head jerk back. He saw tiny beads of blood splash through the air.

"Bastard," Martin heard Greta say above the drone of sirens as the police began to join the fray.

"You're crazy!" he shouted at Greta as he watched her help the Bolshevik she had protected to his feet.

"Help me get him out of here!" she cried.

117

Together they helped the man up and waded through the crowd quickly. By some miracle they reached safety without either the Nazis or the police confronting them. Only when they finally reached the shadowy comforts of an alley did Martin feel he could relax.

"What are you trying to do?" he said at her. "You trying to get us both killed."

She didn't answer as she looked at her Communist. He had collapsed on the ground and she struggled to lean him against the wall. His face was covered with blood and dirt.

"Here." Martin said as he handed her his handkerchief.

Greta began to wipe away the mess that covered the man's face and Martin gazed at the Bolshevik. "Jesus Christ!" he moaned as he recognized the man. "It's Crazy Max!"

Greta looked coldly up at Martin. "He's my father."

* * * *

Martin and Greta took the battered old man to a small house across from a park down by the riverfront. It was a neighborhood familiar to Martin, not far from where he had grown up himself. This working class neighborhood was on the east bank of the Weser, he was from the more rowdy, shoddier west bank. To the people in his old haunts this crowded, poor section was the good side of town.

They had taken the injured man to this house, the house of Greta's youth, but both the man and his daughter seemed out of place. Greta was too good for the place. Crazy Max, Greta's so-called father, was not good enough. He had mumbled continually to her as they struggled to get him home. He had thanked her and cursed her in the same breath, but he was too tired and weak to fight her.

"Mama!" Greta shouted as she pounded the door to the modest little row home.

A tired woman answered the door and silently let Greta and Martin carry the old man into the house.

"What happened now?" she dryly questioned as she watched them deposit Max on the sofa. She stared blankly at Martin as her sad eyes met his. She was a thin, graying figure of a woman, who looked cold and unmoved by scene before her eyes. Her husband was as bloodstained wreck, yet she seemed unconcerned.

118

"I'm Martin Bock," he said to her. "A friend of Greta's"

"I don't really care who you are," she replied.

"Mama, please!" Greta shouted at her. The two looked coldly at each other. Martin could sense the tension.

"Fine," the woman relented. "I'll act civil. Now, what happened?"

Greta spoke as she continued to tend to her father. "The Nazis and the Communists staged a rally at the same time down in the square. This time they almost killed him."

The woman shrugged as she handed Greta a towel. "So, they'll get another chance. He'll always give them another chance."

"It was the worst riot yet," Greta said as she stood and removed her coat.

The mother noticed a fading bruise on her daughter's arm and reached out, grasping Greta by the arm and pulling her closer. "Looks like you were in the middle of it, too."

Greta pulled her arm away. "That's not from today. It was another time. I had a little trouble with one of my marks."

"She was beaten badly by him," Martin added.

"Shut up, Bock!"

Greta's mother turned away disgusted. "I keep warning you, as well. I don't know which is the bigger fool, you or your father."

"Dammit, Mama!" Greta snarled at the woman. "I take my chances, but it's better than what you have. He's the one who's looking for trouble!"

"That's no way to talk to your mother." Martin said.

"I told you to shut up!" Greta now snarled at him.

Greta's mother pulled the towel from Greta's hand. "You wanted me to act decent. You do the same." she bent down and looked at her husband. "Well," she sighed. "At least you look no worse for wear. I'm getting used to seeing you with bruises."

"Ah," Max softly moaned. "It's nothing."

"Nothing!" the woman laughed. "The next time they'll roll you through the door in a wheelbarrow."

Max pushed the woman away and struggled to his feet. "I'm going to get washed up and take a nap. I've got a party meeting tonight."

She watched him as he slowly climbed the stairs to the bedrooms. Martin sensed that the woman had a fondness for the old Bolshevik, though she tried to hide it.

"The party," Greta mumbled. "Damn, fucking party going to get him killed."

119

"It's what he believes in," her mother said.

"They don't give a shit about him, his precious party!"

Greta's mother changed the subject. "I think they're may be violence tonight, Greta. Your brother is delivering groceries for Herr Mueller. Can you go fetch him home?"

"Alright," Greta agreed and turned to Martin. "Now, don't you run away on me? You wait here."

Greta quickly left the house. It was a shabby house, Martin thought as he looked at the worn furniture and faded wallpaper, but not unlike the rest of the houses he remembered from the riverfront. It was clean, he realized, and smelled of cooking and washing. He reasoned that, despite her poverty, Frau Greyer wanted this place to be a fit home for her family.

"Quite a spectacle, aren't we, Herr Bock," the woman said to Martin when Greta had gone. "My husband is a madman. My daughter is a whore. And you're probably wondering what I am." The woman sat down on the sofa looking totally exhausted.

"No, I think you want the best for them."

"I always have," Frau Greyer smiled. "Things didn't work out as I had dreamed."

"I wish Greta weren't what she is as much as you do, Frau Greyer." He said as he sat himself into the torn chair across from the couch. He could hear the springs give way against his weight.

"Can you give her what she wants?"

Bock shook his head. "I don't know, but I'll try."

She looked strangely at Martin. "I sense you're in love with my daughter, Herr Bock. You're not from the riverfront. How do you know her?"

"First of all," he explained. "I am from the riverfront, but worked my way up to better things. And I do love her, Frau Greyer, more than you could guess."

"And how do you know her?"

"I was ordered to find her."

"By whom?"

"By a man who also claims her as a daughter."

"You work for Albert Freyberg," Paula Greyer asked, her voice gaining strength.

Martin nodded.

"Good," she sighed. "But then maybe, your interest in Greta is not one of love, but of duty."

"No, Frau Greyer, I do love her. I love her so much I was afraid to tell Albert the truth. Now, I need the truth from you. Is she really his child?"

"Yes, by birth. But she's mine more than his now. I raised her. In a way I hold myself responsible for what she has become." Paula Greyer sat up and turned her eyes toward the ceiling, as if she were visualizing the past. "Albert came to me and asked for her back when she was eight. I refused. My husband was caught up in the revolution in Russia and I was alone. I needed her then to give me a reason to go on.

"Even as the years past and she grew older and Albert grew rich and important I clung onto her. My husband had returned, giving me a son, and had turned into a devoted Bolshevik and I needed Greta more than ever. I drove her away and into the streets. Maybe we both, Max and I drove her away."

"You could have gone to Albert earlier," Martin interrupted. "Why didn't you?"

"I finally saw that she wasn't going to change. I had to do something to make her change. Maybe realizing that she had a father who cared would help. He could offer her things I can't. I don't know. I still don't know if it's right." Paula closed her eyes, deep in thought.

"When do you intend to tell her?"

"When does he intend to tell her?" Paula asked back.

"I don't know, but it better be soon."

She looked deeply into Martin's eyes. "Why don't you tell her?"

He shrugged. "I don't think she'd believe me."

She smiled at him. "If you love her, if she loves you, then the right moment will come for the truth to be accepted."

121

SIXTEEN

Steven Langley enjoyed being in Albert's house. He enjoyed being with Albert's family. On an extended visit to Europe Steve seldom felt the comforts of home, the sounds of children, and the smell of home-cooking. He was happy and excited when Albert invited him to dinner at the big, old house in the woods outside Bremen. He was beginning to feel like it was his home as well.

In the six weeks since he had met Albert Freyberg the two men had become good friends. They thought alike and had a great many things in common. In some ways their lives were similar, such as the war experiences and the banking business. In some ways the realities they faced each day were the same as well, such as children and a good wife. Mina was very much like Steven's wife; short, slim and younger than he. She faintly resembled Barbara Langley except for the blackness of Min's hair and the coolness in her eyes. Albert's three children reminded him of his own two kids, Steven liked to think. Willi acted just like his own son Jack, and either of the twin girls could be his daughter Joan.

Steve also thanked God that he didn't face the future of hard decisions that Albert faced. He wouldn't welcome the task of having to make the decisions that Albert was now facing. He often wondered, if he were in Albert's shoes, what he himself would do.

Even before dinner began Steven felt at home in the company of the Freybergs. As they talked and enjoyed their before dinner drink Steve relaxed listening to the conversation, sipping wine as if he were in his own home.

"I had wanted Albert to invite some others to join us. Make it a real dinner party." Min cheerfully explained.

Albert smiled as he hugged his wife. "I convinced her that you'd be happier with just the family."

She smiled up at him. "You could have asked only those that were like family. Bock, for instance."

122

Albert shook his head. "Bock thinks he's in love. He's spending his time with his new sweetheart."

"Isn't he your assistant at the office?" Steve asked.

"Yes. And he's quite a remarkable young man. He's loyal, trustworthy and a hard worker."

"Or you could have invited Lucy." Min quickly went on. "I really like her."

Albert looked sourly into his glass. "She's got herself involved with a man as well. Only this one's old enough to be her father. I am seeing trouble there."

"I think it's nice." Min interjected. "Is it anybody we know?"

"Karl Scheuler."

Min seemed to choke on her wine. "Commandant Scheuler!"

Steve had heard Albert speak of him, this Scheuler. He was Albert's commandant in the war and now the man was in trouble with the government. He was angry that Lucy, his secretary, had become involved with him. Even today, Steve knew, the man was hiding out in the secretary's apartment, recovering from an attempt on his life. Albert seldom had showed emotion in front of Steven in the short time they had known each other, but when he had talked about Scheuler there was fear in his voice.

"Enough of that," Albert firmly stated. "Let's have dinner."

It was Christmas dinner this time that the Freyberg's had ask Steve to join them in. Steven had expressed his unhappiness to Albert about not being able to wrap up his business in Europe early enough to get back to the States for the holidays and Albert had quickly extended the invitation for him to join them. Yet Christmas in the Freyberg house wasn't really Christmas.

"We don't really celebrate the holiday." Albert explained over the dinner table sometime later. "To us, it has always been a religious holiday and we long ago decided we had no religion. Contrary to what you may hear in the banking circles around the country, we are not Jews. We are not Christians, either. We have assimilated into German Society. Neither of us being fully Jewish or Christian, have chosen not to burden ourselves or our children with religion. In time, they will make up their own minds."

Steven finished swallowing a morsel of the fine steak they had fed him and asked. "Don't you feel the children should have some background?"

123

"What for?" Mina answered with a question. "What good is religion anyway? I used to pray for things when I was younger and still had faith. None of my prayers were ever answered. And look at the trouble that even a hint of religion is causing us now."

Albert smiled. "We believe that you decide your own fate, Steven. No entity decides it for you. That you must be responsible and make your own decisions, good or bad, that's what we teach the children. That and not to blame anyone or anything for your mistakes."

The Freyberg children listened carefully as their father spoke, or so it seemed to Steven. Whether the younger ones cared or Willi, an apparently strong willed thirteen year old, believed it was unimportant. Albert's children seldom spoke unless spoken to, except to each other. Steven had heard them alone and heard the same childish arguing that his own children tend to do. Willi, it seemed, wanted nothing to do with his sisters and the girls, particularly Marta, the more devilish of the twins, loved to get him upset.

"If your detractors could hear you talk and see your family, they'd quickly change their tune." Steve added in admiration.

Mina shook her head. "It makes no difference to them. I could parade my family all over the city and paint the streets with my words and it would make no difference."

Albert looked coldly at his wife. "I asked you not to talk about it in front of the children."

Strangely, the son broke into the conversation. "You know, Papa, we're part of it too. We get the same insults and such from children at school. A lot of my old friends won't even talk to me anymore."

Albert didn't answer the boy, continuing to gaze angrily at his wife.

"Do things like this go on in your country, Herr Langley?"

Steven knew that Albert would like the conversation dropped, but he felt the boy deserved an answer. "We have our prejudices, too, Willi. There's hate everywhere."

"Do you have Jews in America?" Marta burst in.

"Of course we do."

"We won't have them here much longer," the dark haired girl said. "They're going to kick us all out."

"We're not Jews." Willi told his sister.

"My friends say I'm a Jew." Marta squealed. "A dirty, stinking, filthy Jew!"

Anna, the quieter twin, kicked her sister under the table. "I don't like it when you say that."

Albert's deep voice responded around the room. "That's enough! Sit still, eat and don't talk!" he turned his angry face back to Min. "See what you started!"

"Well, Willi's right." Min retorted. "They are a part of this. They're lives are affected as well. They hear the same words we do, and from children, and you know how cruel children can be."

"They're only mimicking they're parents." Steven interjected.

"Who are bigger fools?" Albert then asked. "These gullible parents mindlessly pass on such vile thoughts to their children or the parents who allow their children to be the objects of the attack?" He again stared coldly at Min.

She looked back, anger growing on her face. "I'm not going to run away. I'm not going to teach my children to run away. We'll stand up to it. Face it and..."

Albert cut into her words. "And what? Maybe it'll go away? Min, you know better than that!"

She waved her hands in front of her. "Enough talk. This is supposed to be a happy occasion. I don't want to talk about it anymore."

"Well, I do!" Albert insisted. "If we ran away every time someone called us a name we'd be running forever."

"We could go to America." Albert said. "Ask Steven, he'll tell you nothing like this could happen there."

"But he just said that prejudice is there, too, Papa." Willi burst in.

"Now, wait." Steve joined in. "I said prejudice, yes! But not like it is here. In America we have freedom of religion written into our constitution."

Albert laughed. "So is it written in the Weimar constitution, until someone stronger comes along to change it. Our constitution is better than yours, Steven, it's so liberal minded it permits madmen like the Nazis to exist."

"Heil Hitler." Marta giggled.

"That's it!" Mina shouted. "No one speaks until we are finished dinner." Albert began to open his mouth. "Not even the adults!" she glared at him.

The cheery Christmas meal turned solemn after that. Every once in a while the twins began to whisper to each other, but the words were cut off by a cold stare from their mother. Neither Albert nor Steven dared to speak either. Everyone finished quickly and the children excused themselves from the table.

125

Once the adults were alone Albert broke the silence. "I'm sorry about the way the dinner turned out, Steven." He apologized as he lit a cigarette. "As you can see, the children aren't the angels we sometimes want them to be. It's a shame your holiday meal was spoiled."

"Actually, I kind of enjoyed it." Steven admitted. "Just being with a family like yours, reminding me of my own family, makes me feel better."

"Even with one that argues so much?" Min questioned as she sipped the last of her wine.

"You all have good reason to worry, Mina." Steve said. "It must be difficult to bear the brunt of the abuse. I mean, on all of you."

"Tell me, Steven." Albert asked as he exhaled smoke throughout the room. "As a man of the world how do you view our country today?"

Steven had to think a moment before he answered. "Things are bad here, but they are bad everywhere. This depression has hurt everybody, every country. Changes are occurring in America too. We'll have a new President in March and Roosevelt has promised us many things to end the depression. Maybe someone like that will take charge here as well."

"The process for orderly change exists in America." Albert said. "The biggest bully on the block doesn't rule the roost."

"But you, too, just re-elected your President."

"Hindenburg!" Min broke in. "He nothing but a senile old man. I couldn't believe the country returned a relic like him to office."

"It was him or Hitler." Albert explained.

Min looked curiously at the ceiling. "Oh, yes! I forgot. But that was no choice! If Hitler's people didn't curse me and condemn me I'd prefer him to the monarchists."

"There is the major difference between your country and mine. Steven." Albert went on. "Here they offered us a radical or the same old thing. At least in America a responsible man stepped forward to lead."

"Personally, I don't like Roosevelt. I think the things be proposes are too radical for me." Steven said. "Despite the fact the he comes from wealth, he appeals to the poor and says he'll break down the rich. I'm rich and I work hard for my money. No one who gets a handout deserves anything from me. But they elected him so I must live with it."

"There's another difference." Albert added. "There someone is elected because they get the most votes. Here, any man can become Chancellor, where the real power is, simply by being able to win more support in the Reichstag."

"Lots of Germans regularly vote Nazi."

"But not enough to elect Hitler as president."

"But enough to cripple the government. No one seems able to control the country." Steve insisted.

"So," it was Min's turn. "What's the answer?"

Albert responded. "The answer is for someone to come along and silence his opposition. If no one speaks out and no one opposes you, you can do anything you want."

"That hasn't happened thus far." Min asked. "What makes you think Von Schleicher can do that?"

"I never said he could." Albert grinned, and then turned more serious. "Mark my word; Von Schleiher's government will fall and Hitler will get his chance. Then he'll silence the Communists, the Monarchists, everyone. He'll do it quickly and the people will cheer."

"And what will you do if that happens?" Steve asked.

"I'll cross that bridge when I get to it." Albert smiled.

Steven looked sincerely at his host and hostess. "I like to think I'm your friend. When that day comes, anything I can do, you just ask."

SEVENTEEN

It had begun as an ordinary Monday for Martin Bock. It seemed like so many other Mondays, but by noon he had known it was going to be different. By noon, Monday, January 30, 1933, the rumors were flying all over town. President Hindenburg had asked Adolf Hitler to form a new government. The Nazis chance had come.

At first, Martin was a little skeptical of the rumor, as were most of the people in the bank office. How could the old man do it? What was really going on in Berlin? The questions kept coming up and no answers were forthcoming from the radio that played loudly throughout the day. Albert had turned up the sound so everyone in the office could hear it, but the music played and no one confirmed the rumor.

"I don't believe it." old Bertha would bellow each time someone drifted in off the street with another new rumor. "They couldn't let those hoodlums run the country."

Lucy, closet to the radio, stared at it constantly. Her face seemed to perk up each time a voice interrupted the music, only to return to the empty stare when the voice shed no new light of what was happening.

Martin finally walked over to her and tried to get her mind off it. "You've always said that it didn't matter who was in power in Berlin." he began. "Why do you care so much now?"

Her blue eyes stared back at him for a long time before she answered. "I'm scared." she finally admitted.

"Of what?"

"I don't know. I'm just scared."

Albert sat in his office all morning trying to work. He kept his office door open, however, which was unusual, and Martin knew he was listening for word as well. Martin finally summoned up the courage to go in.

"It's all that von Schroder's fault." Albert angrily announced when Martin asked his mentor about the situation. "That bastard covered the Nazis debts. They were almost totally bankrupt."

128

Von Schroder, a Rhineland banker, had just recently swung his weight in favor of the Nazis and paid off all the money that the party owed. It was rumored that Schroder and Papen had signed a pact with Hitler that promised that Hitler would be the next Chancellor. It was the straw that broke the back of the von Schleicher government.

"So, what are we going to do now?" Martin asked with a shrug of his shoulders.

Albert lit a cigarette. "I only wish I knew. Maybe the conservatives can control him like they say. Maybe they can't. I don't know."

Just after noon the music playing on the radio suddenly stopped in the middle of the song. The room grew suddenly silent. It was Berlin.

"A special announcement." the announcer started. Lucy reached over and turned the volume up higher on the radio. "From the Reichstag and the offices of President von Hindenburg comes the word that Adolf Hitler, leader of the National Socialist party, has been asked to form a new government. Details of the cabinet appointments are to follow."

From the crowded street, even through the closed windows on this winter day, you could hear the cheers of the Nazis as they heard the news. Yet the voices in the bank remained silent. Martin guessed what was going through everyone's mind. The Adler bank had been repeatedly condemned by the Nazis. What would happen now? Were their jobs safe? Were their lives safe?

Singing could now be heard from the street, but no one talked and no one worked inside the office.

Albert came out of his office suddenly. "Well!" he bellowed, his resounding voice echoing throughout the room. "It isn't the end of the world! Go back to work!" Then he stormed back into his office and slammed the door.

Slowly, almost cautiously, the people went back to work, but their hearts weren't in it and their minds were preoccupied with other things.

Lucy was the first to leave. "I've got to go." she told Martin, tears forming in her eyes. "I can't work."

By two o'clock the room was empty. Nearly everyone had left and Martin stood near the door as he counted out the last five employees.

"I guess we'll have to declare this a bank holiday." Bertha said to him as she too put on her coat.

"I wonder how many of these people are actually happy about what's happened." Martin asked her.

"None of us here." she said. Bertha, a longtime employee, knew everyone in the bank it seemed. "These people know what the Freybergs

129

and the Adlers have done for them and for the worker. No one who works here believes those lies the Nazis say about them. We're not that stupid."

"Still, I wonder how many secret Nazis we have in our midst."

About five minutes later Albert emerged from his office. He didn't seem surprised by the desertion of his employees as he briskly walked up to Martin. "I don't blame them, you know." he said.

"You don't blame who?"

"It's a difficult time, Martin." he explained. "It's difficult to be different in a world that demands conformity and acceptance. These people, my people, have to live with the new regime, continue their lives as if nothing has happened. They're worried, you see, and I understand. I can't blame them for leaving."

"They'll be back tomorrow."

Albert smiled. "Some will. Some won't. The ones who don't come to work tomorrow have the real courage, Martin. It takes courage to walk away from a job when five million people are out of work."

"Maybe so, but in walking away, they side with the Nazis."

"It would appear that way to some." Albert agreed as he put on his hat. "Well, we'll see what tomorrow brings."

"Yes, tomorrow."

Albert looked deeply into Martin's eyes. "Are you seeing Greta tonight?" he asked. "If you are, keep her off the streets. The Nazis will be celebrating tonight."

Martin nodded as he watched Albert walk out of the office. Martin was awed by the man. With the world falling apart around him, Albert was treating it as if it were just another obstacle to be overcome. That took courage.

* * * *

"Listen to them." Greta said as she sat up in bed. "Won't they ever stop singing?"

It was nearly midnight and the Nazis were still at it. Since sundown they had paraded around the city. They had been fairly well controlled, Martin figured; their victory demonstrations hadn't reverted to violence yet. Not yet.

"All over Germany, there is singing in the streets." the radio announcer was saying from Berlin. "Chancellor Hitler greeted his columns of supporters, their torchlight parade still going on, from the balcony of the Chancellery."

Greta reached over to the radio and turned it off. Martin could still here the noise, though, coming from the street. Just like Berlin, the supporters of Adolf Hitler rejoiced in the streets of Bremen.

"They're all fools." Greta said. "These stupid men, marching around in uniforms as if they were still in the army and these stupid boys looking for glory."

"They aren't so stupid, Greta." Martin retorted. "They're just desperate. Most of them are no different than us. The Nazis give them hope."

She sat up higher in the bed and brought her knees up, curling her arms around them and resting her chin on the apex. She stared into the darkness. "Hope! What hope? They've made a lot a promises and nothing's really changed. They're the same empty promises the Communists make; and the Nationalists. They're only empty promises."

"Maybe they need the promises now. Maybe the Nazis promises will come true for them. Maybe some one else with better promises will come along."

"How can you defend them?" she glared at him.

"I'm not defending them."

"Yes, you are."

Martin thought about what he'd said. "Well, I really didn't mean to defend them. I'd like to see this country get put back together, you know. Like the old days. You do remember the old days, don't you?"

She ignored him. "They're brutal people. They're full of hate."

"So are the Bolsheviks."

He could see the look of fear on Greta's face. She was worried for her parents.

He moved closer to her and touched her soft shoulders. She cringed a little and drew away. The sad, childlike pout on her face didn't fade.

"Don't touch me. Not now. Not with all that noise going on outside." she said, brushing his hand away.

"Don't worry," he reassured her. "Your father will be alright. The Nazis don't have total control. It's still a democracy."

He could sense her holding back the tears. "Yes, but for how much longer?"

131

* * * *

Karl Scheuler had listened to the crowds in the streets as well that night and it troubled him. It was what the people wanted, he knew, but did they really know what they were getting themselves in for? So many ordinary people looked upon the Nazis for their salvation now, he felt. Could the madness in the Nazi leadership be controlled? Could the more rational people in Berlin still have the influence to stop them? Were there any sane people left in the government?

Was he wrong? Was he over-reacting to the whole thing? Were his fears justified? He had thought about it over and over again that night and couldn't convince his mind either way. He was a little mad, he knew, but he also knew he was right. A Germany in the hands of radicals was like a time-bomb ready to go off. Only those papers, those incriminating, precious papers, had a chance to defuse it.

Why couldn't Albert see the light? Why couldn't he run away before Hitler came to power? Now may be too late!

And what had he done to prevent it? Karl realized he hadn't done enough and was now hunted and stranded. And worst of all he had dragged Lucy with him.

"I will leave tomorrow." he said to her as they watched the last of the parading Storm Troopers march by.

"Why?" she asked back with surprise. "Where will you go?"

"I've hurt you enough." Karl explained as he touched her face with his hand. She was so soft, so gentle, he thought. How could he ruin her life?

"We're in this together." she replied as her took his hand and held it. "If I didn't love you I would have never let you stay this long. You love me too, I know, or else you'd long ago left secretly and spared me the tearful good-byes"

He smiled at her. "I can't put you in danger any longer. The Nazis! They're going to come after me more vengefully than anyone."

"Nothing's changed, Karl. Outside Berlin, they haven't any power. The ones that chased you, shot you, are the same people. You escaped them before. We'll escape them again."

"I fear for my life, Lucy." he pleaded. "I fear for yours. If I leave now, no one can point to you."

Her eyes smiled at him. "I don't care, Karl. You're all that matters."

He looked away. He had nothing left to say. Because he loved her he knew he should leave. Because he loved her, he couldn't.

She took his hand and coaxed him away from the window and into the bedroom.

"Make love to me," she said as he drew him into his bed. "It's been too long since we've made love."

Karl lay down beside her and kissed her. He could still hear the shouts of the Nazis in the streets.

* * * *

Joseph Strauss worked late into the night. The police headquarters was unusually quiet the whole night and that surprised him. He had expected the Nazis partying to turn into a riot and that he would be pressed into street duty to control the crowds, but the commandant had ordered his men not to interfere with the Nazi celebration no matter what happened and, surprisingly, nothing happened.

It gave Joseph time to think. It gave him time to put the final pieces of the Freyberg file together, though he dreaded the thought of using it. He realized now that the Nazis may not give him an alternative.

He wondered if the people could be right. It may all work out well in the end, he thought. It may be the best thing to happen to Germany. Yet he hated the Nazi troublemakers. He hated the violence they seemed to carry with them wherever they went in the city. He hated the philosophy of hate they professed. He even grew to hate the sound polices they presented for he saw them as lies. How could they bring the people jobs and food and money when all he ever saw them bring was violence and pain?

He had all the pieces they wanted together in regards to Albert and Mina Freyberg. He had all the pieces the Nazis needed to destroy them. He despised the file he had compiled and the way it would be used.

Strauss had the scenario all worked out. Albert was in Martin Luther hospital then, recovering from his war wounds. Both his future wife and the victim were constantly by his side. He had records that seemed to indicate that Mina Adler moved out of Romberge's flat shortly before the murder.

Strauss looked at the pictures of the murdered girl. She appeared to be in her middle twenties, an attractive girl with piercing eyes and flowing hair. In her hospital photograph she even appeared to be appealing. The pictures of her taken by the police didn't do her justice. Pictures of murder victims seldom do. She died from a small caliber wound to the head. She died instantly.

He had two theories. Albert, desiring to share the wealth of Mina Adler, left the hospital and went to the flat and killed the woman who stood in the way of his having the rich heiress. Maybe he loved her, maybe not, but she was poor and in the confusion of the revolution who'd care about one more body, particularly a French girl.

His other theory was that Mina Adler, in love with Albert, eliminated the girl as a rival for the man's love. It made little sense, but crimes of passion seldom do. He thought it less plausible that his first theory.

It was irrelevant, Joseph decided as he folded the file and returned it to his secret hiding place, a false bottomed drawer in his desk. He'd never let the Nazis use the material.

He had made his decision. He would warn Albert Freyberg of the threat. He would hold the file as long as he could and hope Albert did the right thing. He hoped Albert would flee the country.

EIGHTEEN

The mid-February day was clear and crisp. The air was fresh and the whole city glimmered in a bath of welcomed sunshine. Yet Greta knew something was wrong.

Somehow, through the silence of the sparkling middle class neighborhood that surrounded Martin's flat, she could sense the rumblings from the docks. Somehow she knew there was trouble down there.

She hoped and prayed she was wrong. Maybe her fears were getting the best of her, but she could sense it in her soul and she could smell the scent of trouble in the cold breeze. Her mind had told her that there would be trouble today and she now searched for some confirmation of that truth.

"The Reichstag was burning in Berlin!"

"The Communists were to blame!"

That was what the radio had told the people that morning and that was what the people would believe. Their anger at the deed, their hatred against the Bolsheviks would be directed to their stronghold; the riverfront!

As she made her way home to the riverfront, the streets she walked seemed quiet, maybe a little too quiet. The silence hung over the sunlit sky ominously, the only sound being the wind in her ears.

Where had all the people gone? Where were the shoppers and the housewives and the workers? Were they afraid to come out to face the day? Were they, as Greta assumed, afraid of the gangs who would take their vengeance out on the people today?

As she drew closer to her neighborhood she began to hear the shouts of men. She began to hear the sounds of breaking glass and the cries of both anger and pain. She began to smell the acrid odor of smoke.

They were burning the homes of the workers! They were burning her home!

135

Greta could see the cloud of smoke covering her street from the park. On any other day her house, the house she grew up in, the house of her parents, could easily be made out from the other end of the park, but not today.

Today her house was beyond the haze. Today the park was crowded with brown shirts. How could she get there? How could she see if her parents and brother were safe?

"Burn! Bolsheviks! Burn!" the cries of the crowds reverberated in her ears.

Greta knew she'd never make it through the park. The dense crowd of Nazis would never let her pass. She began instead to run around the park. She only knew she had to make it to her home.

"Greta!" she heard a voice call to her. The voice was that of a neighbor. "Come back. They'll kill you."

She ignored the plea and continued to run toward the house.

Out of nowhere a hand reached out and grabbed her arm. A policeman had stopped her and turned her body toward his. "Don't go there." he also pleaded. "Stay back. We'll put the fire out when they leave."

Greta could feel the smoke in her lungs and the sting of heat against her face. "It's my home!" she screamed at the policeman. "My parents are in there!"

She freed herself from the policeman's grip and continued deeper into the blackening cloud.

"No! Stop!" she heard the man call to her, but she kept on going.

At the front steps she stopped, her fears holding her back from going into the house. Greta was deeply frightened of fires. She had always remembered nightmares about fires in her sleep. To this day she had nightmares about fires. Could they have been to prepare her for this day?

She could barely see the front windows of her house through the smoke. She could hear the crisp crackling of fire coming from inside the house. She could hear the laughter and the shouts of the men across the street in the park.

"Burn!" they shouted. "Death to the enemies of the Reich!"

Greta swallowed a breath of air and climbed the steps into the burning house.

She could barely see the room through the dense smoke. She could feel herself choking, the air being sapped out of her body as her lungs filled with poison.

"Mama!" she shouted as she fell to the floor. "Papa!"

The air was clearer near the floor, but the heat continued to grow more and more oppressive. Greta felt around the floor, the stinging smoke and the searing heat blinding her eyes.

She felt the touch of flesh.

In the thickening haze she saw her mother's face.

"Mama!" Greta shouted as she crawled closer to her. She looked at her empty eyes and felt her flesh and knew she was dead.

"No!" she choked, tears streaming down her face. She shook the woman as if to wake her, but she knew all too well it was futile.

Why did you let them do this to you, Mama!? Why!?

Don't leave me alone now, Mama!? I need you!

The smoke was growing thicker, so thick that she couldn't see anything anymore. She couldn't find any air to fill her lungs and felt she was growing weaker. Maybe it was for the best, Greta thought as she felt the life going out of her body. Maybe it was better to die now, with the rest of the family.

A hand reached out for her and shook her back to life. It coaxed her away from her mother's lifeless body and pulled her toward the back of the house. It reached out and handed her a dampened cloth, pushing it against her mouth to filter out the deadly smoke.

She let the hands guide her through the darkness and she crawled to the kitchen. The air cleared a little so she could make out the owner of the hands. It was her brother.

"We can escape through the alley," Gery told her, his breaths short and rasping. His small hands felt strong and sure as they continued to pull her along.

She moved onward toward an uncertain brightness amid the smoke and then she saw another lifeless form sprawled on the floor. She stopped! The body of her father blocked her path and she could go no further.

"Greta!" Gery called after her. "Come on! Only a little further!"

She cringed away from the dead man and began to scream. "No! No! I can't go on! I can't leave them here!"

She felt the sharp slap of her brother's hand against her face. She continued to cry and moan until he hit her again.

"I'll be damned if I'm going to leave you here to die!" he whispered as he grasped her arm and pulled her over the body of her father.

A second later they were in the alley and both of them rolled off the back step down onto the frozen ground. Greta lay there a minute and then

137

felt her little brother's arms around her waist. He pulled her up to her knees and hoisted her to her feet. Greta felt dazed and confused, but the air felt fresh and good as it filled her lungs. The coolness of the outdoors felt so good after the oppressive heat inside the house.

"Come on!" Gery said as she pushed Greta away from the back of the house and down the dirty alley. She stumbled and he had to grab her, steady her and help her walk away from the burning house.

They stopped near the end of the alley and stared at each other's blackened faces.

"What will we do!?" Greta cried to him. "Where will we go?"

She could see the tears in her brother's eyes, but his voice was cold and angry. "I don't know. I just don't know!"

* * * *

Bock found them hiding in the alley. They both seemed dazed and confused, unable to tell him just how long they had been there. Their blackened faces were streaked from the trail of tears they had cried, though when he found them they had long since stopped crying and were simply sitting in the filth of the alley staring blankly off toward the smoldering remains of their home.

When Martin had heard about the rioting down by the riverfront he called his apartment. When he got no answer he realized his worst fears; she had heard about the Nazis burning the leftist's homes and had gone there. He also knew he had no choice but to follow her into the madness.

By the time Martin had reached the neighborhood most of the rioters had left. They had left behind a neighborhood of broken glass and burnt out homes. He remembered the small, brick house of Greta's youth and found it smoldering as well.

Within minutes he had found Greta, silent and drained from her ordeal, and a defiant young boy who seemed threatened by his approach.

"Who are you?" he growled at Martin as he entered the alley and walked toward the pair. "What do you want?"

He ignored him and moved closer, leaning down toward the girl.

"Stay away!" the boy had screamed as he clenched his small fists in front of him.

"I'm a friend." Martin insisted. "Her friend."

The boy sprung at Martin and began to swing his fists wildly at him. With one quick motion Martin threw the boy off him and to the ground. Greta did not move, her blank stare still looking down the alley at the brown pillar of smoke that still streamed out of the back window of her house.

The boy and Martin stared coldly at one another; each now determined to assert their rights.

"Don't you touch my sister, dammit!" the boy screamed as Bock extended his hand toward the girl's face.

"Your sister?" Bock looked at him curiously. Greta had never mentioned having a brother.

"Get back!" the boy demanded as Bock extended a hand to him now.

"Look!" Martin said. "I'm Bock, Martin Bock. I'm... in love with her."

The boy now returned the same curious gaze. Apparently there were secrets that Greta had withheld from him as well. He reached out and took Martin's hand and pulled himself off the ground.

Greta's blackened face moved toward Martin's as he leaned closer to her, but her blue eyes never seemed to see his. He touched her hands with his and felt coldness, almost a numbness come from her skin. Her lips seemed to be mouthing words, but her voice could not be heard.

"What's your name? What happened?" he asked the boy as he continued to look at his love's distressing face.

"I'm Gerhardt Greyer," the boy began. "The Nazis burnt my house, simple as that. My parents were in there. I don't know whether they killed them first or what. Greta went in the house and I had to drag her out."

"She knows they're dead then."

"Yes." his voice choked on the word, his anger giving way to his loss. He had to be no more than twelve or thirteen, Martin knew, yet he acted more mature and had courage beyond his years to follow his sister into the fire to save her.

Martin wrapped his arms around Greta and lifted her off the ground. She felt limp in his arms, but she wrapped her arms around his neck and drew her head up to his shoulders. He could now hear the words she was mumbling.

"Save them," she whispered. "Save them."

"We're you going?" Gerhardt questioned.

"We'll go to my place," Martin huffed as he gathered up the strength to carry her.

He could hear her whispering again. "I'm sorry I wasn't a good girl, Mama. I'm sorry."

* * * *

"I can't believe they really did it." Gery Greyer was saying to Martin. "They killed them. They murdered them."

Martin shrugged. "I guess they're above the law now. I guess they are the law."

"My father's words meant nothing. He couldn't hurt them." the boy sobbed. "My mother never hurt anyone."

The defiance had quickly gone out of Gery Greyer after they reached the safety of the apartment. The anger and hate had left and the boy had started the feel the pain of his loss. Martin knew he was right; nobody listened to Crazy Max Greyer and his wife was no Bolshevik, but they had been marked for extermination just as much as Mina and Albert Freyberg. Martin had begun to realize that it was only a matter of time before they would try to kill the Freybergs too. There would probably come a time when the Nazis would try to eliminate all their enemies.

Greta had come back from her trance just as soon as they had reached the flat. It began as a gentle sobbing, without tears, but soon the tears came and she broke down and cried for nearly an hour. It was good, Martin thought, they both needed to cry it out.

By that evening they both seemed to be back to reality. They had washed away the soot and had managed to eat a watery soup that Martin had prepared. Emotionally they were drained, speaking few words and showing little emotion, but at least, for them, there would be a tomorrow.

The fear was growing inside them now. Martin could see it in their faces each time they heard a car go by from the street, the growl of the engine growing, vibrating through the thin walls, and then fading away as the auto speed by. Each time they heard any sound from the street; the laughter of some passersby, the footsteps on the stairs, they cringed in fear for their lives. Could it be they were coming to kill them also, as they had killed their parents?

When the pounding on the door started both Greta and Gery seemed to draw up within themselves. The girl, curled up in the corner of the bed, began to shiver and the tears started again. Gery, afraid also, tried to summon up his courage as he stood behind a chair, his knuckles bulging as he gripped its spine.

"Who's there?" Martin called as he cautiously approached the door. He felt a little fear as well. The hand pounding against the door to his small flat was strong and firm, its weight vibrating the door with each bang.

"Freyberg."

Martin could feel the sigh of relief in his soul. It was better than he could have hoped for. What Greta needed right now was someone else who cared and, even if she didn't know who he was, she would realize that he cared.

When he first stepped into the room he didn't see her or the boy, they had seemed to fade into the background. He looked compassionately at Martin, his eyes glaring into his soul. "Are you alright?" Albert asked anxiously. "Where have you been?"

"The riverfront."

Albert shrugged. "I thought that's were you'd gone, you fool! Didn't you realize what was going on down there?"

Martin said nothing, slowly walking backwards toward the brother and sister and gradually Albert realized they were there. His face grew surprised, then sad, then concerned.

"What's happened?" he finally asked.

"They burned the Greyer house." Martin said flatly. "Max and his wife are dead."

There was a look of resignation on Albert's face. "I see. Max and Paula are dead." he softly repeated. It was as if he had to say the words to believe it. Yet the look on his face seems to hint he had expected the news.

Greta rose up from the bed, her face curious, and her eyes probing the strange man in the center of the room. "Who are you?" she asked. "How do you know my parents?"

Albert glanced over at Martin. "You haven't told her? She knows nothing about me?"

Martin nodded.

The boy moved toward his sister, his fear of Albert as great as his fear of the Nazis. As they drew near they grasped each other's hands for support.

"Who are you?" Greta repeated.

"My name is Albert Freyberg."

"I know that Bock works for you, but how do you know my parents."

Albert seemed unsure of himself, probing for the words her would say.

"He's a rich man, Greta." the boy said. "He's not from the neighborhood."

Albert stared at the boy. "You must be Paula's son. She mentioned you only once to me. I didn't realize you would be as old as you are."

"Answer the question, dammit!" Greta screamed. "Who the hell are you?!"

"I am...was Paula's brother-in-law."

Martin interrupted. "She needs the truth now."

Greta wrapped her arms around her brother as if to protect him. "What truth? What's the truth?"

Albert stared up at the ceiling. "I am your father."

Gery looked strangely at the man. "Our father is Max Greyer. He's dead. You're lying."

"What's this, some cruel joke, Bock?" Greta hollered at Martin. "You and this man are trying to drive us crazy."

"It's the truth, Greta." Martin insisted. "Listen to him."

"No!" she cried as she released the boy and turned away from them. "After what I've gone through today how can you come in here and lie to me like that."

"Greta, listen." Albert tried to explain. "I never meant for you to learn about me in this way. I believe your mother would have gotten around to it sooner or later, but now, with her gone, what choice do I have but to tell you."

She turned and her face was red with anger. "Max Greyer was my father! Not you! My mother would never be untrue to him!"

"And she wasn't." Albert agreed. "You were never her real daughter. You were her niece."

"Shut up!" she screamed, tears flowing down her face. "Shut up! I don't believe you."

Albert turned to Martin. "I shouldn't have told her. It's too hard. It's too cruel."

"It needed to be done."

Albert turned back to the girl. "I was married to Paula's sister. You are our daughter. You were born on November 7, 1910 in the backroom of our bakery. At aged three your mother died in a fire. Paula and Max raised you as their daughter."

"No!" She cried.

"Your mother came to me some months back and told me what you had become. She begged me to help you. She begged me to be...what was the term she used....yes...your knight in shining armor. I was the one who sent Martin out to find you in the whorehouses."

She stopped shutting out his words. She turned her tearful face toward Albert Something he had said had triggered a memory in the girl.

Albert stepped toward her, his arms outstretched. "Do you remember the days when you were little?" he asked. "Do you remember the smell of beard baking in the shop below your nursery? Do you remember a golden haired woman, much like you, who nursed you and sang songs to you? Do you remember the fire?"

"The fire!" she repeated. "I had nightmares about a fire." her voice was trembling as she spoke to him. "I was very little. There was smoke everywhere. I was crying and a man came and got me from my room. We were running through the flames! Oh, God! It wasn't just a nightmare! It was the truth!"

Albert reached out for the girl and drew her into his arms. As he caressed her he patted her golden hair. "There, there, Greta, my little girl. I never thought I'd hold you in my arms again."

She cried in his arms. Martin didn't know if she realized he was really her father or not, but he knew it was good that she was finally letting it out. There had always been that fear there, he knew, that fire that lurked in the back of her mind from her childhood. It was a pity, though, that it took another fire and more deaths to bring it out.

NINETEEN

Mina thought something was terribly wrong when She heard Albert's voice on the telephone. His deep voice, usually steady and quick, spoke to her slowly, deliberately. As if he was having difficulty finding the words.

"I'll be late," he had said. "I have to talk to you."

What maddening turn of events was she to face now? What bad hand had fate dealt her this time? Mina thoughts turned toward the worst, toward the hopelessness of the situation that had become an everyday occurrence in their lives. She was sure they were being thrown out of the country. The thought of it scared her to death. For Mina, life seemed a nightmare that wouldn't stop.

Before 1932 ended Albert had talked about going on a long vacation. He wanted to be out of the country, away from the pressures of protecting the family wealth. Mina had refused, believing that once he had her abroad he would convince her to sell the bank and never go home. He had talked about that then, but now, since Hitler and his people had come to power, he said it was too late. Albert was sure the Nazis wouldn't let them leave with their wealth, her money, and that they would throw them out once they had taken away everything they had.

Was this, her worst fears, coming true? Was this what had delayed him and was this what he had to tell her?

When he finally arrived he was not alone. Martin Bock was with him, but, if her premonition where true; he had expected him to be with her husband. There were two other people with him, however; a young boy about Willi's age and an attractive blond haired girl in her twenties. It wasn't to be that nightmare, Min realized, but something else she couldn't imagine. By the look on her husband's face she knew it was to be a nightmare as well.

"I'm glad you're home." she said, trying to act as if she didn't notice the strangers as she walked up to Albert and kissed him. "I was

144

beginning to worry. The radio has been filled with reports of trouble in the city."

His stern expression didn't change as he returned her kiss. "I know and I'm sorry to worry you, dear. It was something very important. I hope you understand."

She nodded and turned to Martin Bock. Albert's assistant was holding onto the young girl as if to protect her. Min could sense his feelings went beyond concern. She seemed to sense he was in love with her.

"Good evening, Frau Freyberg," he said to her. "I'd like to present Greta Greyer and her brother, Gerhardt."

She nodded to the strangers. "Welcome to my home."

Neither of them said a word, looking back at her with fear in their eyes. As they stared at Min she realized that they where riverfront people. She saw the same look of fear and desperation on many faces in the streets of Bremen.

"Martin," Albert instructed. "Go find someone from the staff to help you settle Greta and Gery into the guest rooms. Make them as comfortable as possible."

"They're staying?" Min asked, but she wasn't really surprised.

"Yes," Albert answered coldly as he took Min's arm and moved away from the others. "We must talk in private."

Albert and Min retired to his study, the room she despised more than any in her house. It was Albert's room, where he'd always go when he needed to be in control. No one but Albert could dominate in the study, Min knew. She seldom let him take her there, but this time she simply followed him into his lair.

He silently went over to the desk and unlocked it. She turned her back to him and she thought about what he was going to say. If it was only to provide shelter for Bock's riverfront lover and her brother there would be no problem. It had to be more.

"Will you join me for a drink?" he asked. She could hear the clatter of the glasses from behind her.

"Yes," she replied as she stared at his pictures. Why did he keep that picture up? It made Min angry just to look at that damned picture of the four of them; Albert with Francoise and her with Willi. Why did he have to keep a reminder of those times? It was so long ago and so many things had happened since. Why keep the reminders of what could have been?

As he handed her the drink he began to speak. "Tell me, Min, on first impressions, what do you think of the girl?" he questioned.

She took a short sip of liquor. Why, she thought, was he asking? She answered curtly, "I don't know what to think. They're both quite a surprise."

He smiled. It was a sly smile, as if he were hiding something, which she knew he was. He changed the subject. "Mina, how old were you when we met?"

"That's a silly question. You know I was nineteen."

"And I was....."

"Twenty-seven," she chimed in. "What's the point?"

"We never did talk about our lives before we met."

She took another sip from her glass. "What could I tell you? I was only a kid? If you remember, we didn't have much to talk about back then. We had nothing in common."

"But we never talked about my life back before the war."

She shrugged. "So?"

"Haven't you ever wondered about me then? Haven't you ever wondered how I grew up? What I did before 1914?"

"I assumed you told me what was important," she shrugged again, turning her eyes up toward his. "What's the point of this conversation, Albert?"

"Min, when I was nineteen I was married."

She laughed. "And I suppose you're going to tell me that that's your wife."

"No. She's my daughter."

The words stunned her. There had never been much talk about their pasts between them, but she had always felt that he held no secrets from her. She had always felt Albert was the most honest man in the world. Yet, now, he was saying that he had been married before and that the young blond was his child. How could this be?

Min felt a little dizzy and she moved to a chair to sit. Albert pulled up another chair and began to explain the whole story. It was like a dream to her, learning so many things about her husband, things she had never known before. It was like listening to a storyteller, as he went on about his life before the war down by the riverfront. As he explained on and on for what seemed an eternity, she could picture what he said as if it were a dream. No, it was a nightmare.

"So you see now, Min," he went on after telling her today's events. "After Bock and I had called the police and made the arrangements for Paula and Max, I felt I had no choice. I had to bring them here. I had to tell you."

146

"And if you hadn't," Min countered. "If you had left them at the waterfront, don't you think they'd have survived? That girl out there is no child, Albert! She's quit capable of living her own life and of raising the boy."

"But I owe it to her. I need to make it up to her."

Min swallowed the last of her drink. "Don't you think we all have enough problems without you placing another burden on our shoulders?"

"I couldn't just abandon them."

"Why not? What are they to you? What are they to me?"

"Min, please understand."

He was looking at her with those big brown eyes, but this time he wasn't going to win. "I won't accept this. Hell! What am I supposed to tell the children? What am I supposed to tell our friends?"

"I'll explain it to the children."

"The girls are ten years old! How do you expect them to understand?"

"They may welcome a big sister."

"Oh, come off it, Albert! This won't work! She's a grown woman. Let her go."

He stood up and went toward the desk. He poured himself another drink. "I've just gotten her back and I will not let her go."

Mina grew angrier by the second. He was not going to win her over to his side this time. "Go to hell, Albert!" she threw the glass toward him. "I won't have her in my house."

"She stays," he sternly looked back at her.

Min stood up and walked over to the front of the desk. She leaned on it and stared coldly at him, anger in her eyes and in her voice. "Listen to me. If you want to see her...fine. You can set her up in an apartment in the city and visit her anytime you want. You can help her out financially. If she's out of work, you can support her. But she's not moving into my house!"

"She has no job, nothing I will let her pursue. She has no place else to go. She will stay with me if she wants. If I can convince her to stay, she stays," he said as he leaned toward Min, his face also showing anger.

"I suppose you'll tell her that she can live the life of luxury now. She'll have all the money she needs. She won't have to be a barmaid or whatever she was down in those slums," Min growled at him. "Well, she won't have any of my money."

"Your money?" Albert screamed back. "I thought what's yours is mine as well."

147

"It's Adler money and I am the Adler."

"And I'm your husband and where do you think you're money would have gotten you without me. Wasn't I there when you needed me?" he stated coldly as he drew closer to her, their angry faces almost touching.

Min drew back from the desk. He was right. He had been there every time she needed him. He had been her protector. There was also very little she could really do to him. Everyone would side with him; he was the man, after all.

"Mina," he pleaded to her. "Be reasonable. Don't make it harder for me. Don't make it harder for them, or the rest of the family. If you were in my shoes, if the circumstances were reversed, wouldn't you do the same?"

Yes, she thought to herself, if she had some secret child lurking in her past, she would want Albert to accept it. But it was more than that. "You lied to me!" she yelled at Albert.

He took a gulp of his drink. "No, technically not. I could never lie about something like that. My past just never came up."

"You held secrets back from me! I'd never do that to you."

"Oh, come on, Dear," he snickered. "We've all got secrets in our pasts. We both have done things we dare not tell each other."

"You're wrong. I've always been perfectly honest with you." she insisted, but she knew in her heart she was lying. Again he was right. There were secrets that Min had never told her husband, things she'd never reveal.

"I see no point in going on with this," Albert finally said, his patience growing short. "Greta and Gery stay or we all will go, myself included. It's difficult to be alone, Mina. Do you really want that?"

Min could feel the madness growing inside her, but she had no choice but to accept his ultimatum. Angrily, she kicked the nearest thing to her, a chair. "I have no choice! You know that! You win!"

Albert sighed. "Thank you, Darling." he said as he walked over to her and tried to put his arms around her.

Her body shook, shivers running down her spine as his hand touched her hip. She moved away. "Don't touch me!"

"I'm sorry if I've hurt you."

She turned her back to him and started out of the study. At the entrance she stopped and leaned against the frame. "Would you have really left?" she asked.

"I guess we'll never know."

"Bastard!"

He shrugged. "It'll be fine. You'll see."

"Lying, dirty bastard! Never hide anything from me again."

"Yes, dear, I promise," he whispered. Min could see a smile cross Albert's face.

"Albert, by the way,"

"Yes?"

"This girl, this Greta...what makes you so adamant about her not going back to her old job? What did she do?"

He pulled a cigarette out of the desk and lit it before answering. "She was a prostitute."

"Shit." Min murmured as she dejectedly turned and left her husbands lair.

* * * *

The numbness that had shocked Greta's mind seemed to be wearing off as she sat on the strange bed listening to the muffled noises coming from downstairs. Yet there still seemed something unreal about the world around her, something eerie, as if she had left her body and entered that of a stranger. She felt cold, goose bumps covering her shivering body, the voices from below echoing in a strange, whistling silence.

What was she anymore? Who was she? The twisting, chaotic day's events scurried through her mind in quick sequence and baffled her senses. The fire and realization that her mother and father were dead stunned her, but even more than that she felt herself stunned by the revelation that this wealthy man, Albert Freyberg, was her real father. That this man and his diminutive wife live in such splendor while the girl he now claimed as his child lived in the dirt of the riverfront baffled her more. If it were true, how could he have let her struggle so?

Obviously it wasn't an easy time for this man as well, Greta reasoned. The muffled screams of his small wife echoing through the large house told her so. Yet Greta was unsure of his words, unsure of herself as she thought about the events of the day.

For a long time she had been confused by things that were said at home. So long she had felt as if she didn't belong there. Her father, in one of his drunken fits, had bellowed at her that no daughter of his would sell her body on the streets, but she had assumed it was the beer talking.

149

He always knew, she realized now, and with his anger was refusing her as his daughter. Her mother never revealed a thing to her, she realized as she thought back, but Greta herself had always felt so different from them. Could that have been her soul telling her the truth? Was it her mind revealing the truth and reminding her of what it remembered from her early childhood, or was she simply searching now for justification of the facts?

She didn't know what to think. She just had to accept what fate had presented her, she realized. The parents she knew were gone, victims of the Nazis. A stranger now claimed her as a child, maybe giving her hope of a new life? She still had her brother to think of. She still had Bock to love and protect her. She was still alive and was being given a new chance at life.

But what kind of life could it be in this strange house with this strange family? Greta could sense money and contentment even in the thickness of the bed-covers, but could she ever be accepted by these people?

Immediately upon entering the lavish home she had sensed coldness from Albert Freyberg's short, dark haired wife. The woman, who appeared in her early thirties, glowed with the comfort of wealth. Her stylish clothes were simple, yet exquisite, even at home at this late hour. Her voice was cool, educated, and had an icy tone as they spoke to her and her brother. How could a woman like that accept a girl from the streets? How could she know what it was like to struggle through life, to have to fight for everything and have to do things for which you don't feel proud? How could she know what it's like to be desperate?

The angry voice that reached her ears made Greta realize that Frau Freyberg didn't understand and probably was never told of Greta's existence as her husband's daughter. The shouting that reached her ears, though she couldn't make out the words, told her that these people would have as difficult night tonight as would she. The shock that she felt was being felt by them as well.

Would the morning bring new surprises? Would she, Greta wondered, be asked to leave this home in the morning? If that were to happen, what would she do then? Where were she and her brother to go?

"Are you alright?" she heard Gery's voice and focused her eyes on her brother at the doorway to the room. He looked relaxed, his smile beaming into the room. Either he was stronger than she realized, or he was covering his own fears under this cloak of contentment for her sake.

"I don't know." was all she could reply.

150

He came into the room and sat next to her on the bed. He wore an expensive robe over an equally expensive set of pajamas. They fit him well. "It's going to be fine here," He told his sister.

They both could still hear the shouts from downstairs. "How could you say that?" she asked. "Listen."

He shrugged. "I've heard adults fighting before. They'll kiss and make up and go to bed happy. It's no big deal. If that man didn't know he could bring us here, he wouldn't have."

"I don't think we're wanted here."

"Don't worry about it," he reassured her again. "It'll probably be good for us. They've got money and a couple more people in this house won't crowd them. We've got a chance to live really good here."

"I don't want to impose where I'm not wanted."

He looked sternly into her eyes. "Look, Greta! This man is convinced he's your real father. Don't foul it up! Let him think it and let him be it. Let him give you anything he wants. Don't be a fool!"

"I'm too old to be daddy's little girl. He should have been around when I was a little girl. I'm not something that he can own, you know."

"Still, Sister, don't throw this away. It's better than being a dead communist down in the street."

Greta slapped his face. "Don't you dare talk like that, your father....."

He cut into her words. "....was a drunken Bolshevik. Nothing else. This man's got a lot more to offer."

"I will not stay were I'm not wanted!"

"We'll see," Gery said, his voice curiously elated, as he strolled out of the room.

151

TWENTY

Gerhardt Greyer knew he was going to enjoy living in Albert Freyberg's big house. He realized it immediately the first time he saw it and his feelings grew stronger as he roamed the halls and got to know it better.

His only fear was that his sister would blow the whole thing for them.

The first night in the house had been tough, but, he realized, the next days would be even tougher. He felt drained and, after talking to Greta, begging her to accept anything from this wealthy family, he had gone off to a sound sleep.

He awoke to the sounds of little girls giggling. The first sights to his eyes were two sets of brown eyes staring back at him from the faces of the girls. They seemed quite amused as they looked at him lying in his bed in the guest room.

"I think he's kind of cute," one of the girls was saying.

"Shush," the other whispered. "You'll wake him up."

"He's got to get up anyway."

"Where do you think he came from?" one asked.

As Gery's eyes focused in on the girls it became clear that they looked like sisters, but they were almost the same height and weight and, he guessed, the same age. Yet they didn't look like twins.

"Oh, Anna," the darker haired girl replied. "What's the difference? He's probably some slum kid Father brought home."

The other girl turned strangely to the first. "You mean like a stray cat? Does that mean we get to keep him?"

The first girl glanced over at Gery, still pretending to be asleep. She wrinkled her nose. "Who'd want him?"

He heard a louder, adult voice come from the hallway behind the girls. "Anna! Marta! Get out of there! Leave him alone and get dressed."

The girls quickly left and Gery slowly got up from the bed. In the daylight he could better take in the surroundings and realized that the room was more elegant than he had first imagined. The furniture, from the bed to the expensive dresser, was quality like he had seen in the stores downtown. He felt like he had to pinch himself to see if he were really awake.

As he looked around he found some clothes lying out on a chair near a bulky dressing table and looked them over. They, too, were expensive and, he realized, they fit him perfectly. He assumed that he would find a boy about his age in the house along with the two little girls. He worried about that. He could fool the adults and younger children weren't going a problem, but a teenager may be a little harder to deal with.

Gery had grown up tough on the streets of Bremen's riverfront. He knew how to handle himself and was bright and cunning. Fighting the kids who chided him about his Bolshevik father and his sister the whore had made him so. He felt he knew a lot for a twelve year old, enough to survive the streets, the schoolmasters, the older kids, and even the adults he ran into. There was something he realized, though, that he didn't know; how rich kids acted and felt about people like him.

After he dressed and prepared himself for the day he stopped by Greta's room to check on her. She was still asleep and he didn't wake her. She had had a terrible, mind shattering day yesterday, more trying than he himself had faced, and he expected her troubles to continue today. There was no need to bother her yet.

He proceeded down the long staircase and faintly heard noises and laughing coming from somewhere off in the big house. He wondered if those kids were spying on him from around a corner. At the bottom of the stairs he met an older man, a butler he assumed, though he had never seen a butler before. He man nodded at him curtly.

"Good morning," Gery greeted the man.

"Would you care to join the other children for breakfast?" the butler politely asked.

Gery was a little surprised. First, he had never heard a grownup speak so nicely to him and, second, he had half-expected to be shuffled off to the kitchen.

He nodded and followed the butler toward the back of the house. On the way he was met by Herr Freyberg.

"I haven't told my children too much about you yet," he was told. "For now, until it's all explained, you and Greta are here because you're friends of Martin Bock. Is that clear?"

153

"Yes, Sir." he answered. Gery had reasoned that he would be as nice as he could to Herr Freyberg. After all, he was the man who was putting his life on the line bringing them here.

Breakfast was being served in a small room next to the kitchen. Gery guessed that this wasn't the main dining room, but wondered what it could be. Was it possible that the children of the house had a dining room all to themselves? Could it be that the huge house had two dining rooms, one for company and one for the rest of the time?

The room was just the right size for the table and four chairs that were centered in the room. To Gery, who was used to brittle furniture that creaked if anyone sat on it, the furniture was too good for an eating room, yet he knew it wasn't good enough for a formal dining room that he expected in a house as luxurious as this one.

The children of the house sat quietly in their seats and stared at him as he stood in the entranceway to the dining room. He had been right, there was a boy about his age and the boy was surveying Gery with cold, ice blue eyes. He looked very rich and proper, his straight blond hair neatly combed, his clothes pressed and sparkling. He reminded Gery of the kids in the posters the Nazis had plastered all over town, the perfect example of German youth.

The girls were there too, still giggling.

"Won't you have a seat?" the butler said to Gery.

He began to move over to the vacant chair, his knees trembling. He felt a queasiness in his stomach and a little dizzy, but tried to hard to relax after taking a deep breath. He knew he had to give a good impression to these kids. He knew their impressions would mean a lot to the way their parents felt about him.

"I'm Willi Freyberg," the boy said to him as he sat down. "What's your name?"

"Gery Greyer."

"These are my two sisters," he went on, politely, "Anna and Marta." The girls giggled.

Breakfast was quickly brought in by some kitchen help. It consisted of juice, milk, steaming hot cereal and rolls. It tasted as good as it looked and Gery, as hungry as he could ever remember being, gobbled up the food silently.

"Don't they feed you down by the docks?" Willi asked as he watched him devour the food. All of them had barely touched their meals, concentrating on watching the stranger in their midst instead.

"I've heard they eat garbage down there," one of the girls said.

"Oh, shut up!" shouted the other.

"Yes, they fed me," he said with a mouthful of food. "It's just that I didn't get much to eat yesterday."

"Papa said you were burnt out by the Nazis yesterday," the boy went on. "Are you a Bolshevik?"

Gery stopped eating. He wondered how much he should tell this kid. He wondered how much Herr Freyberg had said.

"Everybody says that the Nazis were burning out the Bolsheviks yesterday. If you were burned out, you must be a Bolshevik," Willi explained.

"I'm no Bolshevik," Gery answered. "My father was, however."

"If your father is a Bolshevik doesn't that make you one too?"

"Your father's a banker. Does that make you one too?"

Willi nodded to him, and then asked. "Did my father say exactly why he's letting you stay in our house?"

"Were else would you expect me to go?"

Willi shrugged. "I don't know. Where are your parents?"

Gery looked strangely at the boy. Herr Freyberg apparently hadn't told him enough. "They were killed in the fire," he said coldly.

"No shit!" the boy exclaimed. "That's terrible. I'm sorry I bothered you with the questions," Willi began to apologize. "I didn't mean to..."

Gery cut into his words. "Don't worry about it. That's the way life is."

"Does that make him an orphan, Willi?" one of girls asked.

"Shut up!" her brother bolted back. "Just eat your food and shut up."

There was no more talk around the breakfast table. It gave Gery time to think and he began to think about the deaths of his parents once again. He began to hurt, but he held back showing it to these rich kids. No matter how he hurt inside, Gery resolved, he would never let anyone know. He had to be strong, he said to himself, strong enough to go on and show the world that they weren't going to get him down. Even though he felt like crying he had to hold it in. No one was going to see him cry.

* * * *

Gery tried to occupy himself as best he could that day. He listened to the radio for a while, hearing the reports of more rioting down in his neighborhood and more accusations by the Nazi government in Berlin against the Bolsheviks. He read a book for a while and talked to Greta only briefly. She had spent most of the day in her room and had only one other visitor besides himself, Martin Bock came over late in the morning to see her and he didn't have any words for Gery.

About three in the afternoon the Freyberg children came home from school and were quickly rushed off by their parents to a small room off the parlor. The family was in there for a long time and when they emerged they all looked very serious. To Gery, it looked liked they had talked about Greta and himself. To Gery, they all looked depressed.

A few minutes later Gery went upstairs to his room and a moment after that Willi Freyberg came in a closed the door behind him.

"My father explained it all to me," he started to say. "I don't really believe it, but if he says it's true it must be true."

"What did he say?" Gery asked.

"For one thing, he says you're my cousin."

Gery thought a moment. Technically he and Willi were cousins, he decided. After all, his parents and Albert Freyberg were related by marriage. Strangely, he suddenly felt himself the poor relation from the wrong side of the tracks, just like in some old story.

"He also says that Greta is my half-sister," Willi went on, twisting his face as he said the words.

"That's right."

"It's confusing."

"Yes, my sister is your sister. You try and figure that out."

"I'll tell you one thing, Greyer," Willi went on. "She's a nice piece of ass for a sister. I heard she's a whore, too. How much does she cost?"

Gery rose from his chair like lightning, wrestling the Freyberg boy to the floor. They twisted on the floor for a second before Gery pinned his cousin to the rug.

"Shit!" Willi hollered. "What's wrong with you?"

"Don't you ever talk to me about Greta in that way?"

"Let me up, you bastard!" Willi protested as he squirmed beneath Gery's grip.

"My sister's still better than all of you! You shut up talking about her!"

"She's a whore!"

"Shut up!" Gery screamed as he punched Willi in the face.

"Riverfront trash!" Willi shouted as Gery punched him again.

"Don't you talk to anyone about her! Don't you tell anyone what she was!"

Gery lost his grip on his cousin and quickly found himself pinned to the floor. Willi's sneering face as staring down at him and he waited for the boy to start punching.

"Well!" he prodded him on, "Go ahead."

"Go ahead and do what?!"

"Do this!" Gery shouted as he freed one of his arms and swung at Willi.

They struggled on the floor for a few seconds longer, but again Willi had wrestled Gery to a pinned position on the floor. This time Gery was face down, his nose crushed against the rug.

"You bastard!" Willi said. "I'm not going to say anything. She's my sister too!"

Willi got up from on top of Gery and stood above him. As Gery started to get up the other boy extended a helping hand.

"What was that all about?" Gery asked when he got to his feet.

"I wanted to see how you felt about her?"

"Why?"

"Because I had to know. You defended her. I like that. No matter what they are, a family's got to stick together."

"Yes, sure," Gery agreed. "Friends." he said as he extended his hand to Willi.

"No," Willi said as he took Gery's hand, "Cousins."

"Where'd you learn to fight like that?"

"I've had to learn. I have to defend my family's honor, you know."

"Why?"

"We're accused of being Jews."

Gery was a little surprised. "You say that like you're not."

"My grandmother and great-grandfather were Jews from different sides of the family, but we're not. It's just that the Nazis pick on us."

"I know how you feel," Gery said. "I've been fighting against boys telling me I'm a Bolshevik for a long time. Just because my old man was a one doesn't mean I was one too."

"Right," Willi agreed. "I get so tired of fighting battles that are caused by my parents. Nobody wants to look at you for what you are. They're always saying what you are is because of your parents, but I make my own decisions."

"Sometimes I've felt like running away and becoming someone totally different." Gery told him.

"Don't worry about it, kid, Willi smiled at him. "You're not a communist anymore."

"I guess you're right."
"You're now one of us Jews."

* * * *

Greta was already beginning to regret coming to this house. Although it was only one day, she was already beginning to realize how wrong it was. She was very uncomfortable and lonely. She felt coldness all around her, coming from the people of the house and from the walls of the rooms themselves. To the house, she imagined, she was a foreign body to be forced out. It was as if the house itself didn't want her there.

She had slept in late, her mind and body drained of all feeling and, even after awakening, she felt drained as she wandered around the big house.

Worst of all, she had no one to talk to and she knew she had to talk to someone; she had to talk out the grief and confusion she felt inside herself.

She couldn't express it to her brother, she knew. He seemed happy to be in the house. He seemed quite capable of taking things as they came, but she hurt from the abrupt changes that had been happening in her life. She was stunned by it. Why, she wondered, wasn't he suffering as much as her?

Bock, too, was not the one she could reveal her grief to. He had come to see her that day, but he didn't seem to respond to her urgings for help. She had only hinted at it, that was her mistake, and he didn't pick up on her hints. He had only said that she would recover in time and that she would adjust. He sounded just like Gery, but there was a rumor of regret in his voice. Was he sorry that he had ever gotten involved with her? Was he sorry that he had brought her into the lives of the Freyberg family? Was he thinking that he should have left her where he had found her?

Her new-found father hadn't even talked to her that day. He had gone off to the office before she had gotten out of bed and had yet to return from the city. If he was so happy to have found her and brought her here, why would he have shunned her in this way? Was he too having second thoughts?

Alone in the house, with the servants ignoring her and Frau Freyberg no where to be seen, Greta had time to think about all these things. She was beginning to think that it would be best to take Gery and leave, but something kept her there. She didn't know why, but something in her mind told her to stay.

Mina Freyberg joined her in the parlor just after night had fallen. The small woman looked tired, withdrawn, and Greta dreaded having to retreat from the room. She knew the woman would not want to see her and knew it would be best to get out of her way. Greta remembered the loudness of her cries the previous night as they reverberated through the house and knew the hate and anger than the woman felt for her. She rose to leave the room.

"Wait," Mina Freyberg called to her. "Don't go yet. We need to talk."

Greta slowly, silently sat back down in the chair.

"You must realize how difficult it is for me to accept this," the woman said.

Greta nodded. "It's not so easy for me, either."

"I know how difficult it must be for you, losing your parents and facing Albert for the first time. I know you've had a rough time, but put yourself in my place," she seemed to be pleading to Greta.

"I know, but my mind is spinning from the whole thing."

"You were a total surprise to me. He had never told me."

"How do you think I feel? I discover that my parents had lied to me as well. I discover that this man is my father and that the people I had loved as parents are nothing to me," Greta countered.

"But you don't belong here," Mina said. "I've got my children to consider. I've got my position."

"You're making me feel like I don't belong."

"And you don't. Look around you!" Mina went on, her voice growing angry. "We've worked hard to keep what we have. We've got enemies out there hounding at us. When they learn that Albert has another child, a prostitute, they'll have more ammunition to us against us."

"Is that what's troubling you?" Greta asked. "Is that why you're mad at me? I can't help what I am! Haven't you ever......why am I asking? You have no idea what it's like."

"I'd never allow my girls to sell their bodies on the street. I'd never degrade myself by associating with such people." Mina glared at her.

"You needn't worry yourself. I won't turn your home into a whorehouse. I'm thankful for your help."

"I'm not giving you any help, girl! I want you out of here, but my husband insists that you stay. I wished he had better sense."

Greta began to cry. "If you want me to go, I'll go. I don't want be here if I'm not wanted."

"Now, wait a minute. My husband asked that I not force you out and I won't. Stay if you like, but expect nothing from me. I will not be your friend. I certainly will not be your mother. I won't stand in the way of your staying here, but, I beg you, don't come between Albert and myself...at least no more than you already have. If you have any feeling for this man, don't drive a wedge between him and his family."

"I thought I was his family, too," Greta sobbed.

"We're his family. My children and I are the ones he's been with all these years. We're the ones who deserve his love, not you! The man may be blinded by rediscovering something he has lost, but he'll soon realize that he may be sacrificing a greater love. Only you can stop him from making a big mistake." the woman went on, her voice growing angrier with each word.

"I would never deliberately do anything to hurt him."

"So you say now, girl, but I'll tell you right now that I'll do everything I can to stop you. Do not cross me and take my husband away. I'll show you that I can be a very dangerous enemy," Min concluded as she quickly got up and exited the room.

TWENTY-ONE

Martin should have realized he was getting into trouble the moment Lucy phoned him. Lucy Wagner was the type of girl who could manipulate him and he knew he shouldn't allow her to do that to him again, but he simply couldn't help himself.

"Are you going to be home today?" was the question she posed to him the second he answered the telephone that Sunday morning.

He had planned to go see Greta that afternoon, but there was something about Lucy's voice that made him tell her he would be home. Her voice was tense, quivering on every word and her pleadings overcame his inner feelings to tell her the truth.

"I'm coming over." she told him. "I need to talk."

But Lucy never just talked, he thought as he anxiously waited for her to arrive. Lucy tugged at his senses, twisting him around her fingers like a rubber band. That's why he had broken it off with her in the first place. He had grown tired of being used. He had grown tired of being there when she wanted him to be and being invisible when she willed it. He had grown tired of her using him to get what she wanted, whether it was a better job or simply a good time. He was tired of all that, but, still, he could not resist her pleadings to him even though he knew it would come to no good.

When she arrived at his flat he knew there had been changes in her. She looked older than he could remember, lines now drawn on her face that weren't there before. She looked as if she was still trying to be the old Lucy, flaunting her body in that familiar way, but the fire had gone out of her eyes and her hair, usually perfectly cloaking her face, was mussed.

"What's wrong?" he asked her immediately.

She tried to smile, but it was empty of her old emotions. "Why...there's nothing wrong. I just couldn't see spending a Sunday morning alone."

161

Martin didn't let on that he knew more about what was going on in her life than she expected him to know. It had become a topic of gossip and rumor at the bank, especially since she had gone on leave. The rumors had ranged from her being pregnant to her having some dread disease, but Albert had confided in Martin the truth. He knew she was involved with an older man, a man apparently in trouble with the law. He knew she was in trouble and that Albert had been helpless to save her. He wondered what she wanted from him now.

"I guess I feel the same way." Martin told her as he poured her a cup of coffee. "Spending a winter Sunday alone can be boring."

"Well, at least March is here. Winter's almost over."

"I thought you liked the winter?"

"It's been tough." her sad voice replied. She quickly changed the subject. "How are things at the bank?"

"Don't ask." Bock answered. "It's like working in a morgue. People keep leaving everyday and we all sit around waiting for the axe to drop. They're deliberately trying to ruin the business. It's taking every moment of Albert's time and every ounce of his energy to hold things together."

"That's a shame," Lucy said as she cupped the steaming coffee cup in her hands. Her hands seemed to tremble as she raised it to her lips. "It's so wrong."

"Everything seems so wrong." Martin agreed.

"How is the boss holding up?" she next asked.

Martin had had enough. "Why are we wasting our time with this small talk, Lucy?" he asked her anxiously. "I know you want something. What is it?"

She looked at him strangely, her face curling up into a little girl's pout and her lips trembling as if to hold back a scream.

"You wouldn't come here if you didn't want something." he insisted.

She began to cry, choking out the words between the tears. "I didn't know where else to turn. Help me, Martin!"

"What kind of help?"

She reached over and took his hand. "Help me feel alive again."

He felt her pulling him toward her. He saw in her tearful eyes a desperate need he knew he had to resist. He pulled his hand away from hers.

"Oh, Martin, please!" she pleaded as she reached out for him again, her hands grabbing at his and drawing them to her body.

Martin knew he shouldn't, but he felt himself drawn toward her trembling lips. Something in her voice, in her eyes, something below the

162

desperation he saw in her face drew him to her. He knew he shouldn't, but he couldn't resist kissing her again.

As their lips met he felt himself shaking. His soul was telling him it was wrong. It was saying that he loved another, but Lucy was there, now, urging him on and running her hands along his body and exciting him.

"Oh, yes!" she sighed as their lips parted.

She joined her lips to his once again and he could feel her body growing closer with each breath. She reached for his hand and moved it to her breast, cupping it and squeezing.

As their lips separated she rose from the chair and took both of his hands, gently pulling him from his seat as well. She guided him toward the bedroom.

"This is wrong." he said to her as she pulled him down onto the bed. Yet, despite his words, despite the feelings that told him not to go on, he could not get up and walk away.

"No! No!" she pleaded back as she unbuttoned his shirt. "Not wrong. It's right! It's more right than anything."

He couldn't resist her. He knew he was weak and complied with every wish and every demand she made of him. As they continued, as they made love, he wondered what she really wanted from him. Even during the highest moment of their encounter, their bodies rhythmically moving together with her cries of passion ringing in his ears, he wondered what she really wanted.

* * * *

When it was finally over Martin felt a chill run through his body. He felt ashamed. He felt used, but he had yet to learn why he had been used.

It had been a long, somewhat agonizing session. Martin usually felt revived after having sex, his body alive and anxious, ready for more, but not this time. This time he felt drained and cold and afraid. He had satisfied Lucy, who lay beside him exhausted, and he had been satisfied himself, but his energy was gone and he felt no joy in his heart.

Why had she done that to him? Why was he feeling this way? Had all the fire gone out of his feelings for Lucy or was what he felt for Greta so great that no other woman made him feel good anymore? Was this what love was? Was it not having good sex with someone else?

163

Shouldn't it be that you can't have sex with someone else if you love another? Shouldn't his feelings for Greta have prevented him from having sex with Lucy in the first place?

"Oh, that was wonderful!" Lucy sighed as she rolled over to face him. Her face looked more relaxed now, her eyes clear and sparkling. Martin looked her body over as she lay beside him. She was still a beautiful woman, but he wasn't moved by nakedness. Lucy simply didn't excite him anymore.

"What's wrong?" Lucy asked as she noticed the look of disgust on Martin's face.

He turned away, unable to stare at her any longer. "I just know something else is coming."

"What do you mean?" she asked, her voice feigning ignorance.

"Lucy, you want something. I know you want something." he said as he turned back toward her.

"Well...since you asked." she sighed. He sensed she was self-conscious about asking. "There is something you can help me with."

He turned his face up toward the ceiling. At last he was going to hear the truth.

"Now I wouldn't ask if I'd anywhere else to go, but I haven't and I do still love you, Martin. If you do this for me I promise to stay with you forever and do anything you want."

"In other words, you're offering me your body if I do what you want."

"Well, that's an awful way of putting it. I said that I still love you."

Martin rose from the bed and put on his pants. "Lucy, you should have just asked without that 'I'll sacrifice my body to you' crap. I don't want you that way anymore."

"Fine then!" she chirped. "I need you to help us out of the country."

"What makes you think I can help you do that? And who is 'us'."

"Oh, Martin!" she purred. Martin was used to her tones of voice. This one was meant to make him feel superior. "I know you can find a way for us to get out. You've got a lot of connections."

He turned to face her again. She had a sly smile on her face and her body seemed to be posed in a manner he used to find hard to resist. "Lucy, I can't help you. In the old days, maybe I could, but now, with the Nazis, my position and connections don't mean a thing. I can't help you."

"But...think of us!"

"What 'us'!" he shouted. "There is nothing between us anymore. I know you're involved with this man whom you want to flee the country

164

with. I'm in love with another now as well. You can't use me to get yourself and your lover out of Germany and I refuse to use you."

He could see by the look on her face that she knew he had rejected her. He could see her face turn to tears.

"Oh! Dammit, Lucy. All that shit about needing me and wanting me was nothing but a lie. You were trying to use me again and, frankly, it won't work anymore."

"I had to try!" she cried, her face now streaming with tears. "I'll do anything to get out of here."

"Then go throw yourself at some high level Nazi. Maybe he can help you. I can't."

"You don't know how it feels." she said as she curled herself against the blanket. "I'm so scared. Everyday I wonder if they're going to find us. Everyday I live in fear. Karl, he's so....I don't know. I can't go on like this, Martin. Please, help!"

Martin had finished dressing and was ready to go. He had to get out of there before she got to him once again. "Alright, I'll see what I can do." he told her as he put on his coat. "I'll get back to you."

She nodded to him, but she continued to cry.

"You can stay here as long as you need to." he told her as he walked toward the door. "Let yourself out."

TWENTY-TWO

Joseph Strauss entered the darkened office of the Adler Bank long after working hours, his incriminating, secret file clutched firmly under his arm. In the stillness of the offices he could hear the echo of his footsteps as he walked across the hardwood floor to the executive suite. The sounds filled his head and heart with dread for he still was unsure if he were doing the right thing.

Joseph had always been taught to be loyal and to be devoted to his duties. Now he was torn between being loyal to the state and to his profession and being loyal to his own feelings and integrity. He was torn between his decency and his duty. It sickened him that he had to make such a choice, but to ignore the hatred he felt for the hoodlums who now ran the government, to ignore their evil was something against his heart. He had reasoned long ago not to let them destroy Albert Freyberg and finally had summoned up the courage to confront the man.

He remembered back to that fateful morning when he finally telephoned Freyberg to set up this meeting. He remembered the disgust he felt that it had come to this, but he mustered the courage to call on the man. He also made sure he didn't reveal anything important to him. He worried that Freyberg might panic and that would only serve the evil enemy more.

Strauss had requested a secret meeting and Freyberg had agreed, asking the policeman to come to the bank after hours. The doors would be left open and the watchman would be sent away, Freyberg had said.

It had all worked out as planned and now, as Joseph approached the cluster of offices in the back of the bank, he realized that there was no turning back. He saw the light shining beneath one door and went up to there, his heart pounding loudly in his chest.

"Please, come in." the voice responded to his footsteps even before he knocked on the closed door.

Strauss entered and looked upon the face of Albert Freyberg for the first time. He had seen his pictures, he had uncovered every facet of the

166

man's life and dwelled upon the facts he had found for weeks, but it was different seeing the man in the flesh. It was different watching his eyes follow his movements toward the desk. It was different when he extended his hand to the banker and felt the touch of his flesh as they shook hands. Freyberg was no longer just a case, a picture, a set of facts and figures. Albert Freyberg suddenly became a living person.

"I was a little puzzled, Detective, when you called." Freyberg began. "You were a little vague over the phone. What you have to say is important, I hope." Freyberg gestured toward a chair and stared at his visitor intently as Joseph sat down. His voice was deep, resounding in the sparely decorated office. It showed confidence and dominance, as did the banker's intense brown eyes which continued to watch Joseph's every move.

"I had to keep the utmost secrecy about our meeting," Joseph explained. "What I'm doing is beyond and against the wishes of my superiors."

"Can I offer you a drink?"

"No, thank you, but I don't drink. You may indulge if you like." Joseph answered. He knew that the man might need a drink, several, before this meeting was over.

Freyberg moved over to a table near his uncluttered desk and poured a glass of red wine from a decanter. "I'm very curious what tricks and lies the Nazis have in store for me now." he said as he returned to his seat and took a cigarette from a silver case on his desk. "I'm somewhat amused by the secrecy this time, though. You people have never been able to do anything but gloat every time you set out to destroy me."

"I'm no Nazi, Herr Freyberg." Joseph corrected the man. "I'm a servant of the state, but not of those devils."

That brought a smile to Freyberg's face. Deep down, Joseph understood that Albert liked his honesty. He knew he needed the respect of the man to if he were to accomplish anything tonight.

"Alright, then," Freyberg went on, grey circles of smoke surrounding his crop of silver hair. "What do you have for me?"

Joseph opened the envelope containing the evidence and withdrew a photograph. All day his mind had struggled with exactly how to approach the matter, unable to decide whether to just confront the man or to coax the truth from him. He had finally decided to take things as they came. He had no plan of attack.

"Do you recognize this picture?" he asked as he slid the photograph toward the banker.

The moment after Freyberg glanced at the old photograph his eyes grew wide and a smile came to his mouth. "Where did you get this?" he asked.

"It's from the records of the Martin Luther Hospital. Do you recognize the face?"

His smile grew wide. Joseph could see Freyberg's finger move along the outline of the woman's face. "Yes, I do. She's beautiful, isn't she? Her name is Francoise Romberge."

"I see," Joseph replied blankly. He noted that Freyberg spoke of her as if he thought she was still alive. His mind began to calculate the likelihood that he knew nothing of the girl's fate.

"Back during the war she and I were lovers." Freyberg went on. "I guess I still care for her today. It's a shame that things didn't work out."

Joseph could see Albert Freyberg's mind spinning. On his face was a strange look, his eyes shadowing visions of the past, flipping though the pages of his memories of those days from fourteen years back.

"I had met her in the hospital while a patient recovering from war wounds," Freyberg continued his story, still staring at that old picture. "We grew to love each other. We had planned a great life together after the war was over. Francoise was everything I could ask for. For me, she was a new lease on life.

"But she was an Alsatian, a Frenchwoman living under German rule. Her life was...how should I say it...tormented and troubled. Near the end of the war, with defeat certain, she was troubled by the feelings against France that sickened the country." he looked up from the picture and stared at Joseph. "You remember what it was like, don't you?"

"Yes, I was a soldier then also. I remember."

Freyberg looked at the photograph one last time and handed it back to Joseph. "I don't see the point of this, Detective. What could Francoise have to do with me now?"

"Tell me exactly what happened to your relationship, Herr Freyberg. Tell me what you recall."

"Recall, well I remember it like it was yesterday." Albert laughed, but there was hollowness to his laughter. "In the fall of 1918 I was in the hospital again. I was severely burned and had suffered head wounds. Francoise was there for me, but there was rioting in the streets and the talk of war and revolution. Francoise was afraid of what was going to become of her when the armistice came. Then, for some reason, the day the armistice was announced, she just disappeared.

"Mina, my wife today, was a friend to both of us. She couldn't find her anywhere. I still couldn't leave the hospital and was unable to search for her myself and, as the days went by, it became clear that she had run off or been sent back to France. Mina wrote letters, but the authorities couldn't be bothered in helping to find her. It was a terrible time then; the revolution, the desperation. What did the fate of two lovers mean then?"

"So you just gave up?" Joseph asked.

Albert ran his hand through his hair. He looked exhausted from just thinking and remembering his feelings then. "Oh, I guess after a while the desperation and grief turned to hate. I hated the fact that she didn't have faith enough in me....in what we meant to each other...to stay! I hated that! I hated her for a brief time. Then, once again, I began to love her and to relive the grief I felt at losing her, but I knew that I would never be able to find her."

"And Mina Adler, the present Frau Freyberg, was there for you?" Joseph questioned. He was beginning to formulate a new theory in his mind.

"Min...Yes!" Albert went on. "Without her I don't know if I would have survived that time. Without her I probably would have given up entirely. She stood by me and gained my love. Quickly, we were drawn to each other in our grief...she, too, had lost her beloved late in the war...and were married.

"The truth is, Detective, I still hold what Francoise and I had together dearly. I still care for her in a manner different that what I feel for my wife. You know, in everyone's life there is a great passion...only once do you feel it. Francoise was my passion and no one ever can fully replace her. No matter how much I love my wife, I loved that girl differently. What she and I had was special."

Joseph took a deep breath. He had heard Freyberg's story and began to hate himself even more. He hated what he had to do, but realized it was better now, from him, than from the Nazis.

Albert, too, took a deep breath. His eyes, glimmering in the shadowy light of the office, appeared watery and less commanding than before. "Now, Herr Detective, tell me what Francoise has to do with what goes on in my life today?"

"I'm sorry; sir, but I must tell you that Francoise Romberge did not just vanish off the face of the earth that November. She was murdered."

169

Albert sat back in his chair. Joseph could see the emotion swell in the man's face. He could see him holding back the tears. "Oh, my God, the poor girl. My poor, sweet love. I never knew."

Joseph tried to ignore the feelings he himself felt at that moment. He pulled an old report from his file and recited the facts. "She was killed by the penetration of a small caliber bullet in the head. Death was instantaneous." he hoped that would help Freyberg, realizing that his woman had suffered no pain. "The reporting officer concluded that the death, which occurred in her flat, was in revenge for the defeat at the hands of the French."

He looked back at Albert. The banker, a short time ago so firm and confident, was squeezing his eyes and wiping away the telltale tears of his grief.

"I differ with those reports." Joseph stated.

Albert moved his hand away from his eyes and stared curiously at the detective. "What? Explain."

"There was little rioting in the area of the flat that day. On November 11th there was little or no rioting in Bremen at all. Most everyone welcomed the peace. I can't believe anyone would single out a young French nurse for extermination because of the loss of the war."

Albert leaned closer to the desk and toward Joseph. His face showed interest, the pain he was suffering receding into the back of his mind. "And who do you think killed her?"

"I suspected you."

"That's absurd."

"You were a poor soldier before the war. You came from the riverfront. Mina Adler had money and position, which you share with her today. The only one who stood in your way was Francoise Romberge. It was the perfect time and the perfect excuse to get rid of her."

Albert shook his head. "That's the most ridiculous thing I've ever heard."

"I have to agree after listening to you. You could never kill her. I just can't believe that you were never told of her death."

"How could I have learned of it?"

"From your wife."

"She didn't know anything about what happened to Francoise. She helped me search for her." Albert retorted. He looked angered by Joseph's cross-examination.

"Herr Freyberg," Joseph went on as he stared at the police report. At last, the facts and Freyberg's words revealed the truth. "The person who reported the death and identified the body was Mina Adler."

"What?" Albert said breathlessly as he rose from his chair.

"Not only that," Joseph continued. "But she also arranged for burial of the body."

Albert pounded on the desk, knocking over several pictures that were lined up in the corners. "You're lying."

Joseph pushed the report across the desk toward him. "Look! See for yourself. The person who found the body and called the police was Mina Adler. She later claimed the body. She told the police of Romberge's fear of retribution. She convinced the police of that story they put down to end investigation of the case."

Albert looked over the papers quickly and then tossed them toward Joseph. "How could she hide this from me for so long?"

"At first I thought it was because you two were accomplices in the murder and, as such, it was nearly perfect." Joseph said. "Now, seeing you, I have another idea."

"This is insane!" Albert hollered.

"Now I believe that your wife killed the girl."

Albert waved his hands frantically through the air. "She's incapable of that. They were friends. We were all friends."

"You had said that she had just lost someone in the war. In desperate times, people do desperate things. In a moment of madness...passion....grief.....need, people do such things."

"This is crazy."

"Do you feel she had reason to kill her? Do you feel that the desperation was great enough to drive her to that?"

Albert finally sat down, struggling to regain control of his emotions. "She was desperate. Yes! We were all desperate then!"

"But enough to commit murder?"

Joseph could see the mind of Albert Freyberg race back to that time again, retracing the days, the feelings he felt and his wife felt. "She had just lost Willi. She had lost her father, her brother." he mumbled. "She was..." His words stopped. On his face came the look of surprise. The man had just realized that his wife could have done the deed. No, Joseph concluded, that she had committed the murder.

Albert nervously reached for another cigarette and lit it. He then rose and turned his back on Joseph and faced the one window in the office. He leaned against the wall and puffed wildly on the smoke. He was thoroughly wrapped in his own thoughts.

"Herr Freyberg, I was asked to gather this evidence by the Nazis in an effort to destroy you." Joseph explained. "The Gauleiter of this city seems to have a personal grievance against you, but I cannot fulfill my duties in this matter. I despise the Nazis too much. I'm leaving this file with you to do with it as you like. I must warn you, however, that I can only pretend to work with them for a short time longer. The Nazis grow impatient for me to make some progress. Soon they'll pick somebody else to hunt you down. Decide quickly what you're going to do. I've given you a warning of what you will face."

Joseph got up and prepared himself to leave. He took one last look at the silent figure staring out the window and realized that he may have ruined his life in an effort to save his life. He wondered what thoughts were going through the man's mind. He wondered what conclusions were being drawn, what actions would be taken.

"Detective," Albert Freyberg's voice called out as Joseph neared the door.

"Yes," he replied, turning toward the man again.

Albert, his face still turned toward the window, spoke slowly, deliberately. "Take the file. Hold off using it as long as you can, but do not endanger your job. I'll make my decisions as I see fit."

"If you wish," Joseph said as he walked back to the desk and took the envelope. "And good luck, Herr Freyberg."

"Thank you," Albert mumbled. "Thank you for the truth."

TWENTY-THREE

It was past eleven o'clock when Min finally heard the car coming up the drive toward the house. Albert had been working late into the night many times recently, but this was the latest he had ever come home.

Min worried for her husband. The pressure of trying to keep the bank solvent through the storm had to be taking its toll on him. The daily struggle against those who wanted to take their business away, to ruin them, was consuming him. It dwelled on his mind even during his precious hours at home, she could see on his face. The worry lines were beginning to appear, the signs of stress she had remembered seeing only twice before in her life with Albert. Once was during the inflation, the other time even before that, during the war.

Min was depressed as well, and she, too, worried for their future. She was also lonely, spending much of her time in the big house with no one to talk to. The children occupied with school and hiding their own fears, steered clear of both her and their father. And having that girl in the house brought no comfort to Mina.

The visitors made Min uncomfortable, although they really had caused her no trouble during the two weeks since their arrival. Gery had adjusted well to his new surroundings, joining the children in school and becoming great friends with Willi. Min thought the boys made good companions, after what she saw and heard as an initial combativeness, but she had long since decided not to try to understand the mind of her son. She rather liked Gery Greyer, his polite manners winning her over, and could easily accept him as part of her family if things were different.

Things were very different between her and Greta, however. She didn't belong here, Mina's mind insisted. She was a grown woman, too old to blend in with the children and too independent and different for Min. Thus far she had only sulked around the house, avoided Min as much as Min avoided her, speaking openly only to Martin Bock during his visits. She had left the house only once in two weeks, that being for the burial of her parents, and had contributed nothing to the household.

173

Well, that had its good points, Min thought. At least she hadn't left each night to return to the riverfront, to prostitution.

Deep down Min felt that Greta really wanted to pack up and leave. It was only the persuasion of her brother and Bock that made her stay. As far as Albert was concerned, the girl probably felt neglected. Her husband, preoccupied with the job of preserving their life, seldom talked to his daughter.

Tonight would be no different, Min assumed as Albert came through the door. Greta was reading in the parlor and the two exchanged hellos. Albert sounded glum, a tone in his voice that Min was hearing more and more often. What was wrong tonight?

"You're at the office more and more," Min told him as she approached him to greet him with a kiss. "You'd better be careful. It isn't worth ruining your health."

Albert shunned her as she reached up to kiss him. He skirted past her hastily and started for the kitchen.

Min was puzzled. In all their years together he had never failed to greet her with a kiss. Something was seriously wrong.

She followed him into the kitchen and found her husband rummaging through the liquor cabinet. Silently she watched him find a bottle of inexpensive wine, the kind that numbs your senses quickly and starts your mind to buzz, and watched him gulp down a glassful quickly. He then took out a cigarette and lit it, drawing the smoke in deeply into his lungs.

"Something has happened." Min concluded from his actions.

"Are the children asleep?" he asked, ignoring her statement.

She nodded.

"And the servants?"

"Gone for the night."

"We're alone, then."

"Except for Greta."

"As long as the servants aren't around and the children are asleep." he said. There was a note of distress in his voice as he rattled off the words. He spoke quickly, yet each word sounded as if it required a great deal of thought. Min was sure he had been drinking before he came home.

Min had gone through a lot lately, but she was unprepared for the way her husband was acting. She felt her stomach quiver, unable to comprehend what dreaded news he had to deliver.

She, too, needed a drink and she walked over to the wine bottle and poured herself some of the dark, sour wine.

"I had a visitor tonight." Albert told her as she poured.

"Who was that?" Min asked as she took the first sip.

"The police."

Min swallowed the sour wine hard. It burned her throat and continued to burn as it made a path to her stomach. She turned to him, but the burning throughout her body prevented her from speaking.

"They told me some distressing news." he said after he again gulped down a second glass of wine.

"The police," Min finally spoke. "What could they have to talk to you about? We've broken no laws."

Albert didn't reply. He instead walked over to her and took the wine bottle, pouring himself another glass. His face was puffed with redness, Min noticed. She felt pain in that face as he passed her and walked away. She swallowed the rest of the wine in her glass and poured herself some more.

Albert finally spoke. "They told me what happened to Francoise."

Min nearly choked on a mouthful of wine, but held back a cough as she forced it down her throat. Her body shook as the words rang in her head. *Francoise! That was so long ago!* Surely it was all forgotten, she thought. She had tied up all the loose ends in that matter long ago.

"Mina," Albert's voice called to her. "Did you hear me?"

"Yes, I heard you," Min choked out the words, her voice quivering with each syllable. Don't be afraid, Mina told herself. *There's no reason to be afraid.*

"Well?" he asked.

"What does that have to do with us? She ran off a long time ago." Min said, trying to act unconcerned. She thought back to what had been her story then, remembering the words she had told Albert.

"You know that's not true." he said.

Min's heart raced. For fourteen years that secret had been kept hidden from him. For fourteen years she had lived with his memories of her, with how she knew he felt about her. For so long she had kept Francoise' fate concealed, *Why bring it up now?*

"It's a tough thing to learn that she's been dead all these years." Albert solemnly said.

"Oh, God," Min cried. "How dare they tell you that now?"

"And that's not all they told me, Mina." he went on. "They told me that you knew of it all along."

175

Min's heart pounded in her chest. She raised the glass to her lips once again, her hand shaking so wildly that she couldn't steady the glass as it rose from the table.

"It seems that a short time ago you insisted that you concealed no secrets from me," Albert went on, his voice mellow and calm. "Obviously, that was a lie."

"I couldn't tell you then." Min whispered softly, but the sounds echoed in her ears. "I never got the nerve to tell you."

"That wasn't all the detective had to say."

"Oh, what else is there?" she asked, her mind struggling to keep her voice calm as she again raised the glass of wine to her lips.

"He believes that you murdered Francoise."

The glass fell from her hand and shattered on the table!

"Mina, I believe it, too."

Mina stared at the pieces of glass littering the table, at the wine that splattered on her dress and her hands. The wine, richly red as the blood she had once spilled, formed small puddles and began to run toward the edge of the table.

The anger swelled within her. She madly pounded the table with both fists. The wine bottle wavered, then fell over and broke, spilling its bloody scarlet contends everywhere.

"Min!" she heard Albert's deep voice echo through the room, through her mind. "The truth. Why! Why did you do it?"

She turned toward him, but her eyes were transfixed on her hands. They were covered with wine and splinters of glass. She felt her own blood mix with the red wine.

"Oh, Mina," Albert moaned to her, his fist rising up. "How could you have done such a thing?"

"Oh, God!" she finally screamed, her face exploding with tears. "I was mad! I was desperate! I was going to kill myself. She tried to stop me and the gun! The damn gun just went off! Oh God! I know that the gun just went off!" She reached for her husband with her bloodied hands. "Albert, please! I did what I did, but I love you! I need you just as much as I did then!"

Albert stared at her blankly, unable to hear her cries and pleas, unable to speak. He turned his back to her and placed his empty glass on the sink.

She ran to his side and clutched his arms tightly. "Oh, Albert, Please understand! Please! Don't turn away from me!"

176

She felt his body quiver with her touch. She felt him jerk away, shaking her off as one would a fly.

Again the anger swelled within her body. "No! No! You can't shut me out! You can't! Not now!" she screamed loudly as she pounded her fists into his back.

She felt him wince at the blows, but he didn't waver. "I can't believe you killed her." he murmured.

Again she slammed her fists into his back. "You still love her!" she screamed. "You always loved her! I never won your love, you bastard! You bastard!" She hated herself for saying the words and felt the rush of tears again. She collapsed against his rigid body and began to sob.

Albert took a step away from her. She released her grip. "Let me be. Let me think," he said in a shallow, empty voice.

Min regained her senses, but the anger still consumed her mind. "That damned woman! After fourteen years she still holds you captive. After all we've meant to each other, done for each other...she still holds on!"

"Mina," he spoke again. "Neither of us has ever been committed to each other. We've both been prisoners of the past."

"I put my past behind me while you've kept yours hanging on display. That damned picture...."

"Reminders of the past, thoughts of what might have been...for both of us, Min. For me at least, but you destroyed that for me."

His voice was like a knife, hurting her, stinging her mind and body. All the time they had been together he had never stopped loving Francoise. That picture was more than memories....*That picture*!

Min ran from the room, her mind now determined to erase the last of his memories; the picture that kept his thoughts of her alive no matter how hard she tried to please him.

She raced to his study, his lair. She heard his voice call to her from the kitchen, but she raced on, into the room she hated.

There she was with her haunting beauty and her tall, shapely figure, her arm wrapped around Albert. There, the four of them, enjoying a day in the sun so long ago. Two of them, Willi and Francoise, were dead, but he had kept her alive in that picture while she had blotted out all thoughts of Willi in her mind. That picture was his memories. Was it what kept him from forgiving her now?

She felt the tears again on her face, but her anger was stronger than her grief. She grabbed the picture and lifted it off the wall and threw it across the room.

177

It struck the lamp on his desk and crashed against the chair, the glass shattering into a thousand pieces that glimmered in the half-light of the room. As if in slow motion, she watched the shimmering slivers of glass as they fell like snow in the moonlight.

"So much for our memories." she whispered.

TWENTY-FOUR

Greta had heard the couple shouting from the kitchen and it caused shivers to run up and down her spine. She had heard their angry voices before, when she had first arrived. She had heard her parents fight as well. She knew that she herself could shriek as loudly, as madly as anyone. Yet there was something hellish about the arguing she heard coming from the kitchen. The cries of Mina Freyberg resounding into her ears were filled with terror.

What kind of hell was her father putting her through now? What could cause the pain she heard coming from the woman's soul?

Greta put down the book she had been reading and tip-toed toward the hallway to the kitchen. She tried to listen to the words between the cries, but the big old house turned the sounds into an echoing wail, the words drowned out. How Greta wished she could help Mina, to show her she cared. How she wished she could run to her and comfort her, as she had wished Min would comfort and accept her, but a fear held Greta back. The mournful sounds from the kitchen struck terror in her as well.

Greta hid around the corner when she saw the door burst open from the kitchen. She barely caught a glimpse of Mina as she raced past her toward Albert's study, but from what Greta saw she decided to follow her slowly.

She continued to cautiously approach the room when the crash reached Greta's ears. The sounds of shattering glass made Greta realize that she had better hesitate no longer and she quickened her pace.

When she reached the study Greta found Mina sitting on the floor, her body shaking as she cried loudly. Her hands, stained with either blood or red wine, pounding the carpet. Across the room near Albert's desk was the shattered frame of one of his pictures from the war, its glass littering the desk and the floor.

"Go away!" she heard Min scream between the sobs. "Get the hell out of here!"

179

Greta leaned down toward the woman, gently placing her hands on Min's shoulders. "Can I help?" she asked. It was more than Min had done for her when she had arrived filled with grief. It was better than the coldness Greta had received from her father's wife, but Greta wanted to make the gesture. It wasn't just a device to win Mina's affection, either. Greta really wanted to help the woman.

"Oh, God," Min whispered. "Oh, God, why are my secrets coming back to haunt me?!"

"All the secrets of our past are coming back to haunt us." Greta heard the voice of her father. He stood at the entrance to the study, a firm, somewhat angry look on his face. He didn't move toward his sobbing wife, he was still angry at her.

"Why won't the past leave us alone?" Min cried.

"You wanted it buried forever, but those dreams are gone," he coldly stated to her as he walked through the debris and picked up the shattered picture.

"I let the past die," Min tearfully said as she wiped her face with her hand.

Greta took a handkerchief from her pocket and gave it to Mina. She knelt down beside Min and tried to comfort her by stroking her hair.

"No wonder you hated this room so much," Albert went on. "Every time you came in here you saw her face and were reminded."

"Yes!" Min cried as she collapsed into Greta's arms. Greta felt the woman's body quiver. She unleashed herself from Greta's grip and shakily rose to her feet.

"Well, Mina!" Albert's voice remained angry. "Look at her face! Look at the face of the girl you murdered!"

He reached his hand toward his wife and clutched her black hair violently. He twisted her tear filled face around until she was forced to stare at the remains of the picture, at the face from so long ago.

"Stop it! Stop it!" Greta screamed as she rose up as well and jerked Albert's hand from his wife's head. "Can't you see you're hurting her?"

"Not as much as she hurt me."

Greta kept pulling Min away from the man, curling the small woman in her arms and shielding her face from Albert's mad stare.

"Whatever she did," she screamed shot back at him. "Whatever it was doesn't deserve this."

"You don't know," he retorted. "You could never understand."

Min suddenly burst from Greta's arms. "No, Albert. You don't understand. You don't understand how desperate I was."

180

"What did you do?" Greta asked calmly. She tried to stay calm, knowing she had to keep the two apart. She moved between the two of them.

"Go on, Mina," he said. "Tell her what you did?"

"No!" Min cried.

"Tell her!"

"Yes," Greta tried to reassure her. "Tell me. I'm sure it's not so bad."

Min looked at the girl and her mournful face turned down toward the floor. She raised her stained and bloody hands to her face. "I murdered my friend." she mumbled.

"The woman I loved."

"It was an accident!"

"I loved her!"

"You still love her, don't you, Albert?"

Greta remained silent as the words she had heard began to sink into her mind. Min had known desperation and fear, Greta realized. Greta knew what that was like. Greta knew what it was like to do something you knew was wrong.

"You don't love me!" Min shouted at Albert.

He didn't answer.

"I needed you. We needed each other."

Again he didn't answer.

"What am I going to do?" she cried as she turned and stumbled toward the doorway.

"I don't know how we can go on," Albert mumbled.

Greta felt herself growing angry. She turned toward her father, her eyes piercing his face. "How can you say that? It all must have happened a long time ago. You can't just turn away from her now. You can't! If she needed you then, she certainly needs you now!"

"You don't understand," he said as he waved his hand dejectedly toward Greta.

"I think I do."

Suddenly they both heard the door slam and Greta turned back toward the doorway.

Mina was gone.

"Where can she be going?" Greta pleaded with Albert. "Go after her."

The man just shook his head.

"Fuck you! You inconsiderate bastard!" she shouted as she raised her hand toward Albert's face.

181

He saw her just in time and raised his hand to grasp her hand before it struck him. The cold and angry expression on his face mellowed quickly and he released Greta's hand.

"Go find her," he whispered.

Greta was out of the house in a second, her hair blowing in the stiff, cold wind. She felt the chilled night air and shivered. She saw the shadows of the woods reflecting the dim starlight and saw Min's figure running away from the house down the long driveway.

Greta thought about going inside for her coat, but decided to press on. Any delay and she would lose the frantic Mina in the darkness.

As she raced after her she called to Mina, but the woman didn't stop or turn back. At the bottom of the driveway she disappeared into the darkness of the road.

Greta rushed down the drive, her panting breath leaving clouds of vapor behind her. At the bottom of the hill she turned the corner onto the road and saw Min again, this time lighted by the headlamps of a car.

The car, a large Mercedes, had stopped inches away from the woman and Mina stood paralyzed next to it. Greta also was paralyzed and unable to move. She felt as if something strange was going to happen.

The driver got out of the Mercedes and walked around to Min. In the luminous glow of the headlamps, their faces surrounded by chilled clouds of breath, they began to talk, too softly for Greta to hear above the sounds of the engine.

Then the man grabbed Mina's arm and dragged her toward the side of the car. Though she struggled, Mina was easily pushed by the big man into the car.

In shock, Greta still could not move.

As the driver returned to his side of the car Greta could tell what he was. He wore a black uniform with silver piping. He wore the red armband with a black swastika in a white circle. SS!

"Mina!" Greta finally yelled, but it was too late. The car had started to move and had circled, turning away from the house at high speed.

* * * *

Mina had no energy left. She felt numb and lifeless; the stress of the evening's events had drained her of everything. In her depressed state

182

she didn't care what the Nazis wanted with her. She just didn't care about anything anymore.

As the darkened car sped through the night, Mina felt a sickness come from her stomach. The twisting and turning of the Mercedes on the country roads made her dizzy, queasy and each jolt from the bumps in the road made her head ache and pound. She felt tired and sick, her defeated mind ready to accept any fate the Nazis had in mind.

She could see the dark outlines of the trees passing by through the windows, lighted against the stars from where she had landed when the Nazi shoved her in the car. She had fallen against the back seat, her face against the soft cloth, and she hadn't tried to move. She couldn't will herself to move. She just watched the scenery pass and she watched the unmoving figure of the man beside her, his face cast in shadow as if he were the figure of death. Once, then once again, a glimmer of light entered the car and briefly lit his face, but the slim, silent figure remained clouded by the darkness.

"That's far enough, driver," the figure announced after several minutes. There was something hauntingly familiar about the voice, but Min could not place it.

The car quickly slowed and pulled over to the side of the road. As it stopped Min could hear the rustling of branches against the door and the powerful roar of the engine as it idled.

"Go for a walk," the man in the shadows ordered.

The driver quickly opened the door, got out and disappeared into the night, his footsteps growing softer and fainter as he went.

Mina finally summoned the strength to straighten her body to sit in the seat in a manner where she could better see the man beside her. He neither spoke, nor tried to help her as she struggled to right herself, but she felt sure he was watching.

"What do you want from me?" Min reached down to the bottom of her soul to ask.

The darkened figure was silent.

"What do you want?" she repeated as she reached over to touch the man's sleeve. She felt emptiness and drew away fearfully.

"I want you to see me," the figure said, again hauntingly familiar. "I want you to know your enemy."

Min felt the pain swelling in her heart again and forced herself to hold back the tears. "Why?" she sobbed, unable to control her feelings. "Why am I your enemy? What have I ever done to you?"

183

The man reached up for a switch above his head, his remaining arm turning it and blinking on a dim light. In the yellow light his face looked more like death. He was ungodly thin and his face was covered with scars. He wore a black patch over one eye, but the other was a piercing blue. It was a strained and contorted face, but there was something else there, something Mina remembered.

"Willi!" she gasped.

A sick smile curled up on the Nazis mouth, a grin filled with hate and vengeance. Mina shunned away from the face and the crippled body of the man and tried to get out of the car. The door wouldn't open.

"There's no escape, Min," he stated coldly. "These cars are designed to keep people in, where necessary, not to let people out."

"Oh, God!" she cried.

"I'm no ghost, Mina," the twisted face continued. "I'm real, as real as you. Quite a surprise isn't it?"

Min felt totally sick. *It couldn't be! It couldn't be!* Willi Reinhart, the man she loved so much so long ago, had died in 1918, her mind told her. He had died leaving her alone and desperate in the closing days of the war. He was gone, leaving her unprotected, leaving her so desperate. Yet there he was sitting beside her! His voice! His one remaining blue eye!

"I'm not all of Willi," the one-eyed, one-armed Nazi went on. "But I am him."

"No!" she cried. "My Willi's dead."

"No, my dear," he corrected her. "I was shot down in October 1918, but I didn't die in then. I nearly died, but, as you can see, I am alive."

"How can this be happening?" Min cried, but her mind telling her not to believe, but hearing his words never the less.

The Nazi went on. "I was barely breathing when the English found me. Their doctors patched up what was left of me, but it took many months before I could walk again or return to you. It was the summer of the following year before I came back to Bremen."

"Why didn't you come to me? Why didn't you tell me?"

The grin returned to the Nazis face. "I did come back for you, Mina. I came back as soon as I could, but it wasn't soon enough. I came back to Bremen and searched for you and found you married to another man."

Mina gulped down a breath of air. By the end of 1918 she had married Albert. He'd have not known why. He'd have not known how desperate she was.

"I remember that day," he bitterly went on. "I had found Albert's name in the directory. I was overjoyed! He would help me find you. I had gone to your house, but it was locked up. Yet I was sure Albert knew where you had gone.

"So I went to the riverfront and found his shop and who should come walking out but you. Mina Adler....Frau Freyberg...with a baby in her arms. There you were, arm in arm with my friend...as his wife."

"You should have come to us," Min tried to make him understand. "We would have explained."

"Explain what!" he bellowed. "I stayed around those streets. I asked the neighbors! They told me everything I needed to know."

"Please, Willi!" Min cried. "Let me explain."

"You couldn't wait. You couldn't wait to hop into bed with him. Couldn't wait to tear him away from his woman and screw the hell out of him," he continued.

"No!"

"I may have lost an eye, but I am not blind," he sneered. "I may have lost an arm, but my mind still can reason. You didn't even mourn for me."

"Oh, yes I did! Yes!"

The Nazi reached over and clutched Min's trembling hand, squeezing it tight until it ached. "I waited for this day for so long, Mina. I thought it over in my mind again and again. I want to make you hurt, Mina! I want you to suffer like I've suffered. I want you both to suffer."

"Is this why you're trying to destroy us?"

"Yes."

"But I loved you. I loved you so much. Albert loved you like a brother," she sobbed.

"Apparently not enough," he snapped as he released her hand. "But what does it matter now. We would have gotten around to you Jews sooner or later."

"And what if I am a Jew?" Min shot back. "You know us! You know who we are and that my mother's religion doesn't matter to me."

"What does it matter? It serves me to make it true. It serves me as a way of revenge." he said, emphasizing the last word strongly.

"How can you do this, Willi? How can you be one of those vile people?"

"We aren't so terrible," he explained adamantly. "After i discovered your treachery I returned to Dresden and tried to rebuild a life. It was hell. There was little calling for a crippled airman. Only the gutter was

SECRETS OF THE PAST

left for me until the Nazi party came along. They offered me hope. They gave me a chance to rebuild my life. Rebuild Germany! A Germany without people like you and Albert Freyberg. People who prey upon the innocents and upon the veterans!"

Min saw the rage in Willi's eye. She saw a man she could never know, could never have known and loved. She saw nothing but hate and vengeance. "Please, Willi!" she pleaded. "Albert fought beside you in the war. He saved your life!"

"And, I his."

"Please, leave us alone."

"Never!"

"If there's anything left of the Willi I knew...the Willi I loved, please leave us live in peace."

"That man is dead, Mina."

She realized he was right. The Willi she loved was dead. The Willi she mourned, the Willi that drove her to those desperate acts, was dead. What was left was his shell, encasing a monster who knew nothing of love, of what they once shared.

Min couldn't fight him anymore. She just stared at his face, a face she didn't know, with anger she could never understand. She had nothing left to say to him.

The Nazi reached up with his one arm and flicked out the lamp. A moment later the driver had returned.

"Take this woman home," the voice echoed through the car.

186

TWENTY-FIVE

The rush of warm air felt like pine needles against her skin as Min entered her home. It stung her face wildly, driving away the numbness of the cold quickly. She felt her whole body begin to warm, but her soul still felt a stinging pain. It was a pain that she knew would take a long time to go away.

As she turned and pressed the door tightly shut she bolted the latch, locking out the cold winter's air and, she realized, locking out the past. She had to turn to the future, whatever it held. She couldn't depend on the past, its memories, anymore. The beast she had left in that car had convinced her of that.

She leaned against the door and tried to sort out what was happening in her mind. Because Willi had been killed in 1918, she had killed, but Willi was alive. Yet the Willi she remembered was dead, his body being used by a madman who thought only revenge. She had lied and hidden her sin from Albert, had lived in fear that he would discover the truth, yet now that he had, she didn't know what he would do. Would all that she had done to win and keep his love for so long amount to nothing with only the lies remaining?

Was she as alone tonight as she had been on that morning when she struggled with Francoise over her father's gun and pulled the trigger? Was Albert, in his disgust, in his renewed grief, going to turn her out, abandon her as she had thought Willi had done? Who was she to turn to now?

"Min, are you alright?" she heard Greta's voice softly whisper to her. She felt the touch of the girl's hands on her shoulders. There was gentleness in Albert's daughter's touch, as if she genuinely cared.

She turned away from the door and stumbled aimlessly up the hall. The girl's hands dropped away from her shoulders, but one reached out and grasped Min's hand.

"Where did the Nazis take you?" Greta asked anxiously. "What did they want?"

187

Min ignored the questions. "Where's Albert?" she asked instead.
"In the kitchen," Greta answered.
"And the children?"
"I think they went back to bed."
"Good."

Mina began to walk toward the kitchen door at the end of the hallway, a sliver of light at the bottom of the door lighting her path. She knew she had to face Albert now and fight to regain his love, his protection.

Greta's hand refused to let go as Min walked. "Do you need to talk to me?" the girl asked. "Is there anything I can do?"

"No, I must do this alone," Min said as she shook off Greta's grip.

"I'm here for you, if you need me."

"Thank you, but I must face him alone."

"If there's anything I can do....I think I know how you feel."

Min stopped and turned to face the girl. On her young face, seemingly unspoiled by the hard life she had faced on the riverfront, Min saw compassion. Min saw that Greta truly wanted to help her.

"I doubt you could ever know how I feel," Min answered. "But thank you, Greta. Thank you for understanding. I'll never forget this."

A moment later Min entered the kitchen, the bright glare of the lights blinding her. In a second her sight returned to normal and she saw Albert as he sat at the table with his head down, one hand clutching a half filled glass and the other holding a nearly empty bottle of cheap wine. He didn't bother to look up at her.

"I refuse to get into another shouting match," he slurred. "I refuse to argue anymore."

"There's nothing left to argue about," she told him.

"Yes. What's done is done."

"And what we must face, we must face together."

He laughed a short drunken laugh. "Face together. For better or worse...isn't that what they say."

"And this is our worse."

"Ha!" he choked. He looked up to stare at Min, his eyes reddened and cheeks puffy from the wine. "I've been sitting here asking myself if there was ever a better. Wasn't it always the worst? Mina, weren't we, both of us, just a little afraid to love each other?"

"Afraid?" she questioned.

"Yes, my dear," his voice quaked. "Both of us so hurt by the past...so afraid to give ourselves wholeheartedly to each other just in case we lose that love. We were so damned afraid of losing each other that we couldn't find the time to really love each other."

Min listened to his words and found the ring of truth in them. It may have been those thoughts of the love she had lost that kept her from being closer to him. It may have been the same for him. Maybe it wasn't that he always loved Francoise, but that he couldn't bear losing Min in the same way.

"Care to join me?" he asked, a silly smile crossing his drunken face as he raised the wine bottle.

Min snatched the bottle away from his shaking hands and brought it to her lips. She swallowed the rest of the wine down quickly. Let it do its work fast, she begged to herself. Let it numb the mind.

"Now look at us," his drunken voice loudly wailed. "We have a future we can't face and a past that gives us no comfort. The nightmare...isn't that what you call it...goes on and on, never-ending! With each day it grows worse."

"You don't know how right you are," she mumbled. Dare she tell him who their sworn enemy was? Dare she crumble one other sweet dream of Albert's past? She couldn't take away his memories of Willi, his best friend and companion, though her memories of him had been shattered forever. No! No, she decided. She had hurt him enough for one night.

"And now what?" his voice tailed off to a murmur, "Now what?"

"You tell me," Min said as she sat in the chair across from him. She looked deeply into his bloodshot eyes, searching for the Albert she remembered. Somewhere beneath the grief there still remained the kind, dedicated man she had grown to love.

He ran his trembling hand through his full head of gray hair, shaking his head despairingly. "I don't know. I just don't know."

"Oh, please, Albert," Min pleaded in a slow, steady voice. "Don't give up on me now. Don't just give up."

"What's left to do? What's left for us to say to each other? It's all been a lie. A joke!" he moaned.

"Some of it was a lie, my darling," she said as she reached out and grabbed his hand. "Somehow I think we both meant more to each other than a big lie. Upstairs...asleep! They say we mean more to each other. Willi! The girls!"

He nodded.

"Let's stop wallowing in the past, Albert." Min continued as she rubbed his cold hand with hers, warming it like the wine had failed to do.

"There are other lives to think of besides our own. Both of us may consider our lives shattered, our dreams shattered, but there are other's in this house that have futures. Together we have to think of the children."

"Together?" he looked back at her curiously. "Can we ever accept being together again as husband and wife?"

"We must," she demanded. "For their sake, we must."

Albert's eyes grew wide, awakening to the realization of his children's fate. "Yes, Mina, you're right. We have to think of them."

"Albert. Let's get away from here. Let's get out of this sick country before it destroys everything we hold dear."

* * * *

Steven Langley could see that Albert was very troubled. He could see deep lines on his face, valleys that surrounded his mouth and brow. He could see dark shadows around the man's eyes. He could see a terrible fear in his friend's brown eyes. Steven had seen men look like that before...in 1929, during the worst aftermath of the crash.

Albert's voice couldn't betray the look Steven saw in the man's eyes. The voice struggled to be cheerful and calm, struggled not to give away to the fear one could sense in his face, in the sunken eyes. Yet Steven felt the fear in the voice, no matter how much Albert tried to deny it.

"Even this place has changed." Albert was saying as he spit out a morsel of food. "The food is even worse than what it was before they took over."

Steven could see the rapid changes in Germany even beyond the mediocre food now being served in what once was a fine restaurant. He was startled by it from the moment the train from Brussels had crossed the border. He saw change in the faces of the uniformed Nazis that paraded proudly on every street. He saw changes in the many banners that flew over each town, their bright red colors glistening around the Nazi swastika. The changes meant pictures of Adolf Hitler adorned every shop window.

Steven also felt the change in the people. He felt arrogance in every voice, hatred in every stare...or fear, as in the face that now sat across from him.

"I was glad you telegraphed me, Albert," Steven explained as he swallowed a gritty piece of meat. Albert was right, the food was nearly inedible.

Albert scanned the room before speaking, searching the crowd for the now familiar red, white and black armbands. There were too many about for Albert to speak freely, so he drew closer to Steven and whispered the words.

"You once said you would help," he softly said. "I hope you're true to those words."

"I meant it," Steven insisted. "Anything."

"You know what I have to do."

"How quickly?" Steven whispered back.

"As soon as possible. The hounds are close on my heels."

"But what can they do to you?" Steven asked.

Albert shook his head. "They've hypnotized the people, these Nazis. They've convinced even the best of men that they are right and their cause is just. Those they've failed to turn their way they have frightened into submission."

"But what have you done?"

"It's nothing I've done," Albert insisted. "There are skeletons in everyone's closet, including my wife's. I'm just thankful that there are still some decent people left in this country or else we'd be behind bars already."

"Min," Steven was startled. "That's ridiculous. What could they have on her?"

"Don't ask, my friend," Albert insisted. "Just have faith that it's enough to bury us if placed in the wrong hands."

"Okay!" Steven nearly shouted. Feeling somewhat embarrassed, returned his voice to nearly a whisper. "What's the plan?"

Albert looked around the mirrored restaurant again. He seemed wary of every face, every glance his way. He even looked suspicious of the maitre de' and the waiter, who had acted very pleased when they had arrived.

"I've no plan. I was hoping you did, Steven."

Steven thought a minute. He had offered his help to Albert and his family in any way, expecting that Albert, Min and their children would simply board a train and leave, with Steven helping to clean up financial matters while the Freybergs beat a hasty retreat. From what he now saw and heard from Albert, Steven guessed it wouldn't be so easy.

191

"I've got to sneak out of my own country with my tail tucked between my legs and I haven't got the any idea how the hell to go about it!" Albert almost growled.

Steven thought again. "Well, I do have some connections with the American embassy in the Netherlands. Maybe they could help. And I've established a small office in The Hague. My people there would make themselves available if I asked."

"Good, that's a start," Albert sighed. Steven could see the man's mind beginning to work again. "There were many routes used by people fleeing the revolution to Holland at the end of the war. Some of those paths were well marked. Maybe we could cross out of Germany there, if the Nazis haven't closed them all."

"Albert, they haven't exactly turned the country into a prison. Why don't we try buying your way out?"

"It's bad enough that I'm going to have to sell off the bank and most of our holdings before we leave, at a great loss I'm sure. To try bribing the Nazis..." he shook his head dejectedly. "I'll leave this country penniless."

"Fine, then! Have it your way," Steven relented. "But how do we choose the right spot? Where do we go until we're ready to sneak over?"

"What's this 'we'?"

"You'll need all the help you can get. I'm in this all the way."

"If we're caught, Steven, they'll drag you down with me....American or not."

"You can't change my mind."

"Enough!" Albert firmly insisted. "That can be discussed later."

"The problem remains...we'll need help near the Dutch border."

Albert thought a moment. "I have an old friend, an old comrade, who owns a farm up near the border. He owes me a favor. I'm sure he'll help and I can trust him."

"Then contact him."

Albert glanced around again, his suspicious eyes still scanning every face. "I can't. My every movement is being watched."

"Then let me get in touch with him."

Albert scribbled some words on a scrap of paper. "His name is Helmut Schorner. He's a good man, very handy in a pinch. Helmut knows how to get things done. His skills can work to our advantage. Maybe this will work."

"I'm sure it will. Don't worry. We'll get you and your family out." Steven said as he stuffed the piece of paper into his pocket.

192

SECRETS OF THE PAST

"There is one other thing I think you should know, Steven," Albert added, his voice cloaked with fear.

"What's that?"

"I'm going to be carrying out some papers, very important papers. They would like nothing better than to catch me with them, but I owe it to a friend." Albert explained.

"What kind of papers?"

"I guess you could say they are state documents. Some of it is unbelievable; other parts are much easier to believe. If I'm going to run away, I may as well take something of importance with me."

"Why?" Steven asked. "Why endanger your family for some lousy secrets."

"If I do make it out I want the world to know what they can expect from these people, Steven. The rest of the world, wrapped up in their own troubles, looks upon Germany as a land of fools. They view the strutting Nazis as clowns that don't threaten them. These papers prove otherwise."

"Hitler and his people bark so loudly everyone ignores them. Why should some papers change that?"

"The day will come when they will have to listen. They're training flyers in Russia. They're experimenting with tanks in Russia. They've got plans to rebuild the navy....the U-boats. The military is filled with schemes to get around the treaty, to rebuild them." Albert voice trembled as he rambled on about what he read, almost in fear.

"But this couldn't have come about so quickly? In just two months?" Steven argued.

"They're the plans of rational Germans who dream of a country like the Kaisers Germany. The thoughts of these men combined with the lunacy of the Nazis...it's beyond my..." his voice tailed off as he tried to catch his breath. "If the wild theories brought forth in these papers come to pass, Germany will become a terrible weapon."

"Then take them with you, but be quiet about it. The Nazis don't seem very reluctant to destroy their enemies quickly, I'd say." Steven said.

"We'll have to take this thing slow, Steven," Albert explained on. "Get the right people involved in the sales. People I trust to keep their mouths shut until we're gone. We'll have to act so as not to raise suspicions."

"Okay, friend," Steven switched into English. "You're the boss."

193

"Hum," Albert studied his friend's face, and then spoke in his own halting English. "Until I come to ask you for a job, at least."

TWENTY-SIX

Greta sat alone in the parlor thinking, watching the late winter winds that had come down from the north, blowing across the woods and whistling through the windows. As she stared out at the swaying trees she felt within her a serenity she had never experienced. Inside her soul there was inner peace, despite the turmoil that surrounded her life and the lives of those who touched her.

Yes, she thought to herself, the tiny voice inside her purring. *It's much better now. I've been accepted.*

The strangeness of the house and of the people who lived there had worn off. The feeling of being an intruder into their world had gone, replaced by the feeling of being wanted, needed. She and her brother had become a part of the family, but it was a family torn by the stresses placed upon it by the outside world. It was a family coming apart at the seams.

How curious, she thought to herself, that the moment she finally found her place in life, the place she rightfully belonged, should the fabric of that life be torn apart.

Greta was happy that she could experience that life, even though it may end tomorrow, even though she realized that she must take life as it presents itself. One day you're a whore walking the streets, the next you're a fairy tale princess living in a palace. And tomorrow....who knows.

The tension in the Freyberg household had been thick these past few days, hanging in the air like an impending thunderstorm. It crackled its lightning in every word that Greta's father and his wife spoke. It thundered with the harsh words spoken on the radio, with the headlines in the papers. It hadn't exploded in it's fury since that long, terrible night two weeks before, but even the angry words of that night still hung in the air foretelling of the next storm.

Yet life also went on in the Freyberg house. The children, with Gery now firmly part of their band, would trudge off to school each day.

195

Albert routinely went off to the bank each morning and returned late each night as if it were business as usual. Min and the servants moved about their chores in the house as if all were normal, but Mina seemed as if she were in a daze these days, lingering too long to stare at a cherished memento or a faded picture, her mind lost in thought. Albert and Min barely spoke to each other, Greta noticed, but they tried to put up a good front for the children and for the servants. Greta knew that things were changing in their lives too quickly for them to handle and both of them were constantly plotting for a way out, but Greta, though an adult herself, was not in on their plans.

Her mind began to turn to what her own plans should be when she heard the now familiar creak of footsteps coming into the parlor.

"Are you sitting here all alone?" Albert's voice echoed though the room.

She silently nodded, continuing to stare at the rustling trees as they shook with each gust of wind, the naked branches nodding and bending like the baton of a conductor.

Albert sat beside her on the sofa and looked out to see what his daughter was viewing. "It's quite an impressive view, isn't it, Greta." he said after a moment.

"Yes, it is beautiful."

"You should see it in the fall, when the trees are covered with gold and rust. It's like a painting, bright and exciting."

"I can imagine."

He sighed deeply. "It's a shame we won't see another autumn in this house."

Greta turned to his face. He was sad, his eyes fading away into memories of a better time. Greta realized that the years really hadn't been good to her father. His hair was fully grey even though he was only in his early forties. His face was etched with lines, which seemed to grow with each passing day. Greta even noticed that he had begun to limp, it too growing more pronounced as the days went by and the pressures grew greater. Greta had seen pictures of him in his younger days and saw a different man with deep, expressive brown eyes and a determined, forceful face.

"You look surprised," he said as he noticed her stare.

"A little," she began to explain. "First of all, I didn't expect you home so soon. Now you sound as if you've given up."

He shrugged. "I needed to get away from the bank. There's so little I can do down there. My job is almost done."

196

"Then you have given up."

Suddenly there was a look of determination on his face. "Me! I'll never give up. I've just set my priorities on different things. I've put the bank in order and ready for sale. I've put my life together and made plans for our future."

She nodded, thankful that he had included her, but her mind was troubled by the plans another had for her.

He noticed her expression change as her mind remembered those words. "What's wrong?"

Greta cringed back from her father, shying away because she didn't want to breech the subject. "Albert," she began and then stopped. *Damn! Why can't I call him Papa*, she thought to herself.

When Albert realized that she was going to be silent he began to speak. "Hum, I take it you don't want to leave either."

"No, it's not that."

"Don't tell me that you're worried about how I feel about you?"

She shook her head, but it wasn't convincing even though it wasn't what she was really worried about.

"Listen, Greta, I think it's time I fully explained myself to you," he began as he reached out and took her hand. "I know that I should have done this earlier, but so much has happened since you arrived. I guess you've been wondering what I really think."

Greta opened her mouth to speak, but no words came out.

"When I was younger than you," Albert went on, "I met your mother. We were happy during the time we were married and to this day I feel that, if she had lived, we would still be happy. Then, before the war, I worked on the docks, but I saved my money and brought a bake shop down in the neighborhood. Our needs, my plans were simple. Own a shop, raise a family, live a quiet life. Then that damned fire wiped it all away.

"I didn't want to give you up after your mother died, but I didn't know what to do. I was unable to care for you then, unable to provide a home and to raise you as a mother would. When Paula and Max suggested that I give you to them I, at first, turned them down. There was no way I was giving up my little girl. You were all I had.

"But it became so hard to live. It became, with my working all day and sometimes all night, like you weren't mine anymore anyway. We were living in their house and Paula was taking care of you. I was simply a visitor."

He reached out with his hand, and turned her face toward his. "Greta, giving you up was the hardest thing I've ever had to do. I did it for you."

"I know," she cried. She could see he was close to tears himself.

"Giving you up......" he went on, the words coming slowly. "I still, to this day, don't know if I had done the right thing, but I promised never to interfere. I promised that I would forget that I ever had a daughter, but thoughts about you...memories...never left my mind.

"I kept my promise until your mother came to me, and, believe me, I never want to replace the people you call your parents even though they weren't. When she pleaded with me to help I came back into your life. I only hope that I've made the right decision."

"It's not wrong. I appreciate all you've done."

Albert looked away and stared at the trees as they glistened with the rays of the setting sun. "It's wrong if I've brought you here to be dragged down with me. You could've had a more normal life, one not battling the Nazis, if I would have let you alone. Now you're locked with us and I hope you're not sorry."

"I'm not sorry....Father," Greta choked out the words. She had said it, finally said it! "I'm just glad I could make you happy."

"You don't know how happy it makes me to have you back, especially now. Now you can come with us."

"That's what bothers me," Greta began to explain. "I don't know what I really want."

He looked at her strangely, searching her eyes for an explanation.

"It's Martin," she began to explain. "And it's me, too. I feel like the whole world is crumbling around me and I guess I'm looking for a way out. You've offered one, but Martin's offered another."

"And what's that?"

"He wants me to leave this house and come live with him. He says that we can live without fear...the Nazis, he says, are after you, not me. Not us! If I go and live with him I'll be away from here, away from anything they might do to you."

Albert ran his fingers through his hair, thinking deeply about what she had said, but not replying.

"I don't know what to do. I love him, but he's wrong to expect me to just walk away. I love him, but I can't turn my back on you....on the people in this house who've I've grown to love."

Albert squeezed her hand. "And you won't, Greta. Martin is only thinking of you, and himself, I'm afraid. He has good intentions for he loves you, too. There are other ways to keep you safe and still keep your links to us...and to him."

"What are they?"

"I'll talk to him," Albert smiled. "I'll take care of it."

Albert then bent over and kissed her forehead. She could feel that he cared with his kiss. She could see in his face that he was happy that they had talked, that she had bared her feelings and that he had finally shared his. He would take care of it, she knew.

Greta turned and looked out at the darkness. The sun, now fully set, had shed its last light on the trees. They were invisible now, only the sounds of the wind were left as it whistled around the house. The dark shadows of the swaying trees blended with the darkness and became as one.

Greta, too, became as one with her father and his family.

TWENTY-SEVEN

Steven stared at the map spread across the desk with an unwanted familiarity. He had seen maps of Germany before and knew the terrain well, but he never expected he'd have the need to know it that well.

Now he had to memorize it. He had to remember each road, each town between Bremen and the Dutch border. He had to know each village by sight, each sign post as if it were a warning of what was ahead. It had become an unwanted chore as he and Albert would go over it again and again, struggling to insure that every unpredictable eventuality have an instant solution.

"And don't forget," Albert continued to explain for what seemed like the millionth time. "Helmut's farm must be reached in darkness, after we have led anyone following us off the track. Up this road here," he went on as he pointed. "Then past the village."

Steven nodded. He knew the way very well. He knew it in his sleep. He began to think of sleep, his eyes loosing their focus on the map, his mind drifting off.

"Steven, are you listening to me?"

"Yes, I am," Steven answered as he shook himself back to reality. "Do we have to go over this again?"

Albert stared at him coldly, the harsh glare of the lamp on the desk shining cruelly on his face.

"You know you'll be there to guide the way," Steven explained.

"I want you certain you can go on without me. If they come and get me, you must get my family out."

"I know, I know"

Albert shrugged his shoulders as he walked over to the table and poured himself a drink. "Maybe it's time we quit for the night." he said as he finally realized how late it was. "We both could use a good night's sleep."

Steven could only agree and helped Albert secure the maps in the desk. Both were silent as they prepared to leave, only the sounds of their footsteps echoed in their ears.

The bank was deathly quiet as they walked toward the door. Their shoes against the marble floor seemed to grow louder with each step. Their shadows were long and ghost-like in the large hall, the light barely visible from the nightlights in the ceiling. To Steven, it was like a scene from an old Gothic novel; a castle with its last two knights heading out into the forest to hunt dragons.

At the door they stopped, both of them aware that something was wrong.

"Where's the night-watchman?" Albert questioned.

"I could have sworn he was here earlier."

"Damn! Where could he have gone?"

Their ears picked up footsteps against the marble floor. It was the sound of boots...military boots, Steven guessed. He also began to make out a long, thin shadow moving toward them. It looked strange and black, even in the darkness.

"Who's there?" Albert asked firmly, his deep voice grew even deeper as he continued. "I'm the manager of the bank. Who are you?"

"I've come to talk to you," a voice called back to them. The sound was shrill, crisp....threatening.

"Who are you?"

"I'll speak to you alone, Herr Freyberg," it demanded.

"This is an associate of mine. What you say to me, you can say to him," Albert insisted. It seemed to Steven that Albert had lived this before. His friend remained calm, almost as if he knew that he was in no danger.

The figure stepped out of the shadow and into a cloudy ray of light that shined down from the ceiling. The man wore the uniform of the SS, Hitler's elite party forces. The man was gaunt and frail, but stood with the bearing of a soldier. His scarred face had a black patch over one eye and he was missing his left arm.

Albert looked at the man curiously and began to walk toward him, his eyes straining as they looked at the contorted, scarred face. "Who are you?" he asked, his voice cracking.

"You don't know?" the Nazi asked back. "Your wife," he emphasized the word strangely, "hasn't told you?"

Albert silently shook his face.

"You really don't know do you?" the Nazi said again.

"I take it you've come to tell us something important?" Steven interjected, trying to pick up the words Albert should have said, but the man remained silent and looked bewildered.

"I'm not talking to you!" the Nazi shouted. "I'm talking to him!"

Albert took another step closer to the Nazi so that now he was almost nose to nose with him. "Where.....why do I think I know you."

"Because you do, Albert."

"No....can't be. Yet that voice has something about it...and the face...in better times."

"Think harder, further back into your past," the Nazi insisted as he too stared at Albert.

Albert quickly turned away. "No! It's impossible!"

The Nazis mouth turned up in a slight smile. It was a mean, vengeful smile.

Albert glanced back at the man. "You're dead. You have to be dead."

"Now, Albert," the Nazi cynically grinned. "Do I look dead?"

"You're one of them!"

"Worse than that, my old friend," he went on, again stressing the words strangely. "I'm the one who is so determined to destroy you."

Steven burst between the two men. He pushed Albert away from the Nazi. "Look here, whoever you are! Can't you see you're tormenting him?"

"As I have also been tormented all these years!" the Nazi shouted, waving his hand angrily in the air.

"Not by him!" Steven shouted.

"Stay out of this, or I'll have you arrested!"

"I'm an American."

"I don't care what you are! Mind your own business!"

"He's my friend. He is my business."

"Then I hope he's a better friend to you than he was to me."

Albert seemed to stagger backwards as he heard Steven and the Nazi argue. He leaned against a railing and began to whisper. "Willi, no.....not you...against me."

"Perhaps," the Nazi went on to explain. "I should clarify things for your American friend.

"You see, Albert and I go a long way back. We were comrades in the war. We fought side by side against Germany's enemies then. We were close friends who, more than once, saved each other's lives. We lived as brothers; we cried together; we laughed together.

202

"During that time, when both of us were so different from each other, yet so alike, Albert was in love with a French nurse....Francoise was her name. They truly cared for each other. They were, I assumed, to be married when the war was over. It was all we talked about."

"That was a long time ago," Albert mumbled.

The Nazi glared at Albert and continued. "I, too, was in love. She was a lovely thing; tiny, gentle, giving, and she loved me as much as I did her despite our different heritage and backgrounds. She was more than I had ever wanted or expected in life and I, like Albert, expected to come back from the war and marry her.

"But that was not to be! Was it, Albert?" the Nazi asked.

"We thought you were dead."

"How did you know? How could you know?"

Steven joined back into the conversation. "What does it have to do with what's happening today?"

The Nazi now stared at Steven, his one blue eye penetrating through Steven's body. "If you consider yourself Albert's friend you should know of the woman I once loved. She was called Mina Adler then."

"We thought you were dead."

"You didn't even think to be sure. You couldn't wait do take her from me. You couldn't wait to put Francoise aside and marry Mina. You as good as stole her from me!" The Nazi shouted, his face red with anger, his veins rising up on his neck and face.

Albert stood erect, some of the old life coming back into his words. "The war was over. She needed me and I her. We turned to each other and grew to love each other."

"And forgot about Willi Reinhart and Francoise!"

"Francoise was dead!" Albert now shouted.

"But I was not!"

"And that has nothing to do with what you're doing to both of them now," Steven stated.

Albert walked over to the Nazi, fire returned to his eyes, and reached out to take the man's arm. "That's right! What's done is done. Neither of us can go back to 1918 and start all over again. Why hold against us something that happened so long ago?"

The Nazi tore his arm away from Albert's grip. "Because I came back. I was crippled and in pain to find her and found you with her. Because I felt my life, my plans, our future ruined by you and by her treachery. I had nothing to live for."

"Yet you seem to have lived."

"Yes, Albert! Yes!" the Nazi growled. "I lived because I came to realize that you and your Jewish wife tricked me. You made me weak with your defeatist thoughts and, just as you stabbed the country in the back, you stabbed me in the back.

"National Socialism made me see what you and she had done to me was part of the plan to cripple Germany. I've found faith in those teachings. I've found faith in my determination to make this country strong again so people like you and the Jews can't ever tear it down again. I grew strong with the hate you gave me! I grew strong enough to destroy you as you once tried to destroy me."

"You're insane," Albert looked at him disgustedly.

"No, Albert! I'm saner now than I've ever been."

Albert shook his head. "There was no trick on our part. There was no treachery. You've taken the hate you feel in your heart because of what Min, what she and I did to you and corrupted it to include all Jews and even those like Min and I who are more German than Jewish. You can't relate personal grief to that of a nation."

"The nation is made up of people. The real Germans have been hurt by people like you." the Nazi insisted.

"These people are no threat," Steven rejoined the argument. "Except in your mind."

"We decide who is a threat and who is not!"

"Then why all the talk?" Steven went on. "Why present yourself this way? Why not just take them out, line them against a wall and shoot them?"

The Nazi sneered. "Because it wouldn't be cruel enough and because I don't want him...or her held up by people to be martyrs."

"So the campaign to discredit us," Albert said. "To ruin our business and drive us away."

"You'll never get away. First we'll discredit you and then I'll take care of you."

Albert took a deep breath, "And to think, if not for me you would be dead."

"And if not for me, so would you," the Nazi replied.

"I would've thought those times, those things we did for each other...what we once meant to each other, would account for something?" Albert went on. "Willi, if you have any feelings...any at all....because we were once friends, because of what Min once meant to you, I beg you to stop and let us be."

The Nazi shook his head. "Never, the day is coming soon when you'll come begging to me for your lives...both of you. That's a day I'm waiting for; my revenge!"

The Nazi smiled a vengeful smile at Albert and Steven. He quickly turned and faded into the darkness, the sound of his boots growing fainter as his shadow disappeared out the door and into the night.

"There goes the best friend I ever had," Albert whispered to Steven.

"And your worst enemy."

"Yes, but he's sick. It's a sickness that has grown to consume him," Albert explained. "If you knew him then, before the war, and his wounds, and his broken heart....if you had known him then you would have loved him as I did. Until tonight I had always thought of him as a brother."

"Is all he said about Min and you true?" Steven asked.

"Yes, and more."

"Then we'd better hurry along our plans before that madman destroys you."

"If Mina knows he's alive, which I suspect she does, then he has already succeeded in destroying us."

* * * *

Mina was already in bed when she heard her husband arrive home. She lay in a half-sleep, exhausted from the day's chores and the pressure she felt constantly around her. She heard the familiar noises as he came in, hung up his coat and began to climb the stairs.

She glanced over at the clock. In the dim light from the hallway she could barely make out the hands. *Could it really be midnight? Could it be that late?*

He had entered their darkened room now, his form shifting through the grayness, not noticing that she was staring at him, watching his every move as he neatly returned his belongings in their proper place.

Albert had always seemed to lead such an ordered life, she thought. Everything in its place and every emotion well calculated. How much it must hurt him to have his world turn upside-down by this? How much the confusion and uncertainty must hurt? She knew he was hurt by what was happening, by how much she had hurt him. She knew that the only reason they had anything left of their relationship was because of the children. She knew, at least she thought she knew that he didn't care about her anymore.

Not after what he'd learned she'd done.

Mina shut her eyes, choking back a tear as she thought about what had become of their lives. She needed him so much now. She needed him to feel what he had once felt, what she still felt, but she sensed that all those emotions were gone from him toward her. When she was with Albert, when they touched, she felt a coldness that chilled her heart and deadened her soul.

She felt the rustling of covers as he got into bed beside her. She felt herself shiver, his body touching hers and immediately pulling away. *Oh, please, Albert, why can't you love me now, when I need you so much!*

"Why are you still awake?" he asked as he realized she was watching him.

"I was waiting for you."

"You should try to sleep," he told her, his voice cold and detached. "We all need to get more sleep."

"I can't sleep anymore," Min moaned. "Every time I think about sleeping I think that they'll be a knock on the door. I think every sound in the night is them, surrounding us and forcing us into the street."

Albert's body seemed to shudder, his flesh touching her foot and rubbing softly against it. To Min, it felt so good, it was the closest contact he had had with her since the truth had come out. Her heart begged for more.

"I had a late night visitor tonight," he said. His voice seemed tenderer, not as cold and haunting in the darkness. It was like he used to talk to her.

"I don't think I want to know."

"I was thinking about it," he went on as if he hadn't heard a word she said. "I began to wonder what happened to you that night you ran out of the house and were picked up by the Nazis. Who did you meet there?"

Oh, God! Mina dreaded having to tell him. Min couldn't bear thinking about it herself. It made so many things in her life shallow, meaningless.

"Did you see Willi?" Albert's disembodied voice asked.

"Yes," Mina cried softly. She felt the tears swell in her eyes and the salty wetness inched down her cheeks. "Yes, but he a madman now."

"I know."

"Then he was your visitor tonight?"

SECRETS OF THE PAST

"Yes, and he admits he's the one who torments us. In his madness, in his hate for us, he's turned the government against us."

"I know, but what can we do. He's beyond reason."

Albert turned the lamp on and then turned to Mina. He looked at her, the old feelings showing on his face, as Min wiped the trail of tears from her cheeks. He gently reached out his hand to her and held hers warmly. "Why didn't you tell me he was alive? Why didn't you tell me?"

"What could you have done?" she cried. "You couldn't have changed his mind. You couldn't have found any remnant of the old Willi any more than I did. Why should I torment you more by telling you that the man I grieved for so much...so much so that I murdered the woman you loved...is still alive."

"You should have told me. You should have shared this with me," Albert insisted. "I can imagine how much it shocked and hurt you."

"Oh, Albert!" she cried. "If I could have thrown myself at him to stop this madness, I would. He hates you and me so much! He doesn't understand."

"And he never will. The truth will never come out. He must never know everything, especially about Francoise."

"How can we stop him from finding out? The police can't....this detective who confided in you can't keep it a secret forever!"

"That's why we must get out now, quickly, before it's too late. If Willi Reinhart discovers that secret we'll die."

Min reached out for her husband and pulled him toward her. "Oh, Albert, I'm so afraid!"

He wrapped his arms around her and held her tightly as she cried, rocking her as he would a small child. His fingers touched her skin and soothed her fear and her pain. Mina could feel her husband coming back to her.

"Don't worry, Min. I'll protect you," he told her, his voice calm and gentle.

"I need you, Albert," she told him as she turned her tearful face toward his. She looked at his brown eyes, their roundness dominating his face. She felt her lips drawn toward his and they kissed.

"Oh, please!" she pleaded as they parted. "Please say that you still love me."

Albert didn't speak. Instead he joined his lips to hers again and she felt his hands caress her and gently move across her shivering body. Her skin slowly began to warm to his touch as his kisses warmed her mouth and face.

Gently, slowly he pushed her on her back. His hands tenderly reached under her nightgown and slowly moved along her warm body, pushing the nightgown up above her breasts. His hands, still moving and still warming her soul squeezed her small breasts tenderly and Min felt her emotions soar within her.

He did still love her.

She wrapped her hands around his back, feeling each ripple in his scarred body as she remembered from all their time together. His body, which she had hated so much when she first saw the patchwork of reddened scars, she now cherished. She knew every rise, every etching on him and welcomed them back to her touch.

"Oh, Albert!" she cried as she felt a warmth enter her soul. "Oh! It feels so good!"

TWENTY-EIGHT

The waiting was over for both Lucy Wagner and Karl Scheuler. The time for hiding was finished. The time for action had come.

To Lucy, it seemed like an eternity that they had been hiding in fear. It was as if they had been crouching in a cave hoping that the beast outside their door would go away.

That was finished. The waiting was finished. If she and Karl could overcome the fear just a little longer there would no longer be anything to fear.

If all their plans worked out alright, that is.

There were only a few avenues of escape open to them and Karl had pursued them all. To leave Bremen by boat had been totally out of the question. The Nazis scrutinized every passenger list and questioned nearly all the travelers and crew as they boarded anything going out of Bremen and Wilhelmshaven. To attempt the perilous journey by automobile was equally dangerous. The border, though not totally closed or guarded, was constantly patrolled. At the crossing points to the west the border police needed all the papers to be in order and properly signed to let someone pass. Even those not running in fear for their lives were often detained, some simply to see if they would crack as they waited for permission to cross. Both Lucy and Karl realized that they would never get out that way.

The trains were the best idea. The trains heading to Brussels and Paris were overflowing with travelers, far too many for the police and Gestapo to check each one. It could be possible to blend with that crowd and make it out. There would be a cursory check by the police at the last stop in Germany, but a falsified passport and a few marks could insure safe passage. This option was the most logical and the one Karl had set his sights on, but many problems remained.

Attempting to board a train in Bremen wasn't going to be easy. Karl had the feeling that they would be expecting him to show up there, so he decided that a hazardous journey to Hamburg by car would be necessary.

From there they would not arouse suspicion; from there the coast would be clear.

Lucy's childish pleadings and advances toward Martin Bock had paid off in that part of the plan. Martin had gotten them tickets on the morning train to Brussels, via Bremen and Leige, under the name of Herr and Frau Kain. With a floppy hat and little, poorly used makeup Lucy felt she could pass for a middle-aged housefrau, but Martin told her that wasn't necessary. Many respectable German businessmen had young, attractive wives, and, he went on to explain, the police would be spending so much time and energy looking at her that they would forget to look at Karl, whom, he figured, was their prey anyway.

Yet the problem remained to get out of Bremen.

To simply get into a car outside her apartment would never be good enough, Karl had insisted. Lucy still believed that they didn't know he was there, but he was adamant. They would taxi out to the best part of town, to a car Bock had hired for them. It would be waiting there, a large, new Mercedes with its gas tank full and money and food in the trunk.

It all sounded so simple, too simple, to Lucy. Just go outside and flag a taxi. Just get dropped off on Oder Strasse and walk around the corner and hop into the car. Just a few hours away park the car at the Elbe station and ride comfortably to Brussels, a rich burger and his young wife on holiday.

It couldn't be that easy.

And Karl was concerned about his precious papers. This obsession was still crowding his mind and still foremost in his thoughts as they neared the beginning of the last leg of their journey. Who would believe it anyway? To Lucy, Germany was still the clown of Europe, struggling within itself to survive. No one expected the Reich to really rise again.

Yet she dutifully called Albert Freyberg for Karl to inquire about the papers and if Albert could get them back to him. In a way she was happy to make the call. Karl should, she felt, take the papers with him. No need to burden Albert with them any longer. Anyway, it would be good hear Albert's voice one last time....to say good-bye.

"Are you alright?" he asked her immediately as she phoned the office.

"Yes, I'm fine. Karl is fine," she frankly stated. "We're leaving tonight."

"I see," he purred. She could visualize his face in deep thought. "Are you sure you can make it?"

"We've a good plan, Albert. I hope it works."

"I wish you all the best...and Karl, too."

"He wants his papers back," she told him.

There was silence on the telephone. "I don't know if that's wise. The Gestapo watches me closely. I'll be leading them to you." he explained.

She listened as he rambled on about his problems. Lucy felt out of touch with her former boss. When she left the bank she felt he had things under control, but now he was telling her that he didn't and that he, too, would flee the country shortly.

"I have to ask," she said when he had finished. "I really don't care, but for Karl...will you, when you go, take the papers with you."

"I've a family to consider, but, yes, I will."

"Then Karl will understand. I'll tell him his information is in the best of hands. We'll meet again when we're free."

"Where are you headed?" Albert asked.

"To Brussels and then on to London. Karl has friends in London."

"If....no, when we make it out, I'll look you up," he finished.

"Yes," she seemed to choke on the word. Why did he have to begin with if! "I'll see you then."

She began to put down the receiver, but quickly pulled it back. "Oh! And boss.....boss!" she called, but heard a click from the other end. She never told him how much she loved and respected him. She never thanked him.

* * * *

The first part of the journey went well enough, Lucy thought. A taxi proved to be very easy to find in the twilight of the evening and the driver asked no questions and, as Bock had predicted, spent more time looking at Lucy than at her companion.

Lucy had dressed well for the occasion. Her spring dress was sheer and silky, outlining her shape to its best advantage. She also made sure that her light jacket remained open despite the chill in the mid-March air. The better to let the men stare at her breasts. She had curled her hair and carefully applied her make-up. When she was done she had looked at herself in the mirror and been proud of herself. It looked as if she were going to a party instead of fleeing her country.

It was at the end of the taxi ride that things started to go awry. As had become the habit of the local party, there was the nightly march through the wealthy neighborhood by the storm troopers, but it went on earlier than usual and the taxi was suddenly stopped by the demonstration.

"Hey!" Lucy heard the shout of one of the storm troopers. "There's one of them!"

The brown shirts ran over and surrounded the car. They began to pound on the windows and shouts slurs at the rich couple in the back seat.

"Hey! Get away from my taxi!" the driver shouted.

"Jew!" shouted one of the men.

"Vultures!" shouted another.

"Hey!" the driver shouted to the men. "I'm a party member just trying to make a living."

He waved his pin to the crowd and they backed away from the car. They still blocked the path.

"Let them out!" chanted some of the demonstrators.

Karl and Lucy tried to appear calm as they sat in the back, but the fear made Lucy's heart pound and she could see the sweat pouring from Karl's face.

"I'm going to have to ask you to leave," the driver said. "They're not going to let me take you any further."

"You don't expect us to walk with them around." Karl asked.

"Get out," the driver demanded.

Lucy thought fast and held Karl's hand as she spoke. "My husband in General VonScheuler of the Reichwehr and if you don't take us to Oder Strasse Berlin will hear about this."

The driver turned around and stared at her. "I don't give a shit if you're Field Marshall von Hindenburg! Get out!"

"You dog!" Karl shouted at the man as he lashed out at him with his fist.

The driver quickly backed away, but leaned over the back seat a moment later with a police nightstick. "Now, do you and the whore want to get out or do you want me to beat the shit out of you."

Before Lucy could close her open mouth Karl had pulled her out of the car and slammed the door.

The gang of storm troopers swarmed around them, their breaths coated with the smell of beer.

"Well, Fatso," one sneered as he prodded Karl with his finger. "What do you have to say for yourself?"

"I am General VonScheuler and....."

"Sure, you are!" he screeched. "You're nothing but a fat pig with his little bitch out for a night on the town."

"You're nothing but a bunch of hoodlums," Lucy told him.

The Storm troopers crowded Lucy and Karl tighter, but, when they heard the sound of a siren, they vanished into the darkness.

A car sped by and when Lucy looked around she and Karl were totally alone on the street.

"How far?" she asked him.

"I don't know."

They began to walk, not really sure if they were walking in the right direction. Lucy was familiar with much of the city, but this neighborhood may as well have been the far side of the moon.

There was a screech of tires and the roar of a car's engine and suddenly the car that had flown past them had returned. It squealed to a halt a short ways up the street and shined it's headlights toward the pair.

The light was blinding, but Lucy followed Karl's lead and tried to act unafraid. She clung tightly to him and grasped his hand. It shook as she touched it. He also was scared, she knew.

There was the muffled sound of doors slamming as two figures popped out of the car. They were shrouded in the darkness and obscured by the glare of the headlights, but their hats bobbed as they walked and Lucy knew they were SS.

"Karl Scheuler!" a voice called from the direction of the car. "You are under arrest!"

Karl quickly swung Lucy around and pushed her away. "Run, Lucy! Run!"

Lucy turned herself around and looked at Karl. The fear in his eyes mirrored hers. She took several steps backwards and turned, running off toward the end of the street.

A shot rang out!

Another!

As she heard the third shot she cupped her ears with her hands. She bent her head down and stared at the damp pavement as she kept running, but her pace was slowing.

It didn't work, she thought! They knew where they were all the time!

Another shot rang out!

Lucy turned and searched up the street. "Karl!" she shouted as she peered through the glare from the now distant headlights and at the shadowy figures moving between the beams of light.

"Karl! Where are you?"

She felt a hand reach out and grab her. Lucy knew it was Karl immediately as his meaty fingers clutched at her arm and tried to drag her on. She left herself losing her balance and felt the cold, damp ground as it rose up to meet her.

"Lucy! Lucy! Get up! Run! Don't stop running!" he pleaded with her.

He reached down to help her up, gently pulling her with his strong hands.

She looked up at his face and saw him smiling at her. It was as if he were helping a child take her first steps. She began to smile, too.

Another shot burst through the air!

Karl suddenly let go of her hands and dropped to the ground beside her!

"Oh, no! Oh, no!"

He struggled to get to his feet again, but the sting of another gunshot sounded in Lucy's ears and she saw a flash of red burst across Karl's face.

She screamed as she watched him collapse onto the pavement!

"Karl! Karl, please!" she pleaded as she crawled over to him. She touched his hand. It quivered and then went limp.

Lucy heard the sounds of boots on the pavement and quickly the shadows of the black-clad figures surrounded her. She reached out and pulled Karl's body closer to her, finally cradling it in her lap. His blood was pouring onto her silken party dress.

Lucy felt no tears. She didn't feel like crying. There was too much shock, too much fear and she no longer could rely on Karl's kind, reassuring words. He was gone, his lifeless head in her lap.

"He's dead," she heard a voice say from above her.

"Does he carry the evidence?" another asked.

"No," Lucy mumbled.

"Then where is it, girl?" the voice asked. "Who did he give it to?"

Lucy couldn't speak. She just shook her head and stared at Karl, stroking his head gently with her fingers.

"We must find those documents!" a shrill voice demanded.

"She must know whom he gave them to," another said.

Lucy looked up at the men. One stared cruelly down at her. He was a thin, angry looking officer. He had a patch over one eye. He pointed angrily at her with his one arm. "She knows nothing! She's just his little whore!"

"Then what do we do with her?" the other man asked.

"You know what to do," the Nazi crisply said as he walked away.

Lucy stared blankly up at the other man. "No," she muttered as she saw him draw his luger from his holster.

"No! Please, No!" she began to cry as the man stared back toward his commander, a disgusted look on his face.

"Don't kill me!" she sobbed one last time.

The man pointed the pistol at Lucy, pointing the barrel between her eyes. Powerless to stop him, she watched as he gently squeezed the trigger.

TWENTY-NINE

The sick feeling that Mina had in the pit of her stomach continued to grow as she sat listening to the men talk. She felt nervous and afraid, her mind unable to accept the words, the thoughts that were being discussed. She knew it would come to this, to this day of decision, but her heart was refusing to accept this.

The men talked around her as if it were like any other business deal. In her ears their words had hollowness, emptiness as if she was in a barrel and each word reverberated as it touched the walls of her chamber. She was there, watching and listening, but she was off in another world.

Her world was crumbling around her and she was helpless to stop it.

Albert and she had discussed the details so thoroughly. Albert and she knew every facet of the transfer and she had long ago agreed to it, but now, as the plan unfolded before her, she was repulsed by the thoughts.

They're taking my life away, she thought. They're taking away everything I hold dear.

Albert seemed to ignore her except when he needed her agreement on some point. He was too engrossed with Steven Langley and Joachim Kahrbach, one of the old bank executives, to notice the fear and confusion on her face.

"I'm so sorry this had to happen this way," Kahrbach was saying, the hollow, empty ring of his words pounding softly in Min's head. "I can't express how I feel."

Albert smiled at him. It was a reassuring smile of understanding. Why did he seem to understand and accept it, Min wondered? Why was it so easy for him and so hard for her?

"I've worked for the Adlers for forty years," Kahrbach explained. "I never expected to have to handle anything like this."

"These things must be done," Albert assured him. "The bank will be left in good hands. I'd rather have you and some of the old guard take over than some of the others who've been clamoring for us to sell."

"I hope this will satisfy them," Kahrbach mumbled. "Josef is turning over in his grave, I'm sure. If he were alive he'd never let them do this to his bank."

"Well," Albert sighed. "We can't go back to the old days and Josef never faced the situation that Mina and I face today. I couldn't say what he would do."

Kahrbach nodded. "I know, but I wish there was something else I could do."

"In accepting the responsibilities you're taking on you're doing everything I can ask," Albert answered. "In giving us a good price..."

Steven interrupted him. "A good price? The bank is worth three times that."

"Anything higher would be unacceptable to the Nazis," Albert said back.

"Yes, yes," Kahrbach agreed. "If we offered more they would think it wasn't a forced sale."

The men fell into silence as they knew only one matter remained. They turned to look at Mina, the unsigned papers resting on the table before her. The stack of words that would force her to relinquish her birthright sat there, a pen resting atop the first sheet.

"Mina," Albert pleaded. "Please."

She stared at her husband. Wasn't there another way, she wondered? There had to be another way.

"Sign," he politely demanded.

"Father would have never let this happen," she mumbled.

"Sign."

She leaned over and stared at the words, their legal jargon not hiding the fact that she knew in her mind. The formality of the sale wouldn't hide the fact that she was handing over her life, her family heritage to strangers.

Min looked up at the men, their faces coldly waiting for her to act. Couldn't they show some sympathy for her? Couldn't they just go away?

Holding the pen in her quivering hand she signed the papers quickly, not wanting to know what they said or what funds they left her. When she was done she leaned back and tried to hold back the tears that were swelling inside her soul.

"It's done," Albert stated as he handed the stack of papers over to Kahrbach.

"Again I'm sorry it had to end this way," he told Albert, his own voice cracking as he placed the papers in his briefcase.

217

"I wish you good luck," Albert said as he extended a hand to him. "I think you're going to need it."

"I don't know, Herr Freyberg," he rambled on. "I'm just a caretaker in my eyes. Someone stronger will come along to lead the bank and take my place. I'm just happy I could be here to help you."

He walked over to Mina and leaned down to her. She had known Kahrbach all her life. She remembered him when he was a young, energetic assistant to her father. She remembered his stern, angry face when she and her brother, then children, would burst into the bank and cause some sort of ruckus. She never thought he'd be the one, but it was better him than some Nazi pawn taking over.

"I'm sorry, Mina," he said as he bent down and took her hand. "I'm sorry it turned out this way and I wish you all the best."

She looked up at him with her reddened eyes and silently nodded. She had nothing to say.

In a moment Kahrbach was gone and with him went their ownership of the bank. In a moment she had been stripped of her wealth and power.

"Now, the other matter," Albert said almost the second the door closed behind Kahrbach. He took out another stack of papers and placed them before Min.

"Are you sure this is the right thing?" Steven asked as he watched Albert place the papers down.

"I don't see another way," Albert insisted. "It may be a sly ruse, but it insures we won't be poverty stricken when we get out of here."

"What is this?" Mina asked. She had never been told there were more papers to sign.

"Mina," Albert said calmly as he sat on the chair next to her. "This sells the house and the belongings, all our personal property and assets inside Germany to Steven."

"Sell my house and my things!" Min screamed. She never thought she'd have to sell that too.

"Of course, my dear, what did you expect to happen to them when you left?"

She stared at the papers, then at the men. She had never thought about that, always assuming that she'd return when the crisis was over, when cooler and more stable heads ruled the country.

"Mina," Steven spoke to her reassuringly as he sat in the chair opposite her. "This way the Nazis won't get your things. I'll take care of them and I can sell them to get you funds if needed. If you left without doing this the Nazis would just take it all."

218

"No!" Min moaned as she banged her fist on the table. "I can't sell my house! My mother and father built this house! I was born here! I can't sell it all. It leaves me with nothing!"

"You have no choice," Albert insisted as he picked up the pen.

"I can't do this!" she moaned again as she pushed his hand away. "I can't!"

"There's no other alternative," he insisted again.

She began to sob, her mind and body unable to hold the pain in. "I know," she moaned as she cried.

"I'm sorry, but it's for the best," Steven also insisted. "I'm your friend and I wouldn't be doing this if I didn't know it was best."

"I know," she cried as she cupped her hands up to her face.

"Mina, please sign." Albert pleaded.

"In a minute," she cried. "Leave me alone for a while."

"Alright," Albert smiled at her as he rose and walked toward the library door. "We'll leave you with your thoughts."

In a moment she was alone in the library. She looked around and her mind began to see the room as it was when her father ruled the house. Her mind replaced the sparse, Spartan furniture with the ornate comfort that her father had wanted and loved. The bare walls were again lined with books and ledgers in her mind and her memories went back to the things she experienced there. She remembered the good times when she and her brother played in the library, angering her father, but only a little. She remembered the whole house as it once was, with her mother with the staff cooking in the kitchen and her father working in his library. She remembered the games she used to play in the house as a child.

She also thought back to the bad times; when her mother was dying in the master bedroom. Her father and her arguing as their wills clashed once she grew to maturity. She remembered the dinners they held there. That was where she first learned about Albert....and about Willi. She remembered the garden where she and Willi first expressed their love.

There were so many memories she had shared in the house. There were memories yet to come that she had hoped her children could have in this house. The house itself, huge and steady, was the cornerstone of her life and, she had hoped, the cornerstone of her children's lives a well, but now it was being taken away.

She stared at the papers and saw drops of her tears fall onto the sheets. She watched the ink smear and run as the teardrops spread across the page.

The house, everything she owned and loved was going away and there wasn't anything else she could do.

Min raised her head and stared toward the still closed door to the outside world. He was behind that door, she knew. He was waiting like a vulture to take away the things she cared about. He didn't care. He didn't know how much it hurt. He was thinking only of the money and the success of the escape. Albert didn't care if he was taking away the things she held most dear.

But there was nothing she could do.

No matter how angry it made her, no matter how upset, there was nothing she could do. She had a pain in her stomach that wouldn't go away, but it was no use anymore. The hell wasn't over yet. She believed that she would lose everything before it was over. She believed she would lose more than Albert would. She already had.

She reached for the pen and signed the papers.

* * * *

The gentle quiet that surrounded the big, old house seemed to carry with it a foreboding. The swelling breeze that rustled through the trees seemed to ring hollow in Bock's ears as he approached the front door. He had the feeling that the house was in mourning somehow, as if it too hurt from some dreadful news like that which he carried with him.

Greta was the first face he saw when he entered the home. It was a sight he had longed for, not having been with her for several days, not feeling her gentle touch on his, her smiling eyes not staring at him. Yet today, she was not on his mind, and her touch was tentative, her kiss quivering with fear and her eyes unsmiling.

"What's wrong?" She asked as she sensed the same sorrow and fear in him.

He ran his fingers through her golden hair before he spoke. "I'm sorry, my love. I'm sorry I haven't been able to come up to see you, but things have been so hectic down in the city. I feel like my world has been turned upside down."

The look in her eyes told him she knew what he must feel like. If anyone would understand how it felt to have their world turned upside down, it was Greta. There was no need to reassure him with words.

They both understood that the madness what was disturbing their lives wouldn't abate for some time.

"I must see Albert," Martin insisted.

"I'm right here," He heard Albert's voice come from the shadow's of the house.

As Albert came into view he looked older, somewhat worn out. His reddened eyes showed he had had little sleep of late. His distraught face said that the man was troubled. Bock realized the news he had would not make it any better.

"Come in, Bock," Albert beckoned him toward the study. "We have to talk. You too, Greta."

When all three were in the room and the door firmly locked behind them Bock felt more at ease, more free to talk. Albert, though, spoke first. "You probably are a bit surprised by the goings on at the bank and have come to inquire as to your status?"

"No, Sir," Martin corrected him. "I realized long ago that you'd have to sell. I'm only a little surprised that you didn't keep me up to date on the sale. I'd have thought I'd have been better informed."

Albert smiled. "That was to protect you, my young friend."

"How?"

"Those that were most involved in the sale are older men with less to lose should the Nazis put pressure on them. You are too young and I wouldn't burden you in such a way. You have a lifetime to live and, if you choose to live it in Germany, I want it to be free of suspicion that you consort with the likes of us."

"But I thought....." Greta began to interrupt, but was cut off by her father.

"We will talk to him about that in time, Greta. I just wanted to keep his options free should be decide otherwise." He stated flatly.

"You mean if I should choose to come with you?" Bock questioned.

"Yes!" Greta exclaimed as she reached out her hand toward his.

Bock stood silently. He loved Greta, and could see in her eyes that she wanted him to join them. He had hoped otherwise, though, wanting her to leave her new found family to stay with him. He knew how difficult that would be in the Germany that existed today, but he hoped that would change as it had so often in the past. Looking into her eyes to search for an answer, he could see that wasn't to be.

"Martin, please," She pleaded with him. "You know we can't stay here. If you love me you'll come with us."

Her lovely face continued to search his soul and easily found the love he had for her. His mind, he thought, couldn't be so easily changed by a woman, but he surrendered to his heart. "Of course I will come with you," he told them. "Could it be any other way?"

Greta threw her arms around him and squeezed him with joy. Her eyes shined again as they had before, but Bock only heard Albert's words echo in his ears.

"Now you can tell me why you really came here."

As Greta moved away from him he found it difficult to find the words. He stammered. "I received word.....I found out...."

"What?" Albert demanded. "Spit it out."

"Lucy's dead."

Albert winced. His eyes turned toward Greta as if he equated her to the girl. As he turned back toward Bock he seemed to be searching for an explanation.

"The police came around to bank to tell us," Martin went on. "They needed to notify next of kin...all that legal stuff. I thought you'd want to know."

"How?" Albert asked and then added. "As if I need to ask?"

"They say that she was murdered by this man, Scheuler, whom she'd been living with. Some sort of lover's quarrel. He's dead too, they say. Murder-Suicide." Martin explained. "I can't believe it's true. They say that Scheuler had a history of mental illness, but I can't believe he killed her."

"And you shouldn't." Albert added. "Karl did have some troubles in the past, but he didn't kill her, or himself."

"Then who?"

Albert sighed. "We both know who, Martin. We both know why."

Greta then spoke. "And if we don't move quickly, I guess we'll all be next."

THIRTY

"Remember," Albert had told Greta. "We must travel light. Nothing that is not important can be taken along. It will be a risky journey and a speedy one. We can't be slowed down with excess baggage."

Greta herself had little excess baggage to bring. She had little of anything to show for her life. Some new clothes for her new life, some photographs to remind her of her old life. She had brought nothing to remind her of her childhood or her times down on the riverfront.

For her, traveling light would be easy, but the words from her father were not meant for Greta. She knew he worried that his family would want to carry all their memories with them. Her assignment was to lighten that burden.

For Mina it would be especially tough. Her entire life revolved around the house and all it possessed. Each item in the house aroused memories and leaving those things, things that evoked memories would be as difficult as leaving the memories themselves behind.

It amazed Greta how she had changed since coming into the family. It amazed her more how she viewed both Albert and Mina since those first days and how they viewed her. Mina would never be like a mother to her, but somehow they had grown closer. They both realized that the link between them, Albert, meant a great deal to both of them. Having overcome the tension and distrust of the first few days, both Min and Greta bonded their lives in a quiet understanding and friendship. It was more than Greta had expected, but what she knew she needed. It was something Mina needed as well.

Greta found Min in the attic that day knowing she had to do the toughest thing she had yet to do. The memories up there were greater than any other in the house. The need to sort through them, to pick out the few morsels she could take along would make the hours seem like eternity.

"I don't think I've ever thrown anything away." Min smiled at Greta as she found her going through a box of old clothes. "I even saved these

223

thinking in the back of my mind that my daughters would someday wear them. I know it seems strange, but that's the way I thought, even as a child."

"I could just see the girls dressed in the long skirts from before the war." Greta mused. "So out of place by today's standards."

"Personally," Min smiled back, her mind thinking back twenty years. "I thought them beautiful. More attractive in some ways than the way fashion forces us to dress today."

Min sighed. "No use worrying about it now. They'll just be burned. I can't keep them around." She seemed depressed at the thought, though resigned to it.

"Can I help?" Greta asked.

Min nodded as she put aside the clothes and opened up a smaller box. In the box was a packet of neatly wrapped letters.

"What have you got there?" Greta asked as she sat on the dusty attic floor next to Min.

There were tears forming around the corners of Min's eyes as she gently opened the old papers. "They were letters from long ago. Love letters from when I was young."

"Oh, Mina," Greta smiled. "You speak like you're someone's grandmother. You're not that old." And it was true. Min was still a youthful woman in her mid-thirties. Despite the stress and turmoil of this time she was still attractive and appealing in men's eyes. In Greta's eyes she was what men looked for in women; smart, pretty, self confidant and mature. It was something Greta wished for herself someday.

"Are these from Albert?" Greta then asked as she took the one Min had just put down. "I'd love to see how he wrote love letters. May I?"

"These are not from your father," Min said. There was a quivering in her voice. "They're from my first love. They're Willi's letters."

Greta could sense the sadness as she spoke his name and also a tinge of fear. She decided not to read the letter, placing it back onto the pile. Instead, she reached into the box and pulled out a stack of old photographs. The one on top was the picture of a young man in an ill-fitting uniform. "Is this Willi?" she asked.

"No," Min said as she took the photograph from Greta. "It's my brother, Felix."

Greta then remembered a picture from Albert's study of the same boy, but in that one he appeared even younger. She saw there were several others of Min's brother among the old pictures. On many there was a small, shy looking girl, who must have been Mina in those years.

"He was two years younger than me," Min went on. "We were close, maybe closer than most brothers and sisters, especially after Mama died."

"He died in the war?"

"Yes, and it broke my heart," she sobbed. "He was only twenty years old."

Greta had found a small photo, like the ones you get at the carnivals, of Mina and another young soldier. He was a handsome boy with close cropped sandy hair and a peaceful smile that contradicted his solemn uniform. "Is this Willi?" she asked and she handed the picture to Min.

Mina smiled as she gently moved her fingers along the outline of the man's figure. "Yes, in a happier time." Greta saw her expression change quickly and sensed a shuttering in her body. "A happier time," She sobbed. "How can I say that? There was the war. A generation of men was dying. Everyone starving. Yet I can say that for me it was a happier time. Oh, I loved him so much. I loved him enough to defy my father and everything I cared about just to be with him. I was ready to put aside everything for him."

"How'd you meet?" Greta asked when she realized that Min needed to talk about it.

"Both he and Albert were in my brother's unit. My brother was an aerial observer and they were both pilots. He brought them home on a leave and I found Willi to be handsome and fascinating. I quickly became infatuated with him and soon it turned to love."

"And Albert?"

"At first I found him a bit gruff and a bore," Min confessed. "Although we grew friendly, it wasn't until much later that my thoughts changed. That didn't come until after the war."

"What happened to him?"

"To who?" Min looked at her curiously, her mind wrapped up in the past.

"To Willi?"

Her face was very serious, her breathing heavy as she spoke. "In August 1918 I saw him for the last time. He was tired and worn out...all the soldiers were by then. He said goodbye to me and walked out of my life. As we heard it later both he and Albert were flying together when they were forced down in No-Mans-Land just days before the end of the war. Albert was hurt and couldn't walk. Willi went off to find help. That was last we heard of him. Albert was saved. Willi vanished. The Willi I loved....gone."

Greta reached out and touched Min's trembling hands. The woman was close to tears. "I'm sorry."

"My mind could not take that, then...not even now," she rambled on. "I was alone by then.....my mother gone...and my bother. My father hated me for just loving Willi. I had nothing to cling to, but needed something, someone to hold onto. I felt I couldn't go on without him."

"But you did, Mina," Greta reassured her. "You and my father built a wonderful life, with wonderful children."

"For what?" she cried. "To have it all come back to haunt us. To be made to feel that every decision I made, everything I did wrong so long ago I must pay for today. For what did I commit those sins?"

Greta didn't understand exactly what she meant, what emotions the letters and the pictures stirred up in her mind. There was something more to all this than what she was telling Greta, but Greta wanted to change the subject. She felt she must get Min off the subject of her lost love.

Greta placed another photograph before Min's eyes. "Who is this woman?" she innocently asked. "She's lovely?"

"Francoise," Mina mumbled as placed the picture in her hands and, cupping it toward her face placed tears on the picture.

"Yes," Greta recalled. "The picture in the study. The one you broke that night. You on Willi's arm and Albert's on hers. Was she my father's love as Willi was yours?"

The look on Mina's face seemed haunted. Her eyes, swollen with tears, seemed far away in the past. She spoke in a quivering voice, but the words poured from her lips. "She was Albert's woman and my best friend. She helped me through the toughest time in my life. I loved her....like a sister and she felt the same toward me. When Willi was reported missing I was all alone, except for her....except for how she tried to help me. I didn't want to go on. I didn't want to live and I didn't want the...." her voice tailed for her a moment.

She bit her lip and continued. "I didn't know if I wanted to live or die, but I was so envious of Francoise. One morning...that morning....I went to the flat with a gun I had taken from my father's house not really knowing why. Things were so crazy then...the strikes and the rioting. Any moment the war would be over and Willi was gone and Albert, who

226

belonged to Francoise, was alive. I don't know whether the gun had
more to do with my protection, my revenge, or my despair."

Mina's tear filled eyes searched the ceiling as she sobbed her body
shaking as she clutched the faded photograph. "I took the gun out of my
purse and showed it Francoise. I don't remember if I meant it or not, but
I told her I was going to kill myself if I had to go on alone. She said
everything would be fine...that I would find someone else to love. She
didn't understand. I screamed at her that she had everything and I had
nothing. She had Albert while I was alone. I became more upset as we
argued and began to wave the gun into the air."

Min's eyes grew wider, her face shocked as she relived the events of
the morning, raising her hands in front of her as if she were firing the gun
again. "She came toward me!" she cried. "She grabbed my hand!"

"And the gun went off," Greta softly completed the sentence.

Min cupped her face in her hands. "Yes! Yes! I still don't know
whether I meant to or not. Was it an accident? To this day I don't know.
Did I mean to kill her?"

"But it was a long time ago. Albert forgave you this accident," Greta
reassured her. "Albert loves you."

"I never told him the truth," Min sighed. "Now he knows, but I kept
it from him....hid my secret from everyone for all these years. This was
what we argued over that night. This is why we are leaving Germany.
My fault. Mine and mine alone."

"You can't say that," Greta said. "It's not your fault."

Mina stared off into the past again. "Willi, the man I once loved.
The man I named my son after. The man I thought was dead. He's the
one who pursues us. He's the one who would use the fact that I killed
Francoise...and that I hid it, to drive us from our home."

* * * *

"Look, Anna!" Gery heard Willi shouting at his little sister. "You
can't take all your dolls on the trip. Only one or two."

Gery agreed with Willi, but didn't feel it was his place to join in the
argument. Gery knew he still wasn't that much a part of the family.

He felt very comfortable in this house, with these kids, but still was
a visitor. This he knew and so when he realized that they'd be leaving
Germany and the house, he wasn't as upset as Willi and his sisters. Willi,

with whom Gery had become good friends, knew what was going on, but both the twins were confused. They had been told they were going on a trip and the rest was left up to their imaginations, which went wild.

"I know if I leave them here I'll never get them back," Anna cried. "I know we're leaving home for good."

"Fine," Willi sighed, "But Papa won't let you bring the dolls either and then I'll get into trouble."

"Good!" Marta exclaimed. "Better you than us. I'll tell Mama and she'll let Anna bring her dolls."

This job wasn't going to be easy, Gery began to realize. Both twins were stubborn and knew more than their parents would like to believe. He and Willi were given the task of getting the girl's stuff together along with their own and Willi had already parted with a good amount of his possessions. He was determined that his sister's sacrifice be the same.

"Go on," Willi taunted his sister. "You ask Mama. She'll tell you the same thing."

"I'm going to tell her that I don't want to go," Marta insisted. "I want to stay here."

"Look, girls," Gery said. "You want to stay here and be treated like some outcast? I sure don't. I want to go where I'm just as good as anyone else. I don't want to be afraid everyday."

"And where's that?" Anna asked.

"Oh....anywhere better than Bremen," Gery replied.

"Maybe we'll go to America with Herr Langley," Willi said.

Anna's face soured up. "I don't want to go there. America is full of gangsters and cowboys."

"And Indians!" Marta hollered. "I don't want to get scalped."

"Oh girls, please," Willi moaned.

"America isn't like you see in the movies," Gery explained. "Everyone isn't a gangster."

"Is Herr Langley a gangster?" Willi asked the girls.

"How do we know he isn't?" said Marta.

"I give up," Willi moaned.

Gery looked both twins in their four brown eyes. "I don't think you've got much say in it anyway. If we're going, we're going. You just have to make the best of it."

He could see Anna's face curl up as if she was going to cry. "I don't want to leave my friends."

"What friends?" he sister turned to her and asked.

"All our friends from school," Anna cried back.

"They all are acting so creepy since....you know who ...with all this Jew business," Marta sneered at her. "Do we have any real friends left?"

"There's Paul! He's still nice to me. And Maria."

"Oh, Anna, grow up," her sister moaned. "I think we'd be better off somewhere else too."

"Then why argue with me?" Willi questioned.

"Who else am I going to fight with?" Marta smiled. "And I still don't want to leave all my things."

Gery threw his hands up the air. "Fine, then! We'll just leave both of them here. They can become servants for the next owners."

"That's not a bad idea, Gery," Willi agreed. "They'll be a lot more for you and I with them not around."

"Do you think your parents will go for it?" Gery asked.

"They're so mixed up right now they won't even notice they aren't with us until we're across the border."

"Then it'll be too late," Gery smiled.

Both boys began to walk toward the door.

"This is a great idea," Gery laughed. "Goodbye girls. Hope you like the new owners."

He could see them both look curiously at each other in disbelief. Then they looked at the boys and shouted in unison. "Willi! Gery! Help us pack!"

THIRTY-ONE

Strauss sat in his darkened office waiting for the last sounds to melt away from the world outside. The voices of the stragglers happily talking about politics or last night's game before going home to their families. He heard the sounds of the streetcar going by and the roar of the engine of an automobile starting up then drifting away down the street. The sound of the night desk below him, accompanied by the static of the radio muffled two floors down.

Strauss waited in the darkness, watching the glow of his cigarette die down, waiting for the quiet that signaled he could make the momentous call.

Finally he picked up the receiver of the telephone and slowly dialed the number.

"Hello," a youthful female voice began as the connection completed on the other side of the line. "Freyberg residence."

"Herr Freyberg, please."

"One moment," she quickly replied. "Whom shall I say is calling?"

"A friend"

There was silence on the other side of the line. Strauss wondered if he should have told the caller his name, but was afraid he may have been too late and that it was a trap. The girl's voice on the other side of the line could have been placed there by the Nazis to trap him.

"This is Freyberg," a man's voice spoke to him across the telephone line.

"This is Strauss," he said, hoping the man on the other end would respond with some sign of recognition.

"Yes, Detective," the man said. "I haven't heard from you since our little meeting and wondered when you would call."

"It's time, Herr Freyberg," Strauss whispered.

"When must you give over the information?"

"Tomorrow, the Gauleiter comes tomorrow and he is demanding that I turn over what I have. I cannot hold them off any longer, I'm afraid."

There was a moment of silence on the other end.

"I hope you are prepared?" Strauss asked a minute later.

"Yes," the voice said after a deep breath. "We are prepared. Do and say what you must to protect yourself, Detective. I appreciate all your help."

"Good luck, Herr Freyberg."

"Good luck to you, Detective Strauss," he heard the voice say. "And thank you."

Strauss hung up the phone and stared into the darkness that surrounded him. He wondered what Albert Freyberg and his family would do. He wondered what he himself would do when his time came.

* * * *

Steven watched as the Freyberg family silently gathered their sparse belongings and put them into the motor car. The warm spring night felt heavy and deadly, Steven thought. The windless, cloud covered sky darkening all around him. Could the heat and the darkness be their friend in the escape?

Steven felt that the Freyberg house was being watched and hoped that the latest ruse would be sufficient. The big black car he had seen up the street must have been them. They watched the house, waiting for unusual activity that would be a signal that the Freybergs were about to leave. Steven began to feel that some normal sounds should echo in the house tonight.

"We should be making some noise." he said to Martin Bock, who had brought the other car to the house. They had decided to leave in two cars, but not the Freyberg's own limousines, which would be too suspicious. Steven had driven one to the house and Martin the other. It was as if they had come up for a visit, but there was no laughing, no sounds to indicate a friendly get together up to now.

"I will take care of it," Martin said as he left Steven's side. A moment later he returned with Greta.

"We'll go into the garden and have a little fight for their amusement," Greta said. "Signal us when we're ready to go."

They vanished and moments later Steven could hear their voices rise angrily toward each other. Mina heard it too and rushed toward the garden door. Steven blocked her path.

"What are they doing out there?" She whispered as she tried to push past Steven. "Someone will hear them."

"As they should," he said. "Let the listeners hear that everything is normal in the house."

Min nodded and went back to gathering her children's things. The cars, hidden behind the bushes of the driveway were slowly loaded by Albert, his son and nephew. Despite the voices of Bock and Greta loudly talking in the garden there was an eerie silence in Steven's ears. It was still too quiet, he thought, and suspicious.

Steven went to the study and turned on the radio. The sounds of music filled the house.

A moment later Albert joined him in the study.

"I just wanted to make it sound normal in here," He explained.

Albert nodded. "I suppose you're right. Unless someone realizes that I seldom listen to the radio anymore."

"Then what is normal at this time of night in the Freyberg house?"

Albert shrugged. "I don't know. I can't think."

"Then let's allow it to be up to their imagination."

Within minutes all was ready. The children were crammed into the first car and told to sit on the floor.

"No noise," Albert whispered to them. "Do you hear me? No fighting. Not a sound." He pointed his finger at the girl's scared little faces, their frightened eyes staring back at him in the darkness.

"It's alright, Papa," Willi whispered back to him. "I'll take care of them."

"Good," he smiled at his son. "You and Gery take care of them."

Min then came over and leaned into the car, draping a blanket over the children. "We'll be with you shortly," she told them softly. "Just keep quiet and listen to Greta and Herr Bock."

"Mama," one of the twins whispered back, her voice almost crying. "When will we see you again?"

"Tomorrow. Tomorrow morning. I promise."

"I love you, Mama," the other cried.

She bent over and hugged all of them and then closed the door of the car.

"Go get Martin and Greta," Albert whispered to his wife. Then he turned to Steven.

"How long after the first car leaves should we go?" Steven asked.

"About a half hour. I think the first car will have the greater chance of success. Whatever happens we must give the children a head start." Albert stated.

Steven could still hear Greta shouting in the garden, but saw Bock come up to them. The girl was keeping up the ruse to the last.

"Are you ready?" Albert asked.

Bock nodded.

"You have the directions to Helmut's farm?"

"Yes. I will get them there as quickly as I can."

"We will leave shortly after you," Steven reminded Bock. "Don't stop for anything."

"Once out of the city no one will question a car on the road." Bock insisted.

"Be sure of nothing, Martin," Albert insisted. "Trust no one."

"I understand."

Greta then joined them in the foyer and quickly hugged her father and Mina. "You must be careful," she whispered. "We'll all be safe soon." Then, just as quickly as she came she vanished into the front seat of the hidden car, covering herself up with a blanket.

"Thank you for a wonderful evening," Bock then announced in a normal speaking voice, just loud enough for the world to hear. "Please say goodbye to Greta for me and tell her I'm sorry."

"I'm sure she'll forgive you in the morning," Albert also spoke loudly, his deep voice booming in the darkness.

"Goodbye, Herr Bock," Min added.

Martin slipped into his car and started the engine. Without hesitation he proceeded down the driveway and out into the street. From his vantage point at the door to the house Steven could see him move past the car on the street. Other than the glow of a cigarette there was no activity from the Gestapo car.

"Oh, God," Min cried as she watched the car carrying her family speed away. "Let them be safe."

Steven and the others went back into the house and silently entered the study where the radio still played the symphonies from Berlin.

"Now we must wait," Albert said as he poured drinks for them all.

"How long?" questioned Mina as she took the glass from her husband's hand.

"Just a little while, my dear," he said.

"Albert," Steven asked after sipping some of the wine. "When you are safely out of Germany, where will you go?"

"I haven't thought that far ahead, Steven," Albert smiled. "Have you any suggestions?"

Steven looked deeply into his wine glass. "I was hoping you'd consider working with me."

"In America," Min added. "I really didn't think about going there."

"I don't think any of us would be comfortable in America, Steven," Albert said. "Someplace closer to home, maybe. As for working for you, I'd be honored."

"We can discuss that when the time comes." Steven concluded. "First let's get ourselves out of here." He felt himself getting jittery at the delay.

"All in due time." Albert patiently stated.

And the time passed very slowly for all three of them. The music droned on and on, melody drifting into melody until the moment came.

At Albert's suggestion they all drifted toward the door to the house. The radio still played in the background and the house lights burned in several empty rooms as the three of them stood at the entrance to the house in full view of the car up the street.

They chatted loudly under the doorway lamp and acted as if it were just the end of another evening. Mina was the first to depart, planting a kiss on Steven's cheek prior to going back into the house where she would quickly slip out again through an open window and into the back of Steven's half hidden car.

When both men were sure she was safely hidden away they shook hands and parted, Albert waiting by the open door while Steven got into the car and started the engine. Then he too quickly went back inside, closed the door and slipped through the window into the car, which at that moment began its movement down the driveway.

They had rehearsed it many times and it seemed to go off without a hitch. To the men up the street it only looked as if Steven had left, or so they hoped.

As they sped past the big black Mercedes Steven couldn't help but strain his eyes into it. The two men were lazily staring at the house, unaware of the deception that had been done to them. They didn't even catch his eyes on them. It would be awhile before they noticed that the lights never went out or that the radio was never turned off and by then it would be too late to catch them.

Steven smiled at turned his eyes toward the road.

THIRTY-TWO

It had been a long night's drive for Steven Langley, winding through the North German countryside toward the small farm near the Dutch border. They speed along the empty roads, slowing down only while passing through the deserted villages; he had made good time and encountered no trouble.

The Freybergs, while remaining hidden for the first part of the trip, now sat with him to keep his mind alert and his body awake. Although Mina slept part of the way, Albert and Steven amused one another with old stories mostly centering on their flying days.

Both Albert and Steven were sure their ruse had been discovered by now, the Gestapo now going through their things and wondering where they had all gone. They also guessed that Bock, traveling the same route with the rest of the family, was still on course just ahead of them.

At daybreak they neared their goal, appearing for the entire world as a happy band on a springtime jaunt, breezing easily through the last towns before Helmut's farm. Rolling though the green countryside of the North German plain toward what looked like a cluster of beaten old buildings in the distance.

As they got closer Steven could see that the farm did look tired and weather beaten, just as he expected, its wooden framed buildings seeming to bend in the gentle spring breeze. Steven could the see the other car by the main house, but did not see anyone around.

As they stopped the silence began to worry Steven. "Curiously quiet," he whispered to Albert. "I'm worried."

Steven brought the car to a stop a hundred meters from the farmhouse. It wasn't that he expected a brass band to greet them when they arrived, but he hadn't expected the eerie silence that surrounded them.

Albert and Steven quietly got out of the car. Were Martin and Helmut Schorner being cautious, Steve wondered, or was something wrong?

"Please move no closer!" A scratchy, gruff voice called out from the farmhouse. "Identify yourselves!"

"Helmut!" Albert shouted. "Have you gone blind?"

"You, the stranger!" the voice called to Steve. "Convince me this is no trap."

Steven looked at Albert and shrugged his shoulders. Albert had a strange, uncertain look on his face. Steven didn't know how to answer.

"Where's Bock?" Albert called.

There was no answer.

"Your name is Helmut Schorner," Steven began, finally realizing what he had to do. "You were a sergeant during the war. You pasted the aeroplanes back together. You married a Frenchwoman after the war. You had saved her from the firing squad with Albert and another man's help."

There was silence from the farmhouse.

"Shouldn't that be good enough?" Albert questioned.

"Yes, I hope so," The man came into view. He was a stout, middle aged farmer emerging from the house carrying a rifle.

Albert walked up to meet the man and hugged him. "Helmut! Thank God! Is everything alright?"

Helmut smiled and nodded. "Yes, all asleep." He then turned to Steven. "I didn't want to wake them and wanted to make sure that Albert hadn't been forced to lead the Nazis here."

"I can understand," Steven said as he shook the man's hand. "And thanks for helping."

"If you knew how much I owe Hauptmann Freyberg, you'd understand."

* * * *

It took several hours for Mina to adjust her senses to the farmhouse. It wasn't that the farm was dirty, there was mustiness about the place and with each step the floor boards creaked. The home was neat, clean and orderly, but the aging furniture was tired and faded and the old house didn't keep out the chill in the morning air or the odor of wet straw coming from the barnyard.

Min guessed that these things had once bothered Marie Schorner, the lady of the house. She is a tall, willowy woman in her middle forties.

She had the signs of age in her eyes, on her face and in her hair streaked with grey. Neither old before her time nor eternally young, she looked her age.

Marie had set about to make her guests comfortable during the first hour they were there, showing them the hastily prepared loft where the children would sleep and the back room were Min and Albert could rest. She helped hid their belongings, just in case, and then began to prepare breakfast while the men discussed their plans.

"Can I help?" Mina asked as she joined Marie in the kitchen. It was a large room, with the customary central cutting table being dwarfed by a huge cluster of dull metal pots hanging from the ceiling.

"Thank you," Marie replied in a French accent mellowed by years living among the Germans. "I haven't had to feed such a crowd in a long time.

She handed Min a stack of steaming biscuits fresh from the oven. Marie then reached for a ladle and began to stir a large kettle. "I'm afraid there isn't much," she apologized, "Times being what they are."

Min smiled, "We appreciate everything you and your husband are doing. We appreciate it more than you know."

Marie reached out and touched Min's hand. "There is no way we could repay all that your husband did for us during the war. These things we do today are only a small tokens."

"Yet I know how difficult things must be for you."

Marie smiled. "No harder than for you and your family."

Min could only nod.

"I think you're so lucky," Marie said as she began to spoon out porridge into several small bowls. "Your children are so beautiful. I....Helmut and I.....never were blessed with children. Helmut's boys are grown now and....well, I was never their mother.

"I could see that your children were scared when they arrived last night. Even the older girl......"

"Greta?" Min interrupted. "Greta scared? I can't imagine."

Marie smiled. "She may not show you, but she is. And I must say Frau Freyberg...."

"Min"

"....Min, she doesn't seem like she could be your daughter."

"She's not. She's Albert's from another marriage. And, as you said about Helmut's children, I can never be her mother."

The woman completed assembling the breakfast of biscuits, porridge and jam and brought it to the men in the dining room. They barely noticed it as they studied a map of the border region.

Albert pointed. "The Nazis have closed all the main roads to Holland....here...here and here. The best route is through the woods, but I expect they'll have patrols out."

"We have to risk it!" Bock concluded.

"If only there was some way of distracting them," Steven added.

"Or avoiding them."

Steven pointed to a small village on the Dutch side of the border. "My people from The Hague have set themselves up in an Inn here. We have to find some way of getting to them. They've papers for everyone. Helmut, for you and your wife, too."

"That's very considerate, but we first must find a way over to them." the farmer smiled. He had a crafty smile on his weather beaten face.

"What have you up your sleeve?" Albert asked as he noticed Helmut's sly look.

Helmut shrugged. "First we eat, and then I'll show you."

* * * *

Steven Langley had never been familiar with farms. He was a city kid who had grown up mean and tough on the streets of New York. To him, grass was something that grew between the cracks in the sidewalk. He felt very out of place on Helmut's farm from the moment he had arrived. He felt uneasy that he would do something or go somewhere that he shouldn't be. After breakfast, when he, Albert and Helmut went outside to the barn, he hoped he wouldn't have to lead the way. Steven wasn't sure he could find the barn.

It was almost ten in the morning before they went outside. Although he had been up all night on the drive to the farm, Steven didn't feel tired. His adrenaline kept his mind alert and his body functioning. The coolness of the spring morning didn't hurt either.

In the bright sunlight, Helmut's farm didn't look much better than it had in the twilight of the dawn. The graying wood framed building seemed to wash away in the glare of day. The buildings all looked dry and tattered, but none more than the one they approached now, a huge sloped roofed barn.

"When I got word you were coming," Helmut explained as the three men walked. "And when I figured out why, I tried to think of how I could best help. What skill did I have that could help you, Hauptmann."

"Helmut," Albert interjected. "Please stop calling me 'Hauptmann'. The war is long over. I'm just Albert to you."

Helmut continued as if he hadn't heard. "How could we be sure to get you across the border? I asked myself that. I almost completely ignored the best answer until one of my pigs got loose from the pen."

"A pig?"

"Yes, one of my pigs ran into the old barn and reminded me of what I had there," Helmut said brightly. He was grinning from ear to ear. "I had got them at an auction so long ago. They were perfectly worthless then. They probably are today, but they may just fit our needs."

With that Helmut swung open the wide door of the barn. The sunlight sparkled against the dust, shimmering against two monsters sitting in the middle of the empty barn.

"My Lord!" Steven exclaimed as he saw them.

As Helmut swung open the other door the light sprayed the huge machines even more and the faded grey and white colors began to glow brightly in the sunlight. Before Steven were the figures of two ancient aeroplanes, flying machines from the Great War. Two magnificent two-seaters.

"Goodness," howled Albert. "Where in the world did you get those?"

"Some private estate had them, back in '23," Helmut explained as he walked around the aeroplanes. "They went bankrupt in the inflation and were giving things away. I paid several thousand marks for them, but the money was only worth its weight in paper. They told me I had gotten shit for shit."

"Maybe they were right."

Helmut leaned against the wing of one plane. "Then they were; now they wouldn't be. I toyed with them for a while after I first got them, and then didn't look at them again until two weeks ago.

"And you made them fly?" Steven finished.

"I made them fly-able!" Helmut explained his smile still brightening his face. "You, Albert, can make them fly."

"I've haven't been in an aeroplane in fifteen years, yet flown one." Albert shook his head. "I don't know....."

"It's like riding a bike," Steven quietly said. "It's perfect. There's one for you and one for me."

Albert walked closer to the old machines. He shook his head. "I don't know how well these things could make it up. I wouldn't risk it with my family."

Steven smiled at his friend. "We've got no choice. These old Albatros's need to make a couple of short, tree-topping flights or we may as well turn ourselves over to the Nazis. This is our best shot."

THIRTY-THREE

Martin and Greta had been given the choicest spot on the farm, or so both of them thought. They would spend their one and only night together at the farm in its creaky old barn. From the loft, overlooking the old Albatros aeroplanes that would take them out of there the next night, Martin and his love cuddled amid the soft hay and thought about their future.

"Do you think we'll make it?" Greta asked as she looked down at the planes.

"Albert and Steven are both experienced flyers and Helmut is a superb mechanic," Bock said, trying to comfort her fears. "I'm sure we'll be able to fly across the border."

"If the Nazis don't catch us first," Greta replied, her body shivering in his arms at the thought.

Greta had changed so much since he first met her, Martin thought. Once she was nothing more than a brazen prostitute, hard and cold to his touch. She had softened so. She had seen death and fear and maybe, through Albert and Min, what love could be.   Maybe it was his love that changed her most, Martin wished. Now no one who would meet her would think of the girl he had first met down at the riverfront. No one would suspect that the woman he would marry was ever a whore.

"Where will we go when it's over?" Greta asked.

"It'll be the chance for us to start over," Martin explained as he gently stroked her hair. "We can go where people don't know about our past and we can settle down. We can forget about politics, about Communists and Nazis, about the gap between the rich and the poor and just be people."

She looked at him, her eyes searching deeply into his. "Can we ever be just ordinary people? Would we want to be, Martin? After everything, could we turn our backs forever on this insane world and pretend it doesn't exist? Will the world let us?"

"Damn! I don't know," Martin shrugged. "I can sure as hell try!"

241

"Where? America? The end of the earth?" Greta sounded more upset with each thought. "Or will the Nazis and their hate follow us even there until we face them and either defeat them or die trying."

Martin couldn't help but laugh. "You sound almost like your.....father...like Crazy Max."

"There's a lot of Max Greyer in me," Greta said. "A lot of him and some of Albert. Neither man would turn away from them."

Martin gently kissed her forehead. "Greta, my darling, I don't want to turn away; I just want some time alone with you. Some time to live without worry, or hate, or fear."

"Me, too."

Their lips were drawn to each other and quickly their bodies drew closer. In the prickly, dried hay of the barn loft Greta and Martin forgot the troubles that surrounded them and the thought of the perilous journey ahead and found their hiding place in each other's arms.

* * * *

Steven had agreed with Albert that the best time to begin their escape would be twilight. The cover of darkness would afford them a better chance of escape. The border guards, should there be any in this isolated corner of the world, would be tired and less alert to the sudden drone of aeroplanes. Once across the border, the problem would be finding a place to set down, but only on the first trip. The others would be well lighted.

Everyone was aware of the chances they were taking. Everyone, save the children, realized this was their last, best opportunity to get out. The border grew tighter with each passing day and Germany's cautious neighbors, flooded with refugees from the new Reich, were not welcoming people with open arms.

This was why they felt that such a brazen attempt might succeed. "No one would expect this." Albert guessed. "No one would think of flying a pair of rickety old two-seaters like this. They're relics."

"And they'd never expect more than one trip," Steven added.

"Should they make it," Albert grumbled as he gazed at the graying war birds in the shadows of Helmut's barn.

Yet the day of waiting, and hiding, now seemed ungodly long. Steven and the other visitors sat in darkness listening to every sound and praying that the rustling of the wind through the trees wasn't the rush of an oncoming automobile.

Thanks to Helmut's aeroplanes Albert's mission became easier and the plan quickly formed in his mind. "It will take three trips," Albert guessed. "The twins on the first trip; they're small enough to fit on someone's lap, therefore two others can go."

"Who?" Min immediately questioned.

"That should be you and Greta."

Helmut thought about that a long time. "I agree."

"I don't agree," Min said. "I think it should be Helmut and Marie."

"No one said we're going," Helmut replied. It was true, Steven thought, no one had invited the Schorner's along.

"Do you want to come with us?" Albert then asked.

Helmut shrugged. "My sons are grown, one into a very loyal Nazi." Steven noticed a cynical tone to the man's voice. "There's nothing holding me here but this broken down old farm." Helmut then looked at his wife. "I'd say it's really up to Marie."

She reached out and grasped his hand, her face smiling. "It's your home, dear. Yet you know I would leave in a moment. My instincts tell me this will be no land for a Frenchwoman to live in."

Helmut turned back to Albert. "Then we go."

Steven brought them back to the business at hand. "Now that that's decided, I have to agree with Mina. Helmut will then be there in case of trouble with the engines and Marie to help with the girls."

Albert turned to Min. "You'll be all alone here while we go over, Mina. Are you sure this is alright?"

Min and Albert stared deeply into each others eyes. "I know it's for the best, as long as you do come back."

"Three trips then," Albert went on. "The girls, Helmut and Marie first round.

"The boys with Greta on the second," Min suggested. "The boys can crowd together in one seat."

"And lastly you two and I," Martin told him.

Everyone had sat silently since those decisions were made. As Steven himself thought about the risks involved he guessed the others concentrated their thoughts on their futures. How uncertain they were for them. They had left most of their things behind. They were going off with next to nothing, only the hope of freedom and a better tomorrow in their hearts.

Maybe their thoughts were on the past, Steven wondered. The good times and the bad. The triumphs of life and its setbacks and hardships. The party seemed to be deeply in thought, each person not speaking, not even looking at one another as they pondered tomorrow and remembered yesterday.

"We've given up almost everything we've ever had," Min had said in another time and place. "We've only our memories."

Finally, it was time.

The sun had begun to set. They would be flying into the sun at treetop level, Steven realized. They were flying unfamiliar planes toward unknown targets with the sun in your face. Not the best of conditions, but Steven liked the challenge.

Helmut and Martin wheeled the first aeroplane onto the clearing. The old mechanic carefully checked out the ancient aircraft. He leaned on the wing, maybe to see that it wouldn't break. He stared at the engine and seemed to smell it as he squinted at the grey, cold steel. He traveled around the machine, looking, poking, and peeking until he was pleased with its condition.

Then they wheeled out the other Albatros and he went through the whole procedure again. He looked like a happy man, Steven thought. This was what he loved, what he did best. Inside, Steven felt, Helmut was less a farmer than a tinkerer.

"Alright," Albert seemed to sigh. "Let's get to it."

The men began to place their small amount of luggage into the fuselage of the old aeroplane. These machines didn't hold more than a bag or two behind the observer's seat, but enough for what these people had brought. Albert took aside one bag and opened it, carefully removing a large brown envelope.

"Steven, come here," He called.

When Steven was at his side he handed him the package.

"What's this?"

"Secret plans," Albert tried to explain in a soft voice. "These are top secret plans that many people have risked their life for."

Steven was stunned. "You risked your life for this. You're not into this kind of game."

"No, I'm not, but a friend, a good friend, begged me to get these out of Germany for him. I fear he gave his life to see that it happened. I promised I'd try. I'd deliver them to Germany's enemies." Albert went on to explain. "I still want to keep that promise, but if anything should happen I ask you to finish this mission."

SECRETS OF THE PAST

Steven silently nodded and folded the envelope into his pocket.

"I think we're ready," Helmut said his voice without emotion. "Now remember, we can take off right here if we rev up the engines to full throttle, but it's to short a field to land on. The landing field is up over that hill. Better for both landing and take off."

"They why are starting here?" Steven asked.

Helmut smiled. "It's a long, uphill push to make that field. You feel up to it?"

"No."

"Then it's settled."

Albert squinted at the setting sun. "Flown recently, Steven?" he asked.

"A little here and there."

"I haven't been up since 1918. The last time I came down rather hard."

"It's like riding a bike. You never forget."

"That's horseshit and you know it."

The flyers smiled at each other. Steven realized that Albert had the confidence that a flyer needed, yet he knew they both knew they're own mortality.

"Scared?" Steven asked.

"Petrified."

Helmut rotated the propeller of one of the aeroplanes. "Well! Get in!" he called.

Steven climbed into his seat. He stared at the Spartan, unfamiliar panel. Two dials and a stick. Not much to fly by.

Albert climbed up and leaned over toward him. "Works like any plane, but this one flies very sluggish. Remember, nò sudden moves, these C-V's don't like it. Switch is under there." Albert pointed and he climbed down.

Steven turned the switch. "On!" he hollered loudly.

"On!" Helmut yelled back.

"Turn!"

"Turn!" Helmut replied and he pulled the propeller and the engine stuttered to a start.

Helmut climbed up and placed himself into the observer's seat. "Remember," he yelled in Steven's ear. "I'm right behind you."

Albert then lifted little Anna up and placed her in Helmut's lap. "You hold onto Herr Schorner," he told her. "Everything with be alright."

"Papa, I'm scared."

245

"I know, baby." Albert said as he tried to let go of the girl's hand. "But it'll be fine."

Steven felt a tap on his shoulder and felt Albert's weight leave the aircraft. He eased the throttle forward and the old aeroplane inched forward. Turning up the engine he began his journey.

THIRTY-FOUR

The silence, the lovely quiet, soothing silence surrounded Mina like a cloak as she and the others sat in the darkened barn. Mina could look at Greta, Gery and Willi; their eyes staring fearfully back at her through the dim light of a single lantern. Please! Please! She prayed; let us get out of this safely. Please, let it end.

Min knew all of them were afraid of the silence, of every sound that the night brought. The dusty, slightly mildewed barn held no secrets for her; it's creaking with the breeze imbedded in her mind after the first few moments. The wind in the trees and the noises of the animals were also no longer mysteries. She knew them all and could separate them from the sound she hoped to hear, the drone of the engine of an old aeroplane, and from those she would dread. The faint drone her mind thought it heard in the distance could be the sound of the aeroplane. Let it be them, her mind demanded. Let it be them.

Greta's eyes were seized by the most fear, Min concluded. The girl felt alone without Martin beside her. Her fear came from the loneliness, but also from an understanding of just how vulnerable they all were just then, all the men off making the first part of the escape happen.

All the men away, even Bock, preparing the expected landing field they would use for their return. He was two miles to the west, too far to help when the sound she dreaded came closer. Please God! Please! She felt her heart pound. Not now! Her mind raced. Not when we're so close.

Mina didn't know if she had first seen their headlights sneaking through the cracks in the old wooden barn, or if she had first heard their engine's roar to a sudden stop. Could she have sensed their coming even before they arrived? She knew they were there and her mind refused to believe it. Her worst fears could be coming true. Let it be anyone but him, her soul pleaded.

"Sit still," she whispered to the others as they all sensed the danger.

Greta slowly rose from her seat and moved toward a small opening in the wall. The bright shimmer of moving lights briefly illuminated her face as she gazed out. "Two cars." she told them.

Just let it be someone else! It was all Mina could think about. Let it be someone else!

Mina rose from the stool she was sitting upon, her left hand clutching the buttons of the old blue sweater she wore. Turning and twisting them in anguish, she took her fear out on the buttons until one loosened, breaking off in her hand. Her right hand, meanwhile, had reached into the pocket of the sweater and wrapped itself around her father's aging police revolver. Something in the back of her mind had told her to take the gun, unused and hidden since 1918. Oh please! She thought to herself; don't have a need to use it.

The voices from outside had begun to penetrate into the barn. The men, their loud gruff tones barely understandable, seemed to surround them. Then they came closer.

Just let it be someone other than him, Mina thought.

"The barn!" she heard one say.

Greta began to back away from the door. She realized they were coming.

Mina glanced around and motioned to the boys to stay in the shadows as she herself moved forward toward the door. Her hand closed more tightly around the revolver.

The door swung open and the artificial light poured in from outside. The glare of the torches suddenly blinded Min and she strained to see beyond them to the intruders. She saw only the peaks of their hats. They were SS!

"Don't shoot!" Greta shouted. "Don't!"

"Everyone out in the open," One man stated harshly.

Mina seemed paralyzed as she remained bathed in the light from the men's torches. She couldn't move. She couldn't think or react. She felt the touch of a hand on her arm. Instinctively reaching out she wrapped her free arm around her son. Not him, her mind raced, not now. He must never know. He'd never understand.

The lights faded. One dark, tall figure approached Mina, now surrounded by Greta and the boys. Min's eyes, struggling to adjust to the returning darkness, strained to see the face of the man. Soon she recognized it. Soon she recognized the eye patch. It was him. It was Willi Reinhart.

"Where is he?" Reinhart asked.

248

Min remained silent. Why did it have to be him? She tightened her arm around Willi.

Reinhart's face contorted in anger. "It's over Mina. Tell me where he is." His voice remained calm despite the anger on his hideous face. The voice, that of the man she once loved, or maybe always loved, was the same. If only the soul of the man she remembered was still there.

"No one else here," One of Reinhart's men said. "This is it."

"Mina," The Gauleiter went on, "Tell me where he is. Save the heroics for others. For the sake of your children tell me."

"For the children," Mina finally spoke. "If you had thought of these children we didn't have to run." She felt the anger grow within her as she looked at his face. There was still the look she remembered there, a look she saw everyday. Why did he have to be here? Her mind couldn't shake the questions, the doubt, and the anger.

"So tell me where Albert is hiding."

"He's gone."

"No, I doubt it," Reinhart smiled. "He's too much a gentleman. I expect that if we wait he'll be joining us."

"Is that what we're going to do?" Reinhart's man asked.

He nodded. "Join the others in searching the farm, but I expect you won't find him.

After the other man left Reinhart sat himself down on the only chair in the barn and looked at the statues of Min and the others, unmoving in the light of the flickering lamp.

"Introduce me," he demanded.

"Why?" Greta asked. "Who are you?"

"And old friend?" he smiled. "Who are you?"

"Greta Greyer," She said as coldly as she had been asked. Greta stood with her head erect, the defiance she felt for the Nazi seeming to make her glow against the lantern light.

"I am Wilhelm Reinhart, Gauleiter of Bremen," he said coldly. "Here to arrest the notorious Albert and Mina Freyberg, Jews in conspiracy against the Fatherland."

"That's crap!" Greta seemed to spit out the words.

"Greta," Min moaned, "Don't antagonize him."

Mina felt her hands shaking. She felt herself slipping away, as if it were all a dream.

Willi took a step toward the man. "I know your name." he began, a curious look on his face. "I was named after a man named Wilhelm Reinhart. He was a good friend of my parents. You can't be him."

249

"You are???" Reinhart looked curiously at the boys face.

Mina took a step toward Willi and restrained him from going any nearer the Nazi. "This is my son, Willi."

"Willi?" Reinhart gazed at Min.

"Yes," she said. "I named him after you. I wish I hadn't now."

Mina suddenly sensed movement behind her and saw Reinhart's eye shift away. His attention had been fixed on her and the boy, but now it raced to her left. She turned and saw Greta moving away.

Her eyes raced back to see Reinhart's hand reach for his luger, his eye following the girl as she moved.

"No!" Min yelled as she pushed her son away. She stepped between Reinhart and Greta.

She reached for the hand of the man and tried to wrest the gun from it. He quickly shook her off.

"Please don't!"

"Stop!" he demanded.

Min pushed herself into the man with all her weight and felt him move. Again she reached up for his gun hand and pushed it away.

A shot rang out!

"Mama." she heard Willi say.

"Run, Gery!" Greta's voice called.

Desperately she swung her hands in front of the man. Her eyes shut, her heart pounding, Mina frantically tried to stop him.

She felt a shove and then the cold steel against her face.

Then the pain!

Then the ground!

"Dammit!" she next heard Willi Reinhart's anger. "Where is she?"

Mina's vision cleared. Reinhart stood above her, his eye red with anger as it searched the barn for the girl, his gun outstretched, searching as well.

Mina felt her head and when she moved her hand away saw the blood. She felt dizzy again.

"Mama," Willi said as he knelt down next to her. "Are you alright?!"

"Go look for them," Reinhart ordered as his men entered the barn. "Two of them, the girl and a boy, have escaped.

* * * *

Gery Greyer had perched himself in what he felt was the best spot to watch what went on. He knew his own skills and agility could keep him alive in the slums of Bremen. He felt sure he could climb higher, run faster and think more quickly than the men who chased him, yet he was scared beyond any fear he had ever experienced.

The only sound he seemed to hear was that of his own heart pounding in his chest. The only sight before his eyes was a fuzzy feeling of fright as he caught his breath surrounded by the leaves of the tree.

He had climbed a huge tree next to the barn. The tree, big and overflowing with limbs and leaves, rose up next to the barn and rested itself against it. From this spot he could observe everything that went on below and he could hear the sounds coming from inside, where Mina and Willi Freyberg were still held captive.

Why hadn't Willi run? Gery asked himself. Why did he have to stay by his mother's side? He could have done more good out here, Gery thought. He could have lured the SS outside and given his mother a chance.

Yet Gery sensed there was something holding the Freybergs in there beyond the physical grip of the SS. Something sinister and eerie about the way Frau Freyberg looked at the SS leader. Something curious that Gery couldn't figure about the way the SS leader looked at Willi Freyberg. Willi had said that he was this man's namesake. Could that be true?

It was the fixation they had on each other that had given Greta and him time to move and left little for the SS to react to. Now Greta was solidly hidden in the woods and Gery in the tree.

Now he watched the SS scatter to find them, but he felt sure they wouldn't. He could see from his perch where Greta was and luckily the men were moving away from her.

He could also hear the words coming from inside the barn.

"Damn!" the SS man was cursing. "I let my guard down for one second. I let myself be gracious and human and this is what I get for it."

"Please leave us alone," Min's voice cried.

Gery swung himself silently over closer to the barn. He could see down through an opening from his new position. He could see the SS leader, gun drawn, staring at his prey.

"You will go out there and tell them to surrender," he was ordering Mina.

"Why?" she questioned as she rose from the floor and moved away from the man. "Why would I want to do anything like that?"

251

"Because I'm ordering you to or....."

"Or what," Min cried. "Would you kill me?"

"If I must!"

"Is there anything left of your soul?"

The man reached out and grabbed Willi's arm. Gery watched as he swung his one arm around and enveloped Willi Freyberg and somehow still managed point the gun at the boy's head.

"Willi!" Min screamed.

"I can hurt you, Mina," Reinhart stated, his voice filled with rage. "Or I can hurt your son."

"Please, No! No, Willi! No!" Mina began to walk toward them.

"Take another step and I'll kill him."

"Please, No! Don't hurt him! He's your son!"

Gery couldn't believe what he heard, and neither could Reinhart.

"He's your son!" Mina cried again as she crumbled to the ground.

"Impossible!"

Gery tuned his ears onto Mina as she cried. Her words, soft yet echoing in the barn, reached him in his perch outside on the roof. "That's why Albert and I married; for your son, Willi. He's your son."

Reinhart began to drag Willi Freyberg toward the outside. The boy struggled, but he couldn't release himself from the Nazi's grip.

Gery could hear Mina's cries as she was left alone in the barn, but the sounds from outside, rising up clearly in the night to his ears, soon drowned out her sobs.

"Yes! Yes!" Reinhart said as he struggled with Willi. "I can see it now." He turned the boys head toward his with the barrel of the pistol. "It is my face. You could be mine."

"No!" Willi grunted as he struggled to free himself. "I'm the son of Albert Freyberg. Not you....."

Reinhart laughed. "Ha! To think! All these years! All the lies they had to live with."

"Leave me alone," Willi grunted as the struggle continued. Gery was amazed how the one armed man could hold onto the teenager. He realized how the strong this Nazi was.

"Now, my son," Reinhart said as he pushed Willi further from the barn. "Tell your friends to give up. Tell them or I'll go back and hurt your mother."

"No."

"Tell them!"

Suddenly out of the darkness Greta ran out and reached for Reinhart's arm. The startled Nazi had little choice but to release his hold on Willi and confront the girl.

"Run! Run, Willi!" Greta called, but the boy didn't move.

Greta and the Nazi fought for the pistol, and Gery realized that it was his time to act. He knew Greta couldn't beat the Nazi, even with two arms, and doubted if he could. He wasn't sure the both of them together could, but he had to act. Someone had to.

Gery jumped down from the tree. As he felt his feet hit the ground he knew something was wrong. His knees collapsed and he crashed down. He was stunned, but it wasn't as if he had hurt his legs. He felt sick and paralyzed. Is this fear? He wondered.

Greta and the Nazi continued to fight over the pistol. They were a confusion of arms and legs as they struggled and Gery, struggling himself to move, called to Willi. "Run! Do something! Help her!"

Yet Willi simply stood there and looked at them.

"Oh God!" Greta screamed. "Help!"

Gery finally felt himself move. He ran over to them and reached up to join the three other hands fighting over the pistol.

Then the gun went off!

Gery seemed to see the bullet come out of the barrel and drive itself right through his left hand. He saw the bullet burst out the other side followed by droplets of his blood before he felt any pain.

Then the pain, a searing white pain that blinded him, shot through his consciousness!

"Gery, No!" he heard Greta's voice.

Gery grasped his left wrist with his other hand and stared at the mass of bloody flesh that was there and thought he heard himself scream.

Then he heard another shot ring in his ears and the world went white and silent.

* * * *

Mina Freyberg recovered her senses as she heard two shots sound from outside the barn.

"Willi," she mumbled. "Willi, please be alright."

Her senses weren't fully aware of the meaning the gunshots. Her mind concentrating on what her son had heard. Would he forgive her for

253

the lies? Would he forgive her for the truth? If he was alright, would he understand?

Mina felt the same fears she had felt that cold and hungry autumn as if that emptiness and foreboding had suddenly returned. She felt the same as she had then, when she had maneuvered Albert into marrying her. She had kept that sin, all her sins hidden for so long. Could that be why she ached so now, now that it was in the open.

What would Willi think? How would he react when he realized that he was not Albert's son? Not the son of an honorable man that a boy can love and respect, but the son of a monster of a man with a swastika armband? If he was unharmed, she wondered, would he still love her?

There was a deadly silence now from outside. The gunshots, the last sounds, had stunned Mina back to reality. Whatever happened, she realized, she must go on and protect herself and the young people left in her care.

The revolver was now in her hand. The long neglected weapon with which she had killed once could now be her salvation if she had the courage. Mina realized she had to have the courage.

She pointed the pistol at the entrance to the barn, determined to stop anyone from harming her and, she hoped, anyone from harming her son. "Willi!" she called. "Willi, are you alright!"

The first figure through the door was one of the SS. Mina quickly squeezed the trigger.

The gun sparked and bucked and the man's face exploded before her eyes an instant later.

Mina felt the droplets of blood spatter her hands and arms, but she steadied the gun with both hands and stared at the doorway again.

Another figure!

Another SS!

Another gunshot and again the splash of blood as the bullet hit its mark.

"Willi," Min called. "Greta! Gery! Someone!"

The door to the barn swung wider and she saw a pistol turning to point at her.

She squeezed the trigger again. The pistol flew from the hand of the man who carried it and seemed to explode in the air. The Nazi, clutching his face, staggered into the barn and toward Mina.

She bit her lip and pointed the gun at the approaching Nazi. She fired and watched him crumble to the ground.

"Oh, Lord!" she moaned, tears now running down her cheeks. "How many more?!"

"Mina." she heard a voice.

She looked up and saw a figure enter through the doorway. She raised the revolver, one hand gripping the other to steady her trembling hands. Quickly, instinctively, she pulled the trigger.

"Mina! No!" she heard. Beyond the barrel of the gun was Greta's face.

She watched as the bullet struck Greta in the chest. It seemed to lift her from the ground and toss her onto her back.

Mina was frozen, the smoking gun burning her hands. "No! No. Forgive me." she murmured as she watched Greta's body quiver and roll from side to side on the floor of the barn.

THIRTY-FIVE

The three men, their spirits high after the completion of the first part of the mission, seemed to bounce down the wooded path back to the farm. All of them, Steve realized, where elated over the ease with which it had gone off. He and Albert had guided the aging, overloaded aeroplanes over the border as if they had been doing it all their lives. They skimmed the trees and crossed into Holland and away from the clutches of the evil Nazis in only a few minutes.

Effortlessly they set the aeroplanes back down to earth in a quiet field and unloaded their passengers and cargo.

Checking the maps to determine where they were, they arranged for the return on the second trip with Helmut and prepared to go back to Germany.

Albert said goodbye to his daughters, probably realizing that there was a chance he'd never be back, and both of them lifted off again.

Martin waited for them back in Germany on a field chosen because of its long slope and its obscurity, and lit the torches when he heard their approach. The pilots easily brought the Albatros's in.

Now they were on the way back to the farm to get the second group. If the danger weren't so real, so near, they'd be laughing and shouting to the night sky their good fortune. As it was, the spirit in their steps and the smiles on their faces told the story in silence.

Steve realized that something was wrong as they neared the farm. He could see the silhouettes of two sinister cars. He felt his heartbeat quicken and prayed they still had a chance.

"Stay back," Albert insisted. "Stay in the shadows. I'll go up and see what's happened."

Steve sensed that Albert was not as alarmed as he could, or should be. Could it be that he had somehow known that this would happen. Steven had been sensing defeatism in his friend, as if he expected things couldn't go according to plan.

As requested, Steve and Martin waited in the shadows as Albert went up to the barn.

"I can't just sit here," Martin said. "I've got to know if she's......"

His words were cut off by a single gunshot.

Then another crackled and echoed through the woods.

Neither Steve nor Martin could stay behind any longer as they rushed up to the barn. As they ran gunshot after gunshot echoed through the woods. Whether there were a total of five, six or seven shots, Steven couldn't be sure.

Panting for breath as they neared the doorway, they heard another shot ring out and saw Albert's figure as it pointed a pistol into the barn.

A moment later Steven had joined Albert in the doorway, before him was a sight to sicken any man. Three Nazis lay around the entrance to the barn, all of them dead.

Yet the sight that sickened Steven most was Min and Greta, the young girl nestled in Min's arms, covered in a blanket of blood.

In an instant both Albert and Martin were knelling beside the two women. Min was stroking Greta's hair, helpless to do more.

Greta's body was shaking and she struggled to speak. "It hurts," she whispered in a shaky voice. She lifted her head up and looked down toward her chest. "I'm shot! God, I'm shot. Son-of-a-bitch!"

"Shush, stay quiet. We'll help you," Min tried to sooth her. "Look, Martin's here. Your Father's here."

"Is that all my blood!" She said as she stared at herself. "Dammit! It hurts!"

"It'll be alright, Greta." Martin clutched her hand with his. "It'll be alright."

"Your right," she sighed. "It doesn't even hurt anymore."

"That's good," Martin tried to comfort, reassure her.

"No, it's not," she smiled back at him. She whispered more softly to him. "I love you, Bock."

"I love you, too," he whispered back at her.

She sighed once more and closed her eyes. A second later she was gone.

"No! Greta! Please don't die." Martin pleaded as he stroked her golden hair.

Steven turned away from the sorrowful scene and struggled to hold himself together. He turned to Albert who rose up and stared coldly at the exit from the barn.

Mina sat there, her face covered with tears, the girl in her lap, her hand holding a small revolver.

"Who?" Albert asked.

"Willi Reinhart," Min quietly replied.

"Where?"

"I don't know."

"Why couldn't you protect her?" Albert softly said to his wife.

"I tried," she answered.

If it had been Steven in Albert's place he knew what he would have done. He'd have gone over to comfort Mina, whose eyes showed she desperately needed it. But Albert was a different man and he turned and walked out of the barn.

"Where are the boys?" Steve asked Mina.

Martin took Greta's body and lifted it off Mina. He walked with her slowly to a patch of straw in the corner. There is put her down and sat next to her, still stroking her hair.

Min tried to rise up, then crumbled to the ground and began to sob. Another shot rang through the air.

Steven ran out of the barn to Albert's side.

"Reinhart," Albert screamed madly into the night. "Face me!"

Steven turned toward the angry, desperate man. He was just standing there, the pistol from one of the dead SS men in his hand now, lazily at his side as if waiting for the Nazi to return.

Out of the shadows came two figures, but he quickly realized it was Willi and Gery. Thankfully, Steven sighed.

"You won't find him," Gery said as he walked unsteadily, bolstered by young Willi. "Greta shot him. He's not dead though, but ran off into the woods." Gery held one hand around the other, which was wrapped in a bloodstained cloth. He had clearly been hurt, but the boy bravely stood nearly erect.

"What happened?" Albert demanded of his son.

Willi didn't answer, instead leaving Gery's side and walking past his father toward the barn.

"Mama," he called.

Albert reached back and held him still. "Don't go in there." He told the boy. "Don't....."

The boy looked at his father with a cold, icy stare

Willi shook loose from Albert's grip and started toward the barn again. This time Steven stepped in front of him. "Don't go in there. It's too gruesome."

258

"My mother?"

"She's...she's alright." Steven told him. "But......"

"Greta!" Gery called. "Where's Greta?"

The injured youth had joined Willi. Steven watched their faces turn suddenly white with shock.

"I'll take care of her," he heard Martin's voice behind him. He moved past Steven, carrying the body of the girl, and walked off toward the woods.

Albert and the boys silently, sadly followed.

* * * *

"Helmut will be getting worried," Albert said as he strained to see his watch against the darkness. "We should have gone long ago."

"He'll follow instructions," Steven answered back. "He knows to wait until dawn if need be."

Martin felt himself coming back from some dreamlike state. Slowly his senses began to grasp all that surrounded him again. He still felt hollow and sad, but he shook himself back to reality to help finish this task. He can mourn his lovely Greta later. He can mourn her forever.

It had begun to sink in. She was gone! Her pretty smiling face would never look his way again. Her voice, still alive in his mind, biting at him with her sharp tongue or cooing affectionately, would fade from his memory. Someday, as with all those Martin had lost in his life, the words she spoke would remain, but the sound would fade from his mind. He hated the thought that he someday wouldn't remember what she sounded like.

Martin knew he had to go on. He knew that this night must end with Albert, Mina and the boys out of Germany. Who knows when the Nazis will return? Who knows if the Gauleiter, if he's still lives, will return with more henchmen?

"Steven," Albert gave the American his last instructions. "Get them safely out."

Steven quietly nodded and then climbed into the cockpit of the aging Albatros.

"Can't I go with Mama?" Willi turned to Albert and asked. The boy had been strangely quiet since the incident, concerned over his mother's welfare and oblivious to everything else. Martin realized the shock had hit him hard.

"No," Albert insisted. "You and Gery. Now!"

"Come on, son," Steven called as he extended his hand down to help the lad.

Reluctantly, Willi climbed up into his place.

Martin saw that there could be a problem. "It's a tight fit," he told Albert. "You sure...."

Albert cut him off. "It will have to do."

Gery would be next into the cockpit, squeezing into the back seat with Willi. The boys were nearly grown and the place wasn't made for two people, but Martin knew as well as Albert that there wouldn't be a chance for another trip.

"Martin," a voice spoke from behind Martin Bock. "You'll miss her, won't you?" Gery asked, the emotion of his loss beginning to seep into his mind. His own pain and the shock had made it necessary for Gery to hide the grief, and, strong as he was, it was coming out now.

"Of course," Martin replied. The two people who knew and loved Greta the most held each other for a moment, sharing their pain.

A moment later he was in the aeroplane.

A moment after that they were airborne.

"Now," Albert sighed as the Steve's plane faded into the darkness. "Our turn."

"No," Martin told him. "I'm not going, Albert."

His mentor, his friend, his father figure, looked curiously at him, but didn't utter a word.

"There's no reason for me to run," Martin explained. "It would have been different if Greta were alive. I'd go anywhere to be with her. With her gone, I don't know what to do, but it's not this."

"You've no reason to stay here," Mina, who had been so quiet thus far, said.

"Nor, should you want to," Albert also added. He placed his hand on Martin's shoulder, a serious, fatherly expression on his face. "Germany is becoming a cruel place, Martin. Not the kind the land where you'd want to live. You happily wanted to leave with Greta. There's no reason to stay without her."

"But she's still here," he countered. "She's in the air. She's in the places I'll go and the sounds I'll hear. Out there...well.... she's just not there."

Albert and Mina nodded as if they understood, but they couldn't have because Martin didn't really understand how he felt. Was he doing the right thing? Would he regret this missed chance to leave?

"If you change your mind....."

"I'll look you up, Albert, my friend."

Albert then turned to his wife. "We'd better be gone."

She nodded at him, but their eyes failed to meet. She took a step nearer to him, her body seeming to tremble with each step.

Albert's hand touched her face, turning it until their eyes me. "I'm sorry, Mina." he said tenderly. "I'm sorry for everything that's happened and for what we must do now. I'm sorry I haven't understood always just the way you felt."

She wrapped her arms around him and hugged him tightly.

"It'll be a new start for us, Min," he went on. "It will be a new and safe beginning away from this horror. Together, we'll make it!"

He coaxed her to the cockpit and helped her in.

"Good luck." Martin told them.

"And to you," Albert replied as he shook the man's hand. He drew away for an instant and then came back to hug Martin as if he were his son. "Good luck, boy! And thank you."

Martin help start the motor and the sound of the sputtering Albatros filled his ears. Above the drone he heard Mina call to him. "Don't be long, Martin Bock. Join us soon!"

"Let's go!" Albert's voice stated.

He waved as they passed and waved again as the aeroplane lifted off. As the Albatros disappeared into the night Martin hoped Albert and Min would find their happiness again.

17897470R00139

Made in the USA
Charleston, SC
06 March 2013